IDENTICAL

SASKIA SARGINSON

First published in Great Britain in 2024 by Boldwood Books Ltd.

Cover Design by Head Design Ltd

Cover Photography: iStock

A CIP catalogue record for this book is available from the British Library.

Paperback ISBN 978-1-83603-007-2

Large Print ISBN 978-1-83603-008-9

Hardback ISBN 978-1-83603-006-5

Ebook ISBN 978-1-83603-009-6

Kindle ISBN 978-1-83603-010-2

Audio CD ISBN 978-1-83603-001-0

MP3 CD ISBN 978-1-83603-002-7

Digital audio download ISBN 978-1-83603-004-1

Boldwood Books Ltd
23 Bowerdean Street
London SW6 3TN
www.boldwoodbooks.com

For Alex, with love

PART I

1

ALICE

You can never go back. I know that now. And as I stand on an unfamiliar street, about to enter a house that doesn't belong to me, it reminds me of those other moments in my life when one small step, one seemingly common-place action altered the molecules of existence, stirred up time and reset the future. I think of that last morning at Hawksmoor when I emptied my brother's rucksack of his things and refilled it with my own, slipping my passport into the pocket, and when I stood by the tarn arguing with my sister as snow speckled our eyelashes, blinding us with starbursts of light.

Regret is my familiar shadow, whatever the weather, however the sun falls or the moon wanes, it can never be erased. It has crawled inside me, settled into my bones, a darkness carried forever.

All this flies through my mind as I glance at the address scribbled on a scrap of paper, then up again at the white, terraced house I recognise from a sketch my sister once did for me. Hollyhocks Cottage is squeezed between its neighbours behind an overbearing privet hedge. There's no sign of any hollyhocks. Three strides and I've reached the front door, standing in the shadow of a palm leaning over from next door.

Am I really going to do this?

The hedge prevents me from being overlooked, but I glance over my shoulder just in case, before lifting the bottom of a cat sculpture, fingers creeping underneath to find Cecily's keys. The metal shapes are gritty with earth and attached to a small heart-shaped keychain. I have no idea which one is right. There are four, all different sizes. I slot the biggest one into the top lock. It doesn't fit, and I glance behind me again before trying the next size down. It rotates and the door swings open into a narrow hallway.

I stand on the threshold, muscles tensed for flight, and I think of those other moments, the decisions that changed everything. This is my last chance to back out, or my one chance to make things right. Now or never. Then I'm inside, and the door swings shut behind me.

'Hello?' My voice sounds tremulous.

A sudden shriek makes me jump. Gulls outside, I realise. I give a shaky laugh and slip the bulk of my rucksack off my shoulders, inhaling the aromas caught in its fibres, the different smells that speak of my travels, my life on the road. I'll have to find a place to hide it.

I peer into the living room on my left. It's splashed with spring sunshine and runs the length of the house. Pine floorboards gleam. A bay window is hung with long, cream curtains. There are two sofas, one in front of the window, the other against a radiator, making an L-shape around a coffee table, an orange and red rug below. I touch a yellow candlestick on the mantelpiece, examine a bright, electric clock in the shape of a fish. The only reference to Cecily's past is a framed photo of Hawksmoor. I stare at the hulking contours of the house, the fells in the distance, the dark shadow of the yew in the foreground. And inside I remember the huge wooden crucifix looming out of the darkness at the bottom of the stairs, the smell of dank earth, the sound of dog claws against flagstones.

I rub my face, and blink into the neat, clean room. It feels safe and contained. A tall bookshelf and an upright piano stand either side of the French windows at the far end. I wonder if Cecily plays. She hasn't mentioned it in her letters. We didn't as children; the grand piano at Hawksmoor was hopelessly out of tune, the top merely providing a place to stand rows of photographs.

I explore the rest of the ground floor. There's not much to discover. A cramped cloakroom with a loo under the stairs. The narrow hall leads into a kitchen at the back with white walls and units, a grey tiled floor. My throat is dry with anxiety. I pour myself a glass of water from a filter jug on the windowsill, gulping it down. A large fridge has postcards stuck to it with colourful magnets. There are photos. One of a girl with chubby cheeks, freckles over her nose, and a doleful gaze. A ruddy-faced man with laughing green eyes. It's like a stage set for ordinary family life, except... I know it's a lie. I open the fridge, and stare at neatly stacked shelves filled with food. I shut the door. Oh, God. I'm never going to get away with this.

The half-glazed back door looks out into a small, fenced area of grass, and I concentrate on the patch of green, aware that my breathing is shallow, and my heart is beating too fast – some St. John's Wort and valerian root would be useful, but I doubt Cecily believes in alternative medicine. There's a gate set into the back fence, so there must be an alley or lane behind. Something living rubs against my ankles. I bite my tongue in shock. A large, fluffy tabby cat is winding around my legs. I squat down to rub the cat's head, and she purrs at me. I look under the sink and find a tub of dry cat food, shake it out into the bowl on the floor. The bowl is inscribed with 'Sukie'. I watch Sukie crunching kibble and wonder if she can smell I'm a stranger. 'Bet you can,' I tell her. 'But you don't give a damn, do you? As long as I fill your food bowl.' No morals, cats.

Upstairs, I find a double room facing the street that must belong to my sister. There's a neatly made bed covered with a cream quilted spread and matching scatter cushions. But the things that give it away are the King James Bible on the nightstand, and the silver crucifix on the wall above the bed. She has an old-fashioned dressing table, a bit like the one our mother had, ornate with drawers and cabinets, dark and polished. This is the only room with a reference to our religious upbringing, a reminder of our past. I count five painted icons arranged on the dressing table, each of them inscribed with the usual clichés – a cracked gold halo glistening above a plump Christ child, The Holy Mother holding her hands together in prayer, and winged archangels looking up with earnest expressions. I turn each one over, not wanting to see the images, and pile them in a stack. Sitting on the stool at the dressing table, I try one of the drawers. It's filled with make-up, a hairbrush and some jewellery; I recognise our mother's pearls and a gold brooch. Poor Mummy. Cecily told me she'd finally lost her mind and now lives in an old people's home. I try the next drawer down. It's locked. I pull harder, but it resists my efforts.

I look at myself in the mirror and touch the newly blunt ends of my short hair with a pang of loss. Before the chop, I'd had a long, straggly style; some sections had self-matted into locks, some I'd plaited and woven with beads. My hair had made me feel sexy and wild, telling the world I wasn't compromising, that I didn't follow rules. But I'm already getting into my part, and the regret doesn't linger. The thing about hair is, it grows.

I notice that my cheeks are flushed and hectic looking. I don't bother with make-up usually, but Cecily is the opposite. '*I never go without my eyeliner and mascara,*' she'd said in her latest letter. I try dabbing some powder over the redness, then find a black eyeliner pencil and lick the end. Leaning close to the mirror, I attempt to draw a line, smudging it with my finger, then stoke the mascara wand over my upper lashes. A little wonky, but it will do. Her wedding ring, a decorative watch and a gold crucifix on a chain lie on the surface. I fasten the necklace around me. The metal feels warm, as if she's only just taken it off, and I slide the wedding band over the joint of my ring finger.

Opening the built-in wardrobe on the opposite wall, I discover a neat line of hangers holding clothes arranged in colour order; most of her things are black, grey or blue. Typical uptight Cecily. I lean in and stuff my rucksack into the furthest corner, sticking it behind longer skirts. I can't resist pressing my nose into folds of fabric and inhaling. But she smells different as an adult, and there's a strong chemical scent of fabric conditioner that makes me sneeze. A black hair is stuck to the weave of a jacket, and I pluck it free. It matches my own exactly. There are some clothes laid out neatly on the bed, a push-up bra covered with scallops of silver and lavender lace and a pair of matching knickers that are not designed to cover anyone's buttocks. Interesting. Secretly not-so-uptight then. I step out of my dungarees, take off my vest top and boys' boxer shorts and fasten myself into these pieces of sexist torture. The lace scratches, the underwire digs into my flesh. I pull on the tailored grey trousers and navy shirt she's chosen for me. I like to move through life like a dancer in loose clothes, long skirts, baggy Indian trousers. Cecily's clothes seem designed to be punitive. I touch the crisp navy sleeve, and it feels as if her spiky arms are wrapped around me, bony clavicles grating against mine.

Growing up, we didn't touch each other very often. It had seemed important to maintain that dividing line, the beginning of one and the end of another. We didn't want to be one interchangeable entity, not after we'd spent nine months in the womb, curled into each other, sharing the same tightly packed placenta. We punished people for getting us mixed up, playing them at their own game by swapping identities, confusing pupils, teachers, even our parents. But the fact is, years of separation have etched different habits into us. We share the same DNA, but no longer have the same experiences. And it's that that's made the biggest difference. I don't know what she's thinking any more.

Next door there's a functional tiled white bathroom smelling faintly of cleaning fluid and roses. Cecily's pots of cream are lined up on the shelf above the wash basin. Cleanser, toner, exfoliator, serum, moisturiser, night cream, hand cream. I unscrew a lid and inhale the botanical scent, stick my finger in and rub some onto my hand.

Next to the bathroom is a door with a sign saying 'Keep Out'. I turn the handle and poke my head in. 'Hello?' I try cautiously, just in case. I smell incense. The walls are covered in posters; dirty mugs and women's magazines clutter surfaces; a single bed has an old teddy propped against the pillow, and twists of dark-coloured clothes lie over the floor. I presume it's a typical teenager's bedroom, but I'm not an expert. I recognise Courtney Love's face on several posters but haven't heard of any of the other pop groups.

There's one more flight of stairs, and I walk up, treading softly. The door is open. This must be Gabriel's room. She'd told me they're sleeping apart. One sloping ceiling is fitted with two Velux windows. A low bookshelf is crammed with worn spines, curling art postcards propped up, a collection of smooth pale stones. A double bed is rumpled with half-pulled covers, next to it a table holds a reading lamp, a couple of pens and a glass of dusty-looking water. I nearly trip over a pile of novels on the floor, and bend down to see what he's reading – a volume of poetry and three murder mysteries. Not what I would have expected from a history academic. Several pairs of men's boots and trainers appear to have been kicked across the floor. A scratched wooden desk stands in front of a window, piled with papers and books, a hulking PC, and an Anglepoise lamp. I glance around at the mess. Is this the room of an alcoholic?

I lean across his desk and look out at rooftops, a glimpse of blue water, and a rise of land beyond, patchworked with fields. It's such an English scene. I can't believe that I'm back in this country. It's not rational, but for years I've had panic attacks at the thought of returning. Turns out, it took a cause, a purpose greater than my own fear, to finally get me here. I've never set foot in Cecily's home before, so it's odd that this view and the house itself feel somehow familiar. I guess because Cecily has described them to me in her letters, just like she's described everything else in her life. All those words flying between us, envelopes carried across oceans.

A noise makes me startle and I stand, head cocked, heart thumping as I listen. There are movements below, a rustle, the click of a door shutting. My pulse thunders in my ears. Has one of them come home early? Should I go down and greet them? Isn't that what Cecily would do? A seagull flaps in front of the window, brown-speckled feathers working the air, and I wish I had wings to disappear over those patchwork fields. What if Gabriel's on his way up? Or the daughter, Bea. I slip down the stairs back into Cecily's room, shutting the door behind me, leaning against it with my eyes closed, breathing as quietly as I can, gathering my courage like a burglar. I've taken my sister's identity but standing here, on the brink of greeting either her daughter or her husband, my plan seems doomed to failure.

2

CECILY

The idea of going to hell terrified me, so I tried my best to guard against the seven deadly sins, reciting them like a rosary, counting warnings instead of prayers. Gluttony was definitely the one that would trip me up, pushing me into the fiery pit. We didn't get pocket money, but a banished aunt sent us cash for Christmas and birthdays, and I saved mine to spend in the village shop. Guiltily, I dreamed of Wagon Wheels, unwrapped slowly from their red and gold foil, Cadbury's Creme Eggs so gooey sweet they made my teeth ache, and then there was Jane's Victoria sponge made for special occasions, with jam squeezing out of the middle, icing powder shaken into lacy patterns on top. I coveted them all, and hoarded my pennies, longing for the taste of sugar.

Daddy kept a painting of hell on the wall of his study. It was a world on fire. A place of craggy rocks and cinders, erupting volcanos and molten rivers, where no greenery or hope existed. I tried not to look, but the horror won out, my eye irresistibly drawn to images of blackened toad-creatures whipping naked sinners, pushing them into burning pits and chopping their heads off. Daddy often had a selection of weapons on his desk to study for his book: a long pike with barbed points that curved backwards to better hook and tear the skin, or a heavy, double-edged sword, with a tracing of nicks in the metal where it had hacked at bone. I thought of the damage they would do to fragile human flesh, and how the toad-creatures would enjoy using them.

Sometimes I found myself in that terrible landscape and woke up screaming.

'Jesus loves you,' Mummy said every night after our prayers. 'He's waiting for you.'

'But not yet,' Alice would say. 'We're not going to die yet. We're still only twelve.'

Mummy kissed her forehead and smiled with freckled lips. 'Of course. I meant later. When you're very old and tired of this life, then Jesus will call you home.'

'Will he call us home if we've been naughty?' I asked, worrying about Alice.

'Oh, yes,' Mummy said. 'As long you've repented.'

'So, it's true, we just have to say we're sorry,' I said, relieved.

'You have to mean it, though.' Mummy smiled.

Alice rarely said sorry, and when she did, she often had her fingers crossed behind her back. Mummy said we were lucky to be born with a ready-made best friend. 'Together forever,' Alice used to say to me. 'Whatever happens to anyone else, we'll stick like glue.'

How could I fly up to heaven? I'd be miserable thinking about my sister's eternal punishment somewhere far below. Unstuck forever. Alice would ruin heaven for me, which was typical.

* * *

It was Lent. We were hungry, and it had been raining all morning. Drips fell into buckets set out on the landing, a metallic jazz of plinks and plonks. One of the outdoor cats had got into the house and was sheltering under Henry's bed, feral body pressed flat to the dusty carpet, tattered ears back. Alice had been trying to entice him out by dangling a bit of string, but the cat crouched lower, a warning yowl in its throat.

Henry scratched his ankle. 'Think it's got fleas,' he said morosely.

'Shall we play Sevens?' I suggested. 'Or Monopoly?' Anything to pass the time until lunch. My stomach growled and I placed a hand over it, feeling the rise of my hips, sharp as blades. Did thinking about cake count as gluttony – or did I have to eat it to commit the sin? There were almost no fat saints and every image of Christ on the cross displayed his ribs and gaunt cheeks.

I was standing by the window looking at the weedy front drive below, my view distorted by a maze of raindrops. I felt sorry for the beech trees and the old yew languishing under the torrent, branches drooping with the weight of water. The smoky sky was empty of birds. The distant fells wiped out in a haze of cloud.

Henry stood up. 'Hey, Alice, Cilly, come here,' he ordered. I cast him a sour look which he ignored. All my life, my siblings had given me the nickname. To everyone else's ears it sounded like 'Silly.' I was certain that's why they used it; they didn't think I was as clever or quick-thinking as them. 'Did you know that if you put one hand over one half of your face and then the other,' he was saying, 'you can tell which half is good, and which is evil?'

I took a step towards him, interested despite myself. With the air of a conjurer about to perform a trick, he placed his right palm over the right side of his face.

Alice pointed. 'Your left side's crooked,' she laughed. 'Maybe God went off for his lunch when it came to making that bit of you.'

'Alice!' I worried that one day she would be struck down. God peering through our window at the wrong moment and catching her out in her blasphemy.

Henry, older than us by two years, stared at himself in the small mirror on his wall. 'No, you dolt. This is my evil side.' He turned and leered at us, clawing his hands. 'Now you,' he said, sitting on his bed. 'Do it at the same time. Maybe your sides will be different from each other? You know, like a mirror?'

We stood side by side, covering the left half of our faces with our left hands, switching to our right. Then we covered opposite sides. I sniffed longingly at the memory of breakfast toast on my fingers as I submitted to Henry's scrutiny.

'It's strange,' he said, narrowing his eyes to squint at us. 'I can't tell which side is which on either of you.'

We jostled for space in front of Henry's wall mirror and tried it again. My eyes flicked from my face to Alice's. The same high forehead, one black swooping brow over a hazel eye. Half a straight, slightly long nose with a flared nostril. Half a small, rosebud mouth.

'One of you must be all good and the other all evil.' Henry's voice came from behind us. 'And I bet Alice is the wicked one.'

'Oh, ha, ha,' Alice said, swinging around. 'Quick, Cilly, grab his legs!' she shouted as she rushed him.

Henry let out an oomph as Alice took a leap and crashed into him, sending them both sprawling across the bed. There was a struggle, but she managed to get the upper hand as she knelt over him, her dark hair flopping across her face, ragged ends like a witch's mane. He laughed and writhed, fighting back, grabbing her wrists. She shrieked and tried to jerk away, but he hung on, his older-brother-strength winning. 'I knew you were the Devil's child!' he gasped, laughing as he tipped her off him.

I looked at their thrashing legs and wild-eyed mirth, and then the door. Daddy's study was only on the floor below. He was probably working on his manuscript – his great work – a time he must never be disturbed. I shushed them in an urgent mime, finger to my lips.

Ignoring me, Henry sat up, rubbing his stomach. 'You should play rugby,' he told Alice, ruefully, as he flexed his hands. 'Think you broke one of my fingers.'

'Cilly!' Alice was rubbing her wrist with a wince where Henry's grip had squeezed red marks. 'Why didn't you help me?'

I was remembering our two faces in the mirror – two halves of a whole.

'Earth to Cilly?' Alice pushed the tangle of hair out of her eyes. 'Perhaps you've been turned to salt,' she said sarcastically. 'Like Lot's wife?'

'Or stone, like one of the animals in *The Lion, the Witch and the Wardrobe* after the White Witch has gone by.' Henry suggested.

'Get her!' Alice shouted, jumping off the bed. 'Tickling will break the spell!'

I was standing nearest to the door and let out a squeal as I made a run for it. The other two charged after me, and faster than all of us, the stable cat, a streak of bone and muscle, off down the long, damp corridor with its tail straight out behind.

3

ALICE

I check my reflection in the mirror before I go downstairs and my sister stares back. I have her latest photograph to remind me that now I've had my hair cut, the differences between us are still tiny, and without the other for comparison, unlikely to be noticed. I have a freckle high up on my right cheek, and she has the same one but on her left side; she also has a tiny scar shaped like a nail pairing on her chin. Her bottom lip is plumper than mine. My nose is a little shorter. Our eyes have the same halo of yellow filigree, a starburst around our pupils. The only difference is she has a blemish inside her left eye, the legacy of a childhood accident with a sharp stick. But to see it someone would have to be gazing intently into her iris.

All I need is confidence. If I pass the first impressions test, then perhaps they won't get suspicious when my cooking tastes terrible, or when their washing comes out purple or several sizes smaller. Cecily seems to have turned herself into a domestic goddess, whereas I can't cut a slice of bread straight. I take a deep breath. Here goes.

At the bottom of the stairs, in the narrow entrance hall, I hear the fridge closing, the scrape of chair legs against the floor. I approach the kitchen, and see a figure hunched over the pine table.

'Bea,' I exclaim, despite myself.

A dark-haired girl raises her head, glancing through a greasy fringe in my direction. There's a smear of purple on her top lip. She clasps a hefty white sandwich with both hands, butter and what looks like jam oozing from the middle. She grunts a brief greeting and returns to her sandwich. She has a glass of milk next to her elbow and the cat is sprawled, purring, on her lap.

'Everything okay? You're home early... aren't you?' I take an awkward step closer. 'You're hungry?' I say, thinking I could offer to cook; that would be the maternal thing to do, wouldn't it? An omelette, perhaps. Something quick and easy.

'Yes, I'm hungry,' Bea snaps. 'So what? God. Can't you just leave me alone!' and she gathers up her plate and glass and stalks past me out of the room. I hear her thumping up the stairs. Having slithered from Bea's lap, the cat licks at her back leg with earnest attention.

I sink into the chair Bea's just left. There are drops of milk and crumbs on the table, a sticky jar of cherry jam with the lid left off. I let out a long breath. 'Damn,' I say quietly.

I have the achy hollow pain of homesickness, although there's nothing for me to miss. I have shaped my life purposely to avoid belonging in one place. I haven't settled anywhere since leaving Hawksmoor. Perhaps it's just the tension of pretending. I rub my eyes, remembering too late about the bloody mascara. I told Cecily I'd do this for a week, but suddenly seven days feels impossible. I could leave right now – it would be easy to walk away, catch the next train out of Exeter. I've spent the last seventeen years running away. It's a habit that's hard to break. To stop myself, I consult the little black notebook she left for me. Her instructions are to cook supper, and I read the list of meals she's helpfully included: sausages and mash; chops with peas; shepherd's pie; macaroni and cheese. I frown. She's still cooking food from our childhood. Mostly meat-based, and me a vegetarian. I went veggie years ago at the kibbutz. I forgot to remind her.

I manage to find the ingredients for shepherd's pie and follow Cecily's instructions. There's a lot of chopping, and I'm forced to use several pans. As I wait for it to cook in the oven, the oddness of the situation hits me, the reality of being in my sister's home, the craziness of taking her place. My hands tremble and I have an overwhelming need to get out – to go far away, where I have no responsibilities, where there are no expectations to meet, and no pretence to keep up. The kitchen spins, and I sink into a chair. I focus on breathing, in for four counts, out for four counts. I'm here. Nothing bad has happened. I can do this.

I go upstairs and knock at Bea's door. 'Supper's ready,' I speak through the wood in what I hope is a cheerful voice. No answer. I listen. There's a beat of music. 'Bea?' I call louder. 'Aren't you going to eat something?'

Bea doesn't open the door. 'Go away.'

I want to tell her that I've spent hours cooking something I can't eat, and I've only just managed to clean the mashed potatoes off the pan. I want to tell her that it's taking every ounce of courage just to be here. But she can't know that, and if I'm speaking as her mum, I should probably go on about the importance of protein and vitamins. I hesitate, my hand hovering over her door handle. I don't know how far to take this – should I order her to come down?

I decide to leave Bea to her strop. Downstairs, I lean against the kitchen counter, spooning hot potato into my mouth, trying to avoid the mince. Some of it looks a bit pink. Could uncooked beef cause salmonella? I decide not. I pick at oily salad leaves. I suppose I should wait for Gabriel before I sit down to eat. There's an open bottle of white in the fridge and I pour myself a glass. Every sound makes me cast anxious glances towards the front door. By nine o'clock, I think it would be reasonable to go to bed.

I cover the dish with a tea towel and go up to the bathroom, splashing my face, using Cecily's toothbrush from her wash bag to do my teeth. I skip her long-winded beauty routine. Just this once, I think.

She hasn't left me a note with her contact details. I've searched her room and the kitchen, the two places she might have put an envelope for me. She's normally so thorough and organised; she's left me diagrams of the house and area, lists of chores, and realms of notes on how I should behave, even a map of the town with useful places marked with crosses, so it's strange she's forgotten a detail like her own address. I'm guessing she'll send it to me, or she'll ring when she knows the others will be out. I try not to panic. I'm sure she'll contact me soon.

I pick up the hardback book on the nightstand for something to do, flicking through the first pages. It's a non-fiction tome about the Borgias and despite all the poisonings and betrayals, it makes for dry reading. I learn that cantarella was their poison of choice, probably a compound of arsenic. When it was sprinkled on food and drink, the victim died slowly, growing confused and weak over a period of days. Nice. I try to concentrate on the words, but I'm too tense and I don't want to read about long-ago murders. At last, I hear the front door open and close. I switch off the bedside light and pull the cover up to my chin. I try to decode the movements from downstairs. Are they the footsteps of a drunk? I listen to him coming up the stairs, hear taps running next door. The wall between my bedroom and the bathroom is thin. It feels too intimate. I'm lying so close that I can hear him gargling and spitting, and then the sound of piss drilling into the toilet bowl. I shut my eyes, as if that will block out the images that spool, unwanted, through my mind. A chain flushes. Pipes gurgle in the wall cavities. I hear him come out of the bathroom and walk past my door. A floorboard creaks. I hold my breath.

'Cecily?' comes a loud whisper.

I keep completely still. My heart batters at my ribs. The footsteps move on, up the stairs, and across the ceiling.

4

CECILY

I'd prayed for the miracle of Alice's return. And just to be sure, I'd sent her a letter complaining about Gabriel and his drinking. It wasn't exactly a fib. I'd just exaggerated it, explaining how desperately I wanted to leave him, but that I had no time that wasn't monitored by him. I admit that bit was a white lie. Then I mentioned the word 'divorce'. It worked better than I could have hoped, because she'd suggested the plan straight away, in fact she'd insisted on the swap.

She'd written,

Please let me do this. When we swapped identities as kids, we fooled everyone, remember? I know he's your husband, but if you're not sleeping together and barely speaking, I think I could get away with it. Especially if he doesn't know of my existence. How could anyone who looks so like you not be you? Send me an up-to-date photo of yourself and I'll get my hair cut like yours, get my nails done. You know I haven't set foot in the UK since I left – I guess we all deal with trauma differently – but knowing you need me, knowing I can finally do something to make up for what I did will help me find the strength to come back.

I want to help you break free. Let me give you some time to your-

self, so you can have the opportunity to see a solicitor, look for a job, get started on planning a new life before you tell Gabriel you're leaving him. But the main thing is, by divorcing your husband, you'll be standing up to our father at last. He's controlled you for too long. I wish you could see it. He's a monster, Cecily. Once you've done this, we can be together again. You know we belong in each other's lives.

On my last day at home, I woke up alert and jittery. The feeling stayed with me as I crossed the carpet to open the curtains, tugging the fabric back and staring down at the large privet hedge that guards our tiny scrap of front garden. Goodbye hedge, I thought. Goodbye street. Goodbye seagulls. With any luck, I won't see any of you for a long time.

In the kitchen, Bea was slumped over her breakfast, the cat draped across her lap. 'Morning, darling,' I said as cheerfully as I could, pouring myself a cup of treacly darkness.

Gabriel was there too, buttering toast at the table. He smothered it in marmalade, and bit into it, waving it towards me, 'You should have some.' He chewed and swallowed. 'Carbohydrates are good for hangovers.'

I scowled at him. He knew perfectly well I didn't eat in the morning. I picked an apple out of the fruit bowl and crunched noisily through waxy skin into papery flesh. *There*, I thought. *Happy now?*

I kept munching determinedly, the atmosphere sharp as a knife. I had a shred of peel caught in my teeth and as I picked it out, I remembered an experiment I'd heard about, where two apples were placed in jam jars, and for two weeks one apple was told every day that it was loved, and the other that it was hated. The hated one withered faster, slumping into its rotten heart.

'Have you got plans for today?' Gabriel continued, forcing our stilted conversation, for the sake of Bea, I supposed.

Our eyes met by mistake and slid away. I shook my head. 'Nothing exciting.'

Bea's hand stilled against the cat as she looked up, glancing between me and her father, an anxious furrow between her brows. Milk moistened her top lip in a pale moustache.

'You have some...' I gestured to my own top lip.

Bea blushed and dragged a hand across her mouth. My gaze skimmed her waist. Bea tugged her top down and scraped the last drops of milk from her bowl. My daughter doesn't feel good enough and I understand that feeling well enough myself. Yet, I've never been able to find a way of explaining this to her. Instead, I discovered chocolate wrappers hidden under her bed and threw them in the bin with a sense of having failed.

Gabriel finished his toast and marmalade in two bites, gathered his battered leather satchel, and began the hunt for his keys, playing the part of the forgetful professor with his mop of curls falling into his eyes, haphazardly lurching through the humdrum necessities of life. I'd turned my back unable to watch, loading plates into the dishwasher, but Gabriel approached as if for a goodbye kiss, and I couldn't stop myself from flinching. The wounds under my nightdress hadn't healed. My skin was sore, crusted with dried blood. He saw my expression, and hesitated, frowning.

'Come on, Bea,' he said in his hearty voice. 'Let's leave your mother in peace.'

'Goodbye, darling,' I called after her. 'Have a good day.' Too little, too late.

* * *

It's strange to think all of that happened yesterday morning, and in the afternoon, Bea came home to Alice. But my daughter doesn't look me straight in the eye any more, and Alice will have slipped seamlessly into my shoes. It hurts to think that Bea won't even notice. It hurts that she doesn't understand how much I love her.

It's nearly dawn, and the sky is streaked with red, the distant castle a black wound on the horizon. I shiver and wrap my arms around myself. I'm not dressed for the dank early morning air. It's just me and some foxes in an empty street, but I shouldn't be here, standing outside our house. It's tempting to linger for longer, to watch for the stirrings of activity, the morning routine beginning, just to check that my life is continuing without me. And I have a yearning to glimpse my sister through a window or an open doorway. But the curtains are closed, and the privet hedge blocks the view of the door, and anyway, the whole point of this charade is to slip away unnoticed. It's what I prayed for. And if this is going to work, Alice can't know how close I am. She'll soon discover the real reason I need her to take my place. All I can do is hope that when the time comes, she'll understand.

5

ALICE

I wake with a jolt, as if someone is standing over me. It takes me a split second to remember where I am. I should have set an alarm. Cecily said to get up around eight. I grab the clock on the bedside table to check the time. Seven thirty. I flop back onto the pillow. Above my head, Cecily's crucifix is impaled to the wall.

Two strangers wait for me downstairs. I might look exactly like my twin, but I'm not her. We no longer share a life. In the past, our mannerisms mirrored each other's. But over the years I'll have developed gestures and facial expressions that are different from hers. Won't they guess straight away?

I abandoned Cecily once. Left her alone with our father. I didn't try hard enough to save her from him and Hawksmoor. This is my chance to make it right.

Pipes gurgle in wall cavities, there's a muted sound of activity coming from other rooms, a rustling outside on the landing, and the sudden clumping of someone going downstairs. I hold my breath, listening. I get out of bed and root around in Cecily's top drawer, my hiding place for her little black book. The familiar neat, cramped script of my sister's writing is comforting:

Weekdays: get up at about 8 a.m. Have a shower once the others are done with the bathroom. Put some make-up on. Go downstairs to say goodbye before they leave. Bea gets herself up and sorts her own breakfast (Coco Pops or Sugar Puffs). Gabriel makes a pot of coffee. I have a cup, but I never eat anything until lunch.

She says I don't have to get dressed, but I'm aware of my tattoo, a hummingbird hovering in the dip between the sacral and lumbar bones of my spine. It seems to burn through my flimsy, silky pyjamas. Cecily's pyjamas. I decide to skip the shower. The idea of being naked in the same house as a man I don't know makes me feel weird, even if there is a lock on the door. I run my fingers through my strange, short hair, biting my lip in concentration as I apply a wobbly line of black around my eyes, and then stick some mascara on my top lashes. My new longer fake nails make this a dangerous operation. Being my sister is so much more time-consuming than being myself.

I look through her drawers to find something to wear. Nothing appeals. I delve deeper, rejecting anything that looks too formal, too tight, too uncomfortable. My fingers find soft fabric and pull it free. A voluminous white cotton shirt appears. I hold it up. But it's stained on the back with reddish brown caught in the weave. Puzzled, I lift it closer to my face, smelling a faint tang of metal. I drop the shirt, and push onto my feet, limbs tensed for flight. Blood. But who does it belong to? And why has she hidden the shirt in her drawer instead of putting it in the wash? Fear flickers briefly, muddling my thoughts. I pick it up again and touch the stains. The obvious answer is that she cut herself accidentally, mopped up the mess and then forgot about it. I bundle the shirt back and shut the drawer, trying not to think about the amount of blood, and the kind of wound it would take to produce it. In the next drawer up, I find exercise leggings and a sweatshirt – much more my kind of thing. As I go downstairs, I hear the deep voice from last night again and my heart flips. I remind myself of Cecily's bravery. *Divorce.* In our family nobody would even say the word out loud. To us, it wasn't a solution to an emotional impasse, it wasn't a legal process, it was sacrilegious, forbidden, something that would bring down the wrath of our father as surely as burning a crucifix or saying the Lord's Prayer backwards. Knowing she wants to divorce Gabriel is like a neon sign announcing her intention to stop being Daddy's puppet. She's been his 'yes girl' forever, striving to be the perfect Catholic daughter. If this is her bid for freedom from all that, I have no choice but to answer the call. This is a rescue mission.

They are both there, at the kitchen table, Gabriel and Bea. I'm doing this for her, I tell myself, as I fumble for her gold cross around my neck. I walk in, trying to look nonchalant. I hold my breath, waiting for them to denounce me, at the very least to stare at me in consternation. Bea ignores me, continuing to eat her cereal. The radio is on and a newsreader is talking about Chechnya. Gabriel switches it off and his eyes meet mine, skimming the surface and darting away. 'Hi,' he says, finishing his mouthful of toast. 'How are you feeling today? Better?'

I mutter an affirmative, finding it impossible to form actual words.

He nods to a percolator on the surface. 'Just made. Thought you might need it.'

I go across and pour some coffee, thankful that I scoped out the cupboards yesterday and can recall where the cups live. My stomach rumbles. The smell of toast and butter is torture, but Cecily skips breakfast. I lean against the surface in what I hope is a natural pose, and sip hot liquid, not sure what to say or do.

Bea pushes back her chair and clatters her bowl into the sink. 'I'm off,' she says to the room in general. 'Don't want to miss the bus.'

'Bye, sweet pea,' Gabriel says, as she drops a kiss onto the top of his head. It's a normal scene between father and daughter, tender and every day. I think of the bloodied shirt, and my mouth is dry.

Bea gives me a stony look. 'Bye,' she mutters, brushing past and out of the door.

'Bye,' I say. 'Have... have a good day.'

The front door slams. Gabriel glances at me sympathetically. 'She'll come round,' he says. 'You know she loves you really. Even if you are drinking from her favourite mug.'

I stare at him, then look at the cup in my hand. It was the one my fingers grasped first. It's got a big pink flower on the front and seventies lettering declaring Flower Power. I wonder what other little peculiarities and family habits my sister has neglected to mention.

I begin to wash Bea's bowl for something to do, running the tap to rinse it, turning it over in my hands – how long can I spend cleaning one bowl? I snatch glances at him from the corners of my eyes. He has smooth, olive skin, thick russet hair, and his eyes are an unusual, brilliant shade of green. I can see why Cecily found him attractive. Although not conventionally handsome, he has a good, strong face with broad bones, a wide mouth and a large, slightly squashed-looking nose. He's wearing worn looking cords and a checked shirt, giving him an academic vibe. Not my type.

He gets up and puts his plate and cup in the dishwasher next to me. I freeze, not knowing whether to say anything. Cecily said they hardly speak. He hesitates, scratching his neck, and then takes a step closer. He's stocky, not tall, about my height. My fingers tighten on the washing up brush and I stare at the taps, my body rigid.

'It suits you, I think, to have short hair,' he says. I flinch. A compliment was the last thing I was expecting. I slide my gaze towards him and away. 'Cecily,' his voice lowers. 'We need to find a time to talk, don't we?'

Panic crashes through me. She promised this wouldn't happen. They sleep in separate rooms, live separate lives. I swallow and place the washing up brush in the rack next to the sink. There's a residue of white bubbles on my hands. I wipe them on my jeans and turn slowly to face him.

We stare into each other's eyes. I see his pupils expand and then retract into pinpoints of light. I look down at my feet in Cecily's fuzzy slippers. He sighs. 'We can't go on like this.'

I lift my shoulders slightly and let them fall. 'No,' I agree, as it seems the only thing I can say. I keep my gaze on the furry slippers.

'This evening then?' he suggests. 'Bea has her guitar lesson after school.' He shuffles from one foot to the other. 'I can get home by five.'

'Right.' I'm aware that I'm leaning away from him, twisting my torso, my hip jammed against the edge of the kitchen surface. I dart a glance at him and notice fine lines webbing his eyes; there's grey around his temples and a deep furrow between his eyebrows.

'Okay.' He sighs again. 'See you later.'

I grip the edge of the sink and wait for his footsteps to echo through the hall, for the front door to open and close, quietly this time. Blood rushes through my veins in a tidal wave of confusion. I cut two thick slices of bread and spread them with butter and honey and eat them quickly, not tasting anything. I drink the rest of my cold coffee, my heart surging as if it wants to escape my chest.

'What am I supposed to do?' I ask the empty kitchen. 'Dammit!' The cat gives me an inscrutable gaze as if considering my question, and then turns abruptly to wash her back leg. 'You're no help,' I tell her.

I have six more days to get through.

Bea and Gabriel think I'm Cecily. It almost seemed too easy. But I won't be able to keep up the pretence, particularly if he insists on talking. I mean, how is that going to work? I see disaster looming; I'm going to be outed. I know it. And I feel something else I didn't expect – shame. It creeps inside me, cold and withering.

I need to tell Cecily what's happened. I look for her contact details again. I must have missed the envelope. I search the whole house, reaching into drawers, kneeling to peer under the oven and sofa in case it fell and got kicked out of sight. I even look under my mattress. I find three bottles of vodka hidden in strange places, but no envelope. Why hasn't Cecily let me know how to reach her? And I begin to worry: has something happened to her?

6

CECILY

The morning Mummy was due to drive Henry back to boarding school, I was busy dissecting my kipper. I'd pulled out as many bones as I could, arranging them like needles on the side of my plate. The yellow flesh made me want to retch, but it was a sin to be ungrateful. Chewing a small mouthful, my gaze roved around the breakfast table. Mummy was glancing anxiously at the clock on the wall. Henry still hadn't made an appearance. Daddy snapped his newspaper flat with a sigh and took out his pocket watch. 'Half past.'

Mummy stood up. 'I'll go and fetch him.' Dilly uncurled herself from the floor expectantly, ears cocked, little snout pointing up.

'Sit down, Emmeline, one of the girls can go.'

Mummy sat back on the edge of her seat. I placed my fork on my plate and jumped up. 'I'll go, Daddy.'

I hurried out into the corridor, through the long gallery to the main hall, taking the stairs two at a time; but Henry wasn't in his room. His school uniform was still laid out on his chair. The battered trunk fastened with a padlock waiting on the floor. I padded down the cold corridor to the nearest bathroom and knocked. 'Henry?'

Hesitantly, I pushed the door. He wasn't standing, legs straddled over the loo, glaring over his shoulder, shouting '*get out!*' The claw foot bath was empty, apart from a fat-bodied spider attempting to climb the chipped enamel sides. I glanced at the sink with its brown rust stain. Henry's toothbrush was lying on its side, bristles bent and crushed.

I got back to the dining room, panting, filled with the importance of my task as messenger. 'He's not there,' I told Daddy. 'He's not anywhere. Just his trunk.'

Daddy let out an exclamation of annoyance as he threw his paper onto the table. 'What is the wretched boy playing at?'

My stomach contracted. All of us stumbled to our feet, waiting to be told what to do. We spread out like a proper search party, calling up and down staircases, opening rooms that had been shut up for years, peering across furniture draped with dusty sheets, ghostly shapes stranded in the gloom. A bat flew out of the old nursery, whirring wildly from the curtains. Dilly paced at the bottom of the stairs, adding to the panic with hysterical yapping.

I prayed for Henry to come back. Every second he stayed hidden would make things worse for him.

We congregated in the hall to report back to Daddy. There was no sign of Henry. Daddy's face was as hard as one of the gargoyles peering from St. Mary's roof. 'Right,' he barked. 'Search the grounds.'

We tumbled out of the front door, uncertain where to look. There was so much land – and beyond the walls, the fells. How would we find him? The Labradors, sensing a game, and hardly more than puppies, loped after Mummy as she ran across the front lawn towards the tarn, their barks joyful. I stared after her, thinking my brother couldn't possibly be drowned. Not Henry, the best swimmer I knew. Mummy's hair came loose from her bun, brown strands caught in the wind, wispy and fly-away. Her foot slid, as one of the dogs got tangled in her stride, and a shoe came off. She hopped unsteadily as she came back for it, and stood blinking in the light, as if she had something in her eye. The two big dogs gathered around, confused by the hold-up, sniffing her shins. She fished a hanky out from her sleeve, blew her nose. 'It's all a misunderstanding,' she said to no one in particular. 'He's such a good boy.'

I ran to the yew, certain I'd find him crouched at its dark centre, his back tucked against the warm bark, concealed by swagged branches.

Henry loved the tree, and so did God. It was holy. People used to carry yew branches to church on Palm Sunday. But he wasn't behind the screen of green fronds or hiding inside the split trunk. There was just a mistle thrush, pecking at fallen red fruit, the air sickly with the smell of boiled sweets.

He turned up in the end, a little while later, not floating face down in the black mirror of the tarn but on his two feet and only a bit damp. We were congregated on the front steps to receive the next instructions from Daddy, when the dogs started to bark in greeting. And there he was, coming slowly across the lawn, covered in scratches, jeans muddy at the knees, bits of leaf in his hair. He'd forgotten the time, he said. His lie was half-hearted, his eyes red-rimmed. The dogs panted at his heels, tails wagging, overjoyed, Dilly licking his ankles in ecstasy.

Daddy called the animals to him sharply, the two Labs slinking low to crouch at his feet. 'I won't have a wet for a son,' he said.

At the entrance to Daddy's study, Henry started to untuck his shirt ready for the strap. But Daddy shook his head, turned on his heels and marched upstairs. Henry stared after him, and then followed as if in a trance.

Mummy, Alice and I waited at the bottom with the dogs. My heart lunged into my mouth. I felt sick, the taste of kippers repeating in my throat.

'No. Please!' We heard Henry in the distance. And then nothing.

Mummy raised her hands to her mouth. She called after them, 'Darling? Edmund? Henry's already late for school... Don't you think...' her voice too weak to carry to the top of the house.

There was no reply. We stood looking at each other. The muffled-up silence of the house caught at us, made us glance away, nobody wanting to say it out loud. I was relieved it wasn't me locked in the dark, then immediately worried I was being selfish. Tears dripped down Alice's blotchy cheeks. She dragged a hand across her nose and wiped it over her navy school skirt.

Mummy didn't remind us that we should set off for the bus stop. She scooped up Dilly, struggling to speak. 'Your... your father knows... what's best...' her voice trailed away, and she went off in the direction of the kitchen, shoulders slumped, limping on her left side; she must have hurt herself when she'd slipped. It occurred to me that she looked lonely. We three had each other – but who did Mummy have? No friends or relatives. Her only sister was divorced, so of course, we couldn't acknowledge her. As a result, we'd only met her before she left her husband, and I couldn't really remember because we'd been babies. She still sent us money, which was useful.

I followed Alice to her bedroom. We sat on the floor, backs against the hard metal bar of Alice's bed. I sucked a rope of hair until it caught in my throat. Then I applied my attention to gnawing at what was left of my nails, teeth worrying fraying cuticles, the taste of knives on my tongue. Alice got up and paced the room, kicking the skirting board, pushing her hands through her hair, mussing it into tangles. 'How long is he going to keep him in there?' she asked with a violent pounding of her fist into her palm.

Alice's emotions spilled out in a messy spurts like lemonade from a shaken bottle. It was up to me to be the calm one. 'It's for his own good,' I said in the pious voice grown-ups used.

She spun around, and I shrank from her glare. 'You're an idiot,' she told me. 'You believe everything Daddy says. One day,' her voice was fierce, 'we'll all leave this place. And we'll never come back. Serve him right.'

I knew she'd thump me if I disagreed. But of course, we weren't going to leave Hawksmoor. It was our home. Daddy was doing what was best – he needed Henry to be brave and strong, because Henry was the heir, the last hope – I'd heard him tell Mummy when I lingered outside the door, 'It's all on Henry now. We've reached the end of the line.'

I knew there couldn't be any more sons because Mummy nearly died having me and Alice. She never talked about it, but once, Jane had explained that Alice and I had both been in the wrong position in her tummy, and I had got stuck in Mummy's pelvis. It was lucky we hadn't all died. After that, Mummy couldn't have any more children.

Henry reappeared hours later in his school uniform, limping, smudged with dust. He walked with deliberate care, lugging his trunk after him, the trailing end bumping against each step. There was a cobweb caught in his hair. I wanted to pick it out but didn't dare.

Daddy came stomping after him, eagle-eyed. 'We'll have no more nonsense?' He held out his hand to shake at the front door.

Henry took it. 'No, sir,' his voice hardly more than a whisper.

Daddy grabbed the other end of the trunk and together they wedged it into the open boot, cramming it in next to the empty petrol can, wellington boots and musty blankets. After a moment of hesitation, I lunged forward and hugged Henry. He smelt of damp and mouse droppings. His shoulders were rigid.

Mummy was waiting by the driver's door. 'I called ahead. Explained we'd been delayed.' She went to touch Henry, her hand hovering, and then seemed to lose confidence. Instead, she called out, 'Jump in, darling,' in her best cheerful voice.

Daddy stood with legs apart and arms crossed, the Labradors at his feet. Mummy started the engine and the car rolled away. Daddy's gaze was on the Volvo, the curl of its exhaust, sunlight glinting on the back window as it disappeared around the corner. I thought he looked like the oil paintings in the drawing room come to life, the noble bump at the bridge of his nose, the firm mouth under his moustache, eyes that blazed fire at the world, burning with conviction. In Daddy, I saw all the other brave Deveraux men who'd given their lives for their faith, sacrificed themselves to save their tradition. But today he looked disappointed, and I wished I dared to try and find the right thing to say, whatever it was that would make him feel better. He turned and stomped into the house.

'Bastard,' Alice whispered under her breath, glaring at his retreating shadow. 'I hate him.'

I lunged forwards, clamping a hand over my sister's mouth to stop her blaspheming. Ignoring her furious glare, I kept my fingers fixed in place. It would be bad if God heard, but worse if Daddy did.

Alice jerked away with a muffled exclamation, and stalked off towards the tarn, her attitude clearly saying that I wasn't to follow. I stood alone in the drive, wiping the slime on my skirt, before I examined the small red indentations in the fat base of my thumb where Alice's teeth had found their mark.

7

CECILY

Up here on the hill, the wind flies straight from the channel, grabbing at my hair, whipping strands into my eyes, and across my forehead. It's too short to hook behind my ears and I keep pushing it back, as I squint down towards the distant lights of Exeter. I have a good idea where our street is and settle my gaze in that direction, wondering how Alice is coping and if Gabriel and Bea are suspicious of the woman living with them, confused by the differences they can probably sense. We might be mirror image twins, but I noticed from an early age that people preferred her to me; they smiled at her more, wanted to be her friend. I could never understand what made her more attractive. Even Daddy liked her better – and she despised him.

Since I married Gabriel, I've lived in this town. It's my safe place, my burrow. I never expected to find a sense of belonging outside the Lake District and Hawksmoor. I don't like to think of Alice in my home, touching my things, changing my routine, being me. But I need her. I can't do this without her.

I discover a packet of crushed crisps in my pocket and rip it open, finishing the lot before I stop for breath. I probe the salt-skinned roof of my mouth with my tongue, hooking hidden crumbs from my teeth. When I was a child, I used to worry that gluttony would be my undoing. How ironic. It's such a small sin when I'm already guilty twice-over of the worst of all. *Thou shalt not kill.* Those murder mysteries Gabriel likes so much contain the clues to why and how the crime is committed. The 'why' in this case is obvious; the 'how' less so. I still haven't worked out my method, but I need to get on with it. Two days have already gone by, and Alice must be upset and worried that I haven't left the promised address and telephone number. I have a moment of regret, before I remember that she was implicit in the second sin. I can't take all the blame.

Perhaps God won't understand the balancing act of my reasoning, and this will be the transgression that casts me into hell for eternity. But I have no choice, not after my conversation with Edith Baxter.

* * *

The first time I saw her, it was a Sunday morning after church and I was kneeling on damp grass by the drive, my arms a cross-hatching of bloodied scratches. I heard a crunch of wheels over gravel and watched as a Morris Minor parked in front of the house and a woman got out, straightening her felt hat. I knew we weren't expecting visitors – we hardly ever had them – and I stood up from behind the straggly roses, clutching the trowel, to get a better look. 'Hello?' I said. The stranger gasped and pressed her palm over her heart.

'I'm here to see Edmund Deveraux,' she said, recovering herself. She spoke as if she knew Daddy, but I'd never seen her before. If this woman really knew him, I thought, she'd know that he hated being disturbed on a Sunday, especially this close to lunch.

I gripped the trowel in earthy fingers, dithering. She had a stern, craggy face with an impressive nose and thin mouth. Blinking rapidly, her fingers touched the buttons on her shabby tweed jacket. I didn't want to be the one to tell Daddy there was a visitor. He'd been known to throw something at people who disturbed his work – there were cannon balls and daggers on his desk, as well as books, so it was always a risk. I shook my head and ducked down behind the roses again, spying on her through a tangle of thorny stems and sticky weeds. After tugging on the bell pull, she stood, fiddling with her skirt, muttering to herself. There was a volley of barking. Eventually, the door was opened by Alice. They both disappeared inside. I waited a moment and crept after them.

Alice appeared from the long gallery.

'Where is she?' I asked.

'He asked me to bring her to the library,' Alice said, eyes wide. 'But you should have seen the look on his face when I told him who was here!' She gave a mock shudder. 'Rather her than me.'

A glance passed between us, and we nodded in silent agreement, hurrying down the corridors. The library door was shut, and we waited with our ears pressed to the thick wedge of wood, holding our breath to listen better. Sounds were muffled, but I could make out the low tone of Daddy's voice. He wasn't shouting, but it was worse when he spoke quietly, the threat was in the hush. The woman's voice was weak as it rose and wavered. I could only catch odd words, 'time' and 'cruel.' Then there was the shuffle of shoes approaching the door. We fled towards the back stairs, skidding around the corner, and crouched out of sight behind the wall on the first step, hands clamped over our mouths.

'I've told you before, the matter is settled,' we heard him say. 'You're wasting your time. I'd better not catch you on my property again.'

'Damn you. You have no heart,' we heard her say, and there was a sob in her voice. 'I hope you and your family rot in hell.'

I gasped in shock, and a shiver of excitement ran through me. This was just the sort of thing I should be writing in my diary. It would add some melodrama to the ordinary details about what I'd eaten for breakfast and whether Alice or Henry had beaten me at Monopoly. We hunched on the step, hardly daring to take a breath until both pairs of footsteps had faded away. 'Blimey,' Alice looked at me with her eyebrows halfway up her forehead, 'she cursed us!'

'It wasn't a proper curse,' I said, crossing myself to be safe. 'God will protect us.' But my pulse flickered and jumped. 'Did you find out who she is?'

Alice screwed up her face. 'I think she said... Miss Baxter. Edith Baxter.'

'Doesn't mean anything to me.'

'Me neither.' Alice made a face. 'Wonder what he did to her.'

'Nothing,' I said, getting up from the step. 'She's probably mad. She looked mad, didn't she?'

The gong rang. 'You've got earth on your chin,' Alice told me. 'And you haven't changed for lunch.'

I looked down at the blackened knees of my gardening jeans, and leapt to my feet, scrambling up the stairs, panic rising in my throat, *Mother of God, don't let me be late.*

The innocence of it. Worried about a bit of mud on my knees, about being late for lunch.

8

ALICE

I'll leave Gabriel a note saying I have a headache and keep out of his way in Cecily's room this evening. Meanwhile, I have a day to fill. I wander around the house barefoot, peering into rooms. The whole place is full of bad Feng Shui. The Chinese believe a man's destiny is bound to his environment, so Cecily, Henry and I never stood a chance. But Cecily could improve the flow of energy here. For a start, she's got the wrong curtains in the bay window. Vertical lines on fabric shut out the world like a prison cell, and furniture should never block the outside either. The sofa is right in front of the window. I heave at it, pulling at one arm, then getting all my weight behind it, to push it across the floorboards. I arrange it in the middle of the room looking towards the bay. Then I reposition a small table on the other side of it. For some reason, her house has no plants. I love indoor greenery; it brings life and energy.

If I had my own place, I'd fill it with living things, plants, some rescue dogs and cats, a parrot maybe. But because I'm always on the move, I've never had a pet, never even had a plant for more than a month or so. I can't imagine what it must be like to limit your life to one town, one house, one man. I think of Ekkehard, my latest lover, a sax player I'd met in a club in Berlin. I'd liked the clean lines of his body, his dextrous fingers and generous laugh. Musicians understand how to love lightly and move on – their existence is as peripatetic as mine – they don't think in terms of ownership.

The phone rings in the hall, the sound startling in the quiet house. At last! I rush to snatch it up. 'Cecily!'

But it's just someone for Gabriel, and I scribble their name on the jotter next to the telephone on the table with a dull heart. She should have called by now. It's selfish of her – and what if there's an emergency? There *is* an emergency. The proposed talk. It's almost as if she doesn't care if I'm discovered.

Upstairs, to take my mind off it, I consider the problem of her bed. The headboard is up against the dividing wall of the bathroom. The loo is just the other side, and the soil pipes must run under the bed. Seriously bad energy. I try to move the bloody thing, but it weighs as much as a bus. I manage to shift it a few inches, and then give up. I look out of the window into the unfamiliar street. A blonde woman is jogging past, her tight behind encased in purple leggings, a matching pair of trainers on her feet. She looks up just as she passes under the window and slows a fraction, waving. Surprised, I raise my hand in a jerky mimic. I suppose she knows Cecily. She said most of her friends were connected to the church. This woman doesn't look the type. But then, like drug dealers and thieves, you can't tell by appearance alone.

I look at the fussy little watch I've strapped on my wrist. My sister has the worst taste. I look again and check the thing hasn't stopped working. It's like I've fallen into a time warp. Hours have passed without me realising. I haven't made supper yet. I decide to ignore Cecily's list. I can't face cooking meat. I run downstairs and root around in the fridge, realising I have just enough ingredients to throw together a ratatouille. I leave the food in a casserole on the side for the others to reheat, and delve into a drawer, unearth an old shopping list, turn it over and start to scribble a note to Gabriel, explaining that I'm ill, but I stop after a couple of words, realising he might see a difference in our handwriting. Mine is bigger, more of a scrawl than hers. I throw the note in the bin and try again, trying to forge Cecily's cramped and careful script.

In the bathroom, I clean my teeth, washing my hands and face with the bar of soap on the sink that smells of orange blossom. I ignore Cecily's beauty routine again. Too fiddly and time consuming, and I can't concentrate, my ears straining to listen for the front door in case he comes home early. When I hear it open, his feet on the doormat and rustle of a jacket being taken off, I creep towards the landing, tracking his movements below me as he goes into the hall and kitchen. I retreat into Cecily's room, shutting myself in, wishing there was a key to turn. Has he seen my message yet?

When his feet thunder up the stairs, I know he's seen it. The approaching racket kick-starts my adrenaline. There's a loud knock on my door. I throw myself onto the bed, pulling the covers over my head, breath stalling in my chest. If he comes in, I'll pretend to be asleep. But what if he shakes me awake, or drags me out? Maybe better to answer him now, put on a weak voice, tell him I can't speak for the pain in my head? He knocks again and says, 'Cecily?' I want to put my hands over my ears. He repeats her name, then I hear him sigh loudly. He goes away, muttering.

Later, I hear Bea coming home, the slam of the door, the stomp of her feet. She goes straight into the kitchen. I think of her furious response when I'd asked about her being hungry. They must both be downstairs. When the quiet murmur of their voices rises from the kitchen, I get out of the covers and sit on the bed cross-legged. Bea seems to be relaxed with her father. I hear laughter. Garlicky, tomatoey scents drift upstairs and my mouth waters. I wish I'd thought of making a sandwich and taking it upstairs with me – it's my second night of going to bed hungry.

I learnt yoga on the island of Santorini, and in Kerala I spent time in ashrams where yoga was a daily ritual. With nothing else to occupy my time, I drag a chair over to the door and wedge it under the handle. My feet slip on acrylic tufts of carpet as I practice sun salutations, downward dog, upward dog, stretching out stiff hamstrings, working until my shoulders shake. But when I lie prone in shavasana, my mind refuses to be still. I have five days left.

Next morning, he asks me coldly if I'm feeling better and I can't meet his eyes. He knows I was faking it. Monday can't come fast enough. According to the plan, Cecily will arrive straight after the others go off to school and university, giving us a day together before Bea gets home. I'll make sure I've disappeared by then to avoid any danger of us being caught with each other. That's what we've agreed. I was excited and nervous about it, but now I'm having doubts – why hasn't she rung me? She knows I'm alone here every day.

Watching Gabriel's hunched shoulders as he prepares to leave the house, I decipher the hurt in his body. He hasn't mentioned the talk again. I suppose he's wary of further rejection. I wasn't expecting him to care this much.

Bea avoids eye contact with me. She wolfs down her breakfast, kisses the cat, and escapes with her bag over her shoulder, leaving with her father. She brightens in his company, and I see her smile at something he says, a dimple appearing in her left cheek. After they've gone, I sink into a chair at the kitchen table, idly wiping toast crumbs into my palm. This house is full of the unspoken. And even though Cecily has created a tidy home full of order, the atmosphere reminds me of Hawksmoor. There's something dark under the surface. Since leaving home, I promised myself that I wouldn't be like my parents. I go out of my way to be truthful, never wanting to slip back into a life soured with secrets. Yet here I am, marooned in the middle of the biggest pretence of all.

I pull at the neckline of Cecily's sweatshirt. I feel strangled, claustrophobic. Since childhood, I can't stand to be confined. I pull on a jacket hanging on the coatrack and drop Cecily's keys into one of the pockets. The jacket is a little too big for me, shoulders drooping, cuffs falling halfway down my hands. It must belong to Gabriel. The woollen fabric is worn and soft, smelling of clean earth and the sea. I find a loose button in the other pocket, a small shell, silvered with mother of pearl, a perfectly smooth black stone.

Exeter is a pretty town, full of painted Victorian villas, cobbled streets, and the screaming of gulls. Across rooftops, I glimpse the Gothic outlines of the cathedral, and the ruins of Rougemont Castle on a distant hill, exactly as Cecily described in her letters. As I make my way down the street, the sky opens before me like a thrown tablecloth of brilliant blue, white clouds smudging its surface in floury fingerprints. I'd forgotten how tender the colours are in England. The leaves are out and faces of crocuses and daffodils brighten front gardens. I get to a quay, busy with people. The river is a wide expanse of gleaming water, and I watch a large sailing boat motoring along. I'm guessing it's heading for the choppier open sea.

A breeze catches the water, tossing up starbursts of light and spray. The big yacht disappears around a bend. I imagine triangles of white canvas swelling with wind, carrying the unknown sailors further and further away. My stomach aches, responding to a longing to escape on that boat. I was little more than a child when I left the country, going straight to a kibbutz near the Sea of Galilee, picking apples, and taking a grim pleasure in imagining my father's apoplectic reaction if he knew where I was. Even after the kibbutz, my failed stint as an au pair, and travelling with new-found friends, I still thought I might return home after six months, a year, three years. But then there came a time when I knew it wasn't possible any more.

But this ache is different – it's not just me fretting at my lack of freedom, it's also a hangover from the atmosphere this morning, the tension in the house – but it's not my ache, not my problem. I shove my hands into my pockets and turn back. Bea will be home from school soon.

* * *

I find a health food shop on my way back and stock up on herbal teas, hummus, rye bread and lavender oil, using the cheque book Cecily left me. And there's a flower shop, Blooming Lovely, where I buy a sturdy-looking peace lily and a couple of lucky bamboos and three earthenware pots. I arrange the plants in the living room on the floor by the bay window and put my shopping away in the kitchen cupboards. I'm switching the kettle on when Bea comes in. She startles when she sees me, and I continue to pour boiling water onto a fennel teabag, mashing it against the side of the cup, hoping I haven't chosen another of her favourite mugs or committed some other unknown faux pas.

'Bea,' I say quickly before she can disappear up to her room. 'Can we... Can we talk?'

She gives me a mistrustful look. 'What about?'

'Nothing in particular,' I say, blowing onto the surface of my tea. 'Just. I don't know. Anything.'

She scowls at me. 'Are you going senile?'

I laugh. 'No!' I smile. 'I hope not. It's just, well, I know things haven't been good between us, and... and I want to try and change that...' I push on, 'and the best way is by talking. Right?'

She stares at me, wariness tightening her gaze. 'You start, then.'

I feel a rush of relief. 'First, I want to say sorry for anything I've done to upset you. And maybe we can talk about that when you're ready. No rush,' I add, hastily.

She snorts disparagingly.

'Maybe I haven't been a good listener in the past,' I say, turning the cup in my hands. 'But think of me as... as a new person. I had a chance to really think about things recently. And I'd like to do better.'

'Maybe you can start by being nicer to Dad.'

I wasn't expecting that. 'Okay,' I agree slowly. 'I'll try.' I put my cup on the side. 'I've bought some bread and hummus – want some? I'm starving.'

She shrugs and sits down. I put out a bowl of hummus, slice the rye bread, and throw together a green salad, placing them all on the table with plates and cutlery. She investigates the hummus, scooping it on her fingertip and sniffing it before she spreads it over a slice of bread.

'Tell me about Courtney Love – why do you like her so much?' I pour out two glasses of water for us.

She gives me a suspicious look. 'Why?'

'I'm interested.'

'Since when have you been interested in me?'

'Probably always,' I say. 'But definitely now.'

'Is this about me eating too much?'

'What? No,' I say. 'I really would like to know. Is it her voice, or her lyrics?'

She gives me a look through narrowed eyes, as if she's searching out a hidden trick; but when she sees that I'm serious, she tilts her head to one side. 'There's all this power and vulnerability in her songs,' she says, unable to keep enthusiasm from bobbing up inside her voice. 'And I like her style – kind of grungy sexy, the vintage thing.'

'Yes,' I agree. 'When I was younger, all the singers I liked represented something I was looking for. Especially Debbie Harry. She was a rebel and that's what I aspired to.'

'Never heard of her.' She gives me a puzzled glance and scoops the cat into her lap. 'You're acting kind of weird.'

I laugh. A quick trill of amusement. Ha, ha. My heart is hammering at my ribs, but I want to try and make a connection with her. I feel as if we're getting somewhere. I can't hide in Cecily's room until Monday. I want to at least understand why Bea is so hostile to her mum. Perhaps I can help smooth things over between them.

'So?' I say, through a mouthful of bread. 'About Courtney?'

She makes a noise of approval. 'This is good,' she says. 'You've never bought this... what-did-you-call-it... before.'

'Hummus. It's made of chickpeas. I thought we could try eating simple, healthier things,' I say, with a bright smile.

'So... This *is* about my eating?' She puts her fork down, glaring at me.

'No,' I hold up my hands. 'I promise it's not.'

'It's weird as well,' she mutters. 'You usually make stuff and then don't eat it yourself.' She spreads more hummus on some bread. 'Just sit there, drinking wine and staring at me and Dad.'

'Well, I'm not going to do that any more,' I say firmly. 'And we were talking about Courtney Love. Is there something about her you identify with?'

'I don't know.' She tucks a strand of hair behind her ear. 'I suppose I like it that she's difficult, that she's angry with the world. She's unhappy, isn't she? I can identify with that.'

'Bea,' I say softly, 'is there anything I can do?'

'You can stop trying to make me into a clone of you,' she retorts, pushing her plate away. 'Being skinny won't make me feel better. I'm not you. And I'm not a religious freak.'

A tremor of shock runs through me. I swallow, and falter, struggling for the right words. 'I'm sorry if I've tried to force you into being someone you're not,' I manage. 'But it's not always easy being a mum. That's why I want us to be more transparent, about everything.'

Her body tenses and I worry that she's going to retreat to her room again. Lock me out. Like I've been locking Gabriel out. She squeezes the cat closer and presses her face into long fur. 'You haven't even told me off for picking Sukie up while I'm eating.'

My mouth is dry. I must be careful. 'Yes. Well,' I frown, 'I didn't want to spoil the moment. But now you come to mention it, you should put her down while you're at the table.'

Bea kisses Sukie and puts her gently on the floor.

'And what about that group... The one on a poster in your room... Magic Dirt?' I press on. 'What do you like about them?'

She gives me a cool look. 'I just like their music, Mum.' She scrapes the last of the butter onto a corner of crust and pops it in her mouth. 'I have homework.'

I nod and stand up to collect our dirty plates. 'Go on, then.' She picks up her bag and I think I see a small smile curling her lips. 'But I do mean it,' I add. 'About being honest. About talking. Let's not do the silent treatment any more.'

'And Dad?' she says, one eyebrow raised.

'Yeah,' I say, turning away to stack the dishwasher. 'Dad, too. No more silent treatment.' I can feel her waiting for more. I straighten and turn. 'Promise,' I say quietly.

I hate making promises, especially ones I can't keep.

She nods, as if we've made a pact, and leaves the room.

9

CECILY

Summer at Hawksmoor meant smells of cut grass and honeysuckle wafting in from the garden, the beech trees darkening to deep waxy green and the wood pigeons cooing as if their lives depended on it. It also meant for six weeks, Alice and I were free of school, free from the long bus ride twice daily, scratchy uniforms, nuns in their crow-black habits, and the other girls, full of pimples and snide remarks. Best of all, Henry came home for the holidays.

About the time he was due to arrive, we sat astride the lion statues flanking the front steps, taking one each. Waiting impatiently, I leant forward over the frozen mane, my hand stroking an alert ear; the lion seemed to be listening for the sound of the approaching Volvo too. A rumble of engine made me sit up, and we waved our arms over our heads, whooping in customary fashion, as the car appeared around the corner. Daddy hated driving, so it was always Mummy at the wheel. She pulled up in front of the house, and we waited for the first sight of our brother. Strangely, he appeared from the back seat instead of the passenger side, getting out with his tie skew-whiff, and the top button of his white shirt undone. He fumbled to do it up, glancing at the front door with a look of nervous anticipation. But he needn't worry, Daddy was out.

Before either of us had a chance to rush to him, another boy leapt from the other side of the car, hurried around to the driver's door, and opened it for Mummy. She emerged with Dilly in her arms, smiling. 'Thank you, Jude,' she said. 'What lovely manners.'

We stared at the stranger. He was tall for fourteen, not in the gangly way our brother was, but solid and finished, like a fully grown man. Our whooping felt foolish now, as if we'd been caught playing childish games. He looked very odd in a faded dinner jacket, bright red kipper tie, checked trousers, and a brown trilby pulled low over curling blonde hair.

'Who's that?' Alice hissed.

I could feel her bristling. Nobody had told us Henry was bringing a friend. Both boys heaved their cases out of the boot of the ancient Volvo.

Only then did Henry stroll over and after a split-second's hesitation, play-punched each of us on the shoulder. His hair flopped into his eyes. I caught his shyness and shuffled my feet in the dusty gravel, looking down. But Alice grabbed him, kissing his ear with an extravagant smack.

He struggled back, blinking. 'Jude, these are my sisters,' he said. 'Cilly and Alice. This is Jude,' he gestured behind him. 'He's here for the hols. His father's a diplomat, so his parents live abroad. Spain, at the moment.'

'I'm called Cecily,' I said quickly. 'That's my proper name.'

'How long is he staying?' Alice asked with narrowed eyes.

The stranger put up a square shaped hand with long fingers, and grinned. 'For the whole six weeks,' he said. 'Hope you don't mind.' He raised one eyebrow, as if mocking the idea of objections.

Alice said nothing, but her mouth pulled tight against her teeth. I snatched glances at him, noticing his wide jaw and how his crinkly grey eyes turned up at the edges. He looked back steadily, kindly, and I was caught. Warmth flooded my cheeks.

'Henry smells different, did you notice?' Alice said later. 'Kind of musty and sour.'

Anyone could see that he'd grown inches, too, and even though he was still a bean pole, his neck had thickened, his jaw wider, shoulders broad with new muscle. 'Now we'll have to put up with two heffalump boys with smelly feet,' she said. 'And a stranger here for the whole holidays.'

Her eyes gleamed with watery disappointment.

* * *

Alice lay on her tummy in the long grass near the tarn. She scowled and stabbed a twig half-heartedly into an ants' nest. 'I don't like Jude.'

I was secretly glad. If she wanted to be his friend, he'd end up liking her best. 'I think he's... alright,' I said, trying not to give myself away.

'You think he's alright?' Alice said sarcastically. 'Really? We don't see Henry all term. And now Jude's hogging him here as well. Daddy only likes him because he's on his best behaviour. And you just fancy him.'

'I do not!' I sat up, brushing ants from my shins.

'You do,' Alice said in her most annoying voice, clipped and certain as a headmistress. 'Henry told me his parents are stinking rich. But new rich. His family originally came from...' she paused for mock dramatic effect, 'Ireland,' she finished in a comedy whisper. She patted my knee. 'Anyway, watch out he doesn't break your heart. He can have his pick of any girl.' She looked at me sideways. 'Apparently, he's going to be an actor.'

I wondered how Alice had found out so much. I resisted the impulse to pinch her. 'I don't care. I told you – I don't fancy him.'

'Methinks the damsel doth protest too much,' Alice grinned.

I'd confessed my feelings for Jude in my diary, allowing myself the luxury of complete honesty. But there was no way I'd admit it to Alice. Too much ammunition for her teasing. I turned my back, put the edge of my barely there thumb nail between my teeth and severed it with a sharp twist. I spat out the hard sliver, thinking I'd go inside and leave Alice to stew. It would serve her right. But it was too hot to move. My neck prickled with heat. The sun was burning the tops of my feet. I heard a rustling sound and turned to see her stripped of shorts, knickers and T-shirt, her long, tanned legs marked with white where the line of her shorts stopped. She picked her way to the water's edge.

I glanced towards the distant house, the many blank windows flashing bright in the sun. My pulse quickened. But I reminded myself that Daddy was in his study dealing with farm matters and paperwork on the other side of the building. Or he'd be lost in the writing of his manuscript, a book about ancient weapons he'd been writing for as long as I could remember and was more important than almost anything, except God.

I watched Alice take a running leap, disappearing feet first through the dark surface. Bubbles rose and subsided around a stillness. A dragonfly darted past in a shimmer of iridescence. There was the quiet plop of a fish rising. And just as my heart began to bang out a warning, Alice tore into the air, gasping, beating her hands around her. 'Come on, slowcoach!'

I wriggled slowly out of my denim shorts and striped T-shirt but kept my knickers on. I hesitated over my bra. White and lacy from Marks & Spencer. I'd found it on the end of my bed last week, still in its plastic packaging. It had appeared without explanation, like the sanitary towels I'd found in my top drawer. So far, these remained unused. I knew what they were for because a small booklet had been left with them, and anyway I'd overheard older girls at school whispering about The Curse in the loo. Alice said she couldn't be bothered with her bra, one more thing to put on and take off every day. But I'd fastened mine on at once. I didn't want to ruin it. But the thought of exposing the oddly shaped, lop-sided bumps on my chest to scrutiny from my sister made me cringe. They ached and tingled at night, and I lay in bed with my hands over them, pressing the flesh tentatively. Was there something wrong with me? There was no one to ask. Not even Alice. Nobody talked of such things. Even thinking the word 'nipple' made me hot with embarrassment. If I did have a terrible illness, I hoped God would take me quickly.

Keeping my bra on, I stepped into the water, goosebumps spreading across my arms. The muddy bottom swallowed my feet, and I kicked off with a gasp before crayfish claws could grab my toes. Trailing weeds tickled my thighs. Cold gripped like a fist. Meltwater ran inside these green, opaque depths. Two million years ago, huge glaciers thawed, and the resulting watery rush carved out valleys, the force of icy movement digging through earth and rock. Locals said the tarn was bottomless.

Don't swim like a girl, Daddy said in my head. Something touched my stomach and I shuddered, thinking of eels, but kept going, holding my breath as I turned my face again and again into the grainy, softness finding my rhythm, imagining my father's reaction if he could see me now, powering through the water like a boy. Except of course, he'd be furious I was in the tarn.

I swam up and down as fast as I could. Pausing to catch my breath, I caught the sound of raised voices from the bank. *Daddy.* He must have found out. Shame and fear gripped me, the sin of disobedience like a weight. *Dear God, please let him forgive me.* My legs dangled uselessly, no longer treading water. I sank, icy depths pulling me down, down, the tarn sucking me into its frozen heart. Darkness. A green, black blindfold. My body plummeted feet first as if I was encased in a suit of armour.

My fall was halted by a jerk at my scalp. My hair caught in something. A hand clamped itself around my arm at the same time, and a pale shape moved above me. Another strong yank of my hair was enough to wake me from my inertia and my feet came alive, flailing and flipping as I pushed towards the light, lungs on fire, breaking the surface at the same time as Alice. We gasped and coughed, spitting out mouthfuls of tarn. 'Did you get cramp?' she asked. 'I had to grab your hair.'

I nodded, shivering.

'Are you alright, now? Can you swim?'

I nodded again, and she let go of my arm. There was a dark shape on the bank. Daddy. I blinked into the dazzle of sun, fear closing my throat. But the silhouette broke in half, trembling into Henry and Jude etched against the sky. I let out a laugh of relief. But my joy was short-lived. The boys were holding something up, and with a lurch of dismay I realised it was our cast-off shorts and tops.

'Don't you dare!' Alice was shouting, only her head and shoulders visible. 'Give them back!'

Alice's knickers were in the bundle of clothes the boys were waving aloft. I shivered, teeth chattering. At least I'd kept my underwear on.

Henry began to walk backwards, laughing as he dangled our clothes like carrots before a stubborn donkey.

'Right!' Alice rose out of the water: a maniac Venus, windmilling her arms, naked bottom a white blur, shining limbs peddling through mud and grasses, fingers stretched to snatch at our clothes.

'Jesus! Alice!' Henry dropped his trophies with an expression of disgust and swung around with his hands clasped over his eyes. 'Put some bloody clothes on!'

'That's what I'm trying to do, you bastard!'

Jude turned away too, but not before I saw his fascinated gaze hold

Alice's body in the centre of his attention, examining it like a rare and precious artefact. Her small, marbled breasts, narrow hips wreathed with a slimy ribbon of pond weed, the shadowy gap between her thighs. Then he spun around too, shouting apologies, clapping Henry on the shoulder, and they sauntered off as if they'd done nothing wrong.

As she stumbled into her clothes, Alice yelled insults after them. She even threatened to tell Daddy. But of course, none of us wanted to be a snitch. Daddy despised a tattletale.

I hauled myself onto the bank beside her. 'You saved me.'

'We'll always save each other,' she said, casting a dark glance at the retreating shapes of the boys. 'But those two can go to hell.'

* * *

The July village cricket match was a tradition in our family. Daddy and Henry played on the same team, and this year Jude joined them. When Mummy's bedroom was empty, I sneaked in to borrow her Elizabeth Arden lipstick, pushing up the gold tube and copying the way she applied it, mouth goldfish wide. I replaced it on the dressing table next to the powder compact and the embossed silver-backed hairbrush with Mummy's mousey hair caught in the bristles, then I pulled the top drawer open to investigate her illicit correspondence, shuffling through a pile of birthday and Christmas cards to find the latest long letter, written over pages of thin paper. I skimmed the contents. Like the rest of the cards and letters, it was from our divorced aunt, and as usual, she had nothing interesting to say. I presumed Mummy must write back to her sister, posting her letters in secret. I thought of how I'd feel if I was banned from seeing Alice. The idea sent panic shooting through me. Of course, we'd never be stupid enough to divorce our husbands.

Mummy's wedding dress hung in her wardrobe at the back, next to the moth-eaten brown fur that had been passed down from Daddy's mother. The fur was a drooping shapeless thing, sad as a chained bear, but the ivory dress shone out of the darkness like a lantern. Just holding it up in front of me made me feel like a Hollywood star. It had tiny, covered buttons right down the back and on the cuffs, and was cut close around the waist and across the hips, falling in a column to the floor. I hugged it close and hummed as I swayed in front of the mirror, the folds of silk comfortingly heavy against my legs. It was a shame Jude couldn't see me. On my wedding day, I'd wear the dress with flowers in my hair (instead of the tiara Mummy had worn, long since sold, along with most of her jewellery). Big, creamy lilies with orange hearts, I decided, as I twisted at the hip, turning to admire my reflection from different angles, slender as any of the sinuous saints on Daddy's walls.

I wore my floral Laura Ashley dress to the match; it may not have been film-star glamorous, but the high neck and long ruffled skirt made me feel like Tess of the D'Urbervilles. The event was popular in the village, and the side of the pitch was crowded with onlookers. I recognised a few people from primary school and let my gaze slide across them, aware of whispering behind hands and curious glances in our direction. Alice and I had been considered freaks at the village school for being identical, for wearing darned clothes, and even more for living in the Big House. We'd tried to fit in. Alice had run races with the boys in the playground. She fell once, slamming onto the hard surface, but she'd got up without a murmur, ignoring her gravel-pitted skin and the blood running down her leg. That had earnt her a bit of respect. But we weren't supposed to be there – we were the wrong religion, the wrong class – and the other kids knew it. The Girls High School in town wasn't much better, but at least it was Catholic.

One of the faces in the crowd at the opposite side of the pitch hooked my gaze. An older woman in a headscarf. There was something familiar about her large nose and intense stare, but I couldn't place her. The woman was observing Daddy with unblinking curiosity. When her eyes moved to me, I turned away.

Alice and Mummy and I were sitting on deckchairs in the shade. 'In the old days it really was the Big House against the villagers,' Mummy said, from under the wide brim of her straw hat. 'The servants joining in too. Now it's not quite that. But your father takes it very seriously.'

Alice rolled her eyes without looking up from her book. Daddy treated all sports with a reverence he usually reserved for God.

Every time the crowd clapped, Alice yawned, lolling in her chair, nose buried deeper in her novel. I'd brought my diary. Oscar Wilde said you could never be bored with your own diary. *Something sensational to read on the train,* he'd called it. Now that I had Jude to write about, mine was becoming sensational too. But in the event, I never took my gaze from the game, even though I got confused by the rules, and it went on and on. There was Daddy to cheer and Jude to watch. His handsome face grew puce and shiny as he bowled and batted and rushed to leap into the air to catch a ball. He was as athletic as our brother, blonde as Henry was dark. The sun set his head aflame.

We had no chance of meeting boys at our all-girls day school, and it wasn't even worth asking if we could go to discos in the village hall on Saturday nights. It was disconcerting and exciting to have Jude staying. I'd observed him in secret glances when I'd sat next to him at breakfast, and now watching him from afar, the fact that I could call up the shape of the mole behind his left ear, his slightly overlapping front teeth and the texture of the golden fuzz on his square jaw, gave me a thrill. The knowledge was intimate, as if I owned a part of him.

Daddy, the captain, ran up to bowl, his face creased in concentration. His arm was a blur as he released the ball towards the batsman. There was a collective intake of breath from the crowd. He carved his way through the air in the same focused way I'd tried to carve through the tarn. He'd been a Full Blue at Cambridge. His body was still muscular, his limbs impatient, twitching with energy when he was forced to sit, so that sometimes one of his legs juddered under the meal table, rattling the plates and cutlery. His dark hair had turned a distinguished salt and pepper but showed no signs of thinning, and his moustache sprouted vigorously from his top lip. I couldn't ever imagine him slowing down, giving in to the impositions of age. Daddy would stay young forever.

With Daddy, Henry and Jude on the team, the outcome was always certain. Mummy got up, smiling vaguely at the victorious, sweating men coming off the pitch, their white trousers smeared with streaks of green. Henry dangled the bat from one hand, his other arm slung around his friend's shoulder. Alice didn't look up.

'Well done,' I said, on my feet, clapping as the three of them walked over. I twitched the folds of my skirt and hoped Jude would notice me. 'Well done, Daddy,' I repeated louder, my gaze on his face.

Henry tousled Jude's damp hair, and Jude pushed him away, grinning. There was a friendly scuffle.

'Heavens. Still so much energy.' Mummy smiled. 'You must be starving. Plenty of cucumber sandwiches and scones with cream and jam in the pavilion.'

'Good show, boys,' Daddy said. The cross at his neck glinted inside a scrawl of dark hair. He exuded satisfaction, and there was an imperceptible shift in Mummy's shoulders, in all our shoulders, knowing that the ease of this victory would carry us into the evening.

As Daddy passed me, he paused, and I thought he was going to acknowledge my support from the sidelines, but squinting at me, he reached out a thumb and pressed it against my mouth, turning it to examine the waxy evidence. 'Take this off,' he frowned, 'you look like a slut.'

The imprint of his thumb remained, the way it had crushed my lip against my teeth. Mummy threw me an anxious look as she hurried away behind him, fingers straightening the brim of her hat.

I locked myself in a cubicle in the ladies and scrubbed my mouth with squares of crispy loo paper. Alice, who'd slipped in with me, watched the process with narrowed eyes.

'All gone?' I asked.

Alice nodded. I dropped the stained paper into the loo, and she pulled the chain. 'It's not a sin to wear lipstick,' she said as we watched the evidence disappear inside a gurgling torrent.

'No... it's my fault... we're not allowed... and I took it without asking,' I said, each admission a small desolation.

'Did you do it for Jude?' Alice shook her head. 'Don't waste your time. He can't even tell us apart.' She opened the cubicle door, ushering me out. 'I don't understand why you don't get angry when Daddy picks on you,' she said. 'He's meaner to you than me, even though you're the one who licks his boots.'

'I don't... He isn't...' I leant over one of the porcelain sinks. I felt sick. Heatstroke, maybe. I turned a tap on full. 'You're the one who's mean.' I shoved my hands under the rush of cold, splashed my face. Daddy loved me; that's why he didn't want me to grow up too fast or do anything to disgrace myself. He wanted me to have a place in heaven.

Above the row of sinks, our reflections merged and wavered in the mirror.

'Sorry.' Alice's forehead crumpled. 'Forget what I said. Words come out of my mouth before I think. You're much nicer than me. Much.' She took my wet hand. 'Together forever?'

I nodded, unable to speak. The battering in my chest subsided. The woman in the headscarf came in; she looked startled when she saw us, and slipped into a cubicle, shutting the door.

Alice didn't seem to notice her. 'I'm bored to tears. And Jude and Henry are horribly pleased with themselves.' She rolled her eyes. 'I'm going home. Coming?'

I shook my head.

'You're such a goodie two-shoes,' she said. 'What happened to sticking together?'

I pulled my fingers away. I couldn't risk making Daddy angry – especially not now. I watched Alice leave, feeling deserted. I stood in the ladies staring at myself in the mirror. Was I really a slut? Shame filled me and I turned away from my reflection.

As I left the toilets, I realised the woman in the headscarf was still in the cubicle, and I remembered with a jolt where I'd seen her before. She was the same woman I'd peered at through a tangle of rose thorns. She'd demanded to see Daddy and then cursed our family. I hesitated, wondering if I should bang on the cubicle door, confront her, do something. I didn't like her being here. It felt more than a coincidence.

But in the end, I slunk away like a coward into the tearoom, keeping my head down inside the bustle and chatter. Out of the corners of my eyes, I searched for her in the crowd in case she'd followed me. What was her name? Baxter. Something Baxter. I hovered near a trestle table, a disgusting half-eaten egg and parsley sandwich in my hands. I considered disposing of it in a napkin, glanced around to see if anyone was watching and caught sight of the back of Daddy's head, taller than everyone around him. I'd felt the glow of his happiness and ruined it. I stuffed the rest of the sandwich into my mouth and forced myself to swallow.

I had the awful thought that the Baxter woman might be here to confront Daddy again; it would be terrible if she shouted at him and cursed him in front of all these people. I peered around anxiously but still couldn't see her. Edith. That was her Christian name.

A large person crowded against my side. It was Jude, his damp hair darkened to bronze, the skin of his neck glistening inside his cricket top. A bold, animal smell of salt and iron came from him, like a hot horse.

'Cecily,' he said, bending slightly, 'I wanted to say I'm sorry.' He swallowed. 'About earlier. At the lake. We were completely out of order.' He gave me a quizzical lop-sided smile, crinkling his eyes. 'Will you ever forgive me?'

Warmth spread through me, even my toes and fingertips glowed. I smiled back, hoping I didn't have parsley between my teeth or eggy breath. 'Lake?' I repeated, not wanting to correct him. 'I don't remember seeing you at any lake.'

He touched my elbow. 'You're a sport.' His voice was soft. 'And for what it's worth – the lipstick looked pretty on you.'

'How did you know that I'm me,' I asked. 'Nobody can tell me and Alice apart. Except Henry.'

He narrowed his eyes as if considering. 'There's something... different about you. You're feminine. Complicated. Alice seems more straightforward.' He rubbed his nose with one finger, a slight flush moving across his wide face. Then he grinned. 'Although perhaps I'm cheating, because all your sister ever does is scowl at me, whereas you,' he leaned closer, 'have a lovely smile.'

More heat rushed into my face, a raging fire. Nobody had ever talked to me like that. Those words. *Different. Feminine. Complicated.* He'd noticed me properly, not like a little sister. *A lovely smile.* The flames spread through my body.

'Jude!' Henry was waving at him over heads. 'Jude. Over here.'

Jude gave me a wry look, one eyebrow raised. 'His majesty calls.'

'Then his majesty had better be answered,' I replied, managing to sound normal, and not as if my heart was spiking like a sprinter going across the finish line. We had a bond now, an understanding rich with possibilities. He knew who I was – and it felt dangerous and wonderful. Watching Jude make his way over to my brother, my gaze fell on Daddy again at the centre of the room, holding himself stiffly apart from the people clustering around him. A muscle in his jaw would be pulsing, the strain of this necessary nicety taxing his limited resources of patience. He'd achieved his objective to win the match, and he couldn't see the point in all this social pretence – the cricket tea was irritating the hell out of him. That's why he'd snapped at me. On a golden afternoon like this, he'd be longing to stride around the estate with the dogs at his heels, a cigar between his fingers. I wondered how Edith Baxter had dared to curse him to his face. It must have taken guts, but more likely, insanity.

He took out his pocket watch, and I saw his lips move as he read the time aloud. He would have already told the organisers when he'd be leaving. He'd walk out of the pavilion on the dot. As I watched, he tucked his watch away and made his way towards the door, and I slipped into his wake, straightening my skirt, rubbing my fingers across my lips just in case. 'Daddy?' I called. 'Please can I walk with you?'

He slowed his pace just a fraction without turning his head. I scurried forwards, my mind working quick as a ferret to think of something to say that would make him forgive me. He liked to be asked things best. A question could make him go into a long explanation. Something about the Civil War, perhaps. Something to do with the way the musket replaced the long bow, or the number of men who died of sepsis slowly after the battle was over, long after the bullet had torn through their body.

10

ALICE

I've never done this before. Shopping for a family and meal planning are unfamiliar skills. I can't believe how fast the fridge empties, or how quickly the chore of cooking comes round. Thank God I'm not going to have to keep this up for more than a week. I can already find my way around the local Co-op with my eyes closed. I'm here again, stocking up on some basics – a packet of the sugary cereal Bea likes, and some cat food. And I'm picking out a lettuce, thinking I need something healthy, when I hear a voice just behind me.

'Cecily!'

I spin around. A blonde woman is approaching me. She's in full make-up, her hair a fan of bright yellow around her face. There's something familiar about her, but I can't put my finger on it.

'You look like someone just walked over your grave.' She laughs.

'You gave me a shock, that's all,' I say, playing for time as I hold my basket against my stomach. 'I was deep in thought.'

She smirks at me. 'Like you were last night?'

I frown. 'Sorry?'

She lowers her voice to a pantomime whisper. 'It's alright, your secret's safe with me.' She winks.

My heart crashes through my chest, and I clutch the wire basket tighter. I look towards the sliding doors exit and think of making a run for it. 'What do you mean?'

She lets her gaze trail from my face to my shoes, and nods meaningfully, as if bestowing approval. 'I must say, you scrub up well for a girl who was out on the town until all hours.'

'I'm sorry,' I say, irritated now. 'I have no idea what you're talking about.'

'Last night, in The Royal Oak.' She touches her ear, where a diamond glints through her hair. 'You were downing vodkas like there was no tomorrow.' She laughs again. An unkind sound. 'You were pretty pissed, to be fair.' She is obviously delighted with this information. She gives me a triumphant look, opening her blackened eyelashes wide, making spikes against her pencilled brows.

The understanding makes me gasp. Cecily. She saw Cecily. She's still here, in Exeter. I feel sick. 'That wasn't me,' I tell her, deciding she can make what she likes of it. 'That was my identical twin.'

She gives a throaty laugh and jogs my arm with her sharp elbow. 'You are a dark horse, Cecily.'

I know where I've seen her before. She's the jogger who'd waved up at me in the window. I stare her down, my gaze cold. 'If you'll excuse me,' I tell her. 'I've got to get back.'

'Yeah, to that gorgeous husband of yours,' she says with an edge to her voice. 'And if I were you, I'd consider myself lucky.'

I ignore her, grabbing a bag of carrots and marching towards the till, my pulse thundering in my ears. I can feel her looking at me, her gaze a hard spotlight on my retreating back. My hands are shaking, my knees wobbly. There's a long queue for the till. I can't face waiting in line. I leave my basket on the floor, and hurry through the sliding doors, suddenly desperate to get home. The word repeats in my head. Home.

I half expect to find Cecily there, waiting for me. I stand in the hall, my ears alert, listening, and I sense a change in the air, a scattering of atoms, as if someone has passed through recently. I put my head around the door of the living room and notice something spilt on the pine boards. I go over, puzzled, and squat to touch granules of earth. Tracking the spillage closer to the bay window, I discover three damp half-circles left on the boards. Where are my plant pots?

I stand up, expecting to see that they've been moved to another part of the room. But there's no sign of them. Sukie comes purring around my feet, her loud meow asking for food. She follows me into the kitchen, and I pour out the remains of the kibble, wondering where the plants are and who moved them. The things the blonde woman said about Cecily come flooding back. Why is she getting drunk on her own? An uneasy squirming starts up in my belly. Why hasn't she let me know where she is and how to get hold of her? I'm trapped in her life, but meanwhile, she's not sticking to our plan. What the hell is she playing at?

That evening, I remain in the kitchen, waiting for Gabriel and the threatened talk. I'm not going to run away. I can't fake a headache for the rest of the week, so I wait like a condemned woman. I finish off the rest of the white wine from the fridge as I try to think of what I should say to him. Nothing comes to mind. I have no idea what's gone on between the two of them. I'm completely out of my depth. I tell myself I'll just listen to what he has to say and then try and be as noncommittal as possible in my responses. I tip the dregs of the wine into my glass. It's a bit like waiting to do an exam in a subject that I've neglected to prepare for, that I have in fact, not studied for at all.

Time ticks past. The sky over the garden fence darkens from violet to plum, until an obsidian gleam at the window throws back my reflection, a lone woman at a table, her face an oval smudge. I consider opening one of the bottles of Burgundy. He doesn't come. Sukie jumps into my lap, purring, and I stroke her arched spine while she kneads my thighs with sharp claws. Bea opens and closes her door upstairs, and I hear the lavatory flush and taps running. She comes down to the kitchen and fills a glass of water from the filter jug.

'Gabri— Dad... is late,' I say. 'Have I forgotten something he was doing?'

She shakes her head. 'Wednesday night? Don't think so. He's got choir tomorrow, hasn't he?'

'Choir?' I can't remember seeing that in the little black book. 'Oh, yes.' I smile as if I've remembered. 'Of course. Maybe he's just working late.'

'Yeah.' She turns away from me.

'Bea,' I say quickly. She doesn't deserve to be deceived like this.

She gives me a questioning look.

I shake my head. 'Nothing. Goodnight.'

'Okay. Night.' She hesitates as if she's waiting for something else to happen. The soft curves of her face tighten, and she blinks, and leaves the room.

Was she was going to kiss me? Did she expect me to kiss her? It didn't occur to me until now when it's too late. Perhaps she was put off because I didn't stand up, didn't meet her halfway. Every moment in this house is fraught with possible mistakes, holes for me to fall into. I need to remember that as far as she's concerned, I'm her mum, even if she's angry with me. I should have hugged her, at least.

It's past ten thirty. I'm exhausted. It's too late to talk now.

Much later, I hear the creak of floorboards outside my room, the unsteady footsteps of someone who's drunk too much. He doesn't pause outside my door.

* * *

Next morning, wanting to get my domestic duties over and done with, I get into the kitchen first, unload the dishwasher, and then take the full rubbish bag out to the dustbin in the front garden. As I lift the lid, I see shards of terracotta, broken stems, crushed leaves, a tumble of earth and smashed green. I press my hand over my mouth. The deliberate ruin of healthy plants is shocking – the waste of money, the cruel rejection of my gesture. I wonder which one of them did it.

Gabriel comes into the kitchen slowly, holding his head upright with deliberate caution. He doesn't move his eyes and swallows a couple of painkillers with a gulp of water; he leaves most of his breakfast untouched and disappears without even saying goodbye. I feel stupidly hurt by his coldness.

I take the map Cecily left for me and spend the day walking about Exeter, looking for her. There are a surprising number of women with short dark hair. But none is Cecily. I go home in time to greet Bea when she gets back from school. The soles of my feet ache from walking, and I'm frustrated by my failure to find her, but at least I'm getting to know the layout of the town.

Gabriel is home late that evening; choir practice, I suppose. When I go to bed, I notice that Cecily's icons have been turned the right way round again and rearranged on her dressing table. It unnerves me to know that Bea, or Gabriel, has been in here, poking around while I'm out. I wonder, with a chill, if one of them suspects something. I open the wardrobe and pull out my rucksack, checking inside it. I can't tell if it's been rummaged through; it wasn't exactly neatly packed in the first place. But I reassure myself that this is the only thing in the room that would give me away and shove it back into far the corner of the wardrobe and close the doors.

Friday, he is cool with me again, doesn't meet my eyes, slips in and out of the house without speaking. When Bea is there, he and I conduct awkward, minimal communication. I catch her looking at me, disappointment deadening her eyes, or is it suspicion? It doesn't matter – only four more days to go – if this whole plan goes to hell, it's Cecily's fault for leaving me alone. My job is to fill a gap, a cardboard cut-out propped up in her place, until she comes back. But there's a gnawing unease in my guts. She's supposed to be organising a divorce, finding a job, not drinking alone in pubs. An idea hits me, taking my breath away – maybe she doesn't intend to come back at all? I shake my head. I'm being paranoid. She wouldn't abandon her daughter or betray me like that. And she knows I'd never agree to stay here forever.

11

CECILY

I don't know how long that wretched woman was spying on me across the pub before she couldn't resist sauntering over to get her dig in – 'Enjoying yourself, Cecily?' she said with a smirk, casting an eye on my drink.

I raised my glass of vodka and nodded. 'To life,' I said. 'To getting our heart's desire.'

The drink burnt my throat, and it felt good, that scouring, cleansing hit of alcohol. Necessary, even. Someone like Rebecca would never understand what I'd lost, the magnitude of it. The only person who could is Alice, but I can't talk to her now; I can't risk her finding out what I'm about to do – she could never follow me into this darkness. She thinks she's tougher than me. But I'm the rotten apple.

'You should watch it.' Rebecca wouldn't let it go. 'Alcohol's ageing.'

'Just leave me alone,' I muttered, turning away from her, slumping across the bar.

The rest of the evening is a blur. I can't remember how I got back to my room or falling into bed. But I remember my dream.

I was at Hawksmoor again. The locked gates rose above me, speckled with rust. But when I touched them, the heavy halves creaked open, the chain snapping as if it was made of sugar paper. I ran through, feet pounding the gravel drive, stones spitting from my heels as I gulped the loamy smell of dank undergrowth.

A tangle of lofty, overgrown trees blocked my view of the house, the path ahead scrawled with ivy and brambles. On I ran, turning the corner by the stables, past the great yew, its ancient branches shielding nesting goldcrests, sleeping creatures curled inside its knotty hollows. At last, the beloved shapes of tall chimneys and flinty-faced turrets rose before me, the square tower of the left wing soaring out of tree shadows, battlements grimacing at the icy sky.

It began to snow as I surged towards the front door, pale flakes falling and twisting through darkness. Before going up the steps, I trailed my hand over the heads of two old friends, their snarling stone teeth worn and pocked. The flakes were settling, and the lions were already covered in a soft white mantle. Inside the house, the air was frigid, my breath billowing in smoky puffs, but I didn't feel cold. My heart was lit with flames of joy. A name rushed through me, the name I carried in my blood, hissing syllables to curl my tongue around: *Hawksmoor*. I was back where I belonged, bare feet slipping across the grain of weathered floorboards. I inhaled the rising scent of beeswax, the tender perfume of lilac blossoms wafting from the Chinese vases in the entrance hall.

Glancing into the dining room, panelled in English poplar and bog oak, I regarded the familiar gilded portraits of men and women with the same fine, slightly long nose as my own, the same pouting lips raised in secret smiles. I sniffed at the memory of breakfast kippers and scrambled eggs waiting on the silver heating tray, hearing my mother telling me not to forget to put the covers back. And my father, lost behind his newspaper, watching me without taking his gaze from the printed page. *Daddy*.

Heart thrumming, I entered my old bedroom on the first floor, its two leaded windows overlooking the frozen rock garden, a tumble of shadows, blue-lit by starlight. I could hear Alice and Henry calling to me, their laughter as they ran across the whitened lawn. Pressing my nose against the glass, I watched them disappear into the cover of the beech trees and suddenly I knew where they were heading. I gazed towards the cold eye of the tarn. I had to stop them. I turned and dashed out, towards the main staircase and the wide-open front door, certain I could turn back time, erase a tragedy.

But I'd gone up, not down. I was in the old servants' quarters under the eaves, outside the priest hole. My pulse hammered out a warning, yet I couldn't stop myself sliding my palm gingerly over the chalky wall, bubbles of blown plaster fragile under my touch, creeping my fingers over the solid oak beam. I knew the place that gave if you pressed at the top corner, the beam swinging out, revealing a crawl space.

The heavy limb of timber moved, rising slowly, trailing cobwebs. I squatted on my haunches to peer inside the hole, and the cramped, dank interior breathed out its mildewy, rotten smell of fear and betrayal.

'What have you done?' Alice's voice whispered in my ear.

I reeled back, staggering to my feet, and with one bound I was flying down the staircase, out, out into the river of the night.

Have pity on me, most merciful God.

12

ALICE

On Friday evening, I decide that if Cecily isn't going to contact me, I'll have to make another effort to find her. The blonde woman said she'd seen her in The Royal Oak. I go to bed early, telling the others I've got another headache. It's not a lie, the back of my head is tender. I wince when I tentatively press under my hair; my scalp feels bruised as if I've been struck by something hard. At about nine thirty, when I hear the taps running next door, I take a chance and slip out onto the landing. I creep warily, pausing to listen, hoping to avoid creaking joists and boards. I'm not sure who's having a bath, so I slip quietly down the stairs, aware that either Gabriel or Bea is somewhere in the house. The radio is on in the kitchen. Radio Four. It must be Gabriel. I sidle along the wall, past the coat rack, grabbing Cecily's old puffer jacket, then ease the front door open and shut it softly behind me.

It takes half an hour to walk to The Royal Oak. I push into a thrum of noise, chatter and clink of glass, the heat of bodies and breath. I feel invisible as I squeeze past groups of people, drinks in hand, chatting with flushed faces. I'm scanning the crowded room but can't see my sister. I make my way to the bar and try to catch the eye of the busy barman. He nods in my direction, and calls over, 'The usual, love?'

A jolt of understanding goes through me, and I nod. He places a vodka and ice on the wooden surface with a can of tonic. I hand over the money and pour all the tonic into the glass. I sip my drink and glance at the door every time it opens. An hour passes. Maybe she's not out tonight, or maybe she's at another pub. The thought makes me despair, imagining all the other pubs in Exeter, but she's obviously a regular here, so this is the most likely place to find her. Then I spot the back of a familiar head, a dark woman with short hair sitting across the other side of the bar, talking animatedly to someone. I slip down from my stool and hurry over, reaching out my hand to touch her shoulder. 'Cecily!'

The woman turns, surprised. A large mouth, lipstick bright, opens over crooked teeth. She raises one eyebrow.

'Sorry,' I mutter.

I slink back to my drink. A middle-aged man squeezes onto the bar stool next to me. He leers at me, squinting eyes wandering towards my chest. Saliva gathers at the corners of slurring lips. I turn away, hunching my shoulders, hoping he'll take the hint. People jostle me as they attempt to push past to get a drink, but I keep my bottom stuck to the stool, determined not to give up my position. It's got the best view of the door. I try to make the drink last as long as possible, but I'm getting funny looks from the barman, so I end up ordering another. The liquid fizzes at the back of my throat. I eat the slice of lemon, stripping flesh from the peel with my teeth.

A man ordering drinks on the opposite side of the bar looks my way. When he sees me, recognition spreads over his face. He grins and winks. Hope fires in my chest. I slip from the stool and jostle my way through the packed crowd around the bar. I catch his elbow as he's walking away with two drinks and packets of crisps balanced in his hands. He turns and frowns at me.

'Hi,' I say. 'I just wanted to talk to you. You know me, don't you?'

He shakes my fingers off, his frown deepening. 'Not now,' he says in a low voice. 'I'm here with my wife.'

'What?' I move my head. 'I just want to ask...'

'Look. This isn't the time,' he says, glancing towards a woman sitting at a corner table.

I persist, holding on to his sleeve. 'I just need a moment...'

'Piss off,' he hisses with sudden ferocity, and my grasp falls away. The woman at the table is looking in our direction with narrowed-eyed curiosity.

I go back to my bar stool, feeling disorientated, but it's been taken by someone else. There are no other free seats, so I loiter awkwardly in corners, getting in the way of drinkers. I slink over towards the exit, and hover there, anxious I might miss her in the crowd now that I've lost the vantage point of my stool. Strangers trample my toes and elbow me in the ribs. Last orders are called, and she's a no-show.

* * *

Saturday morning, I'm tired and my stomach is queasy. I have no tolerance for drinking, especially vodka. Last night was strange. The man's reaction when I attempted to talk to him has released a thought in my head, an unnerving possibility that won't go away. What else has she been doing on her nights in The Royal Oak? That man at the bar didn't want to be seen talking to her in front of his wife. It doesn't make sense. Cecily is the last person I'd expect to be unfaithful to her husband. She may not love Gabriel any more, but she always cared deeply about her vows. My sister, the devout Catholic.

I have so many questions for her. But if I can't track her down, there's nothing I can do except hope she'll contact me eventually. I consult the black book to see what guidance she's given me for weekend routines.

> *Saturday. Bea often sleeps in. Gabriel goes for a run. You can do whatever you want. I usually put a wash on and then go to my Step aerobics class. But you can skip that.*

I close the book and tuck it back under the bras and knickers in Cecily's underwear drawer. My fingers touch a rustle of paper and I pull out a small bag. It takes me a second to understand that the tiny, green balls inside are dried peas. Perhaps they're a guard against moths. Mummy had us collect conkers every autumn to sprinkle in drawers and between folded jumpers. An old trick, although in our case, it didn't work. I scrunch the paper bag back into its original twist and slip it into the corner of the drawer.

I envy Gabriel his run. I'd like to go for one too – stretch my legs, get my heart pumping – it might release stress from my body. Yoga hasn't done the trick. Frustration and anxiety have tied hard knots inside my chest, made my head hurt. My muscles feel stiff and tight from lack of exercise. Big gulps of fresh air are what I really need. I could at least go for a long, brisk walk.

I should never have swapped places with her, but I trusted her, believed it would bring us closer. I thought it would create the opportunity to meet again at last. I imagined I was her knight on a shining steed galloping to save her. I'm beginning to feel like a mug.

Bea hasn't come out of her bedroom. I know Gabriel left early, I'd heard the front door close, the slap of his feet hitting the pavement. Now he's back. The shower starts up in the bathroom, and there's the hum of the boiler. A hiss of water hitting shoulders and limbs. If he keeps avoiding me, maybe I can make it through the weekend without 'the talk'. On Monday I'll be free. It's only two days. If necessary, I'll go for countless long walks.

I tiptoe past the bathroom door, inhaling the steamy scent of orange blossom soap and shampoo. He's singing loudly, belting out a song, and I recognise the tune to 'Knock On Wood', the lyrics interrupted by humming when he forgets the words. It makes me smile. Downstairs, I remember my domestic duties, and shove some dirty clothes from the overflowing basket into the washing machine, then empty the dishwasher as quickly as possible, before I pull on the puffer jacket again and leave the house.

A chilly breeze is slicing through the warmth of the sun, and leaves shine in a green that's almost lurid, brazenly hopeful. I get halfway down the street when I hear my sister's name being called.

My heart sinks. I turn. Gabriel is pounding along the pavement, his wool jacket flying behind him, the one I wore at the beginning of the week. He reaches me, panting, his face flushed and shiny, hair in wet curls over his forehead, strands dripping onto his collar. I notice his shirt is mis-buttoned, his collar turned the wrong way.

'Cecily,' he says, his voice breathless. 'Let's get this talk over and done with, shall we? We can't put it off for ever. Can we?'

Trapped, I move my head slightly, eyes sliding left and right, as if I could find an escape route. A gull screams over our heads.

'I heard you leaving the house,' he's saying. 'And I thought, this just can't go on. Avoiding each other every day. It's ridiculous.' He gestures to the open road before us. 'Walking and talking is easier than facing each other over a table, isn't it?' he says. 'And this way Bea doesn't have to overhear anything.' He falls into step next to me. He nods towards the river. 'Where are you going?'

'I don't know. I was just going to let my feet take me.'

He gives a short laugh. 'Not like you.'

'You decide then,' I say. 'I don't care. I just wanted to get some fresh air.'

'Right.' He shoves his hands into his pockets. We keep walking, and I can sense his breath slowing, his stride matching mine.

'So? I'm listening,' I say, needing to break the tension snapping between us.

'It's you that needs to talk, Cecily,' he retorts. 'You're the one who's unhappy. You're the one who changes every five minutes, who warms towards me one minute and then pushes me away. I don't know what I've done. Except,' he rubs his forehead briefly and puts his hand back in his pocket, 'except I know you're disappointed that I don't want to live at Hawksmoor.'

Hawksmoor. A shiver of recognition ignites a new understanding inside me. I force myself to keep walking. 'But Daddy's still alive,' I say cautiously, feeling my way.

'Exactly,' he says with a force of feeling. He pushes a hand through his hair. 'We can't live there yet. The old goat will probably live into his nineties. Cecily, I understand how much you love that house, I really do, but apart from the practical and financial difficulties, do you really want to try and save it at any cost? To us, to Bea? This is home to her,' he waves a hand around. 'Exeter is all she knows.' He shuffles his feet against the pavement. 'Do you realise, you've never said you had a happy childhood? You've never shared good memories of Hawksmoor with me. In fact, you hardly talk about your life there. And yet,' he swallows, 'sometimes I think you're possessed by the place.'

I walk on beside him, recognising the truth in everything he says. I agree with him, but Cecily wouldn't. 'I know we can't move there yet,' I mutter. 'But I can't stop thinking about it. It wasn't a happy childhood. But that's not the point. It's my ancestral home – my inheritance. And now it's Bea's.' It's odd, voicing an opinion opposite to my own. The words are reluctant on my tongue.

'If saving it was a viable option...' he lets the sentence trail away. 'But we're talking crazy money. Impossible money. And when your father dies, there'll be death duties.'

'I know,' I say quietly.

He shoots me a puzzled glance. 'So, what changed?' We walk on in silence. 'You've always been unpredictable,' he says, as if he's talking to himself. 'I used to find it intriguing. Then when you told me we couldn't sleep together any more – that you needed time alone – I respected your decision. But, Cecily, we've been living separate lives in the same house ever since, and you never talk about it. There are times when I see the woman I first fell in love with, then you're cold again, or angry.'

I can't think what to say, so I say nothing. It's uncomfortable to be forced to listen to such private revelations. I wish I could stop him from saying more.

'And then there's the drinking,' he says in a low voice. 'It's not helping you – or us. You know I'll support you if you try and stop.'

'Me?' I exclaim. 'I'm not the one who drinks around here.'

He looks away and hunches his shoulders. 'OK,' he says. 'We won't talk about it now.' We walk on in silence. 'Have you... have you met someone else?' he asks, gruffly.

'No,' I say, thinking uneasily of the man in the pub. 'That's not it.'

He takes a deep breath. 'Well, that's one thing I suppose.'

'Have you?'

He gives a short, humourless laugh. 'Believe it or not, I still love you, Cecily.'

'Maybe,' I say quietly. 'Maybe we've just grown apart.'

'You grew apart from me,' he says, with a twist in his voice. 'And there must be a reason for it. But if you won't tell me, I can't make you. Only you've always said there's no way we can get a divorce.' He stops and swings round to face me, colour flaming his cheeks. 'Cecily, I can't keep going like this.' The green of his iris flares into gold and darkens. 'That's what I wanted to talk about. Either we do get a divorce, or we see a councillor. This... this is killing me. And it's destroying our daughter, too.' He's stopped walking, and we're standing on the pavement awkwardly, our bodies angled away.

'I know,' I manage.

He's trembling and I reach out to touch his arm. It's an instinct. But as my fingers close around the fabric of his jacket, he flinches and looks at me. 'God. Cecily...' his voices breaks. He stops and looks away, clears his throat.

I watch his profile, see a twitch of muscle spasm at his jaw. 'Perhaps I was just too young,' I say gently. 'We rushed into marriage.'

He nods and turns back to me. 'I never forgave myself for having a relationship with a student. It was my fault. I was irresponsible. And then I got you pregnant.'

'It takes two,' I say. 'I was an adult.'

He shakes his head. 'You were innocent. You seemed younger than other students. I think – I think your solitary childhood – your faith – kept you protected from the world. Your father didn't let you grow up.' He shoots me a quick glance. 'And being an only child in that huge old mausoleum... I can't imagine what it was like. You were lonely when we met, I knew that. But you'd chosen to be alone, and I felt honoured that you wanted my company.'

An only child. Breath catches in my throat. I know Cecily has lived with that story since Daddy disowned me, but it strikes me now as a cruelty, to erase me and Henry from her life, to deny us our place in her past. Why did she go along with our father's fiction? She didn't have to obey his wishes. She's always been weak. Her lie deprived me of knowing my niece, of knowing Gabriel. Until now.

I snatch a glance at the man at my side. His eyes gleam with unshed tears. He's a good person. He doesn't deserve to sleep in a separate bedroom, or to live in a house with a wife who avoids him. It's true, he likes a drink sometimes. I remember his stumbling footsteps the other night. But it must be the situation driving him to it. I can hardly blame him. His hands are steady. He seems to be responsible about his work. I don't actually think he's an alcoholic. But in that case, Cecily lied. I shiver, pulling my jacket tighter around me.

'This is a mess,' I say. 'And you're right. We either need to divorce, or seek help.'

'Cecily,' he says, with an outward rush of breath. 'You have no idea what a relief it is to hear you say that.' He moves closer to me. 'I've been going mad.' I hear tears pressing at his throat. 'I always worried that you needed the church so much because... because there's something lacking in our marriage.'

I can't have a conversation about religion. 'Well,' I tell him, sweeping my arm out towards the horizon, and walking on briskly, 'here's to a better future. To clarity. To making decisions.'

From the periphery of my eye, I catch his stare. 'I don't know what's happened to make this change. But whatever it is, I'm grateful.'

We've reached a café, a whitewashed building with mullioned windows. He tilts his head towards it. 'We could get a coffee?'

'Sure.' I smile.

Sitting at a table in an empty room, resonant with the scent of fresh bread, he orders two coffees and a couple of croissants. My stomach rumbles. 'I'm starving,' he says as he takes a bite of the pastry when it arrives and wrinkles his nose. 'I think these are supermarket ones warmed up.' But he eats it with apparent enjoyment, offers me the other one, and when I refuse, remembering what Cecily would do, he eats that too.

He raises his cup and sips, puts it back in the saucer carefully. 'I don't want to push you,' he says. 'But it would be good to know how you're feeling about... about us...?'

'I think finding a good counsellor would be the best way forwards,' I say slowly. 'If you agree?' At the very least, I think, this will buy some time while he tries to find someone. And perhaps Cecily will agree to it once she's back. If she comes back, a little voice in my head adds.

'I still think we can save this marriage.' He looks at me, earnestly. 'We have a daughter. We owe it to her.'

I glance at him over the rim of my cup. I had a completely different idea of who he was, and it makes me uneasy, knowing she lied to me. I don't understand why she did, and what else might be untrue.

'Gabriel,' I say, 'Why did you throw the plants away?'

He frowns. 'What?'

'The three plants I put in the living room.' I falter, seeing his look of incomprehension. 'They were dumped in the bin. I thought it was you.'

He shakes his head, frowning. 'I'd never throw plants out. I'd have them all over the house if it was up to me.'

Bea, then. I'm confused about why she'd do something so mean and destructive, but I remember her anger when I'd asked her if she was hungry. I won't mention it to her, not now we're beginning to get on better.

I try and keep the rest of our conversation light, although I'm aware that anything I say could give me away. But he isn't watching out for inconsistencies. Relief comes off him in waves. He smiles and laughs, his body relaxed. Then he folds his hands around his empty cup, and shifts forward in his seat, the groove between his eyebrows deepening. 'I'm worried about Bea,' he says. 'I think our problems have impacted badly on her.'

'I know,' I say. 'She's unhappy.'

'Perhaps now we're sorting things out, she'll feel better?'

He looks so hopeful, so trusting. I squirm under the weight of my lie. I look down. 'I don't know, maybe.'

'You think she's overweight, don't you?' he asks. 'But she's probably been comfort eating because of us.'

'I'm not the expert,' I tell him. 'Let's take it slowly and not rush her.' I push a strand of hair behind my ear. 'We can all eat healthier things. Stop buying crisps and biscuits.'

He grabs my hand. 'Thank you,' he says. 'It'll be easier to deal with everything if we're on the same team.'

'Of course,' I say. 'Whatever happens, she's our daughter.'

I withdraw my hand, although I liked his fingers wrapped around mine. Warm skin. Just the right pressure. Feeling floods up my arm from the memory of his touch, pulses into my belly. I sit back quickly.

'Do you ever regret our decision not to have more kids?' he asks. 'Sometimes I think it would have been good for Bea to have a sibling.'

I can't answer him. I have no idea why that decision was taken.

He flushes, biting his lip. 'Sorry,' he says quickly. 'I know I agreed not to talk about it. But you're a good mum, Cecily, whatever you think. Anyway, we have our daughter, and I'll always be grateful to you for that.'

I clear my throat and look down at the table.

He's looking at me with a considering gaze. 'You know, there's something else about you that's different.'

I look up, managing to hold his gaze, and give a slight, casual shrug. 'Really? What?'

He laughs. 'I've got it.' He waves a finger in my direction. 'You're not wearing any black stuff around your eyes.'

I touch my face. I forgot to put kohl and mascara on this morning.

'I always liked you better without it,' he says, dismissing the matter and leaning across the table towards me. 'The point is, whatever you've been doing recently. Exercise classes or walking or... I don't know. It's done you good.'

There's no hint of suspicion in his words. It must be Bea who's sneaking into my bedroom and poking around. Throwing away the plants had to be a message. She doubts me. I suppress a shiver.

The waitress comes over to ask if we want anything else, and I slump in my chair while Gabriel asks for the bill and chats to her. The back of my head hurts, and I'm grateful for a break from his attention, for some time to calm my heart. I fiddle with the gold band on my finger, turning it around and around.

* * *

The rest of the day is how I imagine a proper family Saturday. Gabriel spends the morning in the garden 'tidying up.' I watch him kneeling by a flowerbed with a trowel. I'd like to join him out there, get my hands muddy, but Cecily hated the weeding at Hawksmoor more than any of the tasks our father set. Bea appears rubbing her eyes, and I glance at her nervously.

'You're up at last, sleepyhead,' Gabriel says as he comes in from the garden, rumpling her hair in the manner of sitcom Dad. Bea smiles bashfully as she bats his hand away. All of this is lit with a kind of gleaming, sunlit halo. This is what Cecily is running away from? I can't understand why my sister is unhappy, why she doesn't love being with these two people. Her people. I can't imagine having anyone who belongs to me. I never understood why she didn't tell Gabriel that I existed. I suppose she told the lie when she met him, and after that, just felt she couldn't ever admit to it.

I attempt to make a mushroom pie, but it's too complicated for my amateur skills. The pastry is claggy as clay, the thin sauce tastes like I've used the entire contents of a salt canister. I hope Gabriel doesn't have high blood pressure.

'Did you forget to put the chicken in?' Bea asks with a grin, looking at a mushroom hanging limply from her fork. She isn't behaving as if she's suspicious of me. Perhaps she's a good actress. Better than me.

'Actually, I think I might be a vegetarian,' I say.

'You think?' Gabriel raises an eyebrow.

I sit up straighter. 'Yes. So, I won't be cooking any more meat.' I shrug. 'Sorry.'

Bea bursts into laughter, and Gabriel joins her. I look from one to the other. 'Why are you laughing?'

'Nothing,' Gabriel says. 'It's just... you've gone vegetarian a few times – and then you're back to eating meat within a few days.'

'I have?'

'We're fine with it, Mum,' Bea reassures me.

'Good,' I say, clearing the plates. 'Don't worry. I'll get better at making veggie things. And this time I'm not reverting.'

'One of us can always cook,' Gabriel says in a casual voice. 'You don't have to do everything in the kitchen. We'd like to help, wouldn't we, sweet pea?'

Bea nods.

After the meal has been cleared away, we play Scrabble in the living room, and then cards, at my suggestion. 'I didn't know you knew all these games,' Gabriel said. 'I didn't even know that you played.'

'Oh, they're just things I remember from childhood,' I say. 'We were always looking for ways to pass the time, especially in the winter.'

'But you were an only child?'

Heat rushes to my face. 'I... I did have some friends,' I say, getting to my feet.

'Just need to put the washing in the dryer,' I mutter over my shoulder, slipping out of the room into the kitchen. As I pull twists of damp clothing from the mouth of the washing machine, I pause and press my forehead hard against the machine. I must be more careful. I've begun to feel too relaxed.

We get takeaway fish and chips for supper at Bea's request.

'Wow, you really have gone vegetarian,' she says as I unwrap my fish-less portion. We exchange a glance and I try to discern anything inside in her eyes that might lend her words a hidden challenge or question. But she's happily dipping her own chips into ketchup and asking Gabriel if we can watch a film. It occurs to me that a girl of Bea's age should be out with her friends on a Saturday night.

We slob on the sofa and watch the film she's chosen from the basket of DVDs under the telly – a silly, fast-paced thriller. Gabriel sits in the middle. When Bea shrieks at something on the screen and falls across her father's lap, his body presses against mine, our thighs pushed together. I'm trapped for a moment, wedged between him and the arm of the sofa. When Bea removes herself from his lap and he can readjust his position, the air between us is like a cold draft.

Later, in the bathroom, I follow Cecily's routine for the first time, smoothing on different products and taking them off again, adding little drops of serum and patting on a thick cream. It takes ages, but it's strangely enjoyable, almost trance-inducing. As I unlock the door, I'm dismayed to find Gabriel on the landing waiting to come in. He's in checked pyjamas, his feet bare. He gives me a rueful grin. I slip out as he comes forwards, and we're suddenly close. 'You smell nice,' he says.

I can't meet his eyes. 'Thanks,' I murmur. 'Night.'

I shimmy past his chest, holding my body away and escape into my room, shutting the door quietly. I smell of her, I remind myself. I'm the imposter. He thinks I'm his wife.

13

CECILY

Jude was fascinated by Hawksmoor, but as Henry despised the place, it was me who showed Jude the house. We explored the disused servants' floor, the scullery and butler's pantry. I took him across the yard to the game larder, a small stone building for hanging dead animals. 'Why is it hexagonal?' he asked, peering inside.

'To keep it cooler.' I didn't like the game larder; it was dark and full of hooks and smelt of death. I hurried him away and into the kitchen, but Jane, our cook, shooed us out. 'I've got enough to do without you two getting under my feet,' she said.

'And this is the buttery,' I said, opening the door into the cell-like room.

'Where they made butter?' he asked.

I laughed. 'Guess again.' I waved my arm. 'A clue. They kept something here.'

'I don't know. A whole lot of fat butts, perhaps?'

I banged his elbow with mine and rolled my eyes. 'Kegs of wine and beer.'

He was entranced by the hidden chapel in the cellar, the banisters carved into sea creatures, the dark and oily portraits of our ancestors, even the boot room, with its pairs of mismatched wellingtons, cobwebby hooks groaning under the weight of dog leads, shooting bags, mackintoshes stiff with age and waxed cotton jackets full of mouse nests. He thought it was charming that broken windows had been patched with cardboard and rain dripped into rooms.

He couldn't get enough of my stories, especially the ones about the Elizabethans who'd hidden Jesuit priests in the priest hole on the top landing. I explained how my ancestors broke the law to pray in the secret chapel built under the house. I didn't tell him that I saw them; not just Elizabethans, but Victorians and Edwardians too, passing me in the dining room, brushing through me on the stairs – a monk in his brown tunic and cowl, a giggling child dressed as a fairy, a man in a feathered hat with long curls down his back, a sword at his side – and sometimes I heard their voices, felt their laughter and fury as if it were my own.

When I showed him the armoury, he stood blinking in the swinging beam of the overhead light, and I sensed his interest quicken. Shadows moved across the killing devices on display, the space musty as a sealed tomb. This was forbidden territory. I strained my ears for the sound of Daddy and closed the door behind us quietly.

'Wow,' he breathed. 'Henry didn't tell me about this. It's... it's epic.'

'Yeah.' I trailed my fingers casually over the gun display cabinet, relishing the moment. 'Daddy's writing a book about ancient weapons – he collects them, and some of them have been in the family forever.'

I picked up a heavy mahogany box inlaid with ivory and opened it. 'Duelling pistols,' I said. 'French.'

Reverently, Jude picked one out of its green baize hollow, weighing it in the palm of his hand. The long barrel gleamed blue in the light. 'Do you think they've been used?'

'Of course.' I took it from him, put it back, and closed the box, wiping the edge with the sleeve of my blouse.

'You're so lucky to have all this.' Jude paced the flagstones, staring at the walls, at horned heads with glassy, reproachful eyes, swords slung from hooks, a flintlock rife with silver engraving. 'My parents do their best to pretend our relatives never existed. Like we've just hatched from an egg or something.' He leant against the gun cabinet. 'Every time we move country, our house smells the same, of plastic and air freshener. Everything brand new. The best of the best, as my parents are always boasting. I'm glad they let me come here in the hols. Not that they care about seeing me. As long as my grades are good, that's all they're interested in. Wish I lived here always, with you lot.' He nudged me with his elbow. 'You could be my sister.'

My heart pumped with gladness and confusion. I couldn't think what to say, how to explain to him that he was more than another brother to me. Much more. *I love you.* The words sounded simple but saying them was complicated and fraught with danger.

He paused before the serrated jaws of a large trap. 'What was this used for?' He reached a finger towards the sharp edges. 'It's big enough for a bear.'

'It's to catch men,' I told him.

'Seriously?'

'Yeah,' I said, standing next to him, our hands just an airy whisper apart. 'Poachers.'

I revelled in his attention, the power of being the one to keep him enthralled. 'Until the 1800s it was legal to catch poachers and trespassers with these. Sometimes they caught other people by mistake, innocent ramblers, the master of the house, even. And animals of course.'

'Must be over six foot long.' Jude whistled. 'We could use some of these at school. That would give the monks a nasty shock.' He laughed without humour.

'It was fixed in the ground and covered with leaves and grass.' I pointed to the central plate. 'When someone trod just here, the steel spring sprang shut. You'd lose your foot, wouldn't you?'

'Yeah,' he agreed with an odd twist in his voice. His brow furrowed as he stared at the device. I wished there was some old family story I could conjure to keep him enthralled. Perhaps I could invent a tale about an ancient relative. But Henry's voice came from outside, calling for him.

He blinked, his expression clearing as he looked at me. 'Better run.'

The door creaked open and shut. I kept my gaze on the rusted edges of the trap. I imagined I could see blackened blood there, a century-old stain.

I didn't notice my father, not until he was standing right beside me, and his fingers had encircled my arm in an iron grip.

14

ALICE

On Sunday morning I wake late with a sour mouth. When I get out of bed, my knees are strangely sore. In the bathroom, I splash my face and pee, and wonder if I'm coming down with flu. I stumble downstairs feeling as if I've been poisoned.

Gabriel comes into the kitchen, looking at me in my pyjamas making coffee and screws up his forehead in surprise. 'No church today?'

Church! My body clenches. It's been years. When I left home, it was the first time in my life I'd missed Mass, then as the years went on, I met people from different faiths, and the prayers Father Michael intoned in our chapel seemed like spells and incantations.

Gabriel is still waiting for an answer. I touch the skin above my eyebrows with a hesitant fingertip. 'I woke up with a headache,' I falter. 'Thought maybe I was coming down with something.'

It's true. I do have a thundering headache, like a hangover, but without the fun.

He frowns. 'Not like you to miss Sunday communion.'

'I wouldn't want to give the rest of the congregation a bug,' I say, a defensive note creeping into my tone. I lift the lid of the bread bin and take out a loaf, avoiding his eyes.

'Should you be in bed?'

'No, turns out it was just a headache,' I say. 'I'm feeling better.'

I can sense his puzzled look, but Monday is almost close enough to touch. I just hope that Cecily shows up as arranged. I push the doubt away. Of course, she will come.

'What do you want to do today, then?' he asks, getting two cups down from the cupboard and sliding them across the counter to me.

Before I can answer, he slaps his hand theatrically to his forehead. 'Choir practice. We've got a performance coming up soon.' He glances at me. 'Want to come along?'

'To the practice?' I pour coffee into the two cups. I've told him I'm feeling better, so I can hardly refuse. 'Why not?'

'Really?' he looks so disbelieving and pleased; it makes me laugh.

'Really,' I confirm with a smile. 'Is that so strange?'

'Yes, actually,' he says, giving me a puzzled glance.

Luckily, I don't have to respond because Bea appears. Instead of the baggy tartan trousers and loose jumper she had on yesterday, she's wearing a figure-hugging pencil skirt that ruches over her curvy hips. She has bare legs, and her clumpy DMs are brightened with short, glittery socks. She's lined her eyes in thick, black kohl, winging it out at the sides.

'Going somewhere nice?' Gabriel asks.

Lots of dads might protest about the skirt or eyeliner, but his face is open and uncensorious. I can imagine our father's reaction if he saw us dressed like that. Cecily and I had to be careful what we wore around him.

'Megan's house,' Bea says. 'She's having some people over. Just to hang out.' There's a glow about her, a barely suppressed excitement.

'Want me to do your hair?' I ask. 'I used to be pretty good at back-combing.'

She looks at me with disbelief. 'Okay,' she agrees slowly.

After she's eaten her breakfast, we traipse upstairs, with me hobbling behind. Maybe I fell out of bed last night. I slip into the bathroom and swallow two paracetamol from a packet in the cabinet and find Bea in the sanctuary of her room. Wielding the comb, I work upwards through her hair with short strokes, remembering Cecily shivering in her silver dress between my knees. I tease Bea's thick, chestnut hair into a messy mop, pulling strands out to frame her face. When I've finished, she looks in the mirror and turns her head from one side to the other. 'That's amazing,' she says. 'Didn't know you could do that. Thanks.'

'Very Courtney Love,' I say.

'You don't think I look silly?' she says, suddenly doubtful.

'You look gorgeous, Bea.'

'Do you think I should bleach my hair, like she does?' She scrunches up her face, and gestures towards the poster on her wall. 'Not sure if Dad would be happy, though.'

'I like your hair the colour it is,' I say. 'But if you're going to experiment, get a professional to do it. And talk to Dad first.'

She nods into the mirror. 'Maybe I will.' And she flings herself towards me in one sudden movement. I'm pressed against her solid, warm body, inhaling hairspray, the ends of her hair tickling my nose. I put my arms around her shoulders and squeeze. As I shut my eyes and hold her, the complications fall away, and it's just me and my niece sharing a hug. An unfamiliar feeling wells up inside me like a wave, a surge of joy. But then I remember, and the hug suddenly feels corrupted, false.

When she pulls away, she wrinkles her nose. 'You smell different.'

'Do I?' I say, deliberately vague. 'I don't think I put any perfume on this morning.'

'Yeah, I can smell your skin,' she says. 'Maybe that's it. I'm not used to smelling the real you.'

* * *

Gabriel drives Bea to her friend's house. When he gets back, we eat a sandwich for lunch. I force it down, thinking that the food will help my unsettled tummy. Then we get back in the car to cross town, and as we drive along suburban streets, I gaze out of the window, searching for a familiar silhouette, hoping to recognise her walk, her profile. Cecily feels distant, unattainable as shadow, and yet she is my other half, known before oxygen, before the world claimed us. As children, whatever our disagreements, being different from everyone else united us. I should have an instinct for what she's doing. I should be able to sense her whereabouts.

Gabriel parks up near a large hall next to an Anglican church and gets out clutching his songbook to his chest.

I follow him inside, limping a bit. The drugs have helped. My headache has gone. A group of people have gathered in ages that seem to range from early twenties to seventies. They are drinking tea and chatting. Gabriel introduces me as his wife to a couple of middle-aged women, who shake my hand and look at me with curiosity. Gabriel waves towards some chairs pushed against the back wall. 'Make yourself comfortable,' he says. 'Take some biscuits and tea.' He smiles. 'I won't blame you if you want to slip out before the end.'

A young man with spectacles claps his hands, and instantly, the group arranges itself, gathering sheet music, waiting expectantly. I make my way over to the back of the room and choose a chair in the middle.

I try to feel where Cecily is now – she could be nearby, passing this very hall, turning at the bottom of the street – I could be missing her by moments. There's not the slightest trace of her in my consciousness. Even in a small town like Exeter, the odds are against me bumping into her by chance. If only I had the address of where she's staying. Why didn't she leave it for me like she said she would? There's no reason that makes sense.

The music plucks me from my thoughts. I'm surprised by how good they are. I was expecting hymns, but each song is different: a rousing gospel prayer, a lilting folk song, a run of pop and rock songs, Elton John's 'Benny and the Jets,' Seal's 'Kiss From A Rose'. And then a gorgeous, soaring version of 'Amazing Grace'. The harmonies are lovely, and I close my eyes to listen better. A female voice sings a solo, before a deeper voice takes over, and I open my eyes. It's Gabriel, his face alight. His voice is bright and strong. The music moves me, creeps inside me, opening something in my chest, my heart.

'You sat through the whole thing,' Gabriel says, coming over to me, beaming.

'It was wonderful. You have a beautiful voice.'

He looks pleased and slightly embarrassed. 'It's a really nice thing to be part of – singing with other people is therapeutic, bonding.'

'I can see that,' I say, feeling almost envious.

Outside, the early evening light is full of the throaty cooing of wood pigeons, the nascent, fecund promise of summer, and I'm back at Hawksmoor again in the August holidays, swimming in the tarn with Alice, the boys playing cricket on the lawn. Those moments glow gold in my memory, a seam of goodness inside darkness. My chest squeezes tight. Gabriel's talking, but I don't hear him as we walk to the car together. His swinging hand brushes mine, and I step away, pushing my fingers into my pocket.

15

CECILY

As soon as Daddy caught me in the armoury, I knew what would happen next. Mutely, I followed him up the main stairs, along the landing, and up the last narrow flight into the old servants' quarters. He opened the priest hole and waited for me to get in.

The stink of damp and decay hit me. Terror lived in the hole. A monk had died in there while he was hiding from searching soldiers. As he prayed to be released, he suffocated to death. There was a plaque with his name in the chapel.

I crossed myself, and stooped low, bending my head to duck under the beam, then getting onto my hands and knees to crawl into the tiny space.

'Consider your sins,' Daddy said, before he closed the secret beam, leaving me sealed inside. I could hear his voice, muffled through the thick slab of wood, praying for my soul, and then his footsteps moving away.

I groped for the gold cross under my shirt. *Dear Lord, have pity on me.*

The metal was hard and unforgiving between my fingers. Daddy's face swam before me. His noble nose and eyes as bright as a flame. Like the face of Jesus, without a beard. The two faces slid across each other, became the same.

I was lost inside blackness, compressed into a shape smaller than an upright coffin. Just the sound of my own heart hammering against the walls of my body. I forced myself to breathe slowly, to wait for my eyes to adjust to the pitchy blindfold. I knew that eventually I'd be able to make out the faint glow of my own hand in front of my face, like the promise of a candle flame. I must be calm. I must wait for this suffering to pass. But I was crying like a baby, salt stinging my cheeks.

The only way to fit was to sit hunched over, hugging my knees tightly, spine against the wall. If I lifted my head, the top of my skull hit dusty plaster or a wooden beam. I kept my nose lowered to my kneecaps. The smell of damp mortar, rotting wood and animal droppings crept into me. My body was my anchor, the bone and flesh scaffolding of myself. I dug my fingernails into my shins reminding myself that I was still alive. I took sips of stuffy air, worried about running out of oxygen.

My mind fragmented, drifted.

A little girl clambered onto my knees, slipping into the tiny gap between my legs and my chest and leant her trusting head against my shoulder. She was wearing fairy wings, and the gossamer stretch of them folded against my ribs, the fragile wire crushed and mangled, meshing us together. I hummed a tune into the delicate curl of her ear, and she echoed the sound back to me, holding me with starfish fingers, her sweet breath mingling with my own. We sang together, her voice pure and wavering, until I realised it was only my voice I could hear.

There was something wrong with me. I should be punished. Suffering was necessary for my soul. I must endure my punishment and pray for forgiveness. It was for my own good. I tried to think of something I could do to make it up to Daddy. I would have to convince him that I was obedient, that I was dutiful and committed to God.

The little girl was crying, her sobs shaking my body as they sounded from my mouth. She pressed her burning forehead against mine. We wanted our mama. Our lungs faltered and heaved, our heart stuttering like a candle about to go out.

Not much longer, and he'd open the door.

But minutes and hours didn't exist. I'd fallen through time and thought I could hear the voices of soldiers shouting commands, footsteps echoing through the house, the clatter of horses' hooves outside on the drive. And there was another person inside the hole with me. Someone in rough textured robes, whose rasping voice muttered prayers in a language I didn't understand. His bony finger brushed my cheek, and I spoke his prayers for him, knowing they would save me.

16

ALICE

It's my last night in this house. The dark insinuates itself, cat-like, against the kitchen window. I can sense Gabriel upstairs in his room, leaning over his desk, his reading glasses slipping down his nose as he concentrates on his marking. I'm scared of what I might say or do if I see him. I want to confess the plan, tell him who I really am, tell him that Cecily lied about his drinking, lied about everything. But this is not my life. It's safer to shut myself away for the evening.

In her bedroom, I collect a dressing gown to take into the bathroom. When I go to the window to draw the curtains, there's a figure on the other side of the street. They're standing in the shadows. Someone with a hood up. They seem to be watching the house. A shiver runs through me, and I close the curtains with quick tugs.

I spend ages in the bath, whiling away time until I can go to bed. I have almost nothing to pack for tomorrow. Everything belongs to my sister. I'll get my dungarees, Birkenstocks and sweatshirt out of my rucksack after the others have gone, change into them and take the old black puffer jacket that hangs in the hall. The forecast is for rain. Before I get into bed, I peer between a crack in the curtains; the figure across the street has gone. Relieved, I unfasten the gold cross, slipping off the wedding ring and watch, and put them on the dressing table for her to find when she gets home. I frown at the icons, at the painted faces of angels and baby Jesus. What if she doesn't come?

She has to come. I have a plane to catch. I'm sticking to our plan, even if she isn't.

* * *

Monday morning. Of course, Gabriel and Bea have no idea that it might be the last time I ever see them. It's only been a week, but I've grown fond of them. A sharp pain presses at the centre of my chest. Who am I kidding? But that's another reason why I've got to leave. They are not my family. A steady patter of rain against the windows. The sky is dull with cloud.

In the kitchen, Gabriel is the only one there. 'No Bea?' I ask.

He shakes his head, gesturing with his toast. 'Maybe she slept through her alarm.'

There's the snap of the letter box. 'I'll get it,' I say, as I go into the hall. 'And I'll check on Bea.' There are two letters with stamps on, addressed to Gabriel, and I put them on the hall table. As I swivel for the stairs, I notice a folded piece of paper on the floor near the mat. It's addressed to Cecily. I unfold it.

Need to stay longer. Just a few days. Cancel travel arrangements.

I gasp. Cecily? I wrench open the door and run to the end of the front path, peering around the privet hedge to look up and down the empty street. There's no sign of her. A tall man is letting himself into a car parked further down the road.

Gabriel calls from the kitchen, 'Cecily? Everything alright?'

'Yes,' I say quickly, shoving the note into my pocket. 'I... I'm just going to wake Bea.'

I escape upstairs, banging on Bea's door as I go past. 'Are you awake? It's late!' Then slip into Cecily's room and close the door. I sit on the bed and squeeze my eyes shut. I'm trapped. I don't know what to do. And my flight, I think. I won't get my money back now. I look at her message again. So casual. No explanations or apology.

I hear Gabriel shouting up to say goodbye. I listen to the front door opening, the hiss of rain on a pavement, the door closing. I go to the window and catch a glimpse of him moving away under a large black umbrella to his car, parked further along the street. I wonder why Bea hasn't left yet, and then I see her, slipping out just after her dad and walking in the opposite direction with her head down; her backcombed hair is pulled into a messy ponytail, and she has no umbrella.

After they've gone, I continue to stare through the rain-splattered glass, looking down at the sodden privet hedge and the water overspilling drainage channels, rushing towards the river. I chew my lip, frustration making a tight knot in my belly. She hasn't bothered to let me know where she is, and she's changed the plan, again, without asking. It feels as though she's playing with me.

For God's sake. I close my eyes.

Do I go? Or do I stay?

17

CECILY

The shelves in the pantry were full of stacked tins, neatly labelled jars of preserves, pickles and chutneys, dusty sacks of greening potatoes and pulses. I pounced on the bag of dried peas and stuffed it into my pocket. As I went back across the kitchen, Jane glanced up with a puzzled look but shrugged as if to say she didn't have time to find out what I was up to, so long as I wasn't taking any of the pies left on the table to cool.

Jane's mother had been a maid at Hawksmoor when Daddy was a child. She'd left to marry the gardener. Jane said she'd grown up with stories of the big house and always presumed she'd work there herself just as soon as she could escape school. In her mum's day, there'd been a cook and a scullery maid, housemaids, two footmen, a housekeeper and butler. Now there was just Jane. She'd looked the same for as long as she'd worked for us: tall and bone-thin in a striped apron, her hands almost as big as Daddy's, with knobs of red knuckles. She had the inflamed, broken-veined cheeks and nose of a drinker, which Mummy said was unfortunate because to her knowledge, Jane never touched a drop.

With the door of my bedroom closed – and just to be sure, a chair dragged over and jammed under the handle – I took the dried peas from my pockets and arranged the withered balls on the floor next to the fireplace. I tested one with my finger. *Holy Mary, Mother of God. Forgive my sins*. It was dry and hard, slipping under the pressure of my touch. *The cross of Christ bears all pain, transforms my pain into love.* I'd just finished reading 'The Lives of the Saints', and I longed to see a vision of the Virgin. If the Blessed Mother visited me, it would be a sign that my faith had been recognised and rewarded. There were girls around the world who'd had visions, who'd received heavenly messages, found their palms bleeding with stigmata. Miracles really could happen to the faithful, and they seemed to happen to teenage girls a lot.

Also, I needed to ask God to give Mummy strength. After I came out of the hole, I'd taken some of her sister's letters from her drawer and left them on Daddy's desk. It was wrong of her to write to a divorced woman and wrong to disobey her husband. She'd be happier without her sister in her life, and it was only right for Daddy to know the truth. But Mummy had been crying ever since, drooping around the house, listless and dull as a rag doll without its stuffing.

I hitched up my skirt, steadied my eyes on my crucifix, and cautiously lowered my bare knees on top of the dried peas. I gasped, let out a cry. Knives thrust through my flesh into my bones, hot needles of agony, blades of pain. I fell to the side, rubbing my indented kneecaps. I sat for a moment, breathing hard, telling myself I could do it – had to do it – and tucked my hair behind my ears, tried again. Suffering was necessary. Purifying. Shockwaves forced my body to become rigid, to shut down, but I remained kneeling, fists clenched, jaw grinding, eyes squeezed tight.

Make him love me. Make him love me best.

I was thinking of Jude, but it was Daddy's face that slid before my eyes.

* * *

I woke up. The dogs were barking. Pale luminescence slid over the carpet through the thin gap in the curtains. I stared through the darkness, wondering if the Labs were barking at a fox. Something felt different. My skin prickled. I pushed back the covers and went to the window, moving a curtain aside to look down at the drive. A shape moved. Bigger than a fox. I caught my breath. There was a person down there, and they seemed to be staring up at the house. A splash of moonlight caught their features, blurring and brightening the dips and hollows of eye sockets and cheekbone, making a mask of their face. I gripped the edge of the curtain, wondering if this was my visit from the Virgin. But the figure turned away and scurried into shadows, their body ungainly and human in its urgency. I heard an engine start, a crunch of tyres.

When I woke the next morning, I thought I must have dreamt it. After breakfast, Alice and I got our satchels and coats to walk to the bus stop. As we shut the front door, Alice let out a scream. Something hung from the wood. Blackened, matted fur, a drooping lifeless body. It dangled by a nail through the scruffy end of a tail. 'A cat,' Alice said between gasps. 'Fuck.'

I crossed myself. The body was oddly flattened. 'I think it's been run over,' she said, looking closer. 'But why would anyone nail roadkill to our door? They must have come all the way up the drive to do it.'

I looked away from the snarling mouth, white teeth like tiny tusks. Black cats were the Devil's creatures. A dark drip of congealed blood hung like a pendant from its tongue. I thought of the figure standing in the moonlight. 'We should throw it away before Daddy and Mummy see it.'

Alice prised the nail out using a flint from the drive and held the dead thing's tail by the tips of her fingers. It dangled gently next to her as we made our way down the long and winding walk to the end of the drive. 'We should bury it, really,' Alice said.

'We don't have time,' I said.

Alice pulled back her arm and swung, letting go of the tail. The cat flew in a heavy arc across some hydrangea bushes and fell with a soft thump into the undergrowth. Alice brushed her hands against her school skirt, a smear of blood on her left palm.

As we stood at the bus stop, I hoped it was just a coincidence, asking for a sign, and getting a squashed cat. But that poor, tattered creature hanging on our door wasn't a heavenly miracle bestowed by the Virgin, or an evil joke from the Devil. A living person had hammered it into the wood. It was a silent curse from someone, or a warning, and the woman in the library came into my head. Edith Baxter.

18

ALICE

I go out, shutting the door behind me and double-locking it before slipping the keys back under the stone cat. The rain is unrelenting; fat drops bounce with the force of their fall, soaking me in an instant, plastering my hair to my scalp. I hoist my old rucksack onto my shoulder, shrugging up the hood on Cecily's puffer jacket, and turn in the direction of the station, walking with my head down. Water seeps into my boots and the bottoms of my jeans. But although I should be hurrying, I can't make myself walk fast. My feet drag, getting slower and slower, until I come to a stop. I look up into the unforgiving sky, the rain blinding me. 'Damn you,' I whisper. 'Damn you, Cecily.'

I turn around, stomping back to the house through puddles. I fit the key in the lock, and almost fall into the hall. My hands are shaking with anger. How can I abandon Bea and Gabriel? What would they think, coming back to an empty house, with no explanation waiting for them? No hint as to where she's gone or when, if ever, she's coming back. I snort at myself. This is my own fault. My sister took off the burden of her responsibility and passed it to me, and like an idiot I accepted it.

I drop the rucksack on the floor, shrug off the sodden jacket and hang it on the newel post at the bottom of the stairs, where it drips onto the floor. Then I grab the straps of the rucksack and go upstairs to Cecily's room, trailing the bag behind me. There must be a clue to help me fathom what she's doing, what she's thinking. When we were children, I might have been able to get a better feel – we could often read each other's minds – but it's been too long a separation and when I try and concentrate on listening for a sense or a vibration from her, I tumble into an emptiness.

I get out her crumpled note and reread it, seeing another sentence written at the bottom that I missed in my panic.

P.S. My turn to do the church flowers this coming Wednesday. Details in notebook.

She must have planned this if she's written instructions for doing the flowers in her little book. When I'd stipulated, I'd only do a week, she already knew she'd force me to stay longer.

'Liar! You bloody liar!' I rage at the empty room. She's tricked me into being her – the whole 'poor me' thing, the whining about needing time, wanting to get a divorce – I don't believe any of it any more.

I open her wardrobe and rifle through her clothes; every item would fit me perfectly, but I'd never choose to wear any of them. We've always had different tastes. I'm realising that my sister's choice of clothes says a lot about her personality: stiff and sensible on the outside, and then the surprise of her hidden underwear, all that lace and wire, torturously, secretly sexy. What else is she hiding in her life? I check the shoe boxes lining the bottom of the wardrobe, lifting lids. I'm frustrated. I don't know what I'm looking for. There's nothing here that gives me a hint about why Cecily really wants me to take her place. I drag over the stool from the dressing table and stand on it to look in the top cupboard. It's filled with a couple of folded blankets and an electric fan with the cord neatly wrapped around its base.

I get down and push the stool back into place. Then I kneel and look under the bed. There's a large wicker basket right in the middle, the kind you take on a picnic. I lie down and stretch my arm and shoulder to pull it out. Inside, instead of travel cutlery and plastic plates, there are sketch-books. A whole pile of them. I sit with my back against the bed and open the first one, leafing through pages, finding drawings in Cecily's familiar precise and delicate style.

There's a sketch of a cavalier in breeches with long curling hair, a sword at his side. As I turn the paper, my pulse skips. Hawksmoor. She's drawn the house with the yew tree making a burgeoning darkness in the foreground. Then there are close ups of the battlements and Pele tower, the front entrance with the steps leading up to the balustrade. She's made details of one of the stone lions, the frozen curls of its mane, its pricked ears. She's sketched Mummy, the two Labs, Dilly with her pointed snout and low-slung belly. There's me and Cecily together, our faces close, but one a simulacrum of the other, a fainter tracing of the same features, a shadow sister. I can't tell which is which. It's eerie. I lick my finger to flick forwards, and I'm looking at Henry. I trace the contours of his face, the firm nose and chin, his intelligent, dark eyes, his teasing half-smile.

There's a smaller pad at the bottom of the basket. A younger Bea holds a kitten on her lap, and on the next page, a little girl holds up the hem of her dress; she seems to be in a fairy costume. I compare the two faces, and I don't think the girl in costume is Bea. Then I'm staring into Gabriel's features. Underneath his portrait, she's written in small, cramped letters:

Till death do us part.

I shut the book quickly. Does she love him, after all? Or did she do the sketch before she lost interest in him? My heart flaps like panicked wings inside my ribs. My body is liquid with nerves, and I have a strange sense that a cage is closing around me. I unfold my legs, wincing at the stiffness in my joints as I pace the room, recalling Gabriel saying that Cecily was angry with him for not wanting to live at Hawksmoor. But did she really expect him to move to the other side of the country, leave his job and take on the responsibility of a decaying pile of bricks?

I sit on the bed and return to the pages of her sketchbooks, finding images of our father; she's made him look almost Christ-like. I can't look at him, and I skim pages fast. Here's the interior of the chapel, the statues of the saints, the painted Madonna staring down at her child. Mouldy damp and musty incense clogs my throat.

She's written words over and around some of the drawings. Sentences worm across the page in no obvious order: '*Offence against the natural law... no impact on legal status... a marriage continues in the eyes of God. Never ending. Never. Never.*'

'*He'll hate me. Disown me,*' she's written in bold, underlining it with such hard strokes she's torn the paper. And she's right. Divorce would be the death-knell for her relationship with our father. On another page there's one word written over and over, criss-crossing, overlapping: '*DIE, DIE, DIE, DIE*'.

I push the sketchbooks away from me, stomach flipping with shock. Cecily had appeared rational in her last letter. She was upset and worried, but she hadn't seemed unbalanced. These scribbled sentences tell a different story, and it seems suddenly obvious that she's not going to leave her husband. Of course not. She's Daddy's daughter and a devout Catholic. So why lie to me about it? I know the answer to that – she guessed rightly that mentioning divorce would shock me into swapping places with her. She knew I'd understand what courage it would take, that it meant rebellion. The question I can't answer is why does she really want me here?

I haul myself up onto numb feet and hold my shaking fingers before me. I can't keep them still. The books lie around me, pages splaying open, jumbled up sketches and snippets of sentences. I don't know what's real and what's pretend any more, and I sit down hard on the bed, shivering. The room tilts, blurs as if air has become liquid and I am falling through it, drowning.

* * *

A bang wakes me. The sound of the front door opening. I sit up and glance at the time. It jolts me back into the day. The afternoon has flown. I realise the rain has stopped; there's a glimmer of weak sunlight gilding the wet window, the glitter of a rainbow. The sketchbooks aren't lying around me any more. I kneel by the bed and pull the wicker trunk from under it. Opening the lid, I see that they are there, piled up neatly. I must have tidied them away. I push the trunk under the bed again, straighten my hair and go down to greet Bea.

She stoops over the kitchen counter, spreading butter over slices of white bread. She glances over her shoulder, cheeks bulging. There's a ripped packet of chocolate digestives open next to her. Our eyes meet, but her gaze is shuttered, blank. Remains of yesterday's black kohl is smudged onto her cheeks. She turns away and goes back to slathering cherry jam on top of the butter.

'Bea,' I go towards her. 'Is something wrong?'

She shrugs. 'No.'

She's piled a plate high with slices of bread and biscuits. She begins to make for the door, pushing a biscuit into her mouth.

'Bea,' I try again. 'Remember, we agreed – we said we'd talk to each other?'

She stops, swallowing hard. She drops her chin. 'I can't.' She walks on. 'I'm alright,' she mutters.

I listen to her going slowly upstairs and her door shutting. I follow, knocking briefly before entering. She's sitting on the floor cross-legged, and she looks up with a furtive expression, mouth sticky. She scowls, chewing. 'You can't just come in here,' she says, already reaching for more food.

'I know it's your space, and I'm sorry. But I can't ignore this – something's obviously happened.' I perch on the edge of her bed.

'Stop pretending you care,' she says. 'Go away.'

I take a breath, 'Please tell me, Bea. Did something happen yesterday?'

'Why should I tell you?' she says, her voice breaking.

I look at my hand. My palm tingles. I seem to remember it making contact with her face. But I've never hit her. It was me that got hit. My father's arm pulling back, the impact sending me sideways. Red roaring in my ears.

I sit for a few seconds, collecting myself, breathing deeply. 'Whatever I've done to upset you,' I say slowly. 'Can we put it to one side for a moment? Just tell me, honestly. Did something happen at Megan's?'

She shoves the plate away from her. 'I... I think I'm going to be sick...'

She pushes herself up and rushes next door into the bathroom. I can hear retching and the flush of the loo. I give her a minute and then follow. She's leaning over the sink, wiping her mouth with the back of her hand. She turns on the cold tap and splashes water onto her face.

'Okay,' I say. 'I'm really worried now. What's going on?'

Her face crumples, and she drops her head into her hands. I've crossed the space between us in a second and folded her inside my arms. She's rigid at first, but then she slumps against me. I press my face into the wild bird's nest of her hair, reeking of stale perfume and cigarette smoke. Her body shudders, ribs and shoulders heaving. She cries in big gulps, sniffing and spluttering. Her sobs become hiccups, and I pass her a length of loo roll. She blows hard into folds of white.

'Let's go downstairs,' I say. 'I'll put the kettle on. We both need a cup of tea.'

I remember how Jane and Mummy would drink tea as if it were a cure for everything. Jane ladled sugar into hers and liked it milky; Mummy drank hers black with lemon.

Bea is sitting opposite me at the table, her mug untouched. She picks at her cuticles, then rubs her cheeks hard. 'I… I was an idiot… there's this boy…'

I grip the handle of my mug.

'David. I thought he liked me.' Her voice cracks and she presses one hand over her mouth. She looks at me as if assessing whether she really can tell me.

'It's okay,' I say, leaning forwards slightly. 'Go on.'

'There were a few of us hanging out at Megan's… and he said… he said he fancied me; said I should trust him if he was going to be my boyfriend…' she shudders. 'We went upstairs.'

I lean over the surface and place my hand over hers. 'Did he, did he make you do anything?'

She shakes her head, and I let out the breath I was holding. Her nose is running, and she wipes it with the ball of loo paper. 'I got frightened when he put his hand under my top. I stopped him. Said I wasn't ready.'

I wait for her to continue.

'He tried to persuade me. But I pushed him away.'

'You did the right thing,' I say.

'But he didn't really like me,' she whispers. 'As soon as he realised I wasn't going to let him... you know,' she blushes, bites her lip. 'After that, he changed. He laughed. He said... it was all a joke. He didn't fancy me. I was too fat to be anyone's girlfriend.' She stares at the table. 'I felt so stupid. They all knew. They were laughing at me.'

Anger builds in me. Where the hell were Megan's parents while this was going on? I swallow my fury and try to stay calm. 'You were brave to say "no".'

'I feel like an idiot,' she whispers, tearing the loo paper into shreds.

'You're not an idiot, Bea,' I tell her, speaking slowly, wanting every word to reach her. 'You did the right thing by stopping him. And what he said isn't true. You're beautiful and kind and clever. He didn't like being rejected, so he said mean things. He's the idiot. More than that – he was abusive, cruel.'

'The thing is,' she says quietly, 'the reason I stopped him wasn't because I didn't want him to... It was because I was embarrassed about my body.'

'When you meet the right person, you won't be embarrassed. It's important you understand that people can't touch you unless you want them to,' I say slowly and carefully. 'You must value yourself. And you have, Bea. You were right. He was wrong.'

I'm wondering how I can get this boy's address, his house phone number, how I can contact Megan's parents. Adults need to know what he's done. He should be punished. My fingers twitch.

'Don't do anything, will you?' Bea's eyes are wide with alarm as if she can read my mind. 'You mustn't speak to anybody about this, or, or I'll never tell you anything again.'

'Okay then, but we have to tell your father.'

She shakes her head violently.

'He needs to know.' I try to sound gentle and reasonable. 'He would want to know.'

'No,' she shouts, spittle on her lips, fear contorting her face. 'You mustn't... I... I couldn't bear it,' she says in a barely there whisper, tears brimming and falling. 'I should never have told you.'

'Alright.' I sit back, defeated, squeezing my hands together. 'I won't say anything.'

'Promise me?' she asks.

I nod reluctantly. 'I promise.'

My chest aches with sorrow for Bea, for what she's gone through. But she's talking about it – and that's the beginning of healing. Cecily and I couldn't talk about what happened to us, not even to each other. Bea raises a quivering smile for me, and I want to tell her everything will be alright, that there are people out there as kind and considerate as her, and she will find them. But what right do I have to counsel her or look after her? I'm the pretender. She needs her real mother.

19

CECILY

The boys, in their final year at sixth form, were back for the Christmas holidays. Every morning, Daddy took Henry into his office and shut the door. Henry was tight-lipped about it, but through snippets of overheard conversations, I gathered that the hours he spent with Daddy involved learning about land management, unearthing historic documents, going over ledgers full of accounts, and discussing the methods by which Henry would save his inheritance from ruin. As part of the plan, he had to study 'something useful' at Oxford. Henry emerged from these meetings looking grim and desperate. Instead of coming to find us, he and Jude would go off together, walking in the fells, not coming back till supper time, exhausted, their clothes soaked through, smelling of earth and stone, of wild wet air and sweat.

Alice and I pretended to each other that we didn't mind being left out, that we had other important things to occupy us. Mostly it was to do with keeping warm. It was December, and the gardens were wreathed in freezing fog. Venturing out meant traipsing through soaking grass, drips of water splashing down from wet leaves and branches. Inside wasn't much better. Our breath puffed before us, dissolving into misty trails as we walked the corridors. We piled on layers of moth-eaten jumpers, pulled on several pairs of socks, resorted to hats and ear mufflers. We spent as much time as possible in the kitchen, the only warm place in the house thanks to the crouching bulk of the range, ancient and temperamental, but tamed by Jane, even though we had to wash pans to pay for the privilege. We sat at the table to draw or play an illicit game of cards, listening to Jane complaining about her arthritis, gossiping about goings-on in the village. Mummy took refuge in the kitchen too, making mince pies and marzipan for Christmas, working out food budgets on the backs of old envelopes.

Sometimes we went back to bed straight after breakfast, piling on slippery eiderdowns and musty blankets, hot-water bottles hugged to our chests, dog-napping Dilly for a wriggling extra source of heat. We worked our way through the books in the library, turning mottled pages, reading Dickens, the Brontës, Eliot and Hardy. For books written in the last twenty years, we needed to get the bus into town and go to the library. But that meant walking for miles and waiting at a deserted bus stop in the cold and wet for hours for a bus that may or may not arrive. Rereading the classics was a more appealing option, although we'd managed to get hold of Edna O'Brien's *The Country Girls*, and read all three books several times, keeping them hidden under Alice's mattress.

* * *

'*Jane Eyre* is better than *Wuthering Heights*,' I said, waddling like Mrs Michelin in layers of jumpers, thick tights under my trousers.

'Rubbish,' Alice said over her shoulder, leading the way down to breakfast. 'Emily Brontë writes from the soul. The ghost of Cathy haunts you forever once you've read the book. She's like... like the voice of the wild moor, something beautiful and free.'

I stomped past. '*Wuthering Heights* is a long-winded muddle. *Jane Eyre* is better written. And Jane is a better character than Cathy – she succeeds against the odds.'

The boys were already in the dining room, Jude lifting the silver tops to the hot plates. 'Henry?' He gestured to a dish. 'Kippers?'

'Damn right. I'm starving,' Henry said.

'Language,' my father warned from behind his paper.

Henry muttered an apology as he poked at two anaemic looking chipolatas sitting in a pool of grease.

Our family didn't use bad words, not ever. No swearing, no taking the Lord's name in vain, and absolutely no mention of sex. We were not to talk about periods, breasts, or any bits of the body contained in underwear, not even whispering them in private. Henry's choice of language had begun to test Daddy's patience; I didn't know why he did it, it would only bring him pain in the end.

Alice and I nibbled at toast as the boys ate rubbery scrambled eggs, kippers and stringy sausages. After breakfast, instead of disappearing off on their own, Henry winked at us. 'Come to my room,' he hissed. 'We've got things to discuss.'

Alice and I followed, surprised and pleased. With the door closed, Jude lit a Camel cigarette and opened the window a crack, blowing smoke into the chill of the morning, flicking his ash over the windowsill.

Henry's room was untidy, clothes flung over the backs of chairs. A mustard waistcoat, a Liberty print tie. I'd noticed recently that he'd started to adopt some of Jude's flamboyant style. There were posters tacked to the wall: Queen, Stevie Wonder, and Ziggy Stardust with a gold and red zigzag painted over his face. The chest of drawers was piled with novels, an ancient bottle of Old Spice, a purple zippo lighter. His tarnished silver christening mug was being used as a pen holder. Every object nestled in a layer of dust. A battered teddy bear lay on the floor, button eyes adrift in a blank face.

'Well?' Alice asked, hands on her hips. 'What's to discuss?'

Jude laughed at her impatience, while somehow managing to keep his cigarette jammed in his mouth. And Henry dropped a vinyl onto the record player and placed the needle in the groove.

'All in good time,' he said with a wink.

'Kung Fu Fighting' blasted into the room. 'Come on! We're celebrating!' he shouted above the din, and began to stomp around his bed, kicking his heels high at imaginary foes. Jude put his cigarette out in the christening mug and joined him, singing along. Alice leapt up, not knowing the lyrics, but making up for it with enthusiastic stamping and punching the air. Jude grabbed Alice by the waist and twirled her round and round until her feet left the ground in giddy leaps. She shrieked and clasped her arms around his neck, laughing. Henry turned the music up even louder and jumped on and off the bed. I stared at them. They were like drunkards with their red faces and determinedly riotous expressions. My disapproval evaporated. I wanted to be part of it, to catch the momentum of this sudden joy, but I was too embarrassed.

'What are we celebrating?' Alice panted. 'Please tell.'

'We'll let you two in on the secret,' Henry gasped, falling onto the rumpled bed, 'if you swear not to tell?'

'Swear,' said Alice quickly, her chest heaving, cheeks pink.

'Swear,' I muttered from my place at the window as they all turned to look at me.

Henry nodded, acknowledging our promise. 'The first thing is, I'm not doing any of crap the old man's planning,' he announced. 'When I leave school, I'm setting myself free.'

Jude sank down beside him, fumbling for another cigarette and lighting it. Henry took it, puffed a drag, and handed it back.

'The second is, I'm going to be a writer. And the third is, we're going to a kibbutz,' he announced. 'Me and Jude.'

'A what?' I asked, thinking I must have misheard.

'A kibbutz in Israel, near the Sea of Galilee.' Henry spoke through a cloud of smoke. I tugged at the sash to let the smell out.

'But… why?' asked Alice hesitantly. I knew she was as hazy as me as to what a kibbutz was.

'Because I've got to get away from here. And that's the place that wil cause the biggest stink I can think of.' Henry gave a wry smile. 'Just wish could be a fly on the wall when he reads the letter I'm going to leave. He going to be apoplectic.' He handed the cigarette back to Jude. 'I'm nc going to saddle myself with hideous debt trying to save this moth-eate old pile.' He waved a hand around the room. 'I've had enough of guilt and I've had enough of God.'

I gasped, cringing for the inevitable crash of the sky, a flash of ligh ning bolt shooting through the window to stab its silver point throug Henry's heart. I closed my eyes and made the sign of the cross. 'But…

don't understand... what about Oxford and your degree? What about saving Hawksmoor?' My voice broke.

The others ignored me. It was as if I hadn't spoken. 'We wrote to them, and they said you get to live and work with people from all over the world,' Jude was saying. 'It'll be good for Henry, give him material for his novel.' He nudged Henry with an elbow, grinning. 'He's going to be a famous author one day.'

'The sea is actually a huge, freshwater lake,' Henry's voice rose in excitement. 'There are hot mineral springs. Mountains in the distance. The land there is fertile. They grow figs and olives.'

The Sea of Galilee was where Jesus gave his Sermon on the Mount. If the boys really did go to the Holy Land, they'd be treading the same earth Jesus walked on – but that didn't seem to be the reason they were going. I looked out of the window, opaque with condensation. Shapes of naked trees could be seen through the mist; they gestured towards the house with dark fingers.

'There's shooting and bombing,' Alice said, frowning. 'I've heard about it on the news. Aren't the Israelis stealing Palestinian land? Won't it be dangerous?'

'It's not violent everywhere,' Henry said, crossing one leg over the other. 'Lots of tourists go.'

'You two should come with us,' Jude said. 'We could write to the community again, ask to book you in at the same time as us?'

'Yes,' Alice said quickly. 'We'll come.'

I startled. 'We can't,' I said. 'We won't have finished school.'

'I don't care about school,' Alice said. 'This is much more important.' She looked at Jude. 'I'll talk Cilly round.'

I scowled at Alice's assumption of power, her use of my nickname. My sister put out her hand to shake Jude's, sealing their agreement. His thumb lingered over the milky patch of skin on her wrist where blue veins converged. My chest tightened. 'Daddy won't forgive you,' I said quickly. 'You won't be able to come home again. Not ever.'

'I hate this place.' Henry's brows drew together, his mouth set in stubborn certainty. 'Once I've gone, I'm never coming back.'

My mind scrabbled in confusion. How could I leave Hawksmoor and

Daddy? But if I didn't go, I'd miss out on the adventure, I'd miss out on being with Jude.

'The other thing is,' Henry said, leaning forward over his knees. 'We're planning a party. To celebrate. Soon as the old man and Mummy go off next weekend to stay with the Jensons, we're opening the place up to some action.'

Jude tilted his head back and blew a smoke ring. It drifted towards the ceiling, breaking apart into uncertain wisps.

'A party?' I dragged my mind to another startling piece of information. 'Without asking Daddy?'

Henry rolled his eyes. 'Learn to live a little, Cilly.'

'With dancing?' Alice was asking, bouncing her bottom on the bed, making the springs squeak. 'What a great idea! Who will you invite?'

'We've put the word out. Boys from school are coming – people from the village pub. Whoever can get here.' He took another drag on Jude's cigarette. 'You can invite anyone you like. Girls preferably.'

'We don't really know anyone,' Alice was saying.

I frowned, that wasn't the point. This was a terrible idea. If Daddy discovered our plan, our punishment was certain. But the other two always teased me for being boring – and I didn't want Jude to think so too.

'Nothing exciting ever happens,' Alice said. 'And now two things! It's all rather marvellous!'

'A last hurrah before we leave this bloody house.' Henry's cheeks looked feverish. 'For good.'

'Amen to that,' Jude said. 'We're off to have an adventure.'

'And we're coming too,' Alice said. 'Aren't we, Cilly?'

I turned away, pretending interest in rubbing a patch through the condensation on the window. The decision to run away seemed easy for Henry and Alice, but Daddy would be devastated. It couldn't happen. I needed to work out how to stop them.

The other three were talking about the party as if it was already decided, which room to use for dancing, which music to play. They didn't need my permission. I worked my teeth around a raw fingernail, ripping off a sliver of skin. Daddy and Mummy were going to stay the night at the Jensons. An early Christmas celebration. The Jensons' place was far enough away to be safe. I could organise a clean-up on Sunday morning before our parents came back. Listening to the others making plans for moody lighting and alcohol supplies, I wondered why it was always left to me to be the sensible one, and in what world the name Cilly could reasonably be applied to me, when it was the others who were foolish.

Jude strolled over. 'What's so interesting out in the mist?'

I turned away from the glass, startled to find him close. 'Nothing.' I breathed in the warm, saltiness of him, the slight whiff of the lemony cologne he used, the musk of his sweat. I could see moisture shining on his forehead, the rise and fall of his chest. He was still hot from the exertion of twirling Alice. I wished it had been my waist he'd held between his hands, my mouth pressed to his neck as the room spun round and round.

He touched my arm gently, and I realised I'd been sucking my hair like a baby. I pulled it away, a strand catching between my front teeth.

'I know you. You're busy worrying, aren't you?' His ash-grey eyes softened. 'It's going to be alright,' he said quietly. 'We belong together, the four of us. Come back into the room.' He took my hand and squeezed. 'We have a party to plan.'

Gladness leapt in me, a bird winging through air, a sudden brightness. I understood now. The party was my opportunity. With the lights turned low and romantic music playing, I'd have my chance at getting close to him. Slow dancing in each other's arms, with my cheek pressed against his chest, he'd realise we belonged together in a different way. Nothing about my feelings could possibly be a sin; they came from a place of goodness. Love for Jude made me see everything else as a wonder, even tiny things like the moths flying out of my jumper, a drop of condensation rolling down a window. I didn't need to worry about Alice. She was just having fun. Once she understood that I had proper, grown-up feelings for Jude, she'd leave him to me.

I raised my eyes and let myself look at him. An unbearable yearning gripped like a stomachache, a longing to put my arms around his narrow, muscled waist, push my fingers through his thick, glossy hair. With a beat of relief, I realised that when he became my boyfriend, he wouldn't abandon me to run off to Israel. He'd forget the ridiculous kibbutz idea; and if Jude stayed, Henry and Alice would too.

* * *

I devoted myself to planning what I was going to wear to the party. My Laura Ashley dress was too short now and it made me look young and ordinary. Nothing was good enough. I was sure Jude liked girls in feminine clothes, after all, he'd liked me in Mummy's lipstick. The evening had to be perfect. I had to be perfect.

While I fretted about clothes, the others were busy secretly collecting and storing cases of beer and cheap wine in the old coach house, hiding preparations in the gardening sheds. Alice had bought a catering box of paper cups and strings of festive bright lights from Woolworths. They discussed music choices in the privacy of their bedrooms. They were ready to spring into action the moment Edmund and Emmeline left the house. I didn't take part in any of the preparations. When I wasn't worrying about dresses, I listed all of Jude's attributes in my diary with reasons why we'd make the perfect couple, concocting possible romantic scenarios that could occur between us at the party, confiding in luxurious detail how I felt. I decided I would give him my virginity and wrote it down as a solemn pledge.

I got the bus into town with Alice on a rainy Saturday. We hurried out of the wet into Oxfam, into a fug of old clothes and moth balls. Other people's cast-off lives and memories thickened the air. Racks groaned under the weight of fabric. Everything was mixed up, with boxes of old records, musty books and ornaments piled higgledy-piggledy on the floor. I pushed hangers apart, examining every item, careful not to miss anything, because miracles did happen. Alice paraded around in ludicrous things – a pair of baggy striped overalls, a yellowing wedding dress with a rip under the arm, men's evening trousers gone shiny at the knees that she had to hold up with a scarf tied tight around her waist. But for me, this was a serious hunt. A gleam of silver caught my attention, and my searching fingers extracted a narrow shoulder strap crushed between a woollen coat and a brocade tunic. I pulled the rest of the dress out carefully, like a sea creature fished from the depths: shining folds of fabric sewn with the glittering scales of hundreds of sequins. With a flutter in my chest, I checked the label. It was my size. I tightened my grasp, slipping behind the dingy curtain to try it on, waving Alice away. I wanted her to get the full impact when I stepped from behind the curtain. After zipping it up through contortions of shoulder blade and elbow, I scrutinised myself in the mirror, running a hand over my gleaming hip. The dress was short, but not outrageously so. It skimmed my body, emphasising my curves, making me look willowy instead of thin. The sequins reflected light onto my pale skin, made my eyes luminous, flattered the ebony depths in my hair.

Alice let out a long breath when she saw me. 'You'll have all the boys queuing up to dance with you.'

I smiled into a grubby mirror leaning next to a pile of boxes. There was only one boy whose attention I wanted. And it occurred to me, as I stared dreamily at my reflection, trying to imagine what it would be like to finally kiss Jude, my first real grown-up kiss, that Daddy would approve of the match. Jude's family were rich and Catholic, and Jude was handsome and polite. I remembered what Alice had said before, that he was from new money, but really, I sucked the inside of my lip, even Daddy had to understand that you couldn't have everything.

* * *

It was three o'clock before the Volvo's boot was eventually packed, and Mummy and Daddy climbed into the front seats with Dilly. The Labs had been left behind. The ancient car spluttered down the drive, Mummy waving one hand from the driver's window, Daddy staring straight ahead. Dilly would be on Mummy's lap, her sharp little muzzle resting on the steering wheel. Daddy refused to touch the dachshund – saying she wasn't a real dog, but really it was because she was prone to nipping anyone who wasn't Mummy.

We watched from the front steps. 'At last,' Alice said out of the corner of her mouth, waving and smiling. 'Thought they'd never leave.'

The car disappeared inside a smoke screen of fumes, and as it turned the corner by the weeping willow, Jude and Henry whooped and high-fived each other.

'Quick,' Alice said. 'Let's get started.'

The three of them sprinted towards the sheds and coach house to retrieve the hidden supplies, shouting instructions to each other. The Labs barked at their heels surprised by the change of atmosphere. I stayed on the steps, leaning against the cold grain of a lion's back. This was to be the evening that would change everything. I knew I would never forget it, the moment before my real life began. Mist lapped the base of trees, floating like the hem of a wedding dress over the spangled lawn. A flight of rooks left the far thicket of beeches in a startled rush, paper cut-outs whirling from an opened hand. I listened to the racket they made as they spiralled up in a vortex of confusion above the tarn, not paper, but raucous living creatures with wings of white bone, feathers shot through with petrol gleam. I tilted my head to watch them disappear into the darkening air and shivered. All around me, the light was turning purple, dense with the coming night.

* * *

It was eight o'clock and the house was ready. The long gallery was hung with loops of flashing lights, inviting baubles of jewel colours, guiding guests towards the ballroom. We'd sellotaped paper chains to the walls as high as we could reach. The mahogany table had been covered with a spider-encrusted oil cloth found in the cellar, wiped clean and set out with crates of beer and red wine. Alice had arranged stacks of paper cups in white towers and tipped salt and vinegar crisps onto paper plates. Flickering nightlights in empty jam jars threw shadows across the cavernous room. It looked romantic, but would enough people turn up to fill it? It seemed vast and cold as a Russian wasteland. (I was reading *Doctor Zhivago*.) But hopefully the icy temperature would get people dancing.

I'd put No Entry signs across the staircase leading to the upper and lower floors to keep the party to the ballroom and entrance hall and contain the mess. The Labs had been fed and locked in the boot room.

I changed into the silver dress in my bedroom, which was as freezing as Yuri and Lara's ice palace. My teeth chattered and I shivered convulsively with cold and anticipation. My numb fingers fumbled with the zip behind me, tugging but failing to reach past my shoulder blades.

'Here. Let me.' Alice had put her head around the door. She zipped. 'There,' she said. 'You look like you should be on *Top of the Pops*. Want me to do your hair?'

I sat on the floor between her legs, a blanket from the bed wrapped around my shoulders. She brushed as if her life depended on it, making my scalp smart and my hair snap with static. 'Very Debbie Harry,' she said approvingly as she backcombed it into a wild mane, spritzing with Mummy's Elnett spray. Alice's own hair was slicked back into a ponytail; she was wearing velvet flares and the yellow blouse with bell sleeves she'd brought in Oxfam. She looked stylish, I thought, but I was glad I was the one in the silver dress, even if my skin had turned into something resembling chicken flesh. I'd warm up soon. Slipping my feet into the only pair of heels I possessed, I sprayed both of us generously with my Rive Gauche cologne. I was usually circumspect with it, wanting to make it last, but this was a special occasion. Sneezing in the descending mist, Alice waved her hands in front of her face and wrinkled her nose. 'Are you trying to kill us before the party's started?'

'Alice,' I said, clutching my sister's hand. 'Do you think Jude likes me?'

She hesitated. 'I expect so.' Then she grinned. 'He'll definitely fancy you in that dress.' She pulled her hand away. 'Come on,' she said over her shoulder as she moved towards the landing, 'let's see if anyone's arrived.'

We went down the winding back stairs together, with me tottering around the steep corners on unstable heels. 'I'll just check that the front door is open,' Alice said as she went off towards the entrance hall. I thought of the balloons I'd tied around the neck of one of the lions earlier. It was hard to imagine now that we were really going to have a party. Perhaps nobody would come.

I paused before I went into the ballroom, straightening my shoulder straps, patting the candyfloss of my hair. I'd hoped to make an entrance, but as I crossed the threshold, nonchalantly as possible, both boys were occupied; Henry leaning over the record player and Jude fiddling with some wires leading out of one of the speakers. I stood, disappointed and shivering. Then with a crackling roar, a blast of sound erupted, and the boys cheered. Bowie's 'Golden Years' filled the space. Jude began to gyrate, head bobbing to the beat, as he dance-walked his way across the expanse of floor, a cigarette dangling from one hand. He'd put dark glasses on, which I thought was a bit affected, but if anyone could get away with it, he could. I waited anxiously near the door.

He stopped with an appreciative whistle. 'Cecily,' he called over the music. 'Looking hot tonight.' He gave me a thumbs-up. 'Damn hot.'

I flushed with pleasure. I couldn't see his eyes through the beetle-like lenses. But I imagined them gleaming with admiration. I was trying to think of something witty to say, when he switched direction and danced towards the table on the other side of the room. Across the floor, I watched him lift a beer bottle to his mouth, his hips swaying, feet as sure and nonchalant as a cat's. His body knew what to do to the music. He was different tonight – more offhand, elusive.

But he'd noticed me. 'Looking hot,' I repeated under my breath, biting back a smile, and running a hand over my waist. 'Damn hot.'

Four young men came in, and greeted Jude and Henry with awkward handshakes, proffering bottles of beer. School friends, I guessed, gawky and polite, one of them in spectacles, one of them with a disastrous rash of spots. I wandered over and was introduced by Henry who bellowed everyone's names above the music. The four stared at me, and the sensation of their gazes licking me was akin to a dog's beseeching tongue on my naked skin – shockingly physical and needy. It made me uncomfortable, and then tremulously excited. I tried biting my bottom lip, jutting one hip to the side, and watched their reactions. Perhaps I could make Jude jealous. The seven of us stood in a group, gulping our drinks, breath making white puffs, unable to hear each other over the noise from the speakers.

I was just about to wander over to Jude, try to start up a conversation about music perhaps, when Alice entered at a jog, arms windmilling, gesturing behind her. 'More people are arriving,' she shouted. 'Carloads. And people on bikes and walking! Loads of them!'

We turned towards a shuffling march of footsteps approaching from the corridor, a mutter of drunken voices coming closer. I had almost forgotten that we were expecting other people, and had a sudden instinct to bolt, but a flood of strangers had already burst into the room. People pushed past me, laughing, gesticulating and talking. A man pinched my bottom as he sidled past. I smelt the sickly stink of weed. I couldn't see Jude any more, or Henry, or Alice.

I had no idea what time it was. I was stuck in a corner of the room, unable to move. Even more people had arrived, and the ballroom was packed. I had no idea who any of them were. They must be gate-crashers. Jude and Henry couldn't possibly know all these people. The party was raging out of control, the room heated to a roaring blaze by a crush of bodies and beery breath. Someone changed the music from the Bee Gees' 'Night Fever' to a heavy metal track, turned it up as loud as the speakers would go. A drumbeat juddered through the soles of my feet into my bones. It hurt my ears, got inside my heart, making it race. I felt hunted. I couldn't think. I tried dancing for a while, but with elbows jabbing at my ribs and shoulders jostling me, it wasn't any fun. Something cold splashed my legs, liquid dribbling down my thighs and calves into my shoes. I retreated, pushing through whirling bodies. It was like drowning, the lack of air, the current of energy trying to tug me under.

To my horror, there were people perched all the way up the main stairs from the entrance hall, huddled in groups and couples, chatting and smoking, and I could hear movement and laughter further up the house. Jesus hung his head in anguish; metal thorns pierced his skull for eternity, nails through his precious feet. Someone leant over the balcony and dropped a bottle down to another person in the hall, I winced at the thought of it catching Christ's shoulder in the fall. It missed Jesus but smashed onto the flagstones. Someone laughed. My No Entry sign had been crumpled and tossed aside. My chest tightened with fury. I had to climb over trespassers to get to the first landing. I glared at them as I went. 'Do you mind?' I said sarcastically. But they ignored me or looked irritated.

It was like a kind of Hell, or Sodom and Gomorrah. What if something valuable got broken and Daddy found out? He would always find out. I forced the terror away, sliding a hand over my dress for courage. Sequins bristled and crackled under my fingers as if they were alive. It was too late to worry about the house now. It had stood through hundreds of years and a Civil War. A party couldn't destroy it. The purpose of the evening was Jude. I caught a waft of romantic music floating out of the ballroom, Minnie Ripperton's high pitched voice. At last, a song we could dance to together.

I flung open Henry's bedroom door, peering in, and found a couple making out on his bed. I didn't recognise them, and they didn't pause in their exploration of each other's mouths. There were people everywhere in the house: boys in studded leather jackets sat slumped on the landing floor, shoulders propped against the walls as they rolled cigarettes, dropping ash on the antique rugs. A girl was passed out in the blue bathroom, a mess of tangled hair over her face, one shoe missing. I crouched down, my hand hovering over the girl's back, the creased red top ridden up to expose a slice of pale skin. There was an imperceptible rising of ribs, the slightest movement in the strands of hair caught around the girl's mouth. She was alive at least. I left the room. There was a splatter of sick at the bottom of the second flight of stairs. I'd never get the house clean in time for Mummy and Daddy's return. I wasn't even sure if we'd be able to eject all the partygoers before our parents got back. The only thing that would save the evening from complete disaster would be if I found Jude. Having his arms around me would be worth the punishment that was bound to follow. We'd broken our promises to Mummy and Daddy and told lies, but worst of all, we'd invited strangers, let them get drunk and have sex in a place where people had suffered and died for their faith.

I escaped to the top of the house, into the narrow corridors that ran like a maze for anyone unfamiliar with Hawksmoor. Here the proportions were different, the ceilings low, the carpet thin; narrow doors shielded cell-like rooms, where housemaids and footmen had once slept. Even the windows were smaller and set higher in the walls. I went quickly past the hidden priest hole, careful not to brush against the big beam that operated the secret entrance point. I navigated by the faint milky glow of the moon seeping through glass. There were no intruders this far up, and tension slipped from my shoulders. I paused to examine my legs where liquid had splashed, licking my finger, and rubbing it over my sticky shins. Red wine. My shoes were soggy with it. 'Idiots,' I muttered under my breath, wishing I had a way of making them leave – or better still, disappear in a puff of smoke, with all evidence of the party gone with them.

The music from the ballroom was reduced to a quiet hum up here, a shiver in the frigid air of the old servants' quarters, a place where the ghost of a monk wandered, lost and afraid, trapped between this world and the next. But I wasn't frightened of him. His bony frame kept me company in the hole, his prayers becoming my own. I ached for Jude. Where could he be? The one person I wanted to see. The thought of him was the only thing stopping me from locking myself in my room and stuffing cotton wool in my ears. I looked at my watch. Midnight. Not too late to turn the evening around. I'd have to go downstairs if I was going to find him or the others. Where was Alice? I'd glimpsed her a couple of times at the beginning of the evening, had briefly danced with her. We'd had a short, shouted conversation after she'd checked on the Labs and reported back. But I hadn't seen her for hours.

As I turned to go down, I heard an indistinct murmur of voices, and a low, rumbling laugh. I stopped, confused, head cocked. It was coming from above, from the roof. My chest swelled with indignation. How dare people invade this part of the house. Were there no limits? Bloody gate-crashers. I hoped they'd slip and fall, splatter themselves onto the gravel below. Except that would mean a scandal for Daddy, and he'd never forgive me for being part of it.

The hidden valley roof was the best place to sunbathe, or just read and relax. Alice and I climbed up there sometimes. It was a secret sanctuary raised above ordinary life and its problems. The laugh came again, soft and deep. The way to get onto the roof was up a short ladder into a section of dusty attic and then clamber through another hatch which led directly outside.

I climbed into the attic and then wriggled my head and shoulders through the next hatch that had been left propped open, looking out at the valley space and sloping slates either side. At the end, between chimney stacks, something was outlined against the cloudy sky. A creature with two backs, which became two people standing close, arms around each other, faces almost touching. The way they held each other made my mouth dry. I understood that I was an intruder, a voyeur at something private and intimate. The desire between them was palpable. They seemed to disappear inside each other, and in the stillness of the night I heard mouths working, skin sliding across skin, heavy breathing. My body flashed with violent heat, need twisting in my belly. A tingling rushed between my legs, the same feeling that came when I was alone in bed with thoughts of Jude.

The clouds moved, revealing a rash of stars, unveiling the moon: a heavenly spotlight casting a search beam. I saw a splay of tender fingers caressing the back of a neck. Inside the new transparency the couple's features glowed, unmistakable, unforgettable.

I stifled a gasp and stumbled back, skinning my knees on planks of rough wood as I shrank through the second hatch, half-falling down the ladder onto the corridor. I crouched on the floor, cowering from the sight lasered onto my eyes. My heart reared inside my chest and fell flat. I couldn't breathe. It was as if I was dead. What I'd seen was impossible. Jude and Henry, together, kissing with their mouths, not like brothers or friends, but lovers.

* * *

I watched the police car arrive from the landing window, its flashing lights striping the mist with blue. I felt weak with relief that the party would end at last. Our parents' Volvo arrived almost at the same time, drawing up behind the squad car, Daddy's long legs stretching out of the passenger side. It turned out that there was a drug dealer on the premises, but none of us was taken away in handcuffs, although I almost hoped for it.

I was numb when Daddy questioned me, still raging about the house being full of Lefties and drop-outs. '*You did the right thing to phone. Now tell me who planned it? Who were the ringleaders? Did you know about the drugs?*' I could hardly answer. 'I don't know,' I said over and over. 'I don't know.' And I didn't. Everything was blank except for a reel that played on repeat in my mind: Jude and Henry, their bodies pressed against each other.

I'd once heard Daddy talking to Father Michael about a man in the village who'd left his wife for another man. I'd been sitting quietly on the floor behind a chair with a puzzle, and they'd forgotten I was in the room.

I wasn't sure exactly what they'd been talking about, except it was to do with the sin of lust. Father Michael had called the two men sodomites, and Daddy had said it was a perversion against God, and both had gone very quiet and drunk more from the decanter, and I'd understood how serious this crime was, the crime of a man choosing another man for a wife. Henry and Jude would burn in hell. But inside my skull, my brain was screaming as if it was me falling into the scorching furnace, my head being pierced with devilish pitchforks.

The next morning, sunlight exposed the William Morris wallpaper, clawed as if a lion had gone berserk, and I remembered the men in leather jackets stuck with metal studs. There were burns in Persian rugs and ancient tapestries. A shameful mess of spilt alcohol, crushed crisps, cigarette butts, puddles of vomit, shards of broken ornaments and shattered bottles littered floors and stairs. Someone had stuck a trilby hat on the suit of armour, a fag dangling from the mouth gap; worse was the moustache drawn with pen onto the portrait of a seventeen century Deveraux Baroness.

Veins pulsed at Daddy's temples. He loomed over us while we kneeled with buckets of soapy water and rags to clean and scrub; he watched us sweep and hoover. He made an inventory of the damage, calculating the cost, which he said we'd have to pay back. But when we heard his howl of outraged horror and fury coming from the bowels of the house, I knew at once that someone had broken into his wine cellar. I felt no fear. Nothing could be worse than the secret festering inside me. I was in shock, my limbs oddly leaden, my mind whirling and jerking like a broken machine. I kept my head down, focusing on the sensation of the wooden scrubbing brush in my hands, the bite of detergent on my knuckles, scrape of bristles against stone. I couldn't look at Henry or Jude. I wanted to find the words to tell Alice what I'd seen, but it was impossible. I was alone with the knowledge. Nobody asked me what the matter was; everyone presumed my stunned silence was down to the party being found out, the trouble we were in.

When it was my turn to be locked in the priest hole, I huddled inside, crow wings feathering my eyes, hoping for the cavalier or the child to comfort me. But they didn't come, and I was alone with the memory of my brother and Jude. I moaned and bit my knees, trembling at the sounds of their murmured lovemaking and quickened panting.

Forgive them, Father, for they know not what they do.

My heart sliding shut. But they did know. And they did it anyway.

Perhaps they laughed about me together: *Poor little Cilly. Daddy's girl. Boring old Cilly fancying Jude. What an idiot.*

How could I ask God to forgive them when I couldn't forgive them myself?

PART II

20

ALICE

I'm glad I didn't leave. I'm proud of Bea. She's bravely going to school and facing David, Megan and their crowd. The silent watchfulness in the house has gone. Gabriel and I make jokes as we share clearing up duties after a meal. The three of us spend time talking at the kitchen table, and yesterday after supper, we all sat down to play a game of cards – I'm teaching them the games I remember from my childhood.

This evening, when Bea goes to bed, Gabriel says he's going to play some piano in the living room and I wander in after him, holding my tea. He keeps his music piled on top of the instrument. I flick through, finding 'The Well-Tempered Clavier' by Bach, some Mozart and Chopin, and a book called *Jazz Songs to Learn and Play*.

'As you know, I'm not an expert,' he says, flexing his fingers, knuckles cracking. 'Haven't practised for ages, so keep your expectations low.'

I lean against the piano as he strikes some chords, then he looks though a *Classics for Piano* to find what he wants. He arranges himself more comfortably on the stool, sits up taller, and reading the music with great attention, plays 'Liebestraum No. 3' by Liszt. He stumbles over some notes but goes back and corrects himself. I clap when he finishes, and he gives a little bow. 'Need a bit more time on that one.'

I wave his songbook for choir. 'Can you play *and* sing?' I ask. 'I'd be really impressed then.'

'Ha,' he says, taking the book from me. 'You've thrown down the glove now.' He skims through the book and settles on something. 'Should be able to manage this,' he says, squinting at the music and nodding his head before he presses his fingers on the keys, and I recognise the opening chords to David Bowie's 'Heroes.'

'Sing with me?' he asks. 'This *is* your idea.'

I perch on the stool next to him. He begins the first verse and then digs me in the ribs; feeling self-conscious, I join in, leaning close to read the lyrics. But it's fun, and after a while, I'm bellowing the chorus. The song ends and his hands rest on the keyboard. He raises one eyebrow as he turns to me, 'I don't think I've ever heard you sing before.'

'Nobody has ever heard me sing before.' I laugh. 'And there's a reason for that.'

'No,' he disagrees. 'You can hold a tune.'

The moment enfolds me in a warm glow. I'm aware of the slight pressure of Gabriel's leg pressing against the length of my thigh. I look down. The sheen on his worn cords is as familiar to me as the shape of his strong fingers. It's as if I've known him for years. This familiarity makes no sense. I'm confused by my sense of belonging.

Nothing here is mine.

* * *

Wednesday morning comes around. Grudgingly, I flick through the notebook and find 'Flower Arranging Duties' underlined near the back. She's given me the name and address of the church, where to access the key, and the name of the priest. I suppose I'll have to buy flowers, as there aren't any spare plants in the tiny garden. I think of the riot of blooms and greenery available all year round at Hawksmoor, and how our mother picked armfuls to place in the Chinese vases: lilacs and hyacinths in the spring, roses in the summer, springs of holly with red berries in the winter.

I revisit Blooming Lovely in the high street and take four bunches of daffodils out of a bucket of water and choose a larger bouquet of purple anemones and alliums, adding cheaper leaves to bulk it out. I walk for fifteen minutes, my arms overspilling with blooms, stopping twice to consult the hand-drawn map Cecily left for me. The scrap of paper is hard to read over the heads of flowers, and the ink is soon blurred with drops of water from the stems, but I find The Church of the Sacred Heart at the end of a street, a large grey stone building with a bell tower like Rapunzel's turret. I squint at the address of the key holder. Ambrose Stone lives three houses down.

He opens before I can knock, giving me the unnerving idea that he must have been waiting behind the door. Ambrose is a middle-aged man, tall and thin with a concave chest. He's wearing tailored grey trousers with creases down the front and a plain white shirt like an overgrown schoolboy. His dark hair is combed flat around a balding crown. He looks at me with an earnest expression through oddly bulbous eyes, colourless as seawater in cupped palms.

'I was worried you were ill,' he says in a nasal voice. 'You never miss church. Have you been sick?'

'Yes,' I say quickly. 'Terrible flu.'

'But you are quite recovered?'

I nod over the profusion of petals, glad that they make a natural barrier between us.

'Thanks be to God,' he says, breathing brown breath over me. 'You've been missed at the Sacred Heart. But I'll see you later?'

'Later?' I frown.

'This afternoon,' he says. 'At the Exposition and Benediction of the Blessed Sacrament.'

'Oh,' I step back. 'Maybe. If I can get away.'

'Is there something wrong, Cecily?' He peers at me. 'Are you still not quite yourself?'

'Maybe not...' I agree. 'I do have a headache.'

'Would you like me to pray for you now?' He reaches out a bony hand as if to touch my forehead. His fingers hover close to my skin. He's shut his eyes and is muttering things I can't catch.

'No.' I shrink away. 'No, thank you,' I say. 'I'm in a bit of a hurry.'

His eyelids snap open, revealing the disconcerting irises. 'I've missed our praying together,' he says, and his voice drops a fraction. He leans closer towards me, his nostrils flaring slightly. 'But I prayed for you, in your absence. I prayed for your health and your speedy return so that you could continue to serve our Lord, Jesus Christ, with all your strength.'

'I'd better get on.' I move my arms in a helpless gesture, shifting the flowers up and down.

Ambrose has tilted his head to one side like a dog intently listening, and I can feel his scrutiny burning my skin, searching deeper, hunting for my soul. He knows something is off. I turn and walk away as fast as I can, without breaking into a jog.

'The church key?' he calls.

Damn. I turn slowly and go back, dragging my feet over the pavement. I know he's studying me. He presses the key into my palm with clammy fingers, his touch remaining too long. Then, grasping my hand, he's muttering again, with his eyes closed, 'Lord, my friend is struggling with a difficult trial. I can see her strength is faltering—'

I tug away from him. 'I really have to go,' I say, hurrying towards the church, petals drifting over my shoulder, wet stems crushed against my chest.

I fit the large key into the lock of the heavy door and push into the empty church. My heart is thumping after my encounter with Ambrose Stone. A narrow red carpet leads through pews to the altar, above it a stained-glass window depicts Christ surrounded by angels. I keep my mind firmly on my task of finding the vases, then emptying and refilling them and arranging my bunches of fresh flowers as quickly as possible. Being in the church is making my pulse erratic. My palms are damp as I snip stems and cram them into water. I complete my duty with a sigh of relief, but as I turn to leave, the priest enters.

He comes straight over and clasps my hands in his. 'A beautiful job with the flowers as usual, Cecily,' he says, without looking at the arrangements. 'But I was concerned that you were absent from Mass. We missed you. We were short on ushers last week. And you were not here for the Sacrament of Reconciliation?'

'I was ill. Flu,' I tell him, my hands lying limply inside his.

'I have some time now, my child,' he says. 'I can hear your confession if you wish?'

'No.' I snatch my fingers back, and take a step away. An iron band circles my chest. It squeezes tighter. 'No. I have to... get home.'

He indicates the screen. 'Are you sure?'

I grab the pew nearest to me for support. The atmosphere of the church is seeping inside me, the smells of dust and stale incense dragging me back to a place I can't think about.

Darkness closes around me, and I blink, struggling to stay upright.

My father presses his face close to mine as I shrink from the entrance of the priest hole. His mouth trembles. *It's your duty*, he tells me, *Your Holy duty,* and he slams his hand on the wall next to me.

I turn on my heels and stagger up the aisle, using the ends of pews as support as I lurch from one side to the other. I can't do this. I can't let myself go back to that place.

I see my father as he nods towards the hole. *'Get in.'*

The threat of damnation hung over us; stories of devils and whippings and ever-burning pits of fire. *You are going to hell, Alice.*

The priest is watching me, and I know there's a similar puzzled expression on his face as the one Ambrose wore. I might have fooled Gabriel and Bea, but the church recognises me as a fake. My father beckons me. *We will pray together, Alice, pray for your sins.*

When the church tower is out of sight, I stop and place a shaky hand over my heart. I decided a long time ago that my soul isn't connected to an institution where men in robes decide if I'm forgiven or not. My soul is my own business.

* * *

After meeting Ambrose and the priest, I change my mind about staying. I can't live a life where I'm expected to belong to a church. I can't pretend to be a devout Catholic. But Cecily and I have yet to agree a change-over plan. In her note, she'd asked for a couple more days. I wish I knew what she was planning – what this whole charade is for.

Pacing around her small kitchen, my body thrums with adrenaline, a riot inside my veins. I push my hands through my hair, press the heels of my hands against my eyes. Her disappearing act has made me as helpless as a flipped-over beetle.

I need to get out. I grab Gabriel's woollen jacket and leave. The rain has cleared, leaving the world rinsed, smells of wet earth and fox pee evaporating into the air. I walk along the street, and my feet take me down to the river, where I pace the bank, watching the boats, watching the freedom of others, as gulls circle above.

Perhaps I should come clean and tell Gabriel who I really am? He wouldn't believe me at first. When he eventually did, the thought of seeing the confusion and pain in his eyes, is unbearable. What would he do? He'd be angry, of course, and he'd turn away from me, and I wouldn't blame him. And Bea? How would the truth affect her, especially after confiding in me about David? She's vulnerable. It could damage her forever, making her lose all trust in the world. I must stay true to the plan, for their sake. Maybe Cecily will call or put another note through the door. If she doesn't contact me in the next couple of days, I'll have to do something, but what? I could go to the police – but she wouldn't qualify as a missing person, not after she's sent me two notes, and has been spotted alive and well, even if drunk, by the blonde woman.

Gabriel comes home early, saying choir rehearsal has been cancelled. After Bea goes up to do her homework, he refills our glasses of Burgundy and sits at the table with me. He shuffles his chair closer to the table, anticipation twitching the corners of his mouth. 'I wanted to tell you.' He's watching my face. 'I've found a marriage counsellor.' He pauses, looking more uncertain as he catches my expression. 'I made some inquiries in my department – don't worry, I didn't say it was for us – and someone recommended her...' he trails off.

I take a gulp of wine. 'That's, that's good.'

'Is it too soon?' Disappointment dulls his voice.

'Sorry. Maybe.' I squeeze the stem of my glass. 'Maybe I'm not ready, yet.'

'But...' he swallows, and I see his struggle for patience in the spasm of nerves at his jaw, the clench of his teeth. 'We've been in limbo for a long time, Cecily.' He leans towards me. 'And we're doing better, aren't we?

Talking really helped. But we need someone professional now. I think there's a lot still hidden between us. Things that maybe... maybe you find hard to express to me.'

I glance at him, but his expression is earnest, uncomplicated by irony or suspicion. When I think of the things Cecily wrote in her sketchbooks, my guts cramp and knot. What does she want from him? From their marriage? I chew my lip, frowning.

'I'll do what it takes to make it work between us,' he's saying. 'Please think about counselling. We can have a one-off session to see if we like it.' He sits back and takes a swallow of wine, his eyes on mine, meltwater clear.

I nod, unable to speak. Events are hurtling towards me, to keep me here in this house, in the wrong life. Most of all, this is not fair on Gabriel. I glance at him from behind my hair, through the bulb of my glass, and feel a rush of anger towards her.

We go up to bed at the same time, and when I turn at the top of the stairs to say goodnight, I find him inches away, close enough to make out the strands of grey in the russet of his hair. The sudden proximity of his sturdy, solid chest, takes my breath away. His eyes are full of a question I can't answer. I step back. Disappointment flickers across his features, hurt following it. He rocks forward, plants a chaste kiss on my cheek. My skin burns, the impression of his lips branding me a liar. I step away with a gasp, muttering, 'Night,' as I hurry into Cecily's bedroom and close the door.

Later, when I think the coast should be clear, I slip out of the house, creeping past the cat who watches me from under the privet hedge. There's an hour before closing time. I hurry back to The Royal Oak. It's not as busy as last time, but after scouting around the place and looking in the ladies, I realise she's not here. I stay for a drink, perched on a stool by the bar, watching the door.

I leave at closing time, aware of someone close behind me. There are heavy footsteps following on my heels, the sound of a body in motion, the rub and rustle of fabric. I walk faster, my head down, only relaxing when I think they've gone in a different direction, but as I turn the corner into a deserted street, someone grabs me from behind, yanking me to a halt. I yelp, twisting around, trying to free my wrist. A man towers above me, and I crane my neck, staring up into a puffy, pale face. Small, dark eyes look back. I've never seen him before. 'Let me go.' My heart rattles in my chest.

His grip is an iron band. He's smiling. 'Hey, hey, easy,' he's saying in a Scottish accent. 'It's only me. We had fun the other night, didn't we? I've been thinking of you ever since.' A blast of sour, beery breath envelops me.

'Let go.' My throat tightens. 'I don't know you.' I strike at him with my other hand, hitting out at an impassive block of muscle. Straining to get away, I twist and jerk, tendons burning as if they're going to break. 'Leave me alone,' I pant.

His broad shoulders shake as he laughs. 'Playing hard to get?' His other hand has slipped around my waist and gropes my bottom. 'You know how to turn a man on.' His voice thickens, and he stoops, pressing his lips over mine. The world shrinks to the horror of his bruising teeth, the wet push of his insistent tongue.

I bring my knee up sharply into his groin. With a grunt, he releases me. I turn and run. My feet fly along the pavement, as I sprint past sleeping houses and parked cars, not looking back. I hear angry shouts behind, but there's no sound of him giving chase.

I stop outside Hollyhocks Cottage, leaning over, trying to recover my breath, supporting myself with palms braced against my trembling legs. When I straighten, I wipe the slime of his mouth away with the back of my hand. He thought I was Cecily. And I remember the winking man from the other night. His fear that his wife would see. The knowledge of what she's been doing fills my throat with bile.

I can't stay in her house any longer. I can't be her. I smell disaster coming like thunder over the horizon, a cordite stink swarming closer, a shock wave about to strike. Things are out of balance. Pressure building inside my head. I need her to come home, whatever she's doing, she needs to stop.

21

CECILY

Christmas was cancelled. New Year's Eve passed without celebration or acknowledgment.

On New Year's Day, we sat in silence at the breakfast table, picking at cold toast, sipping tea. Jude was still staying because there was nobody else who could have him at short notice. The boys were due back at school in a few days.

My job that morning was collecting litter from the garden. It was incredible how far some of the party revellers had ventured, wandering through the darkness into the grounds dropping cigarette butts and bottles. I hunched inside my coat, hands in my pockets, tramping in slow circles, searching the damp grass.

The boys had hardly spoken to us since the party, their faces closed against the rest of the world, and it seemed to me that they'd made a pact, had retreated into a mutual determination to endure, to get through the next few days before they could escape to school. Or perhaps they'd decided to go to the kibbutz earlier? To run away and not wait until the end of term. I could tell they were being careful not to touch each other, not to look at each other with lustful eyes in public. But I knew how they kissed behind closed doors.

Alice kept asking me what was wrong. 'You're being particularly weird. Has anything happened?'

'Daddy hates us, and everything is awful,' I said. 'Isn't that enough?'

'But we're going to run away,' Alice whispered. 'It isn't long till we have our freedom.'

I couldn't tell her that I'd never go anywhere with Henry and Jude. They were dead to me. I wanted to confess what I knew. But the words burnt my mouth. It wasn't possible to say such things aloud. Not even to her. A sudden breeze picked up, rustling the last of the skeleton leaves clinging to the beech trees. I stood up straight and looked across the grounds towards the distant peaks of the fells where flat grey clouds bandaged the horizon. A soft mizzle misted my eyelashes, catching in my hair and leaving a dew on the nap of my coat. A whispering of the deluge to come.

'Cecily.' I turned at the sound of my name. Henry was walking towards me, his footsteps marking the grass. I fought the urge to run, curling my fingers into fists, standing my ground. 'Are you alright?' he asked. 'Alice said she was worried about you.'

I managed a shrug. It made my tummy feel funny to stand close to him, as if I'd eaten too much cream or sugar, a queasy fizzing distaste.

He looked puzzled. 'I'm sorry,' he said quietly. And at first, I thought that he was apologising for what he'd done with Jude. 'It was my idea to have the party,' he went on. 'It was always a risk that we'd be found out. I suppose Jude and I were so excited by our plan to escape – the party wasn't just a celebration, as Jude said, it was a fuck-you gesture to our father, and to the whole rotten lot of them... I don't know... priests and landowners and the filthy rich.' He grimaced. 'Everyone who keeps the establishment lie going.' He rubbed his eyes. 'But it was wrong to drag you and Alice into it. Especially you. You never wanted it.' He blinked. 'I told Daddy it wasn't your idea, that you were never involved in the preparations or anything.'

My heart pulsed with relief. But I remembered the silver dress. My stupid romantic expectations. Jude and Henry kissing on the roof. And it felt as though Henry was laughing at me. He blinked again.

'It's alright,' I lied. 'It doesn't matter now.'

'That's decent of you, Cecily.' He gave a ghostly smile. 'Jude is sorry, too.'

I stared at my feet. My throat tightened. 'I'd better get on.'

'Jude and I – we want to try and do some good in the world,' he blurted out. 'And I can't do that if I'm trapped here.' He paused, and I sensed him looking at me, but refused to meet his gaze. 'I hope you'll understand one day, Cecily,' he finished, quietly.

His hand rested lightly on my shoulder before I heard him moving away. The ache of an absence hung where he'd been. His footprints were already fading from the wet grass. But where his fingers had pressed, it was as if his touch had penetrated my clothes and scalded me. How dare he pretend that he was being fair and kind! How dare he apologise to me for the stupid party! I put a bitten stub of fingernail in my mouth and scraped at the swollen skin around it with my teeth. 'Damn,' I said aloud. 'Damn you, Henry.' My words shook the spangled beauty of the garden like the death of a small bird.

I bent to the task of finding rubbish again, moving across the lawn, numb fingers grasping an empty plastic lighter, crumpling a beer can inside my fist. Under the canopy of the yew tree, the earth was dry and bare. As I left its shelter, the mizzle had turned to needles of hard rain. It was only as I stood with water lashing my eyes, that I realised that my brother had called me by my name. My proper name.

* * *

The rain came down harder, making puddles on the lawn. I went back inside, the rubbish bag dangling from my frozen hand. The house was different – the atmosphere strained and tense, ringing with electricity, as if the storm outside was about to crack open the walls and go raging through the rooms.

'Cilly.' Alice's pale face appeared out of the dark corridor. She beckoned with urgent, frightened motions. My heart thumped a tattoo as I shrugged off my wet coat, pushing back my dripping hair.

'Something's happened,' Alice whispered. 'Daddy called Henry into his study. And now... Now he's in the hole.'

'Where's Jude?'

'Daddy locked him in one of the attic rooms.'

I put my hand over my chest, steadied myself, and took a breath. 'What did they do?'

Alice shook her head. 'I don't know. Daddy's in his study on the phone to somebody. He's angry. Even more than he was on the night of the party – even angrier than he was about his wine.' Alice's gaze wavered, water spilling from her eyes. 'I don't understand,' she whispered. 'I have a bad feeling.' She shook her head. 'Mummy said we should stay out of the way. We're not allowed to communicate with the boys. She wouldn't explain anything. She's gone to her room.'

Alice groped for my fingers and squeezed, but I couldn't return the pressure.

* * *

The rest of the day slipped into the grainy blur of a slow-motion film. The Italian clock spoke into the hush, its mechanical noise marking the hours. Daddy shut himself in his study. An atmosphere seeped under his door, a thick miasma of fury, a reek of desolation. The two Labs waited on the floor outside for him, ears down, whimpering softly.

'Cecily?' Daddy's voice rang out through the silent house. 'Come in here, now.'

Fear galloped through me. I looked at Alice helplessly, and she shook her head, whispering, 'Have you done anything to make him angry?'

'I don't think so,' I whispered back.

'Don't let him see that you're scared,' she said. 'Be brave.'

A fire roared in the grate behind him. Above that, the painting of hell. The devils turned to me, alert and interested. He sat behind his desk, his craggy face impassive. In front of him was my diary. I stared at it. 'This,' he said, putting one finger on the cover, 'is filth. Disgusting filth.'

My feelings for Jude were there, spilled out in privacy over its pages, all my deepest yearnings. My skin flushed hot. The floor shifted under my feet. The devils were laughing. I remembered that I'd also written what I saw on the roof. I'd written what I saw Henry and Jude doing. It was the only space that had felt safe enough, the one place I could spell out their sin.

'Is it true?' His voice was tight. 'What you wrote about your brother and Jude?'

I nodded. He looked at me as if I was the one who'd committed the sin, and then he picked up the diary between his finger and thumb like a dead rat. He went over to the fire and tossed it in. The flames rushed to explore this new object, licking around it, snuffling inside, loving the crisp thin paper, the cardboard covers. My words crackled and burnt.

'You are never to write a diary again, do you understand?' Daddy said. I bent my head. 'You have a sewer for a mind.'

As Henry was already in the hole, Daddy locked me in the game larder. I was grateful that there were no venison carcasses, but a pheasant and three rabbits hung from the smaller hooks, bloodied mouths gaping. I huddled on the icy, slate floor, avoiding looking at the glassy eyes above me. It was dim and cold in the small space. I shivered, wanting the cavalier or the monk to come; they were stronger, braver people than me. It was the child who came instead, tugging at my hair and crying for her mother, and I held her close, needing her living warmth, tasting her tears. When Daddy let me out, I had no idea how long I'd been locked in, but my legs were stiff and numb, and I had to crawl over the slate floor onto the grass outside. I crouched below him, squinting into the sudden daylight. 'Get up,' he told me. 'We will pray together.' He watched me struggle onto my feet. 'We must pray for your soul.'

I followed him across the yard into the kitchen, past the scullery, the butler's pantry and boot room, through the green baize door, down the steps to the chapel. I glanced at my grubby skirt and tried to brush away the dirt, the stink of death.

* * *

Jane brought out lunch and supper and left them on the silver heating platters in the dining room. Only Daddy ate anything, none of us had any appetite. We heard him entering the dining room, then moving back to the study. The dogs followed him hopefully, then settled again outside his closed door with heavy sighs. Jane's eyes were red as she collected Daddy's dirty plate and the leftover food. She moved along corridors with her usual heavy tread, trailing greasy smells, but she wouldn't let us into her kitchen. 'Not today,' she said, shutting her door too.

Early next morning, I heard tyres on the drive and called Alice. We hurried to the first-floor landing window and stared out an unfamiliar, smart black car parked below. Jude appeared out of the house in his coat, bags in his hands. Daddy strode ahead of him to open the back door of the car and waited with folded arms. I couldn't see the driver. He, or she, didn't appear. Jude moved like a broken puppet. He stumbled as he walked to the car, his feet dragging through the gravel, broad shoulders slumped, head down. Tousled blond curls fell into his eyes. He glanced up just once before he got into the back seat, and his desperate gaze slid past our faces, as if we were part of the house and invisible to him. He was looking for Henry, I thought. But Henry was still in the hole. He'd been there for nearly twenty-four hours. The longest any of us had spent in it.

Later, after the car disappeared around the bend in the drive, I heard Daddy going up to the top floor, steps creaking under his weight. It must mean that Henry was going to be released. Henry, who'd been crushed into the tiny space, unable to move, hardly able to breathe with no food or water. Probably his legs wouldn't be able to support him, I thought. His muscles would cramp and shake and refuse to unbend from the positions they'd been forced to keep. He would blink and wince in the light. He would be hungry and thirsty. He might even have soiled himself. He must be sorry now, for what he'd done with Jude. I prayed with all my heart for him to be saved.

22

ALICE

I remember that Cecily kept a diary when she was child, but after that Christmas, I don't think she wrote one again – at least, she mentioned that she'd given them up in one of her letters. When I asked why, she told me they were childish, that she'd outgrown them.

I could do with one of her diaries now, and I'd feel no guilt at reading it. Then I might have a clue what she's doing, an insight into what's going on in her head. I knew her marriage was a lie, but the whole of this safe little domestic set-up is a sham. I've never felt so utterly cut-off from her.

But while I'm stuck here, playing the role of mum, I'm not going to watch Bea struggle without trying to help her.

I'm already in Cecily's workout clothes when Bea gets home from school. 'Want to do some yoga with me?' I suggest.

She looks at me as if I'm mad.

'Oh, go on.' I put my hands on my hips. 'It'll be more fun if we do it together.'

'I didn't even know you did yoga? Isn't that some weird hippy thing?'

'No.' I laugh. 'It's a good way of getting fit and, I don't know, being more in touch with your body and mind. Thought I'd give it a go.'

Her expression has softened from refusal to doubt, but she's glancing towards the kitchen, her after-school habit of eating sandwiches and chocolate biscuits hard to break.

'You can leave anytime you want…' I try to make my voice cajoling but light.

'Oh, alright then,' she shrugs, 'just for five minutes. But if you laugh, I'm going.'

I hold up my hands. 'I'm not going to be laughing at anything. Not when I'm breathing with my mouth closed and trying to remember what comes next.'

I've found an old exercise mat in the understairs cupboard, and I lay this over the pine boards in the sitting room for her – I'll have to make do with the floor. I'll make it a short session, I think. Start with some gentle movements that will allow her to feel her body, mobilise her joints, get the blood flowing, nothing that's too difficult.

We've been practising for twenty minutes, and she hasn't given up in frustration or boredom. She's following my voice guides and movements, giggling sometimes when she gets it wrong or overbalances. We're doing a sequence of sun salutations, and I've raised my arms above my head in high mountain, when a flicker of movement outside the bay window catches my attention. I turn my head, startled by the outline of a person, a dazzle of evening light behind them. I bite my tongue in shock, blink and refocus. There's nobody there, just the play of brilliance and shadow against glass. It gave me a fright, and my heart hasn't caught up with my head, my body jittery with adrenaline. I don't want Bea to notice, so I draw in deep breaths and move into the next part of the flow, bending forwards over my legs, 'Keep your knees a little bent,' I say, 'just let your head hang heavy.'

After another ten minutes, I wind the session down. I'm thrilled that she's stuck with it, and it's a struggle not to grin in triumph. We lie on the floor in corpse pose. 'This is the best bit.' She sighs.

I roll onto my elbows. 'Wasn't so bad, was it?'

She sits up, hugging her long T-shirt around her waist, folding her arms across her chest. 'It was alright,' she says. Her skin is flushed and rosy; she looks pretty.

'Great.' I smile. 'Maybe we can do it again, sometime.'

I'm not going to push her into it. Better if she asks me. As I roll up the mat, I glance at the window again. Any intruder would have had to walk around the privet hedge to gaze into the house. It seems an unlikely thing to do. I must have imagined it.

* * *

The kitchen is full of acrid fumes. The smoke alarm is shrieking. 'Shit,' I yell, rushing past Gabriel as he gets home. I open the oven door. Charcoal clouds fill the air as a blast of heat burns my face, stinging my eyes. I flap a tea towel ineffectually and unlock the back door, throwing it open. I set the blackened food in the middle of the table. *Who's smug now?* Cecily's voice says.

Gabriel looks at the burnt meal in surprise, and I'm about to apologise when the doorbell rings. 'Good timing,' he mutters, rolling his eyes.

The bell sounds again. 'I'll go,' he says, leaving the room.

I hear a female voice and for a heart-stopping second, I think it's Cecily. But then Gabriel's lower tone comes in, and from his calmness, I know that it isn't her. I stare at the charcoaled dish in the centre of the table, wondering if any part of it is edible, and knowing it's not. Carcinogenic, I think. Bea comes in, coughing at the smoke. 'What's going on?' She stops when she sees the ruined vegetable lasagne and laughs.

There are footsteps, and he reappears with the woman who accosted me in the Co-op. She's dressed in snakeskin patterned leggings, a pink sweatshirt and matching leg warmers. Her eyes are heavy with make-up below plucked brows. Her fuchsia pink lips widen into a knowing smile when she sees me.

'There you are,' she exclaims. 'I was worried about you, Cecily.'

I stare at her, and glance at Gabriel, hoping for guidance. He supplies it. 'Rebecca was wondering why you haven't been at your exercise class.' He winks at me.

'You've missed two of my step classes,' she says. 'And you're usually so dedicated.'

'I've just... been... busy,' I offer, pushing my hair behind my ear.

'Ah, yes...' she gives me a meaningful look. 'Busy,' she repeats slowly, wagging a finger at me. 'I know how you're keeping yourself *busy*, Cecily. And it's not good for your health,' she says. 'Naughty girl.' I go cold at her implication. Has she seen Cecily drinking at night, again? Worse, has she seen her with another man? The smell of Rebecca's sugary sweet perfume overwhelms the stink of burning and prickles my nose. She puts a proprietorial hand on Gabriel's arm, her nails a glossy purple that matches her jumper. 'You don't want your gorgeous wife to let herself go, do you?' she smiles. She wrinkles her forehead at me. 'You have to work at it, hon, especially as we're not getting any younger.'

'Mum's doing yoga,' Bea volunteers.

'Yoga!' Rebecca exclaims. 'That won't be burning any calories!'

I force a smile.

'Good of you to call in, Rebecca, but...' Gabriel glances meaningfully at the laid table.

She gives the burnt lasagne a dubious look and pats his arm again. 'I can take a hint!' She flicks blonde wisps, gives a quick head toss. 'Darling,' she says to me, with no warmth. 'Don't be a stranger.' She glances at Gabriel through lowered lashes. 'It would be good to see more of both of you. Why don't you come to dinner soon? I'll be in touch,' she says, looking at me again. 'Ciao. Enjoy!' She waves a manicured hand, and turns. 'I'll see myself out.'

We don't move, waiting for the sound of her heels to disappear, the front door to shut. And then we look at each other and burst out laughing. 'We'll be going to dinner over my dead body,' Gabriel says.

'A tricky manoeuvre,' I say, straight faced.

'What an awful woman,' Bea adds. 'No wonder you don't go to her classes any more.'

'And what's this about yoga?' Gabriel is looking at me and Bea quizzically.

'We'll tell you,' I say, gesturing to the table. 'But first I need to chuck this out. Sandwiches, anybody?'

'Why did she keep going on about you being busy?' he asks, as I scrape the meal into the bin. I'm glad he can't see my face.

'I have no idea,' I lie.

'It was probably an obscure dig,' he says. 'She's obviously taking it personally that you're not going to her class.'

'Yes,' I agree, gratefully. 'I think you're right.'

* * *

I search Cecily's room again. I rattle the locked drawer in the dressing table and try picking the lock with a hair pin I find in Cecily's make-up bag; but it doesn't work like it does in films. The hair pin snaps. The key must be hidden somewhere, so I go through the room systematically, sliding my hand into the back of drawers, checking under ornaments. I pick up the two books on her bedside table, flicking through pages in case there's a hidden cut-out. I don't find a key, but a piece of loose paper wafts out of the Bible. The paper is covered in her handwriting. I sit on the side of the bed to read it.

There's a chunk of text about yew trees, which she must have copied from a book.

Druids held them sacred in pre-Christian times. They have been used as symbols of immortality, but also death and omens of doom.

I think of the yew tree at our childhood home – the thick, gnarled branches, the split trunk. It was supposed to be over three thousand years old. Our father found a Civil War cannon ball lodged inside it when he was a boy.

The toxicity of the leaves is due to alkaloids known as taxines. Eating even a small quantity can be fatal. The victim is unable to breathe properly, becomes confused, has convulsions, and falls into a coma. There's no known antidote.

When we were children, we'd dared ourselves to eat the red yew berries. They'd smelt of pear drops but tasted disappointingly of nothing much. We'd rolled them on our tongues, spitting out the deadly seed before swallowing the flesh. Afterwards, we'd have a raging thirst and run inside to gulp water from the kitchen tap, laughing with the relief of being alive. Why is she researching yew trees? Perhaps she's finding facts to impress our father with – she did it all the time as a child – always thinking of what she could do to pacify and please him, bringing him snippets of information like a dog bringing a stick to its master.

There's a name with a question mark after it. *Edith Baxter?* A phone number and address scribbled underneath. I can't think where I've heard the name before. I frown, concentrating. There's a brief flicker in the shadows of my mind, the shiver of something lost.

Another name, this time underlined. *Mary Deveraux.* No address or telephone number. She must be a relation. Her portrait might even hang at Hawksmoor.

The next name makes me gasp. *Jude O'Clery.*

We'd crouched on the landing by the window that terrible morning and watched him getting into an unfamiliar car. He'd cringed as he walked past our father. He'd looked beaten, forlorn, not like the Jude we knew with the easy grin and broad shoulders, cigarette clamped between his lips as he rolled a cricket ball over his thigh. We never saw him again. He didn't come to Henry's funeral. I haven't thought of him for years.

She's got an address for him too, and a phone number. I stare at the number. I have an urgent desire to call him now. I'm sick of the passive waiting game she's forced me to play; he might know where she is. It's late, but not too late. But I can't ring him from the house phone, it would elicit questions from Gabriel that I can't answer.

I check that I have enough coins to pay for a call and slip out of the front door into the darkening evening, hurrying to the bottom of the street where I remember seeing a phone box. Inside, I hold my breath against the stink of urine, and dial the number on the paper. He answers straight away. 'Jude?' I grip the greasy receiver tighter, reeling from the sound of his voice, the memories it releases. 'It's Cecily,' I say after a beat.

'Cecily?' He's surprised, but not in a good way. 'I don't think we have anything else to say to each other.' His voice has become cold. 'Do we?'

A whirly-gig of panic. I clear my throat. 'I'd like to see you, Jude. Just to talk.'

There's a moment's silence. 'No,' he says. 'I don't think so.'

'One more time,' I say. 'Please. It's important.'

He sighs, 'It's difficult for me. You must understand that.' His voice breaks. 'I don't want to go over it again.'

'I promise I won't make it difficult,' I say, cautiously, feeling my way. 'And... and I'll never bother you after this.'

There's another echoing silence. The hiss of the connection. 'Alright,' he says, grudgingly. 'But you'll have to come to me again. I can't get away during the week.'

'That's OK,' I say, remembering that he lives in Bath. 'That's fine. Where should we meet?'

'Same place as before?'

'Remind me.'

A restaurant. I repeat his words. We arrange a time and date, and I replace the receiver. I remember her shivering in her silver dress the night of the party – *do you think Jude likes me?* – she'd been bright with hope that night. But nothing happened between them. Not then. If she's started to have an affair with him all these years later, that could explain the subterfuge and mystery. Perhaps he's married too. But it sounds as if the relationship has ended. Or at any rate, he's ended it, and Cecily's pursuing him, refusing to take no for an answer.

As I push out of the phone box and walk home, I think I hear footsteps behind me, but when I turn, the footsteps stop and there's nothing there, except a liquid swill of shadows. But I feel a prickle of knowing. A sense that I'm not alone. A rush of adrenaline makes my muscles tense, and I'm primed to run. I walk quickly, with the keys in my hand. The footsteps pad behind me again. When I get to the house, I glance back up the street, searching the inky darkness between pools of streetlight. Nothing, except the cat who comes slinking from under the privet hedge. Perhaps it had been my own stuttering heartbeat I'd heard. I open the door and slip into the hall, Sukie at my heels.

23

CECILY

It had been snowing heavily since Henry's funeral, and I woke up to an eerie nebulous feel, ghostly white light reflecting through my window. It was still early, but I couldn't go back to sleep. I pushed my feet out of the sheets, stepping into a freezing draft, and tugged a cardigan around my shoulders. I didn't want to be alone. I'd slip into bed with Alice until it was time to get up. Unlike me, she never had trouble sleeping. She'd harumph when I woke her, but she'd lift the cover as she always did, shifting over for me to clamber inside. We'd stay snug, pressed hip against hip, our feet entangled. She'd wince at the touch of my icy toes, but she wouldn't really mind. Now that Henry was gone, we needed each other more than ever.

I padded along the corridor on bare feet. 'Alice?' I whispered, shivering on the threshold. But I could tell the room was empty as soon as I stepped inside; there was an Alice-absence, a lack of energy in the frigid air. The covers were neatly pulled up on her bed, the pillow undented by her head. I walked over to the wardrobe and wrenched it open. Empty metal hangers jangled as I ran my hands across them. I sat down heavily, mattress springs creaking. She'd threatened to run away, and now she'd done it. I gulped down a sob. Images flickered behind my eyelids: Alice trekking through a rocky landscape, stopping to pluck figs and olives from trees, Alice murdered by Arabs, Alice swimming in the Sea of Galilee. A hysterical laugh formed inside me and died before it could express itself in sound. How could I survive without her? She promised she'd never leave me. We said we'd be together forever. And now she was gone.

She'd left before I could tell her the truth about Henry – about what I saw him doing with Jude and what happened afterwards. I needed to tell her, but I'd been plucking up the confidence, rehearsing the words. Pressure squeezed my ribs, a constraint around my throat as if hands were squeezing. I thought I might cry, and waited for tears to fall, but my eyes remained oddly gritty and dry.

The room was freezing, and I pushed my numb feet under her covers. I lay down and pressed my face into her pillow, searching out the last traces of scent. 'Alice,' I moaned through chattering teeth. 'Why did you go?'

Tears escaped from under my lids, trickling along the edge of my nose, making a salt path across my cheek, slipping into my ear. It was a relief to cry, to feel my body taking charge of my emotions.

* * *

Daddy banished all traces of Alice and Henry from Hawksmoor. Silver-framed photographs were swept off dressers and sideboards, images of Henry and Alice in christening gowns and school uniforms were removed from the grand piano. Henry's sporting cups, his clothes, his books, and Alice's abandoned possessions disappeared. Coats, wellingtons, and shoes were taken from the boot room, along with the grimy shape of Henry's ribcage etched into the lining of his gaberdine mac, the shape of Alice's long hands, continuously shoved into pockets, worn into the soft, tweedy blue of her coat. Their tennis racquets and riding hats vanished too, the strapped handles and inner silks darkened with their sweat. Nobody was allowed to mention their names. It was as if they'd never existed.

My shock and rage became grief, and then a quiet despair, a cold emptiness. Severed from my twin, I existed inside solitude, removed from everyone. But I had to take on the weight of the others. I had to somehow make up for their disappearance. Daddy needed me. I was the last one left, the only hope for future.

Mummy became one of the ghosts wandering the corridors, Dilly padding at her heels. She murmured under her breath as she went in and out of empty rooms as if she was continually looking for something. Daddy was a man made of ice, his expression rigid, teeth clenched, eyes dead. He locked himself in his study to work on the book and nobody dared disturb him. He'd thrown an axe at Jane's head when she went in to retrieve his tray, and she'd given her notice, saying it was the last straw.

Then a letter arrived for me.

Dear Cecily,

I've arrived at the kibbutz. It was a long journey, and sometimes frightening. I pretended you were with me to give me courage. I know you're angry with me for leaving. But I didn't have a choice. Please forgive me, darling Cecily, and remember it's not too late. I wish with all my heart you'd come too. If you change your mind, I'm here, in the place where Jesus walked – just think of it!

Tell Mummy that I'm fine and not to expect me home for a long time. There are people here from all over the world – America, Japan, Canada, Germany, France – and loads more. It's incredible mixing with different cultures and religions. Everything is shared equally between us – all the chores. We work hard, but there's lots of fun too, drinking sweet Israeli wine, and dancing. We're going to go on a pilgrimage to Jerusalem soon. There's a little Arab village nearby, but sadly no communication between us. My shoulders ache from picking fruit, but I'm already tanned and stronger.

Please write back to me. I've enclosed the address. I miss you.

Love, Alice.

I missed her too. She was right, I was angry with her, but having her letters gave me hope – and I told myself that I could go to her if I wanted. But my life was here, at Hawksmoor, and I knew I wouldn't leave. I wrote back, and that was it, the beginning of our secret correspondence.

In my last years at school, without Alice to outshine me, I found I wasn't as stupid as I'd believed. I worked hard. I aimed to go to university and do history, Daddy's favourite subject.

I took a short typing course at school, for girls who wanted to be secretaries, and plucked up enough courage to suggest to Daddy that I could type up his manuscript for him. He refused at first, but after a couple of days, he agreed.

'Three evenings a week,' he said. 'You will sit in the office with me. But I must have silence while I'm working.'

He grumbled about the noise of the typewriter keys, and then seemed to get used to them. We sat together at opposite ends of the desk, the sound of wood pigeons cooing on the roof. The massive manuscript was impenetrable. Daddy's handwriting was almost illegible and scored through with crossings-out, the pages jumbled in the wrong order, but I worked through it methodically, doing my best. The Labs lay at our feet, farting and sighing. Daddy smoked and scratched his chin, scribbling furiously, consulting some of the history books he kept piled on his desk. Sometimes there would be a weapon laid out before him which he'd take to pieces and sketch, labelling the parts.

It didn't matter if we didn't speak, I was happy to be engaged in a joint project, to be allowed in the same room. He'd ask me to hold the end of a tape measure, or a cannon ball he wanted to weigh. I wrote things down for him – measurements, numbers, making sure my handwriting was clear and accurate.

After a couple of weeks of sitting in silence, he began to talk. And it was as if he couldn't stop. He spoke about the tragedy of the Great War, the three Deveraux sons that had been killed in it, and how the youngest, who remained, had gambled some of the estate away. He told me about General Deveraux who'd lost his eye in combat and was promoted to Field Marshal. He described the grand shooting parties and the balls that had been held in the Edwardian era, and his memories of being a boy in World War Two when the house had been requisitioned by the army, how he'd tried to lie about his age so that he could enlist, and how the house had been left badly damaged, and the family uncompensated.

I listened, asking questions, feeling a surge of satisfaction that I had been the one to bring Daddy back, to relight his burning, blue gaze. His impatient movements returned, and his ringing, imperious voice. The others had betrayed him, but it was my faith that had saved him. 'This family has been in residence at Hawksmoor since William the Conqueror,' he said. 'Of course, it looked very different then. Country houses didn't exist. It's been built and added to over the years. We've survived wars, disease, the Industrial Revolution, taxes, the Crash of '29. And I'm dammed if we're giving in now.' He'd given me a look that made my stomach turn over. 'The Deveraux are tough. The world has tried to erase us. But we fight back.'

He threw back his head and laughed, and I laughed too, feeling euphoric with the sense of being chosen, the knowledge of his approval. But I kept a watchful eye out for his sudden switch into anger, or despair.

24

ALICE

It's a long trip to Bath, so I'll only have time for a quick lunch before I'll have to rush for the return train. I've left Bea something to heat up when she gets back from school, and a note explaining I'll be late. As I walk briskly through the spring sunshine, a chill runs down my spine and across my scalp; I turn quickly and stare behind me. There's no one there, except a woman on the opposite pavement walking her dog, and someone with their hood up turning down a side street. What if another of Cecily's one-night stands comes after me again? I hold the keys in my fist, ready to stab. I'm not defenceless. I've spent years surviving alone.

At the station, I queue to buy a ticket from the booth, and feel a crawling sensation over my skin, a prickle of knowing – as if someone's gaze is on my back. A few people wait in line behind me, and I look at their faces. They seem unconcerned and bored; one man taps his foot and looks at his wristwatch. A group of chattering women walk past with wheelie suitcases, and a few people are reading the departures board. There's a tall man with his back to me, studying one of the posters on the wall on the other side of the hall. I take my ticket and hurry onto the platform. As I find a seat on the train, I tell myself that my imagination is working overtime.

The restaurant is near the station. It's a French bistro done up in red, with gold lettering picking out the name; inside there are spindly wooden chairs and checked tablecloths, waiters in white aprons. I recognise Jude at once. He's sitting at a corner table, consulting the menu. He's thinner, making the wide bones in his face more prominent; his mop of hair is a little less luxuriant, but he's as handsome as I remember. He stands up politely when he sees me, but his expression is wary.

'Well,' he says, gesturing at the other chair. 'It's an awfully long way to come for lunch.'

The strength goes out of my legs, and I sit down and pour myself some water from the bottle on the table. I gulp half a glass, using the time to collect myself. The waiter comes over and we order; I pick the first thing my finger points to on the menu and wait for the man to move away.

'Jude,' I say quietly. 'I'm not Cecily. I'm Alice.'

He stares at me. 'What?' He searches my features with guarded curiosity. 'If this is joke,' he says slowly. 'I don't think it's funny.'

'It's not a joke.' I keep eye contact with him. 'I promise.'

He continues to scrutinise me in silence, then, 'My God,' he lets out a breath. 'You were always identical. But this...' his hand moves to describe the curve and planes of my face, sketching me on an invisible canvas. 'I only saw her a few weeks ago – I'd never have been able to tell the difference if you hadn't told me. It's a subtle thing. More a feel than anything.'

'Jude,' I clear my throat. 'I need to ask you something. Are you having an affair with Cecily?'

I may as well have slapped him. His stunned expression tells me everything I need to know. 'Sorry,' I say quickly. 'It's just... you didn't sound too pleased to hear her on the phone, and she's been acting strangely—'

'No,' he says in a clipped voice. 'I'm not having an affair with your sister. I'm frankly amazed that would have come to that conclusion.' He sits back and tilts his head. 'I think it's you that has some explaining to do.' Distrust is back in his voice. 'Why this charade? Why pretend to be Cecily?'

'It's a long story,' I say. 'But I offered to take her place for a week, so that she could make arrangements to divorce her husband.'

'You're pretending to be her in her own home?' He raises his eyebrows. 'And the husband and daughter... they don't know?'

I nod.

'Why did she need a week? Surely, she could visit a solicitor in a day?'

His words start a buzz of anxiety at the base of my skull. 'She was feeling trapped. She seemed desperate.' I fiddle with my napkin, folding and unfolding it. 'But now she's missing. At least, she's been seen in Exeter, but I can't get hold of her... I don't know whether to be worried or not.' I screw the napkin into a ball.

'I'm surprised,' he says. 'About the divorce. The Cecily I know is a devout Catholic.'

'Yes.' I nod. 'She still is, I think. But she told me that Gabriel – her husband – was controlling. An alcoholic.' The starkness of her deception hits me as I say the words. 'That's why I said I'd take her place,' I finish, quietly. 'Only now she's disappeared.'

'Are you safe there?' His eyes narrow.

I remember Gabriel standing close on the landing, my longing to rest my head on his chest. I nod. 'The thing is, she lied. He's not controlling. He's not an alcoholic.'

'But are you safe from her?' he says. 'From your sister?'

'From Cecily? What do you mean?'

'She seemed... disturbed when I saw her. And she said some things. Things I can't stop going over, asking myself, was she telling the truth?'

'About what? What do you mean?'

'She told me she'd killed Henry.'

The waiter returns with our food. We sit back in silence while the man fusses with salt and pepper, checking if we want mayonnaise or ketchup. Our plates are placed before us: goats cheese salad for me and an omelette and chips for Jude.

I wait for the waiter to move away. I lean forwards. 'That's crazy. He jumped. It wasn't anything to do with her.'

He turns his wine glass, fingers gripping the stem. 'She said it was her fault. She said, "I murdered him, it's my fault he's dead."'

'But... She didn't. She wouldn't.'

'It's what she told me, Alice. Those words exactly.' He swallows. 'It was hard to hear. I kept asking her what she meant, but she didn't elaborate, kept insisting that she was sorry. She said she hadn't understood about love between men. She'd been disgusted by us, she said, at the time. She'd thought it was a sin. She asked me to forgive her.'

His words are like balls, thrown at me hard and fast. I'm shocked by the flash of implications. I stare at him. 'You mean... You and Henry?'

He glances at me sharply, as if he thinks I'm mocking him, but something in my expression makes him relax. 'My dear,' he says quietly. 'Didn't you know? Your brother and I were lovers. And your father found out.'

I catch my breath. Why hadn't I guessed before? My mind reels back, snatching at memories, trying to see what I'd missed. I settle on one image – Henry taking Jude's lit cigarette and putting it in his mouth. There had always been such ease between them. I reach across and touch his hand on an impulse. 'I'm so sorry, Jude.'

'That's what she said,' he looks down at my hand over his. 'She kept saying it.'

I startle. 'She knew back then... about you and Henry?'

'Yes.' He withdraws his hand and sits up taller. 'Yes, apparently, she knew.'

'God, I wonder how she found out?'

'She must have seen us. We tried to be careful. But there would have been moments when she could have glimpsed us through a doorway or in the garden, behind the branches of the yew tree.'

Cecily was a watcher. She moved quietly through the house, listened behind closed doors, wandered the garden with a book. It could have happened; she could have seen them. And I can imagine her reaction. It would have mirrored Daddy's. 'I wish she'd told me.' I spear lettuce leaves with my fork; a tomato bursts, spreading seeds across my plate.

He looks at the tablecloth, his face older, dragged down by gravity. 'She said that your father found out because of her diary.'

'Her diary?' A cog clicks into place. I nod. 'He would have had no compunction about reading it. But he would have made Henry's life hell.' I remember Henry locked in the hole for the night. 'He would never have accepted a gay son. He probably threatened to send him into the army or something. Maybe conversion therapy.'

Jude gives a weary shrug and picks up a chip with his fingers, eating it without enthusiasm. He's hardly touched his omelette. 'It hardly matters now.'

'Did Cecily say anything about her plans – about what she was doing, or where she was going?'

'To be honest, I was in shock after her confession. I think she said she was going away for a while, that she had important business to attend to. A task, I think she called it. Something long overdue. But she was cryptic, didn't give me any details.' He moves his plate away from him. 'She seemed nervous. Highly strung.' He looks at his glass of wine. 'She drank a lot. Threw it back.'

I shake my head. 'I can't believe that she really killed him – I just can't.'

He rubs his forehead. 'I don't want to believe it, either. But those were the words she used.' His fingers have left red marks on his skin. 'Whatever the truth, I think she's unbalanced. She's not well, Alice. I'm afraid she might be about to do something terrible.'

My chest tightens. He's right. Cecily's behaviour points to a kind of madness or sickness – her drinking at night, the strange men – and she must have an ulterior motive for the swap, something she's not sharing with me.

'It's all such a mess. I wish I could go back in time and change what happened.' I fiddle with the salt cellar. 'The party was the beginning of the end, wasn't it? The beginning of it all going wrong. But I didn't understand. I never knew why you were both in such trouble. Why you were sent away.'

'I'll never forget it,' he says. 'Your father marched me to the top of the house, locked me in a room and refused to talk to me. I may as well have been a mass murderer the way he treated me. My parents sent someone to collect me the next morning, and I was packed off to live with relatives in South Africa. Nobody talked about it, but I was told I would never see Henry again.' He takes another gulp of his drink. 'And I never did. I found out about his death months later, from an old school friend. It nearly killed me.'

There seems to be nothing more to say. We are silent for a while before we stumble onto other subjects. I listen with half an ear while he tells me about his design business, and the man he lives with. I offer some details about my life since Hawksmoor. He wants to know what it was like at the kibbutz, and as I speak, he pushes his hands across his eyes. 'If only we'd made it there too,' he says, with a catch in his voice. I give him a moment to collect himself before I look at Cecily's watch. We call for the bill, and he insists on paying. When I stand to say goodbye, he scoops me towards him. His chest has a new barrel-shaped weight, and I'm enveloped by the scent of his cologne, the fresh tang of washing power in the fibres of his crisp, patterned shirt. 'Those weeks at Hawksmoor were my happiest,' he murmurs. 'I sometimes think your brother was the love of my life.'

There are tears in his eyes when he lets me go. I lean in to kiss his still-beautiful, sculptured cheek.

25

CECILY

Dear Alice,

I'm here, at Exeter University! I didn't do too badly in my exams (not so Cilly!) but in the end, I got the place through Clearing. 'Stay clear of Lefties and druggies,' Daddy said, when I told him I'd been accepted. I thought he might have been pleased. He probably is underneath – you know how he finds it hard to say 'well done.' Mummy held my hands so tightly that I had to tug to get them back. I think she's worried because Exeter is so far from home, but I think that's for the best. I'm settled in Halls, and I've worked out how to get around the campus, which is huge.

The other students wear cool clothes, and they all seem to know each other. When they're chatting in groups it sometimes feels like a language I don't understand. I haven't made any real friends. Nobody here could understand how growing up Catholic and coming from Hawksmoor sets me apart. Anyway, I don't know how to connect with other people. I'd never needed to make friends before. I always had you. I miss you.

I hope this letter will reach you. I'm sending it to the Paris address you gave me – are you still working as an au pair? Maybe you could visit me at Uni? Paris isn't so far away. I know you don't want to come back to this country – but Daddy doesn't have to know – and I'd be here to welcome you. Think about it!

Love Cecily

It felt like a relief at first, being at the other end of the country to Hawksmoor. I didn't have to walk past the place on the gravel where Henry's blood had spilled around him like a red cloak unfurling. His head had been turned to the side, the shattered half hidden, just one eye visible. I kept seeing that open eye staring at me through its glaze of dirt. Sometimes I'd tried to imagine what his last thoughts and feelings had been as his feet left the tiles, as his body hurled towards the gravel. But I always stopped myself before my thoughts spun into the darker corners of my mind.

I was homesick at university. It was too expensive to get the train back to the Lake District in term time. I longed for Hawksmoor. I tried to recall the feel of the carved banisters, the heraldic creatures and sea monsters rearing under my fingers. It was only in Hawksmoor that I knew who I was.

I introduced myself to other students as an only child. No one would call me Cilly again. The pressing problem was how to make a success of my life. It was wrapped up with saving Hawksmoor. It was the key to everything. Here, at university, it occurred to me that I could be the one to make money from a career, to marry well. Why not? This was my chance to be noticed, to be the one to make Daddy proud. I was enjoying my current module: The Occult in the Victorian Age. But when the students in my class joked about the ludicrous spectres conjured up by psychics – the green phantasma, the children who crawled under tables to knock on the underside of the wood – I kept quiet, thinking of the ghosts I'd seen on the stairs at Hawksmoor, remembering the sound of the monk's laboured breathing in the priest hole, the feel of the little girl clambering onto my lap, their voices coming through me like a strange haunting.

'She's a typical only child,' I heard one of my flatmates say, talking to a friend in the tiny kitchen. I'd paused outside the door, listening. 'Selfish. Doesn't share her stuff. Standoffish.' Then a short laugh. 'Always chatting away to herself.'

I realised with a small shock that they were talking about me.

'Really? I think I've met her at the Student Union,' the other person said. 'She seemed okay – kind of fun.'

I let out a breath, relieved it wasn't me they were discussing. I'd never been to the Student Union – it was full of crowds of confident students and impossible social demands.

My favourite lecturer, Gabriel Greenwood, was younger than the other tutors, fresh from his PhD, and handsome in the way of an academic, his hair a little too long and tousled, as if he spent the day pushing distracted ink-stained fingers through it, his back slightly stooped from leaning over books. His nose was interesting, crooked at the bridge, with flared nostrils, his mouth large and lush, quick to smile. I had to try extra hard to concentrate when he was talking, wanting to study him instead of his words. His collar was open at the neck showing a glimpse of smooth, golden skin, and I remembered the reddish hairs gleaming on Jude's tanned forearm. But this lecturer wasn't like Jude, I was sure of that. I was more experienced now. Could tell these things. And I'd heard the other girls talking about him. They all fancied him, discussed him in the canteen, guessing what his personal life was like. 'No wedding ring,' they'd discerned.

I was certain he wasn't gay, because for the first time in my life, I saw gay people around me, even two boys holding hands, walking hip to hip like an ordinary couple. I was shocked at first, outraged by their flagrant disregard for convention. I looked around, expecting to see other people's reactions mirroring my own. But hardly anyone raised an eyebrow, and God didn't strike them down. A handwritten banner hung out of a dorm window: 'Gay Rights!' it proclaimed. 'Equality for All'. As the weeks went on, although I wasn't comfortable around homosexuals, their affection for each other didn't make me feel sick either and after a while, it began to feel almost normal. I realised Henry and Jude could have been happy too. I'd made a mistake, a terrible mistake.

It was my habit after lectures to wait for the crowd to disappear before I got up, that way I avoided being jostled, and could leave in my own time. I was in the front row after one of Gabriel Greenwood's lectures, sinking low in my seat, occupying myself by rereading Alice's latest letter. She'd left the kibbutz and it was about the two French children she was looking after, and their handsome father. The lecture theatre rang with students' voices, shuffling feet, seats being flipped up. I glanced at the podium where Dr Greenwood was doing up his briefcase. He caught my eye and smiled. My lungs faltered. I glanced down at Alice's letter and then back to find that he was still looking at me, but now it was with something like concern. I guessed he'd noticed my isolation, my lack of friends. He probably pitied me.

26

ALICE

All the way back on the train, I go over Jude's words. I can't accept that Cecily pushed Henry off the roof. Not on purpose, not in cold blood. Maybe they'd had an argument? Maybe it was an accident? But he was only on the roof because someone let him out of his room. It had never occurred to me before, but as he'd been locked in by Daddy, and it wasn't me who unlocked the door, and Mummy would never have gone against his wishes, there was only one other person it could have been. Realising she'd lied about that makes me wonder if she'd lied about where she was and what she was doing when he fell too – the police had come and interviewed all of us, and we'd had to say where we were and what we'd been doing at the time he fell. Daddy had told us not to say that Henry had been locked in his room.

I'm aware something is different as soon as I walk into her bedroom. I look around, puzzled, and notice that the window I thought I'd left locked is slightly open. I walk over to it and shut it, feeling a sense of concern – have I left it open all day? I think of the person watching the house from the shadows, the image of someone at the bay window.

My clothes smell of trains, a pong of dirty air and grease and stale sandwiches. I shrug off the blue blouse and tailored trousers I chose from Cecily's wardrobe this morning, pulling on one of her sweatshirts and pair of black leggings. Thank God for her exercise clothes. I think with longing of my own things stuffed into my rucksack and glance down at the pair of trainers I'd left on the floor. Except, they're not there. I must have tidied them away. I open the wardrobe, check the shoeboxes, look under the bed.

I put my head around Bea's door. She's at her desk, working, an exercise book open. She looks up and smiles.

'Did you, by any chance, borrow my trainers?'

She wrinkles her forehead. 'Your feet are half a size bigger than mine, remember?' She looks at her clumpy DMs. 'And no offence, Mum. But your trainers aren't really my style.'

'Right.' I force a smile. 'Of course. I must have mislaid them. No problem.'

She glances down at her textbook.

'I'll leave you in peace then.' I turn to go, and pause, looking back at her. 'Is everything okay at school?'

'Yeah.' She twirls her pen between her fingers. 'Better, thanks. I ignore Megan and that lot. I've made friends with a girl called Lily. She's been in my class for a year, but because she's a bit of a wallflower, I'd never spoken to her. But she's really nice. And interesting.'

'I'm glad,' I say. 'Funny, isn't it, how we can miss good things right under our noses.'

She shrugs a shoulder and turns back to her work.

I hesitate for a moment, watching her, and then nip into Cecily's room, quickly rummaging through my rucksack to pull out a book. I slip back into Bea's room and place the book on her table. 'Thought you might like this,' I tell her.

'*Yoga for Beginners*,' she reads. She grins at me. 'Thanks. I wondered how you'd learnt all that stuff.' I am warmed by her smile, rosy as a Greek sunrise.

Back in Cecily's room, I lock the window. What if someone did break in? I check the bedside drawer. I'd left a stack of bills in the corner. They've gone. I check again. My heart thumps. Someone has taken fifty quid. But our mother's pearl necklace and gold brooch are still there. Perhaps the thief got disturbed and left. Perhaps it was Bea coming in from school that frightened them off? The thought of her alone in the house with a criminal dries my mouth. I'll have to own up to Gabriel. We might need to call the police.

'I'm afraid I left a window open when I went out today,' I admit, as I meet him in the kitchen. 'Could you check your stuff and make sure nothing is missing?'

'I'm sure everything's fine,' he says, lifting the lid on the casserole dish on the stove with a tea towel. 'This isn't exactly a crime-ridden area.' He takes his jacket off and hangs it on the back of a chair. 'I'm starving.'

'I'll serve it out – *after* you've made sure nothing's missing,' I say, holding my ground by the stove. I wave the wooden spoon in the direction of the door in a bossy fashion. Did Cecily ever behave like this?

He raises his eyebrows at me, clearly thinking I'm being paranoid, but does as I ask. He comes back five minutes later. 'All present and correct,' he says, slipping into his chair at the table. He's eaten a couple of mouthfuls before he looks at me, and I can see he's trying to find something positive to say about the food. 'Interesting,' he manages. 'Nothing of yours is missing, is it?'

'No,' I say, hiding my face in my glass of water. 'Nothing at all.'

'Okay then,' he says. 'All's well that ends well.'

Why did I lie to him? It just slipped out. I can't retract it now. Maybe I'm mistaken. Maybe I put the cash somewhere else, and I've forgotten. Like the trainers lined up neatly on the doormat.

* * *

As I get ready for bed, I stand on something small and hard. It digs into my sole and I yelp, bending down to unstick a tiny, green ball from my skin. I stare at it on my palm, and then realise it's a dried pea. I remember the bag of them stuffed into Cecily's drawer. I guess this one went astray and has been lying around all this time, and I never noticed it. Or has someone been through Cecily's drawers and disturbed her things? I remember Ambrose Stone. How he'd looked at me so intensely, interrogating me silently. He was suspicious of me. I open all the drawers and look closely at the things inside. Have they been tampered with? I can't tell.

I lie awake in my sister's double bed. Street lighting seeps through the blue curtains, bringing a faint colour, making the room oceanic, drowned shapes of furniture becoming water-logged, benthic. I can't sleep.

All those drawings of Hawksmoor, Cecily's memories pinned to paper, revisited and reshaped. The words she wrote about divorce and sin. The word 'DIE' written over and over. Is she still here in Exeter? Is she downing vodkas in a pub right now, having sex with a man? Was it her who came back to the house, who went through the drawers, took the cash, and moved her trainers? The puzzle goes round and round in my head, never falling into a pattern, resisting any sense. But one thing I do know is that the bond between us has gone, the invisible thread snapped. I thought it had been broken seventeen years ago, that snowy morning by the tarn when we'd argued. But then we'd found each other again through our letters, and I believed the connection between us had been restored, the shining cord pulled tight and secure again.

She's keeping secrets from me. Perhaps she always has.

27

CECILY

Nothing happened between me and Gabriel Greenwood for the rest of that year. Nothing that seemed in any way momentous. We smiled at each other in the lecture hall, and if we bumped into each other on the paths around campus, we stopped for a moment to talk about unimportant things, the weather, my studies. I tried not to say or do anything that would give him cause to pity me, or think me an oddball, and I took care to laugh in the way other girls did, with my head thrown back, and to look at him from under my lashes.

But however ordinary our conversations, our mutual awareness of the other was almost tangible, like a note resonating in the air, pinging back and forth between us, atoms fizzing and dancing. It was healing to have his attention.

One day he asked me why I was always alone. And I'd been truthful, no hair flicking or eyelash batting. 'I don't need anyone else,' I told him. 'I'm not like other people.' I waited for him to be repelled or embarrassed.

But he'd nodded. 'I can see that,' he'd said. 'I admire you for being true to yourself.'

Dear Alice,

I have something exciting to tell you! Yesterday, I was in Exmouth shopping centre when it started to pour, so I dashed for the nearest coffee house to get out of the rain and crashed into someone just inside the entrance. I was beginning to apologise when I realised who it was. Can you guess? The tutor I told you about!

'We may have to stay put for a while,' he said. 'Can I buy you a coffee?'

You can imagine how much I wanted to shout 'Yes!!' as loudly as I could – but you would have been proud of me. I managed a shrug and a casual, 'Okay. Why not?'

We sat at a corner table, making our drinks last. I'd been prepared for him to act the lecturer and do all the talking. But it was a proper conversation, with both of us taking turns to ask questions, listening, and answering.

For the first time, I spoke about Hawksmoor, and I could see how much it interested him. He's a historian, so of course the house is going to fascinate him.

He likes me, Alice. I know he does. He had to get back to Uni, and nothing was said or arranged. But I have a feeling that this isn't the end. I think it's the beginning of something.

Write soon.

Love Cecily

I left some things out of the letter. I didn't think there was any point in telling her that I'd lied to Gabriel about being an only child. It would just hurt her feelings and she might not accept that I had to keep up Daddy's pretence. I understood Daddy's reasoning: Henry had committed the sin of suicide, and Alice had betrayed our religion by going to a kibbutz and she'd betrayed our family by abandoning us. It wasn't all my fault.

Once I'd told the lie, I couldn't un-tell it.

* * *

Easter at Hawksmoor. Father Michael, hurrying from his flock at St Mary's to give us communion at home, was more shrunken inside his white and gold finery than ever as he intoned over Easter Vigil Midnight

Mass with trembling hands, his foul breath spewing the stench of cat food and rotting vegetal matter over us as we knelt with bowed heads. Tall candles spluttered, spinning shadows over Daddy's face as he accepted the body of Christ onto his tongue. Then Father Michael was speaking over me, but I couldn't stop my mind from flitting back to the moment in the café when Gabriel had said it was time to leave, and how I'd taken my chance, daring to rest my fingers on his wrist. 'Maybe we could do this again sometime?'

He'd jerked away from my touch, shoving his hand into his jacket pocket, stumbling over his chair as he got to his feet, cheeks flushed, his expression a fusion of embarrassment and regret. 'I... I'm sorry, Cecily. It's probably not a good idea.'

I'd felt my own face redden. Had I got it wrong? Made a fool of myself, again? But I didn't need him to voice his attraction to me. It was there in the way he opened his body towards me, the softness in his eyes, pupils overspilling with darkness. He liked me. He just couldn't admit it to a student. I knew then that something would happen between us eventually. I was certain of it. We would keep meeting, bumping into each other. It was a matter of chemistry and physics. The story of love repeating itself.

Gabriel wasn't wealthy or Catholic. But he could convert, and he loved history, so he'd respect Hawksmoor. He could talk to Daddy about the things he was interested in – great country houses, the Civil War, Tudors and Plantagenets. My mind rushed on, imagining the future. When Gabriel became my boyfriend, and later, who knows, my husband, then he'd direct his passion into Hawksmoor, becoming my companion and support when we lived here.

At lunch the next day, as soon as the blessing was over, my parents picked up their knives and forks. I endured the chomp of teeth and smack of lips, as we concentrated on the meal that a girl from the village had prepared and served. Mummy had whispered to me earlier that nobody could conjure a meal out of scraps like Jane. The Labs lay stranded on their rotund bellies, wheezing under the table. Dilly, now blind, was curled in Mummy's lap.

After a few minutes of silence, I put down my fork. 'I'm doing well at my studies, Daddy,' I said, looking at him expectantly. 'My tutor says I'm on track to get a good 2:1, maybe even a First.'

He shot me a brief disbelieving glare and pushed some carrot and slice of folded meat into his mouth, chewing methodically.

'That's wonderful, darling,' Mummy said, blotting her lips with her napkin, glancing at Daddy.

'I was thinking of doing a law conversion course after my degree,' I went on eagerly. 'I could earn a lot as a solicitor, or even a barrister.'

'The subject of money is vulgar,' Daddy snapped. 'And I won't have idle chatter at the table. Especially on a Sunday.'

Why don't you love me? The childish words caught inside me. *Why can't you see how hard I'm trying?*

I could never replace Alice, never make up for the loss of Henry and all he'd seemed to promise for Hawksmoor, for the future. But the house would be mine, after Daddy was dead, it would belong to me. There were no other male heirs, and although Daddy wouldn't want it to go to a woman, I would find a way to save it from ruin. Daddy must know that, even if he couldn't speak of it to me. He knew how much the house meant to me, how it bound us together.

I forced myself to swallow greasy beef and chunks of potato, soggy with gravy. Leaving anything on my plate would draw more of Daddy's disapproval. He was like a wounded tiger, still hurting from the pain the other two had inflicted on him, still stunned by their betrayal. He'd never been comfortable with expressing softer sentiments. I'd always had to look below the surface, hunting for the unspoken truth of his love for me in small gestures and glances, things that could easily be missed by someone less vigilant.

I walked through the house after lunch, going into the vast kitchen, where the new girl hunched over the sink washing the lunch dishes. I glanced into the cobwebby scullery and empty buttery, remembering Jude's joke about butts. The boot room smelt fusty with old dog collars and piles of wellingtons, ancient soles rimmed with desiccated clumps of mud, although it was emptier without the others' things. In the drawing room, I ran my fingers over dusty furniture, fondling folds of Miss Haversham-style curtains. I stroked the dulled pewter curves and plates of the suit of armour.

In the corridor to the left of the main staircase, I noticed the last of the blood red Chinese porcelain vases was missing. The one with a crack in it, from when Henry had knocked it off with a tennis ball. Between the portraits hanging on the wainscotting, two naked rectangles glared at me. The missing paintings had been my favourites, especially the one by Leon Bonnat of two sisters embracing. My throat constricted. For years, Daddy had been selling off the contents of the house. I placed my palm flat inside the outline of the missing Bonnat and closed my eyes. I thought I could sense a pulse throbbing weakly deep inside the fibres of the ancient oak panelling.

I continued my pilgrimage upstairs and sat on Alice's stripped bed in her old room; the stained ticking mattress sagging beneath me. The wardrobe and chest of drawers were empty of anything except moth balls and withered conkers. I took out her latest letter and unfolded it.

Dear Cecily,

Sorry it's been a while since I've written, but I got your letter about Gabriel just before I left for Greece. (I've enclosed my new address here.) I gave up being an au pair – the father turned out to be a creep, and the kids were hard work. I've been travelling with a couple of the people I made friends with on the kibbutz. They came to see me in Paris and persuaded me to go with them. (Didn't take a lot of persuading!) We're staying on Mykonos and I've got a job in a bar owned by an English couple. I live above the bar, and my room faces the back yard, full of flies and hot as an oven, but the work is easy, and every morning I swim in the Aegean Sea, and meet up with the other two to explore the island. Down on the quay, grizzled old men mend nets, while hopeful pelicans look for a free lunch. Donkeys are led up and down the cobbled streets, the baskets on their backs full of vegetables and olives. There's a boy here, an Italian guy, with the biggest moustache I've ever seen, who says he can get me work in a Mexican circus as a dancing girl! Can you imagine how exciting that would be!

I'm so happy you've clicked with Gabriel. He sounds lovely. Older men are so sexy! Fingers crossed that he asks you out soon.

Have you been back to Hawksmoor recently? How is Mummy? I won't ask about him. But I'm guessing he's as mean and bad tempered as ever. It must be strange to be there without me and Henry. I have dreams about Henry sometimes – I'm there on the roof, and I manage to catch him before he jumps. But in other dreams, he slips through my fingers, and I watch him tumbling through space. I wake up crying.

Love, Alice

I crumpled the letter inside my fist. I'd tried to tell her the truth abou what happened that day, but I always ended up ripping my efforts int pieces. I didn't want her to hate me.

* * *

'Henry?' I'd whispered through his locked bedroom door, my hand fla against the wood.

'Cecily? Thank God.' His voice was just the other side, sharp with fea and hope. 'What's going on? Where's Jude?'

'You're going to be alright. Daddy's sending you to a doctor.'

'A doctor? What do you mean?'

'Some sort of therapist I think he said. I overheard him talking t Mummy in the drawing room.'

There was silence, and then his voice came again. 'Unlock the doo Cecily.'

'I can't.' I'd taken a step back, scalded by his request.

'Please. I just want to talk. I want to hear more about the doctor – wh Daddy said about the therapy.'

The key was in the lock. What could be the harm? After all, I had goo news.

His clothes and hair were still gritty with dust from his punishment i the priest hole, cobwebs draped over his shoulder like a ghostly han He'd looked at me with such need, it made me feel important. I'd sat c the bed next to him. 'It's alright,' I'd said again. 'You're going to be cured of your illness. You'll go away for a bit. There are special drugs.'

'What about Jude? Where is he?'

I'd thought about what I'd seen that morning – Jude's expression as he'd got into the car and been driven away. 'He's gone, Henry. He's been sent away.'

Henry had let out a low moan. 'Did he leave a message for me? He must have left a message?'

The hunger in his face seemed wrong, embarrassing. I'd looked away, thinking quickly about the right thing to tell him. 'He said he didn't want to see you again,' I'd said. 'He said to forget him. He knows it was a mistake. What happened between you. It was deviant. Sinful.'

'No,' he'd shuddered, 'I don't believe you.'

'I'm sorry, Henry, but it's true.' I'd held his desperate gaze with a steady return, reminding myself that I must not blink or look away. He had to believe me.

Then Henry's face contorted, and a twist of anguished sobbing came from him, rising into a visceral howl. I was afraid it would bring Daddy thumping up the stairs and shushed him. He took no notice. Bent over, as if he'd been punched, he slumped with his face in his hands, the howl breaking down into snuffles and choking sounds, his shoulders juddering. Next to him, I'd clasped my palms between my thighs, my body rigid, wishing he'd stop and behave normally, make a joke, swear, call me Cilly. Anything but this awful display of emotion.

'Henry. You'll be fine,' I'd said briskly. 'You'll be normal again.'

He'd straightened, scrubbing at his snotty face with his knuckles. 'Normal?' He'd given a short half-laugh, then he'd stood up with sudden intention and walked towards the door.

'Where are you going?' I'd trailed after him. 'Daddy will be angry if you leave the room.'

'Stay here.' He'd rounded on me, his voice fierce. 'Don't follow me.'

'Are you coming back?'

He'd given me a long look and shaken his head. 'I'm not going to let him win.'

I'd been frightened by the cold, calm set of his features. His dead, dry eyes. All his passion suddenly gone. But perhaps that was a good sign.

After he'd gone, I'd waited a moment, angry that he didn't care about getting me into trouble. He should have been relieved about getting help, pleased about the news I'd brought him. I'd left his room cautiously, looking up and down the corridor. Henry was nowhere to be seen.

I wonder now if I'd heard the creak of floorboards on the steps up to the attic as I'd slipped into my own room – but even if I had, how could I have known his intentions?

I didn't hear him hit the ground. It was Mummy's scream that sent me running to my window, looking down, not interpreting the shape on the gravel at first. Then with a gasp, reeling back in horror.

How could I tell Alice? She wouldn't understand that I'd only been trying to do the right thing.

28

ALICE

The only clues I have are Cecily's drawings and the weird bits of writing she's scrawled around her sketches. I go upstairs and pull the wicker hamper out from under the bed. Sitting on the ground, I examine every drawing again, every sketch, every word she's written. I take out the little notebook and find some blank pages, copying out her scribbled sentences:

Till death do us part.
No impact on legal status.
A marriage continues in the eyes of God.
Never ending.
He'll disown me.

They suggest two simple facts: neither the Catholic church nor our father will accept divorce as an end to marriage. Only the death of husband or wife can end the pact.

She's still bound by her faith, her vows, her need for Daddy's approval. She's not going to divorce Gabriel. She'll only be free when he's dead. '*DIE*' she's written over and over. '*DIE, DIE, DIE*'. I remember Jude's words. *I'm afraid she might be about to do something terrible.* Did he mean something murderous? The greatest sin of all. I can't believe that, and yet, a cold fear creeps inside me. It's Gabriel who needs to die, if she's going to be free.

I sit with my legs sprawled out, unable to make sense of it.

* * *

I wake up on the floor, feeling dehydrated and disorientated, Cecily's drawings spread out around me. I check her watch, and stagger to my feet. My head is spinning and the room lurches under me. Bea will be back from school soon. I go into the bathroom and splash my face with water, gulping it straight from the tap. By the time I hear the front door open, I've managed to clear my head and I go down to say hello. Bea grins when she sees me and drops her school bag on the floor. 'I'll just get changed,' she says, running upstairs to her room. Doing yoga is the last thing I feel like, but I started her on this habit, and it will do us both good.

I pull the curtains, so I won't be distracted by shadows at the bay window. We do forty minutes of yoga; Bea stands in tree pose better than me, keeping completely still and focused. I feel shaky, my balance gone, as if I'm ill. I'm obliged to keep putting my foot down. I'm grateful when we lie on the floor at the end. After we've put the mat away and I've opened the curtains, Gabriel arrives home.

This has become my favourite time, I realise, as we sit together at the table talking about our days, passing each other the salt or pepper, making plans for the weekend. But this evening, I'm not hungry. The food makes me feel sick, and I finish my glass of water and pour out another.

'I've invited Lily over this Saturday,' Bea says. 'Is that alright?'

'Of course,' I say. 'It'll be nice to meet her.'

'I have an extra choir rehearsal,' Gabriel says. 'Cecily, I wondered if you wanted to come?'

'Yeah,' I say. 'That would be great.'

'We're looking for a new soprano,' he says. 'If you wanted, you could give it a try?'

'Me?' I stare at him. 'I'm not sure I could...'

'You wouldn't have to audition,' he says. 'It's just for fun. You can sing in tune, and that's really all that matters.'

'Oh, go on,' Bea says. 'Isn't that what you said to me about yoga? You don't know till you've given it a try.'

'Our daughter speaks words of wisdom,' Gabriel says, only half suppressing his grin.

I get up from the table on the pretext of filling the water jug. The cruellest aspect of this swap is that it's put me at the centre of a family that doesn't belong to me – offered me chances I couldn't take. I blot my eyes on a tea towel. I don't know what's the matter with me. I've never wanted this kind of life.

* * *

After Bea goes upstairs to do her homework, Gabriel and I carry cups of tea into the sitting room with the intention of seeing if there's anything worth watching on television. We put the cups down on the coffee table, but before I can pick up the remote control or slump into the sofa, Gabriel has turned me by the shoulders to face him. His fingers slip down my arms, holding me. We look at each other and the question is there again in his eyes, his longing like a live creature, something leaving cover, driven by instinct and need. I can't close myself against it. This evening I'm not strong enough to resist the expression of his wanting, his honesty. He puts out a hand and cups my cheek, and I take his fingers and touch his palm to my mouth. He lets out a sigh. Our arms are tangling around each other, my fingers in the soft fibres of his hair. His mouth is gentle against mine, exploring, and then firmer, urgent, and I sink into the kiss, the warmth and relief of it.

I pull away, my hands on his chest, breathing heavily.

He looks shocked. He blinks at me. 'God. I'm sorry.'

There's a prickling sensation at the back of my scalp. Something moves in the periphery of my sight. A disturbance of air behind the glass. A pale shape turning away, darkened sockets where eyes should be, a fall of inky hair across a cheekbone. She's behind the bay window. I know it before my mind can catch up, before my body can act. I spin around. The emptiness of night hangs beyond a sheen of reflection. The outside masked. But the impression of her is there, lasered across my vision.

Pushing past Gabriel, I shout, 'Stop!' stumbling around the sofa, into the hall. Three strides and I'm at the front door, wrenching it open. I dash to the end of the garden path, out past the privet hedge, and I'm yelling into the dark street, 'I know you're there!' I think I can see her, a shape moving out of the glow of a streetlight into shadows. 'Come back!' I scream. In the sky, the moon moves behind clouds.

Gabriel is behind me, his hand closing around my arm. 'Cecily, what are you doing? Who are you shouting at?'

'Nobody. I thought... I thought I saw someone...' I'm not wearing shoes. The ground is damp from a recent shower, the bottoms of my socks soggy.

'Darling, come inside.' He guides me back into the house, walking me into the kitchen. I'm shivering. 'Sit down,' he says, and I obey. He kneels at my feet, peeling off my socks. 'You're cold. Maybe you should have a bath,' he says. 'It'll warm you up. I can make you a fresh cup of tea.'

My teeth chatter. I try to stop them, pushing my hand against my mouth.

He's looking at me with concern. Another unspoken question fixed there. A different question, about the state of my mind.

'Sorry,' I say. 'I'm fine. Really. Just... a bit on edge.'

'Did the kiss upset you?' He's still crouching at my feet. 'I don't want you to worry about us,' he says softly. 'We can take this slow. I'm not expecting anything. Not until you're ready.'

He stands and holds out his hand to help me out of the chair. 'I love you, Cecily,' he says simply. We stand facing each other, and I pull my fingers from his grip, shaking my head. 'I'm fine,' I repeat. 'I'll go and have that bath.'

I force myself to walk away. He's not mine.

But she doesn't deserve him.

29

CECILY

Being in love had not been good for my grades. I'd lost focus, despite Gabriel reminding me to finish my essays, despite his offers to help me study. My mind had given up its grasp on work. I hadn't understood the power of sex, how the longing for it stayed with me while I walked about campus and sat in lectures. I felt a constant yearning low in my belly, a tug of desire between my thighs. I wanted him while I stood in line for a sandwich in the canteen, while I brushed my teeth in the bathroom of the dingy flat I shared with three final-year students. I couldn't wait to be in Gabriel's bed, in his little flat in Exeter, where I was the centre of his gaze, the object of his desire. With the sound of seagulls screaming outside the window, I gave myself up to tenderness. He reshaped me with his touch, made me part of his world, erased my loneliness. I felt almost whole again.

* * *

I unwrapped the second pregnancy test, praying the first had been faulty. Sitting on the loo, I squeezed out some drops of urine, catching them on the little stick. I remained on the seat with it in my hands watching the small aperture. Two blue lines appeared.

I stood up with difficulty, legs numb from sitting, the imprint of the loo seat stinging the backs of my thighs as I threw the stick in the bin and pulled up my knickers. I placed my hands over my belly. An alien was growing deep inside me. I tried to imagine what this thing looked like – a cluster of cells, smaller than my little fingernail – I was hazy about the exact proportions. I didn't feel any different, but I understood with a clench of fear, that in Daddy's eyes, I'd be a monster. Unmarried and pregnant made me a whore, a slut, a fallen woman. He would despise me. Mummy would pity me. The thought of him knowing made me tumble onto my knees in front of the loo, bringing up the remains of my breakfast in a sour splatter.

I waited in the cold for Gabriel to finish a tutorial. As soon as he appeared through the door, I got up from my seat on a nearby wall and approached him. He was obviously mid-conversation with a student and looked startled when he saw me striding purposefully towards him. He moved away from the boy at his side, glancing furtively around. For a flickering second his obvious fear made me hate him. I was sick of pretending I hardly knew him when we met in public, sick of lying to my flatmates about where I spent half my nights.

'What's the matter?' he asked in a low voice, careful not to touch me.

'I'm pregnant,' I said, unable to contain it for even a moment.

He took a sharp breath and clutched my arm. Holding me close to his side, we walked swiftly away from the crowd of students, winding through the campus towards the playing fields. It was midday and bleakly cold. There was nobody playing a match, and we huddled together out of the wind behind the changing rooms.

'Are you sure?' he asked, his forehead wrinkled. 'These things can be wrong...'

'I've done two tests. My period is weeks late.' My anxiety wiped out any embarrassment.

He looked down at his blunt hands, and I could tell that he was considering what to say. He cleared his throat and looked at me. 'What do you want to do, Cecily?'

I stared at him. Did he really think I had a choice? 'I can't get rid of it, if that's what you mean.' I shoved my hands in my pockets so he wouldn't see them tremble. 'We... we need to get married. If I have this baby as a single mother, my father will never talk to me again.'

'Are you sure that's what you want?' he said gently. 'You're very young... to be tied down.'

I snapped my head up. 'You mean *you* don't want to be tied down.' Nerves jangled. 'Is this your way of telling me you won't marry me?'

His face widened in shock. 'No,' he caught one of my hands and held it tightly. 'No, of course not. I'm just saying that it's a lot of responsibility to have a kid, and...'

I snatched my hand away, frustrated. 'I told you when we met that I was Catholic. Weren't you listening?'

'I hadn't factored in this situation,' he said, rubbing his forehead. 'Your religion didn't seem to make any difference to us – to how we were together.'

'Well, it does now.' Panic scrawled through me, tangling into knots of terror. Daddy might disinherit me – if he could pretend his other children never existed, he could easily do the same to me. A gust of air snapped around the corner, slapping my cheeks, whipping my hair back. I shivered as I visualised Hawksmoor without me, the house expunged of any trace of me.

'We'll get married,' he said. 'If that's what you want.'

Relief was like a plug being pulled. Fear drained away, taking all my strength with it and I slumped against him. His arms went around me, and I pressed my face into the sturdy, familiar warmth of his chest, the nap of his jacket. He kissed the top of my head.

'You'll have to convert,' I murmured. 'You'll have to convert to Catholicism.'

With a muffled exclamation, he moved me away, gripping me above my elbows. 'I'm an atheist,' he told me. 'I can't become a Catholic or join any other religion. I'd be lying if I agreed to be converted.'

'For me?' I pleaded. 'Couldn't you just go through the motions, for me?'

He shook his head. 'I'll support your choice of religion, but I won't join it.'

Why had I never asked him about converting before? Had I known deep down that he wouldn't do it, and so avoided the confrontation? Or had I simply felt that there was plenty of time to discuss it in the future? The real problem, I knew, was that I hadn't been thinking at all. But I should have checked. As soon as we slept together, I should have asked the question.

I began to bite my fingernails. He closed his hands around them stopping me. 'You've just managed to kick that habit,' he said quietly. 'Look, I can't pretend that this is ideal timing, and I know this must feel frightening, but we'll get through it, Cecily. I'm not going to desert you now.'

Tears stung my eyes. 'I've trapped you, haven't I?'

'We're in this together. Look, we used protection. But it's never 100 per cent safe. I knew that. I took the risk too.' He pulled me close, 'I love you, Cecily. I would have asked you to marry me anyway. This has just speeded things up.'

Dear Daddy and Mummy,

I have some exciting news. I'm going to be married! He's a tutor here at the university. Dr Gabriel Greenwood. A history academic, with brilliant ideas. I know he'll go far. He makes me very happy. I know it's sudden, and I'm sorry not to talk to you about it or introduce you to him, but we've decided to get married soon, without any fuss. But of course, it would mean so much if you could both attend the ceremony.

Daddy wrote back with one line asking if Gabriel was Catholic. I sent a return letter to say that he wasn't yet, implying that he might convert in the future.

Dear Cecily,

Your mother and I will not be attending your wedding. You are marrying outside the faith, and without my permission. The fact that your prospective husband hasn't had the decency to ask me for your hand is unforgivable, as is the fact that he is one of your tutors, a position of trust that he has clearly broken.

My first instinct was to report him to the university, and you have your mother to thank for the fact that I have agreed not to pursue the matter.

You have always been a disappointment, Cecily. But with this marriage you exceed my worst predictions for you.

I cried in my room, the letter crushed in my fist. I'd made a mistake. I could see how I'd been seduced by love, by the relief of belonging to someone, and how it had thrown me off course. I shivered when I realised that my love affair could cost me Hawksmoor and Daddy.

I sat up, scrubbing at my eyes. I'd work extra hard to win Daddy back, to get him to accept my marriage and my husband. I would restore his faith in me; after all, our love for Hawksmoor still united us.

I wasn't ready to be a mother, and I didn't think I ever would be. I shouldn't have got pregnant. There was a darkness inside me. I was afraid for my unborn child, curled up inside the womb of someone like me – I was sure the poor thing would be consumed with nightmares before they even took a breath of air.

The baby began to make itself known to me. I started to experience morning sickness, and the name made me laugh, because the metallic taste in my mouth and my unsettled tummy lasted all day. I sat my finals feeling awful, nauseous and tired, swallowing down bile as I leant over my papers.

I got a Third, and Bea was born seven months later in Exeter hospital. I gazed into the wizened, puckered face of my small daughter with a mix of amazement and fear. A grandson might have swayed my father, I thought.

30

CECILY

Hollyhocks Cottage is in darkness, curtains closed behind blank windows, as if the house itself is shutting me out. I imagine my child dreaming in her bed, beneath her poster of Courtney Love, hair spread on the pillow, drool dampening a patch of cotton under her mouth. It hurts not to be with her, and it's strange to think that she doesn't miss me, that she doesn't know I'm standing here, alone in the damp night. Sukie watches me from under the shadow of the privet hedge with unblinking eyes. Her feline gaze doesn't judge me for prowling the streets when most people are asleep behind locked doors. 'Puss, puss,' I whisper, clicking my tongue. She ignores me, putting her nose in the air.

It's nearly midnight. I'm not expecting Gabriel or Alice to peer out of their windows, but I feel exposed under the streetlight. I walk on, turning my collar up against a dirty drizzle, my feet stumbling over the kerb as I cross between parked cars. The tarmac swings under me, a woozy see-saw motion, and I clutch my bag tighter, concentrating hard on putting one foot in front of the other. Walking in a not-quite straight line, I head uphill towards the castle ruins.

How easily she's stolen my family. They don't belong to her. Alice is only here because of me. She threw her future away and now I've let her take over my life. I thought she could help me, but I should never have agreed to the swap.

When I saw that she'd moved the sofa and table, it upset me, but I'd resisted putting them back where they belonged, and I've left her weird food in my fridge. I don't want her to know I've been there, in the house, or that I go there still. But when I saw the plants in the living room, I had to act fast. She couldn't bring living things into my house. She must know that I can't be trusted to look after them. Things die on my watch, even when I don't want them to.

It's past closing time, and The Royal Oak only do lock-ins on Saturdays. But I have a bottle of vodka in my bag. Drinking alone at the castle gatehouse isn't so bad. I have the foxes and owls for company. I like being high up. Below, the lit-up town takes on a festive sparkle, the navy sky above steeped in a sodium glow. Most of the time, I have the place to myself, unless I take a man with me, letting him fuck me as he pinions me between him and the cold wall, the back of my skull banging rhythmically against stone, the point of a belt buckle digging into my stomach. There are different ways of achieving oblivion.

* * *

It might be the next morning, or several mornings later, that I enter the Sacred Heart. Time jumps and slides, playing games with me, stealing hours, and then catapulting me forward into a new day with no warning. All I know is that my head pounds and my mouth is parched. I slip into a pew and kneel, clasping my hands at my forehead. The calm of the church seeps into my tight muscles, and the sensation is like cool milk running through the avenues of my body.

Forgive my weakness, Jesus. But I have been sorely tested.

I sneak a glance towards the stained-glass window, wondering if the forgiving light of the Lord will shine on me, if the Virgin herself will whisper encouraging words in my ear. But all I hear is earthly murmuring and the rustle of feet moving down the aisle, people shifting on their knees in other pews.

I clasp my fingers tighter. *Forgive me for what I am about to do. I know it's a sin. The worst one. Give me the strength to carry out my task. I have been too afraid. But it must be done, or I will never be free. I will pay whatever penance you ask of me.*

I close my eyes and imagine the Virgin laying her cool hand on my forehead. *I understand, my child.*

'Cecily.'

My eyes snap open. Instead of a heavenly presence, Ambrose Stone looms over me, his narrow face concertinaed in anxiety. 'I don't want to interrupt your prayer,' he says, although he already has. 'I just wanted to say that I'm glad to see you. And if you'd like me to pray with you, I'll be happy to kneel alongside you.'

I bet you would, you dirty old man, I think. But I shake my head and close my eyes again, waiting for him to go away. I have a horrible feeling that he knows what's in my heart. He looks at me as if he can see all my secrets. Did I speak my prayer out loud?

31

ALICE

Saturday morning. Gabriel gets back from his run and has a shower. I'm in the kitchen eating a piece of toast with my coffee. He comes in and helps himself to a cup. He's flushed and damp from the shower. 'Hey.' He touches my shoulder, smiling. 'Morning.' He puts some bread in the toaster. 'I'm glad you've started to eat breakfast again,' he remarks.

I stop chewing, remembering that I'm not supposed to eat until lunch. I swallow. Cecily spent most of her childhood worrying about her weight. She thought Daddy would only approve of her if she was thin, but both of us had the same rangy, bony frames we'd inherited from our parents. She used to prod her stomach, asking, 'Do you think I've got fat?' and Henry would say, 'I can see the wind whistling through your ribs, you nitwit.'

Gabriel sits opposite me and tucks into his toast and marmalade. He wipes his mouth. 'Last night,' he says slowly, and I brace myself for questions about my screams into the dark street. 'When we kissed... it felt different.'

The give of his lips, the push of his tongue against mine. My heart bangs out a warning. I twitch one shoulder. 'Oh,' I say. 'Can't explain that.' Then, aiming for humour, 'Was it worse, or better?' Trying to make light of it. But I want to know.

He laughs again, a throaty wicked laugh. 'Let's just say I liked it. Actually, when I say it felt different, really it reminded me of how things used to be between us.' He gives a self-deprecating laugh. 'It's been a long time, and I suppose I'd forgotten how passionate you were.'

I let out a breath. He's so close to knowing the truth. I can sense it in his thoughtful, searching expression; he can feel the change in me, the differences that go deeper than a more passionate kiss. But he can't possibly know that Cecily has a mirror-image twin. The answer he's looking for will always evade him.

I want to shatter the mirror, tell him the truth. I want him to know who I am so that I can claim his feelings as my own. But he'd feel trickec and betrayed. His love doesn't belong to me. Except, it does. It's me he's reacting to, not her. She doesn't want him.

'You've got a mark in your left eye,' Gabriel is saying.

'What?'

He's leaning towards me, squinting. 'A tiny black mark. Like a scar Have you done something to your eye recently?'

'Have I?' I place my palm over my cheek. 'Oh. No. That was a long time ago. An accident when I was little.'

'I love the colour of your eyes.' He's smiling. 'All the shades of autumn are in them. Conkers and turning leaves, wet grass. Mud.'

'Mud?' I slap his arm and laugh, relieved. 'Very romantic.'

* * *

I make parsnip and apple soup, a simple recipe from one of he cookbooks. I add seasoning and leave it on the stove ready for lunch an go upstairs. Cecily's bunch of keys is lying on the dresser. It occurs to m that she could easily have copied them before she gave them to me – sh could have let herself in, she didn't need to climb through a window t take the money. Maybe she just wanted it to look like she had, making u think a casual thief had broken in, an opportunist who'd spotted a unlocked window. I pick up the jangling bunch, examining the small ke that dangles amongst the other three. One for the front door, one for th back door, one for the garden gate, and this smaller one that I've neve considered before. I'd vaguely thought it might be for a bicycle lock there is a bike under a cover in the garden. My eyes fall on the ornate dresser with the locked bottom drawer. I'd assumed she would have hidden the key in her room somewhere, but she could have hidden it in plain sight.

It fits, turning easily, and the drawer slides open. Below me, something coils in the shadows. I flinch away, but it's motionless, inanimate. Pulling it out, I find a rough, woven handle attached to seven cords, each with a knot tied tight at the end, knobbly and fibrous, like the knuckles of a small, fighting creature. A scourge. It flops across my palm, and I think of the white shirt with the bloody streaks across the back. What was my sister atoning for? It makes me shudder to think of her here in this room, kneeling with her arm raised, clutching the handle, and then a flick, a twist of rope over her shoulder, the bite at her back.

There's something else at the bottom of the drawer, a clump of green. I reach for it, and I'm holding a handful of a wilted, pointed yew needles, dark and musty with age. I suspect that they come from our ancient yew on the front lawn at Hawksmoor, and she's kept them here for some reason, perhaps a memento of home.

The scent of soup jolts me, returning me to the normality of the ordinary day. It seems impossible and dreadful that Cecily whipped herself here in this room like an old-fashioned martyr, while her husband and child moved through the neighbouring spaces, unaware.

I sniff the air. Gabriel must be reheating the soup for lunch. I put the yew leaves away and coil the ropes on top of them. I worry that the poisonous scent clings to my hands, and rub my palms over my jeans, but when I sniff my fingers, there's no odour.

In the kitchen, the soup is bubbling on the stove, Gabriel busy getting spoons and bowls out. The back door is unlocked and ajar, letting in cool air and a splash of sunshine.

'Good idea,' I say, gesturing towards the garden. 'It's almost warm enough to have it open all the time.'

Gabriel is ladling the soup into bowls. 'I didn't open it. I thought you did,' he says.

Till death do us part.

I stare at him, watching as he dips a crust of bread into a bowl and brings the liquid up to his mouth.

DIE, DIE, DIE.

'Stop!' I shout, and grab the bread from his hand, sweeping the bowls of soup onto the floor. They hit the ground, exploding, shattering, coming apart in fragments that bounce and slide, a swill of pale, boiling liquid flooding across the surface, dripping down the cabinets, pooling on the flagstones.

He makes a startled exclamation, and stares at me. I look back, open-mouthed. Time opens like a sinkhole, a smooth, long tunnelling into darkness, with us teetering on the edge. I am dizzy with vertigo.

He crouches, beginning to pick sharp remnants of broken pottery out of the pale-yellow puddles. I squat on my haunches near him, but when I touch a shard, the edge catches my skin, I wince, putting my finger in my mouth, tasting blood. I'd been certain, a second ago, that Cecily had poisoned the soup. But I don't know anything any more. Would she murder her husband to be free of him? My sister? Would she really do that? Would she, in cold-blood, plan to poison Gabriel? We were all going to eat the soup. She wouldn't kill her own daughter, or me – would she?

I push onto my feet and slump over the kitchen surface, faint, confusion spinning inside, my head in my hands. She's tricked me into taking her place. If she's planning his murder, perhaps she needs me to be her lookalike alibi – or her scapegoat. 'I think I'm going mad,' I whisper.

I feel his arms around me, and I'm leaning into him, my face pressed into the solid shape of his shoulder. My head whirls, and I close my eyes tightly and take deep breaths to fight the rising tide of nausea. He doesn't move, providing a sturdy prop to my trembling limbs. When the giddy feeling drains away, I straighten and step back, attempting to arrange my features into a reassuring expression.

He picks up my hand and examines the small cut, then leads me to the sink like a child and holds it under the cold tap. It stings. The tiny mouth oozes red. He wraps a piece of kitchen towel around it. 'You'll live,' he says. He scratches his head as he stares at the mess still dripping over the kitchen cabinets and gleaming on the floor, viscous splashes sliding down the walls. 'I'm sure the soup would have tasted delicious,' he says. 'I know you're a perfectionist, but...'

He's trying to make a joke out of it. I manage a quivering smile. 'Yeah. Forgot to salt it,' I say.

We kneel together with a bowl of soapy water and cloths, soaking up the soup, wiping the flagstones clean; behind his veneer of calm, he shoots puzzled glances at me, and I sense a storm of unanswered questions inside him. He doesn't know that I'm rocked by them, too.

32

CECILY

Finally, after a day's travel, a night in a B & B, and more driving today, we were nearly there. The landscape either side of the motorway had grown familiar in its tumbled shades of green. I could see mountains in the distance, dark peaks pushing into a hazy sky. Excitement fizzed in the pit of my stomach. Home. It had been so long. I hadn't been back since becoming pregnant. As Gabriel turned the car off the main road and we negotiated narrow lanes, I stared out of the passenger window at drystone walls running like grey spines across vast valleys and hillsides, sheep grazing peacefully, a hawk hovering above a verge.

There'd been no murmur from Bea for hours, strapped into her seat in the back. I slipped out of my safety belt to lean between the front seats, craning my neck to check on her. She was asleep, her small, red face scrunched and flickering with unknown dreams. As I watched, she began to whimper and snuffle, turning her face from side to side, rooting for food. In response, my breasts tingled with a warm rush of milk. 'Damn.' I hauled myself back into my seat, feeling slightly sick from the motion of the car. 'Can we pull over somewhere? I need to feed her before we get there.'

'Sure,' Gabriel said. 'I need a pee, too. But we've made good time.'

We had to drive for another five minutes, Bea howling, before we found an open gate into woodland, and Gabriel parked under a beech tree. He got out, hands flat on his lower spine, groaning. 'Back's stiffened up,' he said, stretching his muscles. 'Need any help?'

'No.' I smiled. 'I'll get her out and perch somewhere. Warm enough. You go and do what you've got to do.'

He disappeared into the trees, and I unclipped a crying Bea from the car seat and took her over to a fallen oak. Sitting on the broad, knobbly wings of its back, I unfastened my bra, and tucked Bea's head under the loose folds of my shirt. I winced as she latched on, the agony of the baby's suction still a shock. I tried to relax. Bea had been fretful and colicky since getting back from hospital, weeks ago. Every night was one long round of feeding and pacing the bedroom with a screaming baby. I had never felt so exhausted and overwhelmed – part of me somehow lost, the rest of me weakened, uncertain. But I was going home. Hawksmoor would return me to myself.

Gabriel appeared out of the bushes. He sat beside us, staring down in wonder at Bea's downy head. 'She's been a good traveller, hasn't she?'

'It's been a miracle to have hours of peace.'

'You should have slept too. I kept telling you to.'

'I didn't want to desert you. It's a very long drive.'

He smiled and kissed my forehead. 'Such a stubborn creature.'

We sat together in the sunshine, under a fall of birdsong and leaf shadow. In the distance, sheep baaed, and between us, the contented suckling noise of our child carried on softly. Gabriel put his arm around my shoulder, and I leant into his chest and sighed. All my blank exhaustion and my flaming nipples were worth it for this.

* * *

'We're here,' I inched onto the edge of my seat, craning my head to take it all in. The tall, rusted gates were closed for once, and I got out to heave them open. We drove through, wheels crunching along the drive. The grounds were a wild riot of tangled trees, thick with creepers, and long grasses.

'It's like entering Sleeping Beauty's palace,' Gabriel said, as he changed down a gear. 'Good grief, does all this land belong to yo family?'

'Most of it's been sold off over the years,' I said. 'But I suppose t grounds are still pretty big.'

'Grounds?' he laughed. 'Normal people have gardens, if they're lucky

Thorns shrieked along the sides of the car. Overhead, twigs reach with stiff fingers towards the roof. As we turned the final corner, t house rose before us like a fortress, and there was the yew tree, familiar spreading branches welcoming me home. But it was cordon off with a square of electric fencing. And there was the surprise sheep cropping the lawn, wandering across the weedy gravel. T animals turned yellow eyes towards us, unconcerned, twitching stum tails.

Gabriel parked next to the old Volvo and turned the engine off.

'Darling,' I said, putting my hand on his thigh, 'when you meet n father,' I paused, choosing my words, 'just be aware that he's a bit o fashioned. Manners are important to him.'

'Don't worry.' Gabriel grinned. 'I won't let you down – I'm not complete heathen.'

But I was filled with sudden doubt. When we were children, Dad made us practise shaking hands with him, 'Keep eye contact,' he'd s 'Firm grip.' 'Don't be a sissy, Henry,' he'd say. 'Press harder. You wo make anyone respect you with a grip like that.' And Henry would grima and try again. 'Yes, sir.'

Gabriel ducked his head, tilting it so that he could stare up at the hig grey walls beyond the windscreen. He let out a low whistle. 'I know y explained it was big, but I never imagined this. It's like a castle.'

The stone lions regarded us with implacable gazes. It was a shock understand that I'd misremembered the details of the brickwo forgotten the exact silver and charcoal shades inside the slate. I'd revisit the house in my mind every day since I left it, so much so, that I som times thought there must be a part of me here, a spirit, a dream of mys wandering the corridors.

Mummy appeared on the steps in her tweed skirt and brown stoc ings. She looked older, her hair almost entirely grey, shoulders stoopin

It was the strain of losing two children, I knew, not just the effect of time passing.

Gabriel squeezed my hand. 'Ready?'

I nodded. 'Let's introduce Beatrice to her grandparents.'

And then we were standing outside the car, Bea in Gabriel's arms, and my mother exclaiming and smiling. Mummy put an arm around me and touched Bea's cheek with an uncertain finger. 'What a beauty,' she said, but turned back to me. 'Darling, I'm so glad to see you.'

I kissed her thin, cold cheek, inhaling the familiar scent of Elizabeth Arden face power, and something sour underneath, the rotten aroma of the house itself, and old-dog stink.

'This is Gabriel,' I said.

Mummy put out her hand with polite formality, but Gabriel ignored it and kissed her on the cheek. I saw astonishment widening her eyes. 'How lovely to meet you at last.' She held herself upright. 'Please, do call me Emmeline.'

'Where's Daddy?' My gaze searched the open doorway, trying to penetrate the gloom of the hallway.

'He's been in his study all morning,' Mummy said. 'Now, do come along, darling. We'll have lunch straight away, after you put your bags in your room. I've put you in one of the guest bedrooms. More space for you all.'

Gabriel took our bags and Bea's carrycot from the boot. Trailing after Mummy, I felt like a visitor. A lump came into my throat, a suppressed anguish. I was being ridiculous. 'Cilly.' The nickname came back to me in Alice's voice. Henry laughing, 'Nitwit.' But it was Alice and I that were the pair, so why had the other two sometimes made me feel like the odd one out? I swallowed down the old rivalry. There was no need for it any more.

I looked at the thin ribbon of daylight underneath Daddy's study door, hoping he'd come out, arms wide to greet me. But we were walking on, up the first staircase, past wallpaper peeling in strips and crumbling plaster, under the portraits of my ancestors. I thought I could hear a faint babble of voices pressing against my ears – the ghosts welcoming me back – the same ones I'd known all my life, the ones that came to me when I needed them most, slipping inside me, whispering words of comfort.

'It goes on forever,' Gabriel said, a note of awe in his voice. 'You mu
have got lost here. Just one little girl in all this space.'

I saw Mummy stiffen, and after a faltering step, stride on. The fictio
would be maintained, I realised, passing the empty spaces on the wa
where Henry's team photographs used to hang.

We unpacked in the Pink Room, hanging up clothes in the hulkin
monstrosity of the wardrobe. Gabriel rattled the empty hangers as he p
his head inside. 'This is the kind of furniture that must have inspired C.
Lewis,' he said. 'Did you read those books?'

I nodded. 'Of course.'

'Must have been lonely for you here. Bet you wished for siblings,' I
said gently as he changed Bea's nappy on the faded rose-coloured eide
down. Released from her confines, the baby gurgled and kicked her le
in the air.

'Not really,' I said, sitting on the bed and watching him skilful
dealing with our daughter. I took Bea from him after he was finishe
kissing her cheek and tucking her up inside the carrycot. 'Be on your be
behaviour, little one,' I whispered. 'We should go down,' I told Gabri
'Lunch is on the dot in this house.'

I was nervous going down the stairs. My legs were weak, and I had
sick feeling in my belly. Daddy would be waiting for us in the dini
room. I felt like the prodigal daughter. Daddy's pride had been hurt by m
marriage, and I needed Gabriel to make a good impression. The ne
hour or so could determine my father's mood for years to come, let alon
the rest of our short visit.

We entered the room together, Gabriel holding the carrycot. He put
on the floor and went towards Daddy, who was standing motionless at th
head of the table. My eyes flicked towards the clock, checking we weren
late, and then back to my father's face. He gave nothing away as he shoo
Gabriel's proffered hand, not even when Gabriel omitted to call him 'Si
like I'd told him to. Daddy dwarfed my husband. Gabriel's head came u
to the older man's shoulders. Daddy hadn't shrunk with age, as some me
did. He stood upright, with straight spine and raised chin. Suddenly,
wished Gabriel was taller.

I approached, uncertain of what to do or say. 'Daddy.'

'Cecily,' he gave me a long look under his majestic eyebrows, his pale blue gaze indecipherable, shielded. 'It's good to have you home.'

Encouraged, I touched his hand. 'It's wonderful to be here.' He didn't respond to my touch, and my fingers fell away from the waxy coolness of his skin. He hated fuss, hated kissing and hugging. It was not his way.

We sat down, Gabriel and I either side of the table and my parents taking their positions at each end. Daddy bowed his head and crossed himself. I followed suit, noticing Gabriel's hands lying inert in his lap. 'Bless us, O Lord, for these, thy gifts, which we are about to receive from thy bounty. Through Christ, Our Lord. Amen.' My lips traced the words silently and I crossed myself again. Gabriel scratched his chin and shuffled his chair closer to the table.

A girl from the village came in with platters of potatoes and greens, putting them in the centre of the table, placing a hunk of roast beef before Daddy, before scurrying from the room. He stood to carve, spending a minute sharpening the knife. With weighty ceremony, he severed the string binding the flesh, and then carved each slice with clinical precision. As we took up our forks, I leant forwards. 'Daddy, Gabriel is an expert on the Civil War. He's had a book published on it.' I couldn't keep the eagerness from my voice. I turned to Gabriel. 'My father is writing a book, too. About the history of weapons. The Civil War marked an important change with the introduction of the musket, didn't it, Daddy?'

He nodded and carried on chewing. I thought that he could show Gabriel his weapon collection after lunch. They could take a walk in the grounds, look at the yew tree, and Daddy could explain how he'd found the cannonball wedged in the trunk when he was a boy. It would be alright. My heart lifted.

'Do you have a publisher?' Gabriel asked. 'It sounds fascinating.'

Daddy finished his mouthful, blotted his lips on his napkin. 'Not yet. I still have work to do. The subject deserves dedication. I don't believe a book can be rushed off every couple of years. Worthwhile study takes a lifetime.'

'It would be lovely to have that luxury.' Gabriel smiled. 'But my books help to fund our living expenses. Lecturing isn't exactly lucrative.'

I wanted to kick him under the table. I was sure I'd told him that money was a subject to be avoided at all costs. Daddy gave Gabriel a withering glance and returned to the task of spearing a carrot with his fork.

'There was a Civil War battle right here,' I said, brightly. 'On the front lawn.'

Gabriel made interested noises, but Daddy refused to be drawn. Bea started to whimper and stir. *Not now,* I thought. *Please, not now.* If we left her, she might go back to sleep, but Gabriel was already out of his chair, bending over her carrycot. Mummering nonsense, he scooped her into his arms.

'Don't fuss,' I said. 'She could have slept longer.'

'Too late for that.' He smiled, holding her against his shoulder. 'I think she needs another feed, darling,' he said, peering into Bea's face.

Heat flooded my cheeks. The atmosphere in the room stiffened, bristling with embarrassment. 'Can't she wait?' Mummy said in a low voice.

'This is precisely why babies should not be allowed in dining rooms,' Daddy said.

Gabriel looked at him incredulously. 'She's hungry,' he said. 'And she needs her mother. Cecily can feed her and eat at the same time.'

My heart thumped. Daddy glared at Gabriel. 'This is my house, and we eat in peace. There will be no jumping up and down, juggling infants.'

Gabriel gave me a confused, questioning look, as he bounced Bea in his arms. I couldn't meet his gaze and stared down at my hands on the white tablecloth. Nausea twisted in my belly. Two instincts clashing. But here, in Hawksmoor, the rules had been etched into me since I could walk and talk. I'd smelt the smouldering cinders of Daddy's rage that morning as we'd entered the hall.

Bea began to howl, her sobs ricocheting off the panelled oak, fuelling disapproval, shaking the dust, disturbing the routine and quiet with her demands. I stayed in my chair. I put another mouthful of food between my lips. My child's screams went on. I dared not look at Daddy, keeping my gaze on the wooden wainscoting, the red wallpaper above, the portraits. The painted faces seemed to tremble with indignation. I swallowed with difficulty.

Gabriel walked towards the door; the wailing Bea slumped over his shoulder. He turned at the threshold, his face dark with suppressed rage. 'You're really not coming?'

I gave him a mute gaze, appealing to his understanding.

His shoulders stiffened. 'I'll take her outside then, so you can finish your meal in peace.' There was an ironic twist to his voice, a coldness I'd never heard before. 'Come and find me when you're ready.'

'It's better to let them cry,' Mummy said, vaguely. 'Better not to give in to a child's demands.'

I shook my head. We ate in silence. Bits of gristle got stuck between my teeth, catching in my throat, the taste of blood on my tongue. Bea's sobbing could be heard still, a muted but desperate wail. To my horror, I felt dampness seeping into my bra. I hunched my shoulders protectively, praying it didn't penetrate my shirt. I felt the weight of my breasts, pendulum-like, the spread of my hips on the chair. Gabriel told me he loved my new curves. But now I understood that I had become clumsy and unlovely in my milky fleshy self.

As we finished the meal, scraping up the greasy remains, Mummy made conversation, asking me about Exeter, about Bea's routine, about the weather. I answered without elaborating, my chest tight with anxiety. I felt Daddy's disappointment. My mistake of choosing a husband without his approval was a thing that could not be erased. It was a foolish to think I could talk him round. I'd never had any power over him.

'Your husband,' he said suddenly. 'How close is he to converting?'

'Converting?' My pulse leapt at my temples. I remembered the letter I wrote before the wedding, hinting that Gabriel was considering it. 'Close,' I told him quickly. 'Very close.' I cleared my throat. 'And Beatrice will be brought up Catholic, of course.'

I caught a slight lift in his expression, and he pursed his lips. 'I'll talk to him about it this evening, when I hope he'll have the manners to remain at the table. I've never known such extraordinary behaviour.'

I nodded, numbly, putting my knife and fork together on my clean plate. 'Maybe I can be excused?' I asked. 'I should go and attend to the baby.'

'Your husband will have to go hungry,' Daddy said, indicati
Gabriel's congealed meal. 'And no dogs to give it to. Criminal waste.'

'Dilly will eat it,' Mummy said quietly, the ancient dachshund snori
at her feet.

Daddy ignored her, flicking his napkin, leaving it crumpled on t
table.

* * *

In the Pink Room, I couldn't calm Bea. She twisted away from my leaki
nipples, convulsing and inconsolable. I slumped on the edge of the be
tears slipping down the side of my nose. 'She's too upset.'

'I can't believe you wouldn't feed her at the table.' Gabriel was tig
lipped, his hair sticking up, his collar awry. 'It's been a nightmare trying
console her. Jesus. In this day and age, you can't breastfeed your ov
child in front of your parents?'

'I told you they were old-fashioned,' I said, persuading Bea at last
latch on, hardly feeling the stab of pain connecting nipple to wom
tracing fire through the branching avenues of my body.

'My God, Cecily. Sometimes I wonder who you are.' He went over
the window and looked out at the grounds. 'This place is falling to bit
he said. 'I can't understand why your parents persist in living here.
stinks of damp. It's not good for Bea. All those spores.'

'It's their home. Our home,' I said, cradling Bea closer. 'It's beautif
Full of history.'

'I agree about the history,' he said. 'But it should really be in the pub
domain. Private houses like this are an anachronism.'

I looked at the back of his head and hated him. The feeling took n
breath away, but it was liberating to acknowledge that I despised the wa
could see the tips of his ears through his hair, the way he hummed
himself, the click in his jaw when he ate. Seeing him next to Daddy, I sa
that he was weak. I was ashamed of him.

'Daddy thinks you're going to convert,' I told him. 'I couldn't disa
point him. He'll ask you about it this evening.' He turned to me, and t

look on his face told me that he wasn't going to go along with the charade. Another hateful thing: his stubbornness. 'You can't do it for me?' My voice was small, hard.

'I told you before.' His voice was equally hard.

We glared at each other over the head of our sleeping child.

33

ALICE

Surfacing out of bad dreams, the first thing I see as I open my eyes is Cecily's crucifix above my head. How can my suspicions about her be real? I sit up in bed, rubbing sore eyes. My head throbs. The books she left on her bedside table catch my attention, the King James Bible, and beneath it, the weighty tome about the Borgias. I pick it up and flick through pages about murders within a family, the art of killing someone slowly.

I don't know who Cecily is. All our years of separation have made us into strangers. I'll never know if the soup was poisoned, but I must stop her getting into the house again to tamper with our food. Poison is the number one choice for women who want to kill. The old joke of arsenic in the soup suddenly feels horribly real – and I remember how the Borgias' victims became gradually weakened, suffering from strange aches and stomach pains, as if succumbing to some unknown disease. But there are other methods of getting rid of someone. Gabriel is out and about during the day, walking next to roads and railway lines. It would only take a well-timed push to send him under some fast-moving wheels. What if she's employed someone to do it for her? Maybe that's who the watcher in the hoodie is. The thought gives me a lurch of panic. I can't follow Gabriel around all day, and I need to be here to protect the house. I'm convinced she has a set of keys. She can let herself in whenever she wants.

I double-lock the doors and keep the chains latched in place, check the window catches are secure. When I'm in Cecily's room, I peer out of her window, looking for the figure on the other side of the street.

* * *

Gabriel and Bea are finishing their breakfast when I come into the kitchen, and they both look up and smile. 'Darling,' Gabriel says, coming over and kissing my cheek. 'Didn't you sleep well? You look tired.'

I know from an earlier quick glance into the bathroom mirror that my eyes are bloodshot, my skin sallow and my forehead etched with a crazy paving of worry lines. 'It wasn't a great night,' I admit. 'I was a bit restless.'

He's giving me a concerned look. It's the same one he gave me when I swept the soup onto the floor, and when I ran screaming into the street. He's wondering what other erratic, irrational behaviour to expect from me.

'But I'm okay,' I reassure him.

'You could have a weekend away,' he suggests. 'If you need a break? I could come with you?'

I smile. 'Maybe.'

'Right,' he swings his jacket off the back of the chair. 'I should get going.' He looks at Bea. 'Want a lift to the bus stop?'

'Yup.' She gets up, a piece of toast clamped in her mouth, and grabs her satchel from the floor. She takes the toast out of her mouth to kiss my other cheek, leaving a sticky smear of jam. 'Bye, Mum. Have a nice day.'

I watch them leave, and my shoulders ache with worry. 'Be careful,' I call after them. 'Be careful, you know, crossing roads and things.'

They turn and give me bemused looks, and then, with cheerful waves, they walk out of the house, and are swallowed up by the bright spring morning.

* * *

There's another piece of folded paper on the floor near the doormat. I open it with trembling fingers and stare down at my sister's writing:

Meet me at the castle gatehouse tonight. Next to the entrance. 11 p.m.

I've glimpsed the ruins in the distance, the stone glowing red in the sunset. I've flicked through a guidebook about Exeter I'd found in Gabriel's room, so I know that the castle was built by William the Conqueror into existing Roman walls. The ancient gatehouse is the only segment of the original building still standing; the guidebook said the last woman branded as a witch in England was executed there.

I have a whole day to endure before our meeting. I can hardly control my rage. I've gone beyond wanting explanations, I'm going to tell her exactly what I think of her – she's lied to me, betrayed Gabriel and Bea, and made me take her place under false pretences for some warped plan of her own. Using the kitchen table, I spread out the town map she left for me, and plan my route to the castle ruins, imprinting it on my mind so there'll be no mistakes or getting lost this evening.

I wait until supper is over and the house is quiet. Bea's in bed, and Gabriel is working at his desk upstairs; he's often there until gone midnight. I creep down the stairs, close the door quietly and hurry away with Cecilia's puffer jacket pulled around me, the hood up. I hurry down cobbled streets past closed shops and pubs. I'm panting as I walk up the hill to the castle ruins. The gatehouse rears out of the darkness, a jagged stone shape backlit by moonlight. There's nobody around. A fox slinks past, eyeing me with distrust. I wait by the gatehouse. The air is wild and fresh and minerally green. There's the distant hum of the town below, the rustle of branches and leaves. The night is dense, stars concealed by fists of cloud.

I bring Cecily's watch face close and squint. She's over half an hour late. My anger is seeping away, replaced by anxiety. I have a bad feeling about this. The clouds shift and a skull-like moon bleeds light onto the world around me, and suddenly I can see more clearly, leaves and grass, the texture of the ruined gatehouse. Looking at the wall next to the entrance, I notice a sheen of white, a corner sticking out between the stonework at the height of my shoulder. It looks like a scrap of paper. I pinch the edges with my fingernails to pull it out. In the moonlight I make out the words tumbling across the page.

Remember Edith Baxter.

I'm certain it's Cecily's writing, just scruffier and larger than her usual script – as if she was in a tearing hurry when she wrote it, or angry, or drunk, or all three. There's another flutter of white higher up. I pull it out and unfold it.

Speak to Edith Baxter.

I find four more bits of paper, all with that one name scrawled in urgent capitals.

EDITH BAXTER.

The name on the paper I'd found inside her Bible. I crumple the notes into my pocket. Another rustle in the gloom. 'Cecily?' I hiss.

There's a soft rush of air, like the suppressed sound of someone breathing, lungs working quietly. Is that a human shape beyond the fall of ivy? I'm listening hard, pulling in the smallest noises. The wind moves through the branches, shivering leaves, and the hairs on my neck stand on end. I turn and walk quickly away, stumbling along the downwards path, heading for the lights of the town.

The scraps of paper are still in my pocket. I know I've heard the name, a long time ago. I wish I could remember her, whoever she is, then perhaps I could solve Cecily's riddle. There'd been a phone number and address scribbled next to Edith Baxter's name in paper I'd found in the Bible. I quicken my pace, filled with a new urgency.

34

CECILY

Dear Alice,

Hearing about your adventures and the places you've been makes my life seem very small. That day in the snow, I should have listened to you. You were right. Everything at Hawksmoor was rotten, and we needed to run. But I was under a spell. I couldn't leave. I wish you'd understood that I wasn't as strong as you – I always needed you, Alice. You should never have left me.

When I fell in love with Gabriel, I thought that was my chance to start again – how stupid I was, there was never any hope, was there, not after Hawksmoor. Bea is at school now, and my days are long and lonely. I have my proofreading of academic manuscripts, but it's dull work. There's something wrong with me. My head aches and I feel a hundred years old. I can hardly get out of bed. In the kitchen, I drop pans, stumble on my way down the stairs. Sometimes I think it would be easier to let myself fall – and hope for a clean broken neck. Like Henry.

I've made so many mistakes, Alice. I don't think I can be forgiven for them.

Thank God I was firm with Gabriel about not having more children. He wanted them, but I knew I shouldn't. I'm not fit for that kind of responsibility. We have a kitten, a sweet little thing, but I forget to feed her. Bea is better at caring for her than me. All the house plants are dead. I had to throw them out – desiccated soil and withered leaves – such a waste. I don't want any more living things to look after. No more children, or animals or plants.

Sorry to go on like this. But it's hard to be alone with my memories, and you're the only one left in the world besides me who shares them. Only you can understand. I wish I was with you. I don't even know where you are right now. I bet all your travels help you to forget. You were always the brave one. I'd never have the courage to live a life like yours. You got away, gave yourself a fresh start. If I wasn't so scared, I'd change places with you in a heartbeat.

Please write soon.

Love Cecily

In our letters, we'd talked about arranging a way of being together. We'd come up with the idea of meeting somewhere in Europe – Paris or Amsterdam. But there was the problem of Gabriel. He didn't know of Alice's existence, and I'd have to lie to him, make up a reason to take a weekend off. Anyway, since I'd known him, I'd told him I hated travel, was afraid of planes and boats. We'd never been abroad together. The truth was I couldn't leave England. I'd fled to the other side of the country after Alice and Henry died, trying to escape my grief, but I wasn't prepared to go any further from Hawksmoor or Daddy. I may as well have a chain on my ankle tethering me to them both. I was afraid of seeing her too, afraid of confronting the past. She thinks she betrayed me by leaving, but really, I'm the guilty one.

Alice was curious about my life, my home and family. In my letters, I'd described all the boring details of my existence, sent her regular photographs, sometimes family shots with Gabriel and Bea, and she sent me ones of her. She was always alone, usually squinting into the sun, out of doors, with a café or bustling market or mountainside as a backdrop, and I always wondered who'd pressed the button. In our letters, we remarked on how similar we looked; beyond superficial details like hairstyles and clothes, it was reassuring to know we were still the same. When she asked me to send her a picture of Hollyhocks Cottage, instead of sending a snapshot, I drew the house for her and included a little sketch of Bea. I'd forgotten the satisfaction of sketching – the way it ate up time. When I was next in town, I popped into WH Smith and brought a couple of soft 2B pencils, a putty rubber and an A3 pad. I recreated the faces of Alice and Henry, Daddy and Mummy. I sketched Dilly and the Labs, the gnarled branches of the yew, and Hawksmoor itself with battlements and Pele tower.

The side of my little finger on my right hand became ingrained with charcoal grey as it moved across the paper. I remembered the soft outline of the beech trees, the rooks rising from them. I used short scratches of pencil, little ticks for wings, as I thought about the starlings in their winter murmuration towards the fells, the way they netted the light above the tarn. And I heard their cries, the wild whistle of wind across water.

I hardly went home any more. Daddy disliked Gabriel and Gabriel disliked Daddy. I kept my drawings hidden under my bed. They took on a significance I couldn't explain, but they offered me a connection to Hawksmoor, each one a kind of magic spell bringing me closer to it, unravelling history with every stroke of the pencil, and promising me a different future.

* * *

For the sake of Your name, forgive my iniquity, though it is great. Seven knots for seven sins. But it was The Church of the Sacred Heart that saved me. I went several times a week, attending Saturday confession, Sunday morning mass, and the exposition and benediction of the Blessed Sacrament on Wednesday afternoons. I was involved in the rota for doing the flowers, volunteered with cleaning, and helped at Sunday School, taking Bea with me. Bea didn't like it; she stamped her feet and said she wanted to stay at home with Dad and it took all my willpower not to grab her by the arms and shake her. 'You're Catholic, Bea,' I told her. 'You're part of an old and important family. This is your inheritance.'

'Don't want my inheritance.' Bea pouted.

I hated it when Gabriel watched our weekly struggle, me forcing Bea into her coat, and Bea trying to take it off again. I could see his disapproval, but he was unwilling to interfere. The day I'd told him I was pregnant, he'd promised to support me in my faith, and he knew that meant raising our child as a Catholic. I guessed he was waiting until Bea reached secondary school age. If she didn't want to go to church then, he'd say that she was old enough to make her own choice. He didn't understand that there was no choice. I couldn't let Daddy down.

Ambrose Stone understood my fears. When I joined him in prayer, he knelt so close there was only a whisper of air between us, and I knew he felt the brush of my thigh or elbow as a jolt of pleasure. But he understood me. He listened to my worries about Bea, and he prayed with me, asking God to guide my daughter, to keep her on the right path. Ambrose was a devoted helper at the Sacred Heart; he was the most enthusiastic of the cleaning volunteers. He polished brass and silver with rags, his thin fingers blackening as the metal grew brighter; he scrubbed the engraved flagstones, swept under the pews, oiled the hinges on the great oak door.

I watched him loiter outside the confessional on Wednesday afternoons, saw how he chose his chore carefully on those days, getting to his knees with a scrubbing brush close to the partition of thin wood, where he cocked his head as he worked, absorbing the murmured sounds drifting from behind the screen.

35

ALICE

All the way back from the gatehouse, on the twists and turns through town, I'm afraid I'm being followed, and by the time I reach the house, my fingers are shaking so much I can hardly turn the key in the lock. I slip inside as quietly as possible and put the chain in place. A living thing butts against my calf, and I smother a shriek. Sukie purrs at my feet, winding around my ankles, ever hopeful for a snack. Not now, I tell her silently, as I step past and up the dark stairs.

The floorboards on the landing creak loudly, and I stop for a moment, waiting to make sure Gabriel or Bea haven't been disturbed. I only let myself breathe properly when I'm inside Cecily's room. I switch on the bedside light and slide the loose paper from her Bible to compare it with the crumpled notes she left at the gatehouse. The handwriting is almost identical. According to the address, Edith Baxter lives in the North, not far from the Lake District. I want to make the phone call right away, but it's the middle of the night. I'll have to wait until morning, after the others have left for work and school.

I spend the rest of the night lying awake, trying to remember who Edith Baxter is and failing. When I do manage to drift into uneasy sleep, I dream about ruined castles and shadowy women laughing behind my back.

* * *

When I've waved Gabriel and Bea off and shut the door, I go upstairs to retrieve the paper from the Bible and go back to the hall to dial the number carefully. It rings. My pulse races with fear and anticipation. I stand with the receiver clamped to my ear. It rings for a long time without clicking into an answer machine. I'm about to give up when an elderly, breathless voice picks up.

'Edith Baxter speaking.'

I am shocked into silence. There was a part of me that wondered if this woman was a figment of Cecily's imagination. I try to speak, clear my throat. 'Hello,' I try again, squeezing the receiver tighter.

There's silence on the other end.

'You don't know me, but I'm trying to solve a mystery and I think you might possibly be able to help...' my words tumble out and I frown, realising I'm not making much sense.

'What's that?' the voice says, sounding suspicious. 'Who is this?'

'My name is Alice,' I say. 'Alice Deveraux.'

There's an intake of breath. 'How dare you call me? Haven't your family done enough?'

I have the feeling she's going to slam the phone down. 'Wait,' I say. 'I'm sorry. I don't know what you mean. I don't know who you are or what my family has done to you.'

There's a long pause, and I hear the hum and echo of the miles between us. 'Are you one of the daughters?' she asks.

'Yes,' I say. 'Alice.'

'I've already spoken to the other one.'

'Cecily?' My body flashes cold. 'But she hasn't talked to me. And now I can't get hold of her. She's disappeared. I think this could be important. Please could you tell me what happened, between you and my family?'

'Important?' She repeats the word, as if turning it over in wonder. 'Important to you, perhaps – but when it mattered, your father didn't care how important it was to me. To my sister.'

'Please,' I beg. 'I'm not my father. Whatever happened. I knew nothing about it.'

Silence and distance rushes between us again. 'I won't talk on the telephone,' she says eventually. 'You'll have to come and see me.'

The line goes dead without her saying goodbye.

* * *

I'm in the bedroom when I hear Bea and Gabriel arrive home. I rush downstairs to greet them as Bea passes me on the stairs, an apple clutched in her fist. 'Hi, Mum,' she says. 'I'm going to get started on homework before supper.' She looks as though she's been crying.

'Are you alright?'

'Yeah.' Her voice is muffled over her shoulder. 'I'm fine.'

I go down into the hall, where Gabriel is hanging up his jacket. He hasn't been pushed under a bus. He's unhurt and whole and breathing. I want to hug him. But he dodges me, striding into the kitchen. I follow him, feeling puzzled, as he shuts the door behind us.

'What's the matter? Did something happen?' I ask.

'How could you?' he says, his voice low and angry. 'How could you keep it from me? I'm her father.'

'What?' I ask, a sick feeling gathering in my belly.

'I talked to Megan's parents,' he says. 'Her father phoned me.' He paces up and down. 'He told me, Cecily. Megan confessed what happened that afternoon, after he'd asked her why they weren't friends any more.'

His fury is a fist rammed at my chest.

'I picked Bea up from school,' he goes on. 'Took her to a café and explained that I knew. She broke down and cried. Then she told me she'd already spoken to you.'

I stare at him, waiting.

'And you thought you'd keep it to yourself?' His voice twists.

'She made me promise—'

'She's the child. You're the adult,' he shouts. He turns away from me. 'I thought this was too good to be true,' his voice drops. 'These last few weeks... I had hope,' he looks at me with wounded eyes. 'I thought we could make it work between us. But I was wrong – you're a liar. You haven't changed.'

'No. You're wrong,' I say. 'I'm not her – I'm a different person.' The words slip from my tongue. I want so badly to make him understand. But the truth isn't enough on its own – and now is not the time to explain.

The door opens, and Bea is there. 'What's going on?'

'Nothing,' he says. 'Go back to your room.'

'No,' she says, standing her ground. 'Is this about Mum not telling you?' She's looking between us, anxiously. 'Don't be angry with her, Dad. I begged her not to tell you. I made her promise. She wasn't happy about it.'

Gabriel says nothing, his face is closed, his arms folded.

She goes up to him. 'Dad, don't blame her for this.'

Gabriel sinks into a chair with a groan, his head in his hands. I turn to Bea. 'I think he needs a bit of time.' I keep my voice low. 'Why don't you go upstairs, and I'll call you down to supper.'

She scrunches her forehead, uncertain, standing on one leg and then the other, looking at Gabriel's bowed head and hunched back.

'He'll be alright,' I tell her. 'He just needs a minute. Okay?'

She nods and leaves the room, shutting the door.

'It was such a shock,' he whispers. 'My little girl.' His mouth quivers and collapses. 'It could have been even worse. And then when I knew you'd been keeping it from me—' he shakes his head.

'It's okay,' I tell him, pulling up the chair next to him. I put my hands over his. 'I understand, Gabriel.'

We're staring into each other's eyes. 'Cecily,' he whispers. He leans forward and we kiss, salt in my mouth, his face wet with tears. 'I don't want to lose you again.'

* * *

After supper, and Bea has gone up for a bath, we talk about the incident and what we can do about it. Megan's father has told David's parents, and there's going to be a meeting between us in a week when David's parents get back from France. 'What do we want out of it, this meeting with his parents?' Gabriel asks.

'We need David to understand what he's done,' I say. 'He needs to apologise to Bea, properly.'

Gabriel nods. 'Yes, that's what I think, too.'

'She said "no",' I remind him. 'She was sensible and brave.'

'You're right.' He shakes his head. 'I'm sorry I snapped at you. When Bea told me, I sort of went into freefall.'

We walk upstairs together, and outside Cecily's bedroom door, we pause. The air between us is charged with the unspoken. It crackles like static. His eyes hold mine, the green inside them clear as a mountain stream. He leans towards me, and our lips meet. I fumble behind me for the handle and open the door to Cecily's room; he follows me in. 'Wait,' I whisper, closing the curtains.

He switches on the side light, but I switch it off. I can't risk him seeing the tattoo at the base of my spine. He doesn't complain about the darkness, just takes my face in his hands, and we're kissing again, shrugging off our clothes. His skin is hot, and I rub my cheek against his chest like a cat, kiss the hollow at the centre of his sternum. I put my mouth to his wrist. His pulse jumps against my lip. The fibres of my body thrum with need, the substance of me melding with the bones and sinews of him. I slip underneath his surface like ducking under a wave, swimming through the mystery of him, diving into his heart's core. There is such recognition, such joyful relief. We move together as if we're remembering an ancient dance, as if we're reviving a ritual dense with meaning.

He says her name at the moment of climax, and I hold his shoulders as he shudders against me, our skin slick with sweat, my mouth against his neck; but before our bodies separate, tears are squeezing from my eyes in a silent howling. I love this man. I can't give him up now. I can't give him back. I don't even feel guilty, not any more.

36

CECILY

I took Beatrice back to Hawksmoor for Easter, while Gabriel stayed at home. He didn't celebrate the risen Christ, and the atmosphere between him and Daddy was unbearable for everyone. Bea made a fuss about coming. She got car-sick, and wanted to stay with her father, but I insisted. She was my proof to Daddy that he had a Catholic granddaughter, that I had done one thing right.

'Why do we have to go?' Bea complained on the long journey. 'I don't like Grandad. He's scary. And the house smells bad. I have nightmares there. It's creepy.'

'It's an extraordinary piece of history,' I corrected her. 'Grandad is stern, but he loves you. And if he asks you about going to church, tell him that you go every week.'

'But I don't.'

'I know. But you should. And it will make him happy.'

'It's a lie.'

'It's a white lie,' my fingers gripped the steering wheel tighter. 'God forgive me, but I've let you get away with skipping church too many times lately.'

'But you don't go all the time.'

'Yes, I do,' I glanced over at her, annoyed by her teenage sarkiness. 'Please don't contradict me just for the sake of it.'

She sighed loudly and sank down in her seat, staring out of the passenger window. We had to stop several times for her to throw up. The car smelt of sour milk, and Bea's complexion took on a greenish tinge. I kept driving, pushing my guilt away. She had to go back to Hawksmoor sometimes – had to see her grandparents. I couldn't understand why she didn't love the house, or at least find it exciting, intriguing. Perhaps she'd feel that way if she'd had siblings to explore it with, to discover all the places that are perfect for games of hide and seek. Hiding places. My hands gripped the steering wheel, trying to stop the past catching me, dragging me back to the open mouth of the priest hole.

I blinked and loosened my fingers. That was one hiding place I'd make sure Bea would never see.

The roads flashed past, the names of towns and cities falling away, the sky changing colours from apricot to silver. As we turned off the motorway, a surge of black clouds obliterated the sun. Rain thundered onto the roof of the car, making a river of the road. I slowed down, switching on the headlights. 'Our welcome home.' I smiled. 'Lake District weather is different from anywhere else.' I squinted through the wipers, through the ripple and flow of water.

'I know,' Bea sighed. 'It rains here all the time because of the winds coming across the Atlantic Ocean. Then they reach the mountains, and they lift or something, making the clouds release moisture, blah, blah. It's like a geography lesson, Mum. You tell me every time.'

I didn't bother to reply. As we drove further into Cumbria, I glimpsed the purple smudge of mountains in the distance. Drystone walls made a familiar grey etching over the landscape; sodden sheep were small boulders against the green, the animals inured to the weather, patiently waiting for the rain to stop. Lambs huddled under their mothers' bellies.

By the time we drove through the gates of Hawksmoor, the fierce downpour ceased as suddenly as it started. I tried not to notice the way the place had become even more overgrown, overhanging trees dripping onto the car, the tangle of undergrowth, nettles and weeds pressing up on either side. I looked for golden daffodils, spotting the bright faces of tulips and hyacinths tucked into the dense grass. Signs of Easter. Signs of hope. As we went past the coach house, I pointed out the huge rhododendron blooms, splashes of blood red against the green. 'And there's the yew,' I murmured, as we passed its dark mantle of drooping leaves.

'And there's Grandma,' Bea said. 'She's carrying something. Is it... a toy?'

Mummy waited on the rain-dampened steps, the lions below her. She raised one hand in regal greeting, her other clasped the dead dog tucked under her arm.

'It's her dachshund, Dilly,' I said. 'She had her stuffed. Don't say anything.'

Mummy waved at us again but didn't descend the steps to greet us. She was cradling Dilly, stroking the little dog's head. I slid out from behind the wheel, stretching my spine, smelling wet air, the scent of the fells and wild greenery. I approached my mother and kissed the thick layer of face powder caking her cheek. Mummy's lipstick looked as if it had been drawn on by a clown, a swathe of scarlet over her puckered mouth. 'And who's this?' Mummy turned to Bea, smiling.

'I'm Beatrice, Grandma,' Bea looked startled.

'Your granddaughter, Mummy,' I said in a clear voice. She was getting worse. It must be some kind of early dementia.

'Oh, yes,' she nodded, vaguely. 'You must come in. Is Alice here?'

I shook my head, taking her arm tightly. 'Let's go inside, Mummy. Which bedrooms are we in today?'

'Who's Alice?' Bea asked, when we're alone in the Pink Room.

'Oh, just... a cousin. She died ages ago. Grandmama's getting forgetful in her old age.' I put my weekend bag on the bed. 'Run along to your own room, darling. You know we mustn't be late for lunch.'

I walked the draughty corridor, heading for the bathroom, passing Henry's room on the way. The door was shut, just as it was that day. *Unlock the door, Cecily.* No, I told him across time, across oceans of what-ifs and maybes. Too late. If only I could go back and change what happened that day.

In the bathroom, I sat on the cold wooden loo seat, and let out a long-held pee, hoisted up my knickers and tights and pulled the dangling chain. Pipes groaned and heaved, but for all its roaring, the flush was a dribble, leaving the water lemon coloured. I went over to the rust-stained sink. Turning the tap, it spluttered and spurted out brown water. I smelt metal and old earth. Waited for it to run clear and splashed my face with cold.

Tell me, Henry begged me. *Where's Jude?*

The voices in my head were bad today. I pulled a rectangle of worn towel from the rail, the nap worn into bald patches, and scrubbed my face hard, scratching my skin. I looked at my watch, taking comfort from the thin gold band. I'm not that teenage girl. There were still fifteen minutes before lunch. I'd go and find Daddy. I was a married, grown-up woman with a daughter, I should be able to talk to him like another adult.

I knocked on his study door. There was no answer, and full of my new confidence, I turned the doorknob, putting my head around. 'Hello? Daddy?'

The room was empty. I sniffed cigar smoke, old leather, dark wood, damp wool. I remembered how I'd sat at one end of the desk and typed up his manuscript. How he'd talked to me about Hawksmoor, telling me stories of the past. We'd laughed together. I smiled at the memory.

Emboldened, I went in, running my fingers over the dusty, cluttered desk. A stub of cold cigar lay in an overflowing ashtray. My old typewriter crouched under a litter of loose papers. He was still writing it by hand, I thought, as I picked up pieces of manuscript covered in his dense, cramped scrawl. I peered down. It was more illegible than ever. There was long, cruel-looking sword lying at the other end of the table. I touched the end of it, the handle darkened with murderous sweat, and I finally understood that he was never going to finish this book.

I sat in his chair, the leather softened and worn into the shape of his buttocks and spine, certain of this new knowledge. It made me feel oddly protective of him. I'd been in awe of the great manuscript for as long as I could remember. It was a mantra repeated daily. He must never be disturbed. He had to have absolute quiet. But the truth was that the book was a useless ramble, a vanity project. I'd have to be careful not to damage his pride if it came up in conversation.

All the drawers in his desk had been left open or half-open, carelessly abandoned to droop, with things spilling from them, a mess of weapons, papers, books, pens, apple cores and dog collars. I began to tidy up – closing drawers, shuffling the contents to flatten them. In the bottom one, I found certificates, documents that looked official, important. He should really file these properly, I tutted, picking up a sheaf of them. I began to arrange them into a neater pile. One of them was my parents' marriage certificate. I glanced at it, and then looked again. There was Daddy's name. But where Mummy's name should be, another one had been written.

I stared at the signatures under the printed names. My mind went blank, my skin rimed in cold sweat. It couldn't be true. There must be a mistake, an explanation. The certificate slipped from my fingers, fluttering to the floor.

37

ALICE

I sit up in bed, sliding one leg out of sheets, inhaling the ripe ammonia of sex. I grab a shirt and pull it over me to cover my tattoo as I pad softly towards the door, not wanting to wake Gabriel. I look back at his sleeping face on the pillow. It felt so right between us. But I can't let it happen again, not until I've spoken to Cecily.

Tiptoeing into the bathroom to pee and clean my teeth, I catch something out of the corner of my eye. Big red letters scrawl across the bathroom mirror.

DIE DIE DIE

My heart flips in fright. A cry escapes me. A red lipstick is lying on the side of the sink, the cap off, the stick of colour crushed flat. I pick it up. One of Cecily's from her cosmetic bag on the bathroom shelf.

My God, was she here when I slept with her husband? Does she know what we did? My skin prickles with heat. I look around as if she might be crouching in the bath, standing behind the shower curtain like a scene from *Psycho*. The small bathroom is benign, empty of anyone else. The scarlet letters scream at me.

I rub at them with soap and warm water, smearing greasy colour over the glass. I rub harder, a sob in my throat. She saw me kissing him the other night; she must know about us. Is that why didn't she show up at the gatehouse?

Back in Cecily's room, Gabriel is awake and beckons to me with both arms. I sit on his side of the bed, trying to shake off my shock. I'm still trembling. I plant a light kiss on his forehead. 'Time to get up, sleepy head,' I say as evenly as I can.

'Let's forget everything and stay in bed.' He entwines his fingers in mine. He smells musty and warm.

'Wish we could.' I smile, pulling my hand away and standing up. 'But I'd better get dressed and make breakfast.'

He looks a little hurt. Then he sits up, running his fingers through his hair. 'Cecily,' he says. 'I won't expect to move back in here straight away – I meant what I said before, about taking things slowly.'

I nod and look down at my hands, noticing red stains around my nails, and quickly wipe the waxy residue on Gabriel's shirt, taking it off to bundle into the linen basket. Keeping my back turned away from him, I slip into the clothes I was wearing last night as nimbly as I can, aware that I'm naked and he's watching me. My body tingles with the memory of his touch. I refuse to feel guilty. What does she expect when she's left me alone with him? She's abandoned her family. Her marriage was broken when I arrived – it's me that's picked up the pieces.

Downstairs, as I fill the kettle and feed the cat, I remember his earlier suggestion of a weekend break. It will be the easiest way of me visiting Edith Baxter without having to explain.

He looks surprised when I tell him my plan, then, 'You should go,' he says, encouragingly. 'Of course, you should. You've been... on edge these last few days. Having a rest could be just what you need.' He slips his hands into his pockets, rocks back on his heels, affecting a casual manner. 'Sure you wouldn't like company? We could find a nice little hotel... and then we could stay in bed all day.' His mouth curls into a smile.

'I need some time to think, Gabriel.' I see him flinch. 'Don't worry,' I add quickly 'It's positive thinking.'

'Well, that's a relief.' He takes his hands out of his pocket, and pulls me in for a kiss, and I let him, opening my mouth. He's grinning when we break away. 'And where are you planning to go?' he asks. 'A spa, maybe?'

'I'm going to Hawksmoor,' I say, the idea coming to me as I speak, because I know it'll put him off suggesting that he accompany me again. 'It's time I checked on Daddy; he's getting frail. And I should visit Mummy in the home.'

He makes a slight grimace. 'Doesn't sound like the most relaxing weekend.'

'It's my duty,' I say, sounding like my sister.

* * *

Am I doing the right thing, rushing off to talk to a woman I don't know? It might be a wild goose chase, and meanwhile I'm leaving Gabriel and Bea alone. I still don't know what Cecily's intentions are. Maybe this is a trap? A way to get rid of me for a night?

'Make sure you use the chains on the doors,' I tell him. 'And don't let a stranger into the house. I've heard there's a spate of burglaries happening in the area.'

He raises his eyebrows. 'Really?'

I nod, a little too enthusiastically. 'It was on the local news.'

'You've got extra jumpy since you thought we'd been broken into,' he says gently. 'But that turned out to be a false alarm, didn't it?'

I nod again, tightly. 'But you must be careful, Gabriel. Promise me.'

He inclines his head with a serious expression, but I can see from his eyes that he's humouring me.

'And while I'm not here, why don't you and Bea get takeaways?' I suggest in my brightest voice. 'It doesn't seem fair that I'm eating out i you're not.'

'Alright,' he shakes his head, laughing. 'If it makes you happy, I'm sur Bea and I can endure a Chinese takeaway and a fish and chip supper ove the weekend.'

'I was thinking as well,' I add, 'that maybe we should get the lock changed, just to be on the safe side.'

He scratches his head, making his hair stick up. 'That would b expensive.' He catches my expression. 'But if it will make you feel safer,' he says. 'I'll look into it.' He gives me a straight look. 'Sure you don't want me to come with you?'

'No,' I say, holding his gaze. 'You'd hate it. And you're in the middle of term. You're busy. I'll be fine.'

His forehead furrows. 'It's a long journey.' The furrow deepens into a worried frown. 'I don't like to think of you doing it alone. You're taking the car, of course? I can cycle or take the bus to work.'

'Don't worry. I'll be fine.' I take his hand and bring it to my mouth, pressing my lips to his knuckles. 'Gabriel, whatever happens,' I say slowly, 'I'm glad we talked. These last couple of weeks have been important to me. You're important to me.' I can't stop myself saying it, as me, as Alice. I clench my jaw to prevent other words spilling out. My confession held back.

'Cecily...' his eyes darken, a shadow moving behind the iris. 'There's something else isn't there?' He's frowning. 'Something you're not telling me?'

I shake my head, but my gaze drops.

He pulls me close. 'You know, you can tell me anything,' he murmurs into my hair. 'Anything at all.' His heart beats against my sternum, the pulse finding a rhythm in me.

I close my eyes, inhaling the clean scent of his skin, orange blossom soap, the faint drift of lanolin from his fisherman's jumper. 'One day. I'll tell you everything.' I whisper it softly, too softly for him to hear.

* * *

The doorbell rings early on Thursday evening. I keep the chain on and open the door just enough to see who it is. A familiar figure looms on the step, peering through the crack at me; my instinct tells me to slam the door shut. Instead, I slip the chain off, as I attempt to look neutral and unfazed. 'Ambrose?'

'Cecily,' he says, leaning towards me. 'I thought I'd call in to see how you are.'

'I'm fine,' I say, remembering that I'm supposed to have been ill.

'You've been absent from church for days,' he says. 'I've been worried.'

I cross my arms. 'I've had... family things to sort out,' I tell him, annoyed by his persistence, the unnerving way he has of staring at me with his colourless eyes.

'Cecily, it's in times of stress and uncertainty that you need God as your guide more than ever,' he says, taking a step nearer. 'Pray with me. We can ask Him for his help together.'

'Ambrose.' Gabriel has appeared behind me. He leans to take the other man's hand. 'What can we do for you?'

Ambrose looks put out. 'We haven't seen Cecily at the Sacred Heart recently,' he says. 'I wanted to check that everything is alright.'

'That's kind of you,' Gabriel says. 'But she's leaving very early tomorrow morning, aren't you, Cecily? Crack of dawn. A long road trip. So, I'm sure you'll understand that she has things to arrange now.'

'A trip?' Ambrose repeats.

'Yes,' I tell him. 'To visit my parents.'

Ambrose closes his eyes, bringing his hands together in prayer. 'Lord, look down on us, and on your servant, Cecily. Help her, Oh Lord, to make the right decision, to follow you in your name...'

'Ambrose,' I say gently. 'Gabriel's right. I'm busy. Goodnight.'

We shut the door on him, and Gabriel grins. 'That man has always given me the creeps. Wasn't sure if you needed help getting rid of him, but it sounded like it.'

'Your help was most appreciated.' I smile. 'Although,' I add, remembering that I'm being Cecily, 'I'm sure he means well.'

* * *

I set off on the long drive first thing the next morning, before the others are up, with a packed lunch and a bottle of water. As I unlock the car door I glance up and down the street, checking for anyone loitering near our house. But it's too early even for hooded watchers. The car is unfamiliar and I haven't driven for ages. I keep crunching the gears, swearing under my breath. On the motorway, it's easier. I stay in top gear, cruising along staying within the speed limit, the wind rushing past. The address I have for Edith Baxter is on the outskirts of the Forest of Bowland. I'll circumnavigate Bristol and Birmingham. I don't want to break the trip with an overnight stay; I'd rather keep going if I can.

I switch on the radio to keep me company. The news comes on with a story about a bomb going off in Oklahoma; many feared dead the newsreader says, and then President Clinton's voice vowing swift punishment for the perpetrators. I change channels. Madonna's latest song fills the car. I can't listen to anything, I'm too anxious. I switch it off, tapping my hands on the wheel, wondering if I've done the right thing. I left the photograph of me and Cecily on top of Gabriel's songbook. Two identical girls in plaits. I want him to know who I really am. When he sees the photograph, he'll understand why I've seemed different. He'll know straight away he's been living with the other sister – he'll know who he slept with, who he really loves. Leaving the photograph has blown up the swap and there's no going back. But I can't keep this up any more; it's been going on for too long. We need clarity now, even if it hurts.

I stop twice at service stations. It's at the second one that I notice a red hatchback pulling out after me. I have a strange feeling that it might have been parked near me at the last stop, too. It follows me onto the motorway. As I turn off the M6, the small, red hatchback turns too.

The road cuts through dark forest, and the red car is behind me, twin circles of light dazzling in my wing mirror. My mouth is dry and sweat prickles my armpits. I press the central door-lock down. Something runs across the road, a low body with a long tail. I swear under my breath and brake, watching a form disappear into shadows. But the car behind is closer now. I speed up, and the other car speeds up too. I keep glancing into the rear-view mirror, but the blaze of headlights obliterates the driver. I press my foot on the accelerator, going much too fast down a dark, narrow, unfamiliar road, rushing into the glow of my own lights. I peer ahead, longing for a sign of human life, for houses and streets. Suddenly, I'm staring at bark, leaf shadows, rivers of black. A wall of trees. I slam my foot on the brake, and I'm sliding sideways, trunks sweeping past my window, my seat belt sharp across my chest.

The car stops on the verge with a judder, the engine cutting out. I look up, anticipating the worst – a man with an axe jumping from the red car, a crazy person coming for me – and I bend over the steering wheel and turn the key, but the ignition won't catch. The other car is alongside me on the road. It slows. My fingers fumble with the key, turning it again. A sob rises in my throat. A blur of pale face turns towards me through the driver's window. I twist the key. *Please start.* Then the other car speeds up and I'm watching its taillights disappear into blackness.

Relief swallows me. I sit back, exhausted, hands shaking. I must have missed a corner. The car has slewed up onto a verge, but somehow missed hitting trees. I lean my forehead on the steering wheel, breathing deeply. Night presses in around me. An owl cries. I turn the key in the ignition again, and the engine starts. Insects whirl like atoms inside the beams of my headlights.

My wheels bump back onto the tarmac. Five minutes later, a sign for the village appears. I'm nervously scanning parked vehicles, but there's no sign of the red car. Perhaps I'm imagining things; after all, if the driver wanted to hurt me, they'd had their chance when I skidded off the road. But I need the comfort and security of other people. I've already phoned ahead and booked a room at the pub in the village. I'll stay there tonight and visit Edith Baxter after breakfast tomorrow.

I reverse into a space in the car park at the back of the pub, grab my bag from the boot and hurry inside the building. The murmur of human voices, bright lights and the familiar smells of alcohol and chip fat make me feel better at once. It's all wonderfully normal. My heart begins to slow. The bar is half empty, just a few locals by the look of them, sitting over their pints. A cheerful landlady shows me up to my room. She opens the door and switches on a side light, gives me a key, and tells me breakfast is served between seven and nine.

A double bed takes up most of the space. There's a kettle on the side, a saucer of tea bags and little cartons of milk, two white cups. Heavy beams criss-cross the ceiling and a mullioned window looks out onto the road. I put my bag down and use the bathroom, splashing my face with water, cleaning my teeth.

I'm longing to get into bed, my body aches with tension. I touch my chest, bruised from the seat belt, and walk to the window to draw the curtains. But as I look out, my heart crashes into my mouth. The red car is parked across the street.

38

CECILY

1995, three weeks earlier

I left Edith Baxter at her front door and managed to walk to my car on trembling legs, fumbled with the key and slid in behind the wheel. But I couldn't start the engine. I'd lost my ability to make decisions. I don't know how long I remained inside the parked car, unable to move, staring through the windscreen. It was as if her words had ripped a blindfold from my eyes. For the first time, I understood the real magnitude of the sin poisoning my life. It had taken someone else's story to unlock my own pain, my own rage.

When I roused myself enough to turn the key in the ignition, I knew where I had to go. It was more than curiosity – it felt like the punishment I deserved. A pilgrimage or penance.

* * *

A bored-looking security guard stepped out of his booth when he saw me approach. 'You can't go in,' he said, holding up a beefy hand while he finished chewing a mouthful of pork pie. 'It's dangerous.' I ignored him, looking at the yellow digger, like an outsize Tonka toy, parked in the muddy drive. I had to get inside.

I reversed and drove back along the country lane until I was out of sight of the guard and parked at the entrance to a track. The roof of the old hospital was visible above leafy trees; I could make out a water tower, the skeleton of exposed rafters and broken tiles. I kept the water tower in my sights as I walked down the rutted track through fields, hoping I could get in from the back. A tangled copse of rowan, hawthorn and elder stood between me and the grounds. I pushed through the thicket of trees, edging past overgrown blackberry bushes, and came up against a tall perimeter fence. I ignored the signs screaming 'KEEP OUT, DANGER', and followed the enclosure, one hand bumping over knotted ridges of wire, until I found a hole ripped in the mesh.

Inside, I fought my way through undergrowth and long grass. Coarse blades brushed my shins, brambles snatched at my legs, tugging at my jacket. The hospital grounds were bigger than I'd imagined. The first building I came to was a low, brick shed with a heavy padlock on the boarded-up door. As I walked around the corner, I nearly fell over a couple of charred logs, a circle of burnt earth whitened with ash, a small, deserted encampment with an empty whisky bottle and two crumpled beer cans abandoned in long grass. But I was standing in the shadow of the main building. It rose, gutted and forlorn, into the grey sky. Half the roof had gone. Saplings sprouted from crumbling walls. Weeds pushed through paving stones. I walked the length of it, frustrated. All the doors were sealed with metal. When I eventually found a ground floor window without bars, I half-dragged, half-rolled an empty oil drum over and stood on it precariously, hauling myself over broken glass.

I let myself drop into a long corridor. The peeling walls had been daubed with graffiti, and there was a stink of urine. I wasn't the first to break in. I thought uneasily of the abandoned campfire. I made my way across mounds of rubble, destroyed books, splintered wood, and broken slabs of plaster, breathing in stale, dank air. Either side of me, doorways gaped into dim rooms. I stepped inside one and found myself in a narrow cell. There were stains on the floor and bars on the window; the walls were covered in some kind of padded fabric, frayed and rotted, coming away in chunks like a dead animal's hide. It was as if I could hear the screams and cries that had once sounded there, an old fear surging forwards to reclaim the space, to claim me. I edged away into the corridor, my hands thrown out to grasp the edges of the doorframe as if someone or something was trying to drag me back inside.

She had lived here. She was imprisoned in a padded cell while we swam in the tarn, while we sat in the Deveraux pew with our heads bowed in prayer. Easter and Christmas and summer holidays, she was here. While he lectured me on my sins and failings, she was here. While he locked me in the chapel with him, she was here.

I heard a movement further down the corridor, a shuffle, the noise of old bricks tumbling; I turned and ran, panic compressing my heart. I scrambled to get over the windowsill, but it was too high, and I failed to drag myself up, trying again and again, sobbing, scraping my elbows on the wall as I looked over my shoulder, not knowing what I was afraid of but desperate to get away from it. Finally, I managed to heave my body onto the sill, catching my left knee on a serrated point.

* * *

I only stopped the car when the hospital was far behind. A fine rain was falling, the wipers smearing oily wet across the windscreen. I got out and stood in the road, letting my skin and hair get soaked. Beads of moisture trembled on my sleeves. I longed for the kind of downpour that would strip me clean.

I bent down and touched my knee, finding a rip in my jeans. My fingers came away sticky. Anger burnt, licking at my belly, rising into my throat. He'd ruined her life, just like he'd ruined mine and Alice's. The world slipped and slid, tarmac rocking beneath my feet. Bending at the waist, I vomited onto the wet road.

I sat in the car. My damp clothes clung to my skin, and I shivered, wiping the back of my hand across my lips. I didn't know who I was any more. All the pieces of me were jumbled and broken. The unravelling of everything I thought I knew became the unravelling of myself. I remembered my aunt's letters to my mother, and how as a child I'd destroyed their last link with each other by leaving the letters for Daddy as if they were a gift for an unpredictable God. I thought of Henry, and how I'd judged him by Daddy's standards and got it wrong. If it wasn't for me, he might still be here. I'd tried so hard to avoid being sent to hell, but I was the biggest sinner of all.

The soul that sinneth, it shall die.

He'd used God's name to do terrible things. To lock his first wife away. To punish his children. To lie to his family.

The son shall not bear the iniquity of the father.

But what about the daughter? What about her?

39

ALICE

I can't sleep. I'm listening for stealthy footsteps outside my room, a creak of floorboards, the sound of someone twisting the doorknob. I've locked it and pulled a chair over to wedge under the handle. My body is rigid, senses on high alert, hounded, hunted. I stare into the flickering shadows the streetlight casts over the beamed ceiling, wondering if the driver of the car is out there, sitting behind the wheel, or if they're standing under my window, looking up.

I must have dozed off, because I wake with a start, fragments of a bad dream clutching at me. Morning seeps into the room. I get up and immediately go to the window and cautiously twitch the curtains apart. The red car has disappeared.

Everything seems more normal in daylight. The landlady has laid out a place in the bar for me, a checked tablecloth, and a basket of fresh bread. I seem to be the only guest. She appears from the kitchen, bustling and busy, with a maternal manner. 'What would you like, lovie?' she asks. 'I can do you eggs, bacon? I've got some muesli, too?'

The room carries the tang of last night's alcohol, a dash of bleach. My stomach is bilious with nerves and refuses the scrambled eggs on toast I've ordered. I nibble a corner of crust and manage a cup of tea, spooning sugar into it. After settling up, I leave the pub by the back entrance, throw my bag into the boot, and drive away.

As I leave the village, the red car pops up in my wing mirror again. My belly contracts. I can't pretend it's a coincidence. My fingers tighten around the gear stick, as if that will help me to think, gripping until my knuckles whiten. Should I turn around, drive back to the pub, or better, a police station? But the village won't have a police station, and what could I say if it did? There are plenty of red cars on the road. The driver hasn't threatened me. Nothing has happened.

I keep going, remembering the directions the landlady gave me, my gaze sliding to my rear-view mirror, watching the car behind me. They're keeping their distance today, but I can just make out the outline of the driver, sitting high behind the wheel. The landlady said it was short drive through the forest. The trees look ancient, most of them oaks. Rotting trunks lie at the side of the road, living branches making a canopy above the car. I glance behind. The car has dropped out of sight. I get to some tall gates and turn in at the entrance of The Hall with a feeling of relief. Surely, whoever is following me, wouldn't risk coming down a private drive?

It's a substantial, ugly house with thick, grey stone walls, flying buttresses at either end. Tudor-style chimney stacks tower over the roof; a large, pointed porch almost conceals the heavy front door. Thick layers of ivy climb the walls, gnarled vines sprouting dark green foliage. Overlapping leaves press up against windows, almost completely concealing some. Chunks of mortar are missing, tendrils digging their way into the brickwork.

The red car hasn't followed, and I park and hurry over to the porch. I tug the bell pull. When the door opens, I take a sharp inhale. The woman standing before me in a tweed skirt and brown cardigan, stout brogues on her feet, has hardly changed from the day I opened the door to her at Hawksmoor. I only saw her for a few minutes, but she'd cursed our family as Cecily and I had crouched on the back stairs. The corners of her thin mouth are edged with folds of skin, her chin dissolving into a straggly neck. She scowls. 'You again,' she says.

'No,' I say quickly. 'I'm Alice.'

She stares at me with a suspicious frown. 'You look exactly the same.'

'We're identical twins.' I raise my shoulders a fraction as if to apologise for the confusion and attempt a reassuring smile. 'Mirror image.'

She gives a disbelieving harrumph, but shrugs, opening the door wider. 'As you're here, I suppose you'd better come in.'

I turn to look behind me. Still no sign of the red car.

She shows me into a room dim with viridian light under a vaulted ceiling. Beyond the windows, folds of creeper press against the glass, making it feel as though we're under water. I sit on a lumpy brocade armchair. My bladder is bursting. I'm desperate for a pee, but I don't like to ask. An ancient Pekinese dog wanders in, a small tongue protruding from his panting mouth. He bumps against my shins.

'He's blind,' she says. 'Don't touch. He bites.'

The room is stuffy. The windows sealed with green. Edith Baxter's mouth is a thin trap, a line of disapproval. She seems to resent me, dislike me. We regard each other warily. As far as I know, Edith only visited Hawksmoor that one time. I can't imagine why Cecily wants me to meet her. 'When… when did my sister come to see you?' I ask.

'A few weeks ago,' she says. 'Two, three, perhaps. My memory isn't what it was.'

Folding my hands in my lap, I wait for her to continue. She settles deeper into the sofa opposite me, crossing her ankles, knees pressed together as she stares at a place just over my left shoulder.

I sit forward, clear my throat. 'If you don't mind me asking, what's the connection,' I ask. 'Between you and my family?'

'My sister was married to your father.'

'Your sister…' her words clatter inside my brain. 'And my father,' I repeat stupidly. 'Married. But… when?'

'1956.'

Numbers click through my mind. Five years before Cecily and I were born. Four years before Henry. I'm trying to grasp what that means.

'I think, perhaps, she was happy for a while,' Edith is saying. 'He was handsome, even if he wasn't a kind man. Proud of course. But not cruel. Not then. But she had three miscarriages in quick succession, and th local doctor, a friend of your father's, said it was unlikely she'd be able to carry a child to term.'

'So... she died?' I manage to ask. I'm finding it hard to concentrate on her words. My father. Married to someone else before our mother. It's unbelievable.

'No,' she says. 'She died years later. Physically died, that is.'

I frown, not understanding.

'It was after the last miscarriage that that she became ill, staying in bed, crying a lot,' she goes on. 'Depression, we'd call it now.' Edith smooths her skirt over her knees. 'But your father had her committed to a mental hospital.'

I understand now why we've never been told about his first wife. Never heard her name. I dig my thumb nail into the fleshy part of my hand.

'The doctor agreed she was a danger to herself and needed constant psychiatric care. I tried to stop it, tried to get her out. My parents had died, so it was left to me. But it didn't matter how many times I wrote, how much I begged him, Edmund refused to sign the paperwork. He knew the governors. He blocked me at every turn.' Her voice is strangely devoid of emotion. She sits very upright. 'Within a year, he'd had the marriage dissolved and was engaged to your mother.'

I stare at her, feeling sick. 'What happened to your sister?'

'Mary. She was called Mary. She died ten years after they gave her a lobotomy.' She looks down into her lap. 'It's not far from here. The hospital. But there was a scandal – mistreatment of patients. It's been closed for years.'

'My God.' The room tilts. I glance towards the window, needing air. Beyond the puzzle of ivy, something moves, the shape of a person. I think I see the outline of a face peering in.

'Someone's there,' I gasp. The dog at my feet lets out a short, rasping bark.

Edith doesn't even turn her head to look. 'Perhaps the gardener,' she says, unruffled. 'He comes once a week.'

I'm trying to see through the obscuring leaves. I can't make out the shape any more. My heart rattles in my chest. I sip air, blowing out, trying to relax clenched muscles. I swallow, pushing sweating palms across my jeans.

Any words I can say are inadequate. I feel ashamed. The woman sitting opposite me is reduced, sad, her only rebellion her refusal to meet my eyes. Or perhaps she can't bear to look at me. Perhaps I am too offensive, too much of a reminder of my father.

'I have an apology, too,' she says, examining the backs of her wrinkled hands. 'Years ago, I left a dead cat nailed to your door. I was half-mad with grief. You must understand how angry I was, how desperate.' Her mouth trembles. 'But it was a pointless thing.'

I would like to make her understand how sorry I am. I want to tell her that my father disgusts me, but I can't speak.

She pushes herself to her feet and shuffles across the floor to show me out.

'Your father is evil,' she says, just before she closes the door. She looks at me at last, and her eyes are cold. 'He's still alive, isn't he?'

* * *

Leaving The Hall, I turn onto the forest road, not knowing where to go Should I drive back to Exeter? My mind reels. How easily he has scrubbe people out of his life, erasing them from history if they spoil his idea o how it should look. Edith's words repeat in my head. *Your father is evil.* squeeze the steering wheel, trying to imagine Mary – her terror at bein locked up, her hope that they'd let her out when they realised th mistake. I have a hazy idea of mental hospitals in the fifties and sixtie Did they give her cold baths, electric shock treatments, before they even tually cut out part of her brain? I grip the wheel tighter.

It's then that I see the red car again, tailing me at a distance. My ange at my father leaps into anger at whoever it is that's hounding me. I pres my foot to the accelerator and the car revs, sending me shooting along straight length of road. I swerve around the first corner, the gearstic sweaty under my hand. The road bends and weaves, and I grip the whe tighter, shoulders rigid. The red car has fallen back. The driver is stru gling to take the corners as fast as me; they don't have the same reckless adrenaline in their veins. I slam around the next hairpin bend and spot a Land Rover parked up in a narrow forest turning. I check the wing mirror. No red car. I turn the wheel sharply and skid into the turning, just missing a tree. The wheels lose traction on the slick grass, and I crash through a swathe of young bracken. I jam on the handbrake, parking behind the larger vehicle, my car half-hidden by the empty Range Rover and shoots of acid green. Sinking low in the seat, I turn to look through the back windscreen. The red car flies past, and I catch the profile of the driver. A flash of forehead, nose, receding chin. But that's impossible. It can't be him.

As soon as the car's disappeared, I pull the door handle and tumble out, pushing my jeans down over my thighs, crouching to let out a long stream of urine. I gaze up at the road through the screen of bracken, alert for engine sounds. I pull up my trousers and scramble back behind the wheel. When I turn the key in the ignition, the engine stutters and fails. I try again, nudging my foot against the clutch. The mechanism turns and catches, roaring as I accelerate and reverse out with a squeal of brakes. I'm driving fast back the way I came, checking the mirror; but the red car doesn't materialise. I've lost him.

Was it really Ambrose Stone? Why would he follow me all this way? He thinks I'm Cecily, I remind myself. And she has told me lie after lie.

I go through the village, driving along country lanes onto the moors. I look in my rear-view mirror every few minutes to reassure myself I'm not being followed. The sky is an upturned bowl of silver. Fast-moving clouds coil and uncoil like ribbons in a stream. I don't know where to go or what to do. I park on the verge. Once out of the car, the wind grabs at my hair, whipping it across my face. I can breathe more easily in all this space, and I lean into the push of air, walking across scrubby hillside, hands in my pockets, chin tucked into my chest. I come across a herd of wild ponies. The small, sturdy animals ignore me, tearing grass, broad rumps against the weather, coarse tails whipping at their hocks. I sit on the ground, lying back against springy heather. High above, a kestrel balances inside vaulted hollows, wings holding it against an invisible force, amber eyes hooking its prey.

Why the hell was Ambrose Stone tailing me? Perhaps it wasn't him. Whoever it was, I've lost them. I'm safe.

And I'm starving. I go back to the car and root inside the glove compartment, hoping Gabriel might have left some food amongst the clutter. I'm in luck. There's a chocolate bar. God knows how old it is, but I don't care. My mouth waters as I sit behind the wheel, unwrapping the snack, wolfing down stale wafers covered in old chocolate, licking the inside of the wrapper for scraps.

I need to get home. Make sure that Gabriel and Bea are alright. I've known for a while now, that Hollyhocks Cottage is my real home. For the first time, I belong somewhere, and have people who belong to me. I'm sick of being a wanderer, homeless, rootless. I have nowhere to go, except there – all my instincts driving me to return to the two people and the one place I've come to love.

I start the car and turn in the direction of Exeter. Once I'm on the motorway, I put my foot down, and miles rush past as I grip the steering wheel, staring ahead, my vision blurry with exhaustion. As I drive, I have a strong sense that despite my desperation to get back, I'm doing the wrong thing, that I'm missing something, forgetting something – but I fight the feeling. I need to see Gabriel, feel his arms around me.

When I'm close to Bristol, I pull into a service station to fill up with petrol. I buy a sandwich and black coffee, stirring in three little sachets of sugar, and sit in the car. The caffeine and sugar help to revive me. My mind returns to the problem of Cecily. She must have wanted me to see Edith, to hear the truth. Cecily already knew the story about Mary, the lie we've been told all our life. Our father, the hypocrite. I sip my drink and close my eyes, trying to enter Cecily's mind. What would she do with that information? What effect would it have on her?

She's the one who worshipped him, the puppet who did his bidding without question, the one who believed everything he said and everything he stood for.

'DIE', she'd written in her sketchbooks. 'DIE', she'd scribbled on the mirror.

My eyes snap open. I have a sudden conviction. It wasn't Gabriel she was talking about. It was our father.

I put the coffee down, breathless with urgency as I take the road map from the pocket in the door and spread it across the steering wheel. I estimate that I'm roughly four hours away from Hawksmoor. Retracing my journey is the last thing I want to do, but I must find her. I'm not afraid any more. Whatever she's done, she's still my sister. She needs my help. I can't let her murder our father. If that's what she's planning, I must stop her.

And I want to tell her the truth about me and Gabriel, tell her that this swap is permanent – she can have her freedom. But in return, I will take her life. Her home and family are mine now.

I gulp the rest of my drink and start the car. Driving away from Exeter, I enter the other side of the motorway, following signs for the North.

40

ALICE

It's late and the main street is empty of people, houses subdued under a purpling sky, a faint smell of wood smoke drifting in the air, a few windows lit with gold. I pass the primary school where Cecily and I spent our time as outcasts, and the Anglican church that our father despises.

I drive out of the village down a road that narrows into a lane; my headlights showing a dense hedge on one side of me, the fissures of a drystone wall on the other. I sense, rather than see, the spread of the dale beyond the wall, and the black cloak of the hills rising into the higher fells. Granite outcrops and ridges stand as witnesses to my homecoming. I imagine what they see from their lofty positions: a small car with twin beams of light tunnelling through darkness. Perhaps they can make out the human sitting inside the moving tin box, see how she clasps the wheel with trembling fingers. They have witnessed armies on the march, looked down on gibbets hung with the dead, and farmers guiding tired sheep home. I am nothing to them.

I had forgotten the way this landscape is soaked in history, an ancient stage carved out of volcano fire and melted ice. I had forgotten how lonely it can feel to travel at night, weaving half-blindly across the face of the earth under a fathomless sky.

The gates of Hawksmoor appear on my left, rotted husks of metal standing open. I drive through slowly, the pit of my stomach clenching in anticipation. Bushes burgeon out of the shadows, hydrangeas and dogwood gone wild, their twigs scratching the sides of my car with awful squeals. I can make out the tops of tall grasses, arrow-head fringes glinting in my headlights. The battlements and tower appear out of a scrawl of trees, and I pull over in front of the old coach house and kill the engine. I sit for a moment, collecting my nerve, as the car ticks into silence. Something prevents me from driving up to the entrance, an instinct for stealth, a fear of the past, of him.

I never thought I'd find the courage to come back, never thought I'd have to face him again. My hands are shaking. Is Cecily here? If I'm right, she's already in the house. I hope I'm in time to intervene, to stop her from committing a crime. To stop him hurting her.

I stretch across to the glove compartment and pull out the torch I'd found when I was looking for food. I press the button and the beam comes on. Thank you, Gabriel, I think, as I close the car door as softly as possible and follow the verge, walking across the unkempt lawn, avoiding the noise of the gravel, towards the front door. The whole building is in darkness. The Volvo is parked at an odd angle in the middle of the drive. In the moonlight, I notice flat tires and a lacing of rust around wheel arches, weeds growing against its sides. I suppose it's been abandoned without my mother to drive it.

As I reach the lions, blood pounds in my ears. I can't breathe. It's been seventeen years. Terror grips me. I don't know if I can do this. I don't know if I'm brave enough to walk through that door. I sink down on the cold step, crouching with my forehead pressed against a stone flank. Give me courage, I ask silently. I remember how Cecily and I sat on the lions while we waited for Henry at the start of the holidays. A pang of loss shoots through me. The air is suddenly cold and I'm shivering, nauseous. I close my eyes.

When I open them, my legs are stiff and aching, and I stand, swaying, on the top step. In the distance, the bells of St Mary's toll nine times. My hand reaches out to push the heavy door. It gives with a creak. Hesitantly, I slip through into deeper darkness. I keep still, hardly breathing, waiting for my eyes to become accustomed to the lack of light, listening intently. I can hear nothing but the rush of breath through my body, but I know I'm not alone.

I edge along the outer wall, the big tapestry brushing my shoulder as I feel my way past the Italian clock, past the walnut tables where the Chinese vases used to stand. It's odd not to have the dogs here, tails wagging, hot breath on my ankles, their welcoming barks. The house is cold. The air damp and claggy in my mouth, stale and unused. I make my way past the dining room down the passage to our father's study. I knock softly; there's no answer, so I press the handle, and it swings open. My fingers fumble along the wall for the light switch. But the bulb doesn't ignite. I inch forwards over to where his big, leather-bound desk crouches, a massive shape in the darkness, and find the Anglepoise lamp, but that doesn't come on either. The electricity must be off. I click the torch on and shine the beam around me, lighting up the painting above the desk. Gurning devils' faces leer down at me, pitchforks in hands. I touch the desk, gritty with dust, littered with papers in my father's hectic scrawl, ink blots like blood splatters. Unopened bills and final reminders slide through my fingers. Something rustles underfoot. The torch picks out more papers, scattered as if they've been thrown to the floor.

I make my way along the rest of the passage, down the stairs to the basement, sloping flagstones uneven under my feet. I shine light into the gaping mouth of the scullery, the buttery, the vast, empty kitchen. It's cold. The range must be out. My flickering beam shows a mess of opened tins on the old oak table. I go over and look at empty containers of baked beans, tuna fish and anchovy, sharp lids peeled back like lethal tongues. There's the rank stink of old fish. A half-eaten loaf of bread speckled with mould is surrounded by stale breadcrumbs, a knife smeared with butter. The air is bitter with rot. Something moves in the corner, a scrape of claws against stone, and I step back, expecting a rat, but it's one of the feral cats slinking away.

I go as quietly as I can through the long gallery returning to the entrance hall. The hairs on the back of my neck stand up. Is Cecily here? My father? I stop in the hall, shining the narrow light around. It catches on something at the foot of the stairs, a bristle of spikes, an elongated metal lozenge, wide as a shark's grin. It takes a second before I understand what I'm looking at. The mantrap. The adrenaline in my body accelerates into a cold rush of fear, as I understand how easily I could have trodden on it. I can't leave it there. I stuff the torch in the waistband of my jeans, and cautiously pick up one end of the trap. It's long and heavy. I drag it back backwards through the corridor, my arms straining with the weight. Its edges catch against wood and stone, making a scraping noise, a siren squeal announcing my presence to anyone who's lurking upstairs.

Wedging the armoury door open with one shoulder, I heave it through. I'm trembling. If I hadn't caught the mantrap in the torch light – Jesus – I take a breath, trying to steady myself. Did my father leave it there for me? But he didn't know I was coming. How could he? I go up the back-stairs, shining the light on every step, to be sure there are no more devices left to catch me. I feel my way along the corridor of the first floor, creeping past gaping doorways, past my own bedroom. I don't go in. There's a sour smell of tom cat competing with the aroma of damp. The curtains are open on all the windows, and moonlight filters in, milky between darker pools of ink. I think of shouting out, calling for Cecily. I know she's close. I sense her panic, her fear.

I feel the sudden gathering of energy, the disturbance of air, before I am hit by a rush of bone and sinew. A thump of muscle against my shin. I stagger under the blow, heavy as the fist of an angry man, and the torch falls from my fingers. Pain stabs through my right knee. I look up to see the outline of an animal disappearing along the corridor, tail up, fur on end. Bloody cats. I rub my knee, flexing it cautiously. Nothing seems to be broken, but it throbs like hell.

Where is Cecily? Has he done something with her? An old terror squeezes my throat. His face looms close, his mouth a wet hole of need. Lips twisting with frustration. I raise my hands to my neck, trying to prise his fingers away. *You will be cast down, Alice, into the fiery furnace.*

I can't breathe. I lean against the wall, shutting my eyes, lungs burning. My mouth gasps at oxygen. Flashes ignite like sparks of electricity behind my vision. Darkness pulls me in. The syrupy blackness of the past. A mire of grief and anguish.

* * *

My eyelids snap open. I'm not leaning against the wall any more; I'm sitting on a step. I don't know how I got here or where I am in the house. The faint glow from the moonlight has been extinguished. I fumble for the torch, before remembering I dropped it. I put my hand against a bare surface next to me, then down to touch the rough texture of the step below. No carpet. The width is mean. I'm sitting on the stairs to the attic. I hear a noise and cock my head, ears straining. A rumble of muffled knocks, like distant thunder. The sound is coming from higher up, towards the eaves. I get to my feet and go slowly up the steps, feeling my way with my hands, trying to avoid making the joists creak. I'm in the narrow corridor of the old servants' quarters. A trickle of starlight comes through bare windows, casting patterns on the floor. The sound has gone. I wonder if I imagined it. As I creep forwards, shadows jump at my shoulders.

The noise starts again, a soft, insistent scrabbling to my right, the rustle of long tails, the scratching of sharp claws, rats behind the brick-work. I realise I'm outside the priest hole and understand the sounds are human nails working against crumbling plaster. There's a muffled thump behind the wall – the impact of a foot or fist perhaps. My eye is caught by a long, thin shape next to me. A walking stick? My heart judders as I realise it's a gun. My father's shooting rifle is propped against the wall.

I put my ear to the plaster. 'Cecily?' I whisper as loudly as I dare. 'Cecily. It's me. I'm here.' The scrabbling intensifies. 'Wait. I'll let you out,' I say, feeling across the beam for the secret lever. My toe catches on something, and I bend down, finding a torch at my feet and click it on, shining it over the beam to find the hidden mechanism.

The great wooden limb rises slowly, releasing a foul stench, the contaminated air from centuries-old terror, dust impregnated with pigeon and rat droppings, mould spores, the prayers of the dying. There is a spurt of coughing, and one long, thin leg appears, shoulders squeezing out sideways. A torso eases through, a head appears, and my father tumbles like a broken doll onto the patched carpet.

I step back with a cry. The torch falls from my fingers.

My father looks up at me and scrabbles for purchase with his hands, long fingers clawing. He manages to rock onto his knees and then lurches forward, his forehead touching the floor, as if in prayer. He is shockingly old, thin hair pasted to his balding skull; his cheeks hollow under the drape of skin.

'Where's Cecily?' I can hardly speak, my words squeezed out in gasps. 'What have you done with her?'

I pick up the gun. It's heavy and the muzzle points towards him. He rolls onto his back and the moonlight picks out his cadaver's face, the gaping mouth. His eyes are dark holes. For a second, my finger trembles against the trigger. But I turn away and fling the rifle from me, sending it clattering into the priest hole. I feel along the plaster to find the place to press, and the oak limb slowly closes, slotting into place with a soft click.

I wonder how long he was in there. Not long enough to kill him, at any rate. Something grips my ankle. My father's long fingers are wrapped around me like a shackle. He's shuffled forward on his elbows, and now he's hanging on to me, nails digging in. 'Cecily,' he pants.

Fear and disgust rise like bile. I yank my foot away with a shudder. He's too weak resist. 'I'm not her.' I bend over him. 'I'm Alice.'

He stares up, mouth falling open in disbelief. Then his lips twist, and rage distorts his expression. With a grunt of effort, he swipes for me again, fingers outstretched, but I move back. He begins to drag himself on his belly towards me. I keep just out of reach.

'Liar, liar.' His rasping breath cuts through the darkness. 'There is no Alice.'

Nausea crashes through me, a vortex of confusion. The corridor swells, the floor pitches, rearing up and crashing down like a boat in a storm. I turn and stumble away from him, arms out, lurching blindly from one wall to the other.

41

CECILY

I've fallen to my knees in a narrow corridor. I get to my feet, squinting into the moonlit space. The ceiling is low, the sides sloped under the eaves. I'm at the top of the house in the old servants' quarters and the air around me quivers with a malignant presence. I'm not alone. Someone breathes in the darkness nearby. With a crashing heart, I follow the ragged sounds towards a shape lying prone on the floor. I inch forward carefully over the thin carpet. When I'm close enough to see who it is, I rear back. Daddy. Someone's let him out. It must have been Alice. She's here in the house. I knew it the moment I walked through the front door – I can smell her, sense her. She hasn't deserted me. I glance towards the priest hole. The entrance is sealed up, the beam in place. She's the only other person who knows the secret mechanism. The gun has gone too. She must have taken it.

Daddy lies motionless on his front, legs bent as if he was in the act of crawling. He's moved some way from the priest hole, and it looks as though he's collapsed. He's unconscious, his lungs pulling in shallow, staccato breaths. I stand over him, thinking how easily I could close off his oxygen. I'd only need to place both my palms across his mouth and nose and apply some pressure. It would take moments.

I sink onto the floor beside him, but turn away and pull my knees up, making a cave for myself, like I used to in the priest hole. I cover my eyes, trying to think. Alice is here somewhere. She's answered my prayer – she's come to save me from committing irredeemable sin.

I wasn't going to keep him in there for ever. I was going to let him out after an hour or two. But first, I'd wanted him to suffer, to know how we'd felt, locked inside that place. It had been easier than I'd imagined making him obey me, the heft of the barrel at my hip as I walked him up the stairs towards the attic. One step, then another. His stooping frame ahead of me, his faltering feet in slippers. It had been hard to balance the gun in one hand and keep the torch steady in the other, but he'd submitted silently. It had felt like a dream, as if I was following a pattern that had been laid down for me since the beginning, that for the whole of my life, I'd been heading for this moment in the darkness, on the stairs, a gun pointed at my father's back.

Outside the priest hole, I'd told him to stop. 'You were always the disappointment,' he'd said. In the light of my torch, his eyes blinked furiously, leaking water. Not tears, just the seepage of the elderly. He'd leant towards me, wiping his cheek with the nub of a knuckle. 'It should have been you that died.'

My hands shook so that I'd dropped the torch, but I'd kept the gun on him while I'd felt across plaster and rough oak, finding the place to press.

'Henry was the one Hawksmoor should have gone to. He would have come to his senses. I would have made sure of it.' His ruined face sneered. 'Alice was a fine girl. But you. You had no fighting spirit. No gumption. You've made a mess of your life because you're weak. Always have been.'

'You made me weak,' I'd told him. 'You never loved me, never believed in me. But I'm the one who stayed for you. I've been loyal.'

'I've sold the house,' he'd said. 'Sold it for development.'

'Liar,' I'd said, my heart pounding. 'You wouldn't. It'll be mine when you're dead.'

He shook his head, smiling. 'You'll never have it. Nobody else wants it. The restoration costs are ruinous. And we are ruined. The debt is bottomless.'

I'd pointed the rifle towards the priest hole, watching him bow his head, stooping to get onto his knees, crawling clumsily into the dark as I'd pushed the muzzle against his spine. The wall sealed him up. I could walk away, I'd thought. Leave him there forever. But I'd had a better idea. A terrible idea. I'd seen the red notices from the electricity company heaped up in his study. The power was off. I'd already dragged the mantrap to the bottom of the stairs in preparation. He wouldn't see it in the darkness. The developers would find his body when they came with their wrecking balls.

He's too weak to walk now. He'd never make it down the stairs.

Stop. It doesn't matter. I pinch my thigh, a little nip of pain to remind myself that I'm not here for that. However cathartic revenge would feel, however much I wanted to see him flailing in the trap, if I killed him, I'd have to pay for it. The punishment for taking the matter into my own mortal hands would be eternal damnation. Alice has saved me from that – her intervention came just in time.

All I have left are words. I still have so much to tell him. I prod the shape on the floor beside me with my foot, and he stirs, gasping like a drowning man breaking through waves. 'Alice?' His voice croaks, eyes wide.

'No, Daddy. It's me. Cecily.'

He struggles to get up but can't even make it onto his knees. Floundering like a landed trout, he manages to prop himself up on one shaking elbow. 'What are you—'

'I know about your first wife,' I interrupt, squatting next to him. 'Mary Baxter. I saw your wedding certificate. Remember Edith Baxter? She came here once to beg you to release her sister.' I take care to pronounce each word clearly so that he can't avoid them. 'I went to see her. You had Mary committed to a mental institution because she couldn't have children.'

He blinks at me in confusion. Then the old arrogant look comes into his face, a crafty glint in his eyes. 'She was insane—' his voice breaks off as his elbow gives way, his torso slumping onto his front, so that he lies with one cheek against the moth-eaten carpet. 'The marriage was dissolved,' he mutters into the dust. 'There was no need to speak of it.'

I crouch over him. 'You wouldn't let Mummy see her only sister because she was divorced.'

'I told you... no divorce... marriage dissolved...' His voice is faltering, muffled, breaking apart, and I know time is running out.

'You made me believe I'd made a terrible mistake by marrying Gabriel. I loved him, but you treated me as if I'd committed an unforgivable crime.'

'You can't blame me for... your bad decision...' each word gasped. He can't die yet.

'Marrying Gabriel was the best decision I've ever made,' I get hold of his face with both hands, twisting it on the column of his neck to stare up into mine, needing him to understand. 'But you ruined my marriage.'

I let go, and his skull flops back onto the floor. 'He was... an unbeliever,' he mutters.

'I thought about killing myself,' I tell him. 'Locking us in the priest hole wasn't God's will. But you changed me into someone small and afraid and ashamed. I don't know how to escape the memories. I do bad things to try and block them out.' The hit of vodka, the stranger pushing himself into me. Pain to kill pain. But I couldn't let Gabriel sleep with me after that. I couldn't let him near me. I was corrupted.

'I was going to end it all,' I whisper. 'I was going to poison myself.' The twigs of yew gathered and kept in my pocket, transferred to my locked drawer.

'DIE', I'd written over my sketchbooks. 'DIE, DIE, DIE'. The people I loved would be safer and happier without me. But I had a child. I couldn't leave her.

'You. Fail. At. Everything—' he wheezes.

'It would've made you happy, wouldn't it, if I'd killed myself? Damned forever. That's what you wanted. The number of times you told me that I'd go to hell.' My voice trembles. 'Only I didn't kill myself, Daddy. Or you.' I bend close to his ear. 'I wanted to. But Alice came.'

'Alice?' he whispers with a shudder.

'Yes. She came back. She hates you, too. But she escaped, didn't she? A long time ago. She had the sense to know you for who you really are. And she ran, Daddy. She ran for her life. It's me that's the fool. I stayed for you.'

His eye has closed, his skin bluish in the dim light. I know I should roll him onto his back, open his airwaves, but I can't touch him again. 'I'm not going to hell,' I whisper. 'But you are.' I curl into a ball, clutching my knees, rocking back and forth, wishing the child would come, the cavalier, the monk. They always came when I needed them. I need them now.

A bitter stench of urine fills my nostrils. He is leaking, the vessel of his body giving up, falling apart, the engine running down. His fingers clench against the carpet. I remember them around my throat, wielding a strap, slapping my face with the open span of sinew and bone, the smell of sweat and incense. *We do this to please God.*

I want to take all my unspoken words and press them into his mouth, force him to swallow my pain. I want him to know that I can't stop punishing myself for being the person he's made me; rotten and guilty.

Behind me, I hear floorboards groan under the pressure of a foot stepping and releasing. The sound amplifies in my ears. Someone is coming up the stairs.

I stay still, hoping to melt into the shades of darkness. My heart thumps through the cage of my chest. A blinding light fills the corridor, the beam of a torch bouncing across the floor, searching the space. The circle is dazzling. It lassoes me inside its glare. I cower as I blink up at it, unable to look away. I want it to be Alice, but the shape behind the torch is too large, their step too heavy.

The torch hovers over me, and the eldritch figure squats, a hand reaching. I'm caught, pulled against the width of a chest. Two arms pin me into stillness. I try to struggle, but he's too strong for me. I feel the brush of cotton, the rasp of stubble on my skin. I smell orange blossom. 'Cecily,' he says. 'It's me. Gabriel.'

He's holding me, saying things I can't take in. Relief overwhelms me. I rest my forehead on his shoulder, let it become real. My limbs are stiff, my mind numb. 'Gabriel.' I pull back, confused. 'How did you—?'

'It doesn't matter now.' He's shining the torch onto the shape next to me on the floor. In the flickering light, I see Daddy's chest rising and falling. 'Your father,' Gabriel crawls over to him. 'What's wrong?'

'His heart, I think.'

Gabriel heaves at Daddy's shoulder, rolling him onto his back. 'Edmund, can you hear me? Hang on. We'll get help.' He turns to me. 'We need to call an ambulance,' he says. 'Is there a phone in the house?'

I try to clear the muddle in my head. 'In his study,' I manage.

A sudden gasp of air makes us turn to look at Daddy, and from his chest, the screech of a steel saw against metal. His forehead glistens with sweat, and his hands move, tearing helplessly at his throat. His body starts to twitch, convulsing as if there's a spirit inside battling to get out. Then, with a ghost cry, he goes slack. 'Is he dead?' I whisper.

Gabriel bends over my father, frowns, and quickly places his mouth over Daddy's slack lips. I try to block out the sounds – wet suction and huff of air – then with a rip and a bounce of buttons, Gabriel opens Daddy's shirt and positions the flat of his hands at the centre of Daddy's sternum. Gabriel kneels up and pushes down hard with straight arms. The pale hoop of my father's ribs creak and bend, the old, soft fabric of his body inert as dough under the pummelling. Gabriel pants with the effort of trying to force Daddy's life back into him. The rhythm is sickening, desperate. I want it to stop. Gabriel lowers his face next to Daddy's, listening. He sits back and picks up a limp hand, feeling for a pulse at the wrist. He turns to me and shakes his head.

He puts his arm around my shoulder. 'I'm going to call for an ambulance,' he says. 'Are you alright? Can you stay here?'

I don't have the strength to move. He disappears into the darkness, the bobbing light of the torch going with him. Then I remember what I did. 'Gabriel!' I shout after him. 'Be careful. There's mantrap at the bottom of the main stairs.'

'What?' His voice rises out of shadows.

I repeat myself. 'Use the torch. Go slowly,' I add, sinking onto the floor next to Daddy. I lie beside him, my hand finding his, entwining our fingers. I want to feel the warmth draining out of him, and the cold creeping inside his veins like the slow freezing over of water. His hand in mine is harmless. It's just me in the darkness again. The child and I used to sing in the hole to keep the terror away, her voice whispering words for me, so that she became me, and I became her. I begin to hum.

42

CECILY

Heavy footsteps. Voices. Lights bounce into my face. I squint away from the glare. The comfort of professionals enters the corridor, the practical actions of people who know what they're doing, 'Are you alright, love?' one of them asks me, as his companion kneels over my father. Paramedics. I have a jolt of fear. Will they try to bring him back to life? My heart thumps erratically against my sternum.

Gabriel is talking to them. 'I arrived at just gone midnight,' he's saying. 'He blacked out then. I'm guessing he's been dead for at least thirty minutes.'

They bend over Daddy's body. I look away.

One of them takes my wrist between thumb and fingers. 'I'm fine,' I tell him.

'You're in shock,' he says. 'Hot sweet tea. You need to sit somewhere quiet. Take it easy for a while.'

They lift Daddy's body onto a stretcher, strapping him on, talking all the time as they work out how to get the stretcher through the house to the ambulance. I don't look at him again or say goodbye. And then they're gone, manoeuvring the stretcher down the narrow stairs. Their friendly voices disappear with the reassurance they gave. The hallucinatory feeling returns. Shock, I suppose. I am shivering as if I'm swimming in ice water.

Gabriel crouches beside me. 'Cecily,' he murmurs. 'I'm so sorry about your father.'

I close my eyes, fighting the swimmy feeling, fighting the grip of the cold.

'Hey,' he says gently. 'You're shivering.' He helps me to my feet, his grasp warm and firm.

'Please hold me,' I say through chattering teeth.

His arms go around me, and I resist the pull into nothingness. I want to stay inside Gabriel's arms. It's over. I don't need to run any more.

'Cecily,' he says. 'What's going on? What happened here?'

I shake my head. I can't explain. I don't have the energy.

He holds me to his chest, his mouth in my hair. 'It's alright,' he says. 'We can talk about it later. Let's get out of here.' He steps away. 'Can you manage the stairs?'

I stand taller, strength running into the bones of my legs. I take a step and another, and wince as my right knee buckles.

'Are you alright?'

I nod. It feels as if my knee has been whacked with something hard. But I limp on, with Gabriel supporting my elbow.

We go through the deserted house. On the first-floor landing, there's enough moonlight to see by, and he clicks off the torch as we walk slowly down the main staircase. 'There wasn't anything at the bottom of the stairs,' he says in a puzzled voice. 'No mantrap.'

'She must have moved it,' I say.

'She?' His voice is sharp. 'There's someone else here?'

'Yes,' I say. He gives me a puzzled glance but doesn't ask more questions. We've walked past the place where I'd left the trap, and he's leading me towards the front door. I stop as if I've hit an invisible forcefield. 'I can't leave,' I say. 'Not without her.'

'Okay,' he says, turning slowly. 'This... woman. Where is she?'

'I don't know,' I say.

'If she's hiding, we'll never find her.' I sense disbelief in his voice. 'Too many rooms. Shall we shout?' he looks at me. 'What's her name?'

I shake my head.

Gabriel rubs his chin, looking puzzled. 'Well, we can stay for a while. Perhaps she'll find us. The electricity seems to be off. But I have matches, so if we can find a candle—'

'The kitchen,' I say.

In the cavernous room, Gabriel lights a stub of candle and I slump into a chair at the table. He moves around looking for things on the surfaces, and then exclaims as he manages to get a gas ring to light. 'It's a little camping stove,' he says. 'Your father's been cooking on it. Now, if I can find some tea...'

There's the sound of water filling a kettle, the hiss of flame, the clink of cups being placed on a surface. I stare at the blue, gold flicker of the candle. Daddy is dead. Henry is dead. But where's Alice? I feel her close. She's in the house. She wants me to find her.

Gabriel puts a cup in front of me and pulls a chair over, sitting down beside me. 'There's a lot of things I don't understand,' he says. He gets something out of his pocket. In the candlelight I look at a photograph of me and Alice. We have long plaits. Alice is frowning. I touch the picture and notice a stain. It's crumpled as if it's been carried around in a pocket for a long time.

'This is mine,' I say slowly. 'I took it when I left home to go to university.' I frown. 'Where did you get it?'

'It was on my songbook.' He flips the picture over. Someone has written '*HELP ME*' in big, spiky letters on the back. Did I write that? 'Who's the girl with you?' he asks. 'She looks like your twin?'

I nod. 'Alice.'

'Your identical twin,' he lets out a breath. 'And she's here, now?'

I clasp the warm cup with both hands. 'Yes,' I say.

'Did you come to Hawksmoor together?'

I try to lift the cup to my lips, but my hands are shaking and hot liquid spills onto the table, splashing my lap. My thighs sting and throb. Did we come together? I can't remember. Ever since I drove through the rusted gates, I've been confused, losing time. I think she was here first. She was the one who locked Daddy in the hole.

Gabriel finds an old tea towel, wets it with cold and mops at my damp legs. He takes the cup away from me. 'I'm sorry,' he says. 'You're in shock. You don't need to tell me anything yet.'

'No,' I whisper. 'I want to tell you – but I don't know if I can. It's all a muddle. She came here with me – because she's always with me – except she's far away at the same time.'

'This sounds like a riddle,' he murmurs.

A sob breaks from my chest. We sit in silence. Gabriel takes my hand in his and squeezes.

'I need to see her,' I say, as certainty settles inside me. 'I know where she is – will you come with me?'

'Alright,' he says, standing up. 'But let's take it slowly.'

I lean into his supporting hand. At the main hall, we turn right down the long gallery, shuffling past the boot room, down more steps into the cellar. I stop outside the studded, oak door of the secret chapel, and clasp the heavy iron ring of the handle with both hands. It opens. I walk ahead of him over the smooth, polished floor towards the altar, her voice whispering in my ear, *What have you done?*

* * *

It snowed in the days after Henry's funeral. The grounds were thick with blown powder. Bushes and plants looked cowed, misshapen with white swellings and tumours. The fells had ceased to exist, erased by mist. It wrapped our eyes like wet gauze as Alice and I crunched through crystals. Cold reached into my lungs, scouring them clean. The inside of my nostrils stung.

'We need to talk,' she'd said. 'Let's go outside. Walls have ears.'

The yew was bent under its frozen burden, and clumps fell with a dull thump as we passed it. Before us, the scratched hieroglyphics of bird feet and animal tracks led us through a white wasteland, disappearing into silver haze. We walked to the tarn. A layer of ice imprisoned the dark water, and I thought of the eels and crayfish tucked into the mud far below, their hearts slowed to near death to survive.

'It's all arranged, Cecily,' she said, stopping at the edge of the bank.

She blew on her hands. 'We're leaving tomorrow. I've already packed my stuff in Henry's rucksack.'

'We can't go,' I said. 'It's dangerous there. We can't leave home. Not now that Henry's dead.'

'This isn't a home,' she said. 'It's a prison. And Henry would want us to keep to his plan.' She looked at me through eyes fringed with frost.

I shook my head. 'I can't.'

'Why?' her voice rose. 'I don't understand.' Her pupils contracted, and my reflection, curled inside them, shrank. 'What Daddy does. You know it's wrong,' she said quietly. 'If you stay here, he'll destroy you.'

'I'm not leaving Hawksmoor.'

'It's just a bloody house, Cecily,' she said. 'I don't want to leave without you.'

'Then stay with me.' I swallowed. 'Together forever,' I reminded her. 'We promised.'

She swung away from me in frustration and stared across the ice. 'Cecily,' she said softly. 'Please. I'm begging you.'

She didn't need to turn around to know I was shaking my head. She took a small step onto the skein of frozen water and another, and stood, finding her balance on the slippery surface.

'What are you doing?'

She walked another few steps towards the centre.

'Alice,' I called. 'Don't be stupid. We don't know how firm it is.'

She looked over her shoulder. 'You're a coward, Cecily. But you won't get anywhere if you don't take a risk.' She turned away and took another step. 'Tell me you'll come with me tomorrow.'

She turned to face me, shrugged, and stepped backwards. 'Tell me, Cecily.' She held out her hands, palms up like Jesus. 'Tell me you'll come to the kibbutz.'

'I can't!' I shouted, my voice full of panic.

She smiled, shook her head, turned around and walked further, almost striding, as if she was on a hike, until she slipped and rebalanced with a jerk and flap of her arms. 'It's beautiful out here,' she called, her voice a little shaken. 'But there's a whole world waiting for us, Cecily.' She swept her hand towards those invisible faraway things. 'Deserts. Mountains. Cities. We can't even imagine now.'

'Alice,' I called, my toes creeping on to the ice; every part of me tense and coiled. 'Come back. Please!'

'Tell me we're leaving tomorrow.' Her words a sing-song echo, bouncing from the hard, glittering surface, loud in the stillness. 'I've got the tickets. All you've got to do is pack a bag. You just have to say, yes.'

She was a long way out. The mist wrapped her in tendrils. I couldn't see the details of her features any more. I heard the creak and judder of the ice. 'Alright,' I shouted in desperation. 'Yes.'

'You'll come?' She moved one leg behind her, teasing me.

'Alice.' I could hardly speak. 'Be careful.'

'Promise me!' she shouted.

'I said I'll go with you.' I gabbled it. The meaning of the words irrelevant. I would have said anything to get her to come to the bank. 'I promise.'

She was walking towards me now. Her smile shone. Puffs of silver trailed from her mouth into the gelid air. She looked beautiful, like a vision, like the Virgin Mother. Everything around us was silver. The grass at the edge of the tarn glinted like precious carvings. Clumps of hard mud twinkled with frost. We waited for her, the grass and snow, the earth, and the hushed grounds.

The crack sounded like a gunshot. It ran in a fissure from the ball of her foot, a ribbon unfurling. It branched out. A deadly tracing spreading around her. She stopped, and looked at me, the smile gone.

'Alice,' I whispered.

She kept utterly still, looking at me for what seemed like hours. We'd become statues, my gaze hooking into her gaze, a line shining taut between us. A cord to keep her safe. Don't blink. Don't move. We were suspended in time, two creatures caught in a glacier, fixed forever.

Another gunshot. Cracks opening around her like mouths. The thin black lines fattening, expanding, moving apart. With a long, sharp squeal, the ice shifted and tore itself apart; she lurched and cried out, falling straight down in a slithering of legs, torso, head. A small splash. She was gone.

I fell onto my knees and crawled towards the gaping hole. Under my fingers, I heard fractures race. I flattened myself against the groaning surface. Cold stuck to my palms. The jagged edge where she'd disappeared seemed very far away. I should have brought a branch, a stick, something for her to grab. I pushed myself on a little further, wriggling on my belly, shuffling inch by inch. A shadow moved below me. A fish, I thought, staring down through opaque ice. An oval blur hovered, her eyes and mouth hollows pressed into the pale of her face, and the darkness of her hair, dancing. Her hand was suddenly splayed against mine. A thickness of frozen water between us. Then nothing. The tarn had taken her.

* * *

Gabriel and I pass between the carved pews over the stone flags. Above us, moonlight shifts through the gratings, falling like small coins onto our faces and hands. At the altar, I turn to the right and walk to a section of wall where there are two newer memorial stones. I take Gabriel's torch and shine the beam onto the stones, picking out the engraved writing.

Henry Deveraux, 4th July, 1959 – 2nd January, 1977
Alice Deveraux, 18th August, 1961 – 14th January, 1977
May their souls rest in peace.

'My brother and sister.' I look up into Gabriel's shocked face. 'They're dead. And it's my fault.'

43

CECILY

Gabriel reads the plaques, then he looks at me, his expression full of horror.

'I had no idea. I... don't know what to say.' He shakes his head. 'But we've got to leave, Cecily.' He touches my shoulder, gently. 'Alice isn't really here, is she? Just her memory. But there's somebody waiting for me.' He takes my hand, glancing at the grey light showing through the grating. 'It's nearly morning. Can you make it to the car?'

I nod, and we retrace our steps, up the creaking stairs, along the gallery, past the dining room, into the main hall. I walk through the front door, leaving it wide open behind us, a gaping mouth. The next people to come will be workmen in orange coats and hard hats, carrying plans to erase Hawksmoor and build in its stead little houses with pocket-sized gardens, roads, pavements, and car parks.

The sky above the fells is stained dirty red. The dawn chorus has started. Birdsong comes from the yew tree. I hope they don't chop it down. I hope they let it live, bearing witness, carrying our story in its roots and branches, its deadly bark dense with history. When we reach the car, Gabriel gets behind the wheel. I don't look over my shoulder at the house, instead I lean my head against the seat rest and close my eyes, listening to thorns scraping the sides of the car. Gabriel slows and turns through the gates. Opening my eyes, the craggy profiles of the fells are silhouetted against a star-speckled sky, and I'm crushed by the weight of things I don't know. Sheets of moonlight lie over the dales, the dark shapes of drystone walls throwing long shadows across silver-grey grass. In the sleeping village, I smell woodsmoke, see a cat slinking around the corner of a house.

Instead of indicating towards the motorway, Gabriel takes a left at the crossroads, and I realise we've arrived at St. Mary's church. Gabriel pulls into a parking space and switches off the engine. I look up at the tall bell tower, the ridge of the roof with the grinning gargoyles. 'Why are we here?'

He touches my knee and says something I don't catch as he gets out, shutting the door with a clunk. I watch him go through the gate, past the gravestones, towards the porch. I am suddenly afraid. Something appears out of the shadows of the church. A tall, stooped figure. For a second, I think it's my father, come back to life. The two of them speak briefly and approach the car. As the moonlight catches a beaky nose and thin mouth, I recognise Ambrose Stone. My body prickles with confusion.

'What's he doing here?' I whisper as Ambrose climbs into the back seat.

Gabriel puts his seat belt on. 'He's why I came to find you,' he says. 'He turned up at the house with a crazy story about following you in the car all the way up to Abbeystead, and then losing you.' He leans forward and starts the engine. 'He was certain you were about to do something terrible. He insisted I go to your parents' house.' Gabriel keeps his eyes on the windscreen, although we haven't moved. 'Anyway,' he goes on. 'I'd already seen the photo of you and Alice, so I knew something was wrong. Ambrose drove me up here as I had no car. We must have been breaking the speed limit the whole way.'

'I knew time was of the essence,' Ambrose says apologetically.

It hadn't occurred to me before to wonder how Gabriel had arrived at Hawksmoor. Ambrose has shuffled forward on his seat and stares intensely at me, his bulbous eyes milky pale. 'How is your father?'

'He's dead—'

'His heart,' Gabriel says. 'There was nothing we could do.'

'I'm sorry.' Ambrose crosses himself. 'God had plans for your father all along, Cecily.'

His words confirm my suspicion. He'd heard me through the thin wood of the confessional. I want to tell him that he shouldn't eavesdrop on the sins of others. Except, it's true that I was going to murder Daddy, wasn't I? But I didn't need Ambrose. Alice set Daddy free and moved the trap. It was her that saved me.

'I asked your husband to leave me at the nearest Catholic church,' he's saying. 'I wanted to pray for you. For your father.'

'We'll drop him off on our way. I left his car near Hawksmoor's gate.' Gabriel glances over his shoulder. 'I'd like to give you the petrol money, Ambrose. It's the least I can do. You've really gone out of your way to help us. You must be exhausted from all that driving.'

'Please,' Ambrose says. 'No need for that. God gave me strength. I wanted to help.' Then he clears his throat. 'And I have to apologise. I know you saw me outside your house, Cecily. I'm sorry if I frightened you. I followed you in Exeter, and I followed you in the car because I wanted to protect you. God told me you needed help. It was hard to see your faith faltering.'

We drop him next to a red car and wait for him to get in, and then Gabriel and I drive on. I rest my forehead against the window, and snatch at fitful sleep. We stop at a dismal service station. Standing in the damp carpark, I roll out the stiffness in my neck. Dawn is a smear of dirty orange across dark blue. The passing motorway traffic creates a monotonous roar – a grey noise that presses into my ears.

In the café, we sit across a Formica table with cups of coffee. 'Tell me about Henry and Alice,' he says.

I push my fingers together. My acrylic nails are growing out, the polish chipped. 'Henry was older than us. He was wonderful. A wonderful brother. But he was gay, and I didn't understand. I lied to him, told him the boy he loved didn't want to see him again. He jumped from our roof.'

Gabriel's forehead furrows. 'But it wasn't your fault,' he says. 'You made a mistake. You were a child.'

My throat is tight. I manage a sip of tea. 'And then Alice died,' I tell him. 'She fell through the ice. But she only went on it to force me to change my mind – she wanted me to leave with her, and I refused.'

'Two children, dying so close to each other,' he murmurs. 'Was there ever an inquiry?'

'There was an autopsy for Henry. My father managed to convince them that it was an accident. He knew the magistrate. And Alice... it was an accident. But it wouldn't have happened if I'd agreed to go with her.'

'Why didn't you tell me any of this? Why didn't I even know you'd had siblings?'

'Daddy wiped Henry from the family history and then Alice too. I kept up the pretence for him. He said I was an only child and I suppose, secretly, I liked it – not having the others to compete with – he always preferred them even though I was the one who loved him. The thing is,' I look at him. 'Alice has never left me. Not really.'

'There were letters on your dressing table,' he says, leaning across the table. 'From Alice to you, and from you to Alice. They seemed to go back for years.'

'We've written to each other ever since she left home.'

He's silent for a moment, playing with his teaspoon. 'But she couldn't have written,' he says quietly. 'She's dead.'

I look away from him, squeezing my eyes shut. 'I don't know what's happening to me.'

'I think you wrote her letters,' he says. 'Maybe it was a way of denying her death, of keeping her alive.' He reaches across and wraps his fingers around mine. 'In one, you said that you were afraid of me – that I controlled you, that I drank.'

'I'm sorry,' I whisper. 'I'm afraid of myself. Afraid of what happens to me. I do terrible things. There are all these blanks in my memory. I'm out of control and it feels terrifying – I never know when I'll disappear.' He let's go of my hand and I push my hair away from my face. 'It's been like this for years. Ever since she died.'

'What do you mean?' he asks. 'You disappear?'

'I lose time. Hours. Sometimes days.'

He falls silent and stares down, as if he's thinking. 'In the last letter,' he says quietly. 'You said you wanted a divorce.'

I look at his strong, kind hands. 'I had to please Daddy and he hated you.'

'You're not bound to his will any more, Cecily,' he says in a low voice. 'If you want to leave me, I'll move out—'

'No,' I say quickly. 'I should be the one to leave. You and Bea would be better off without me. I don't deserve you, either of you. We should divorce. I want you to be happy.'

He blinks and rubs his eyes. 'I won't pretend it's been easy these last years, but my feelings haven't changed. I do still love you.'

I swallow hard. There's so much he doesn't know. He wouldn't love me if he knew what I do when he's asleep, when I'm out in the dark world, alone. A bad apple is useless and disgusting. Worse, it spreads rot to other fruit, contaminates like a disease, infecting others with decay.

'All of this,' he sighs, 'it's hard to get my head around.' He rubs his nose with a knuckle. 'But we need to deal with one thing at a time, and it seems to me that the most important thing is to get you help. I think you're ill, Cecily. There's something very strange happening. It's... it's as if you have a split personality.'

'No.' I shake my head. 'No.'

'It's nothing to be ashamed of – I think... the other part of you is Alice.' He gives me a long look. 'You've been struggling with this since I met you, haven't you?' His voice is gentle. 'Even at Exeter? That's why you sometimes seemed like a different person.'

His kindness makes me want to cry. I blink and fold my fingers through his. 'I...I confused people, didn't I? Forgetting things I'd said or done. I was confused, too. And scared.'

He swallows. 'When we met, I knew you were troubled. But I put your changes of personality down to mood swings.' His fingers squeeze mine and let go. 'You don't have to hide it from me any more.' He sits forward, brows wrinkling. 'There must be some kind of therapy, a cure, someone who can help you. We'll find a doctor.'

'Do you think it can stop? Do you think I can be normal?'

'Yes,' he says.

'Gabriel.' I hold his hand across the table. *I love you.* The words stay in my head, instead I say, 'There are things you still don't know about me – things I do – shameful things...'

'There's a lot of stuff we need to say to each other.' He sweeps his jacket from the back of the chair, picks up the car keys. 'But it can wait. We should get going. We still have miles to go.'

We are silent on the motorway. Speed lulls me, the warmth of the car soporific. I touch the webbing of the seatbelt across my chest, feel the smooth glass of the passenger window, clasp my knees in tea-stained leggings. I'm still here with Gabriel – it's just me: Cecily, wife, mother, and survivor. The relief of him knowing my secret is huge. I thought he'd find me disgusting, weird, a freak. But he wants to help me. He still loves me. Maybe that was all it took to dispel Alice's ghost. Maybe now I can stay present in my life. Maybe it was always that simple.

We pull off the motorway, negotiating narrow roads lined with hedges, and then we are driving into Exeter, gulls wheeling above the car, raptor eyes spotting our return. Familiar streets open on either side of us. Home.

'Cecily,' he says, as we stop at a red light. 'We slept together the other night.' His voice is hesitant. 'Do you remember?'

A shock of understanding, then a flare of rage. I bite my lip. She's betrayed me. But I can't blame him. She's easier to befriend, easier to love. She's always taken what she wants. I shake my head. 'That was Alice.'

Gabriel's cheeks are red, and he frowns, rubbing his hand over his forehead. 'This is beyond me.' He sounds hollowed out, exhausted. 'I'm sorry. I don't know what to say.'

'It's alright,' I say quietly. 'It was my body in your arms.'

The lights are green. He changes gear as we move ahead and turns briefly towards me with a quizzical expression. 'I noticed something on your back. Scars, I think. I could feel them. You didn't have any before. But you... or Alice... were trying to hide them from me.'

'Yes,' I tell him. 'I need to hurt myself. I deserve pain.'

He pulls over suddenly, swerving into a parking space at the side of the road, and looks at me. He turns off the engine. 'I don't want you to hurt yourself,' he says, his voice shaking with anger. 'Nobody deserves pain. We will get help, Cecily.'

He takes my hand in his, entwining our fingers, and we sit for a few minutes without moving in the warm, enclosure of the car. It's no longer early morning. The world is waking up. I notice people leaving their houses; a jogger runs along a damp pavement; a woman crosses the road with two terriers pulling at their leads. There are puddles. The road gleams. It must have rained.

Gabriel leans forward to turn the key. 'Are you ready?'

I nod.

* * *

We pull up outside Hollyhocks Cottage. The privet hedge is alive with glittering drops. It takes only three strides to the blue front door. The drooping palm from the neighbour's side drips water onto my sleeve as Gabriel lets us into the little hallway, and the unique smells of our house rush around me like a hug. I feel as if I'm an invalid returning home. Sukie is lying on the pine floorboards, washing behind her ears. Bea runs down the stairs in her pyjamas. Relief and happiness stretch her mouth wide. 'Mum,' she says. 'You're back. Dad let me have my friend to stay. He said he was going to surprise you.'

'Yes,' I say, smiling. 'He did.'

She goes into my arms. The softness of her, her morning breath. But I'm numb with exhaustion. I want to pull away, climb the stairs and fall into bed. 'Shall I get some breakfast ready?' she asks. 'I want you to meet Lily. She's still asleep.'

'Let your mother rest,' Gabriel says. 'We've had a long journey.'

'It's OK,' I say. 'We can have a cup of tea.'

But Alice is at the back of my eyes. Pushing, pushing to get through. She's insistent. She wants this moment as her own. I lean my face into the coats hanging from the rack and summon all my strength to resist her. *I don't want the swap any more,* I tell her. *It's time to go, Alice.*

Do you think you can get rid of me, she says, *when I'm the best part of you?*

Her sentence slides across my tongue, but I refuse her words. I have my own voice. *You don't belong here,* I tell her. *This is my family.*

Bea has gone ahead into the kitchen, still chatting about her friend. I hear the click of the kettle, Sukie meowing for food. Gabriel is there at my elbow. He puts his arm around my shoulder, looking at me with concern. 'Are you sure you're alright?'

I nod, and we walk into the kitchen together. There's a rucksack on the floor. I frown. 'What's that doing here?'

'I found it in your wardrobe.' Bea glances at my face anxiously. 'Sorry. I just wanted to show Lily your clothes, and then I saw it in the corner. It's full of old things.'

'It belonged to my brother,' I say.

Bea frowns. 'Your brother?'

Gabriel has his arm around her. 'Mummy's brother is dead, darling. That's why she's never talked about him.'

I'm staring at the rucksack, packed with Alice's things. She was going to take it to the kibbutz. Seeing it in the kitchen tears something open inside me, and I shiver, my fingertips aching with cold, my toes frozen. Spinning ice crystals blur my vision, crusting my eyelashes with silver. The room is filled with snow. White flakes whip around me, a blizzard of nothingness. Stalagmites fall from the ceiling. The floor tilts under my feet, and I stumble, my hand grabbing the back of a chair.

I can make them happy, she whispers.

'No!' I cry.

'Cecily?' Gabriel is beside me.

He wants me, Cecily. Not you.

My teeth are chattering. She is pressing through me, slipping into the spaces inside my head and body, smothering me, erasing me. She's stronger than me, she's always been stronger than me.

'She's here,' I gasp, as I slide into a chair. But I'm lost inside swirling brilliance, my words erased by the sharp crack of breaking ice.

Don't resent me. I'm just better at your life.

In the distance, she laughs with the others, talking about toast and cherry jam. She's got through, she's with them now. It's like falling through water, as if I'm watching Bea and Gabriel from a long way down, our little kitchen getting further and further away, their faces fading, distorted by ripples and wave wash, a fan of bubbles. And then, blackness.

Together forever, she says. *Remember?*

EPILOGUE

1996

Psychiatrist's Report:

Notes on Cecily Greenwood.

The patient has been diagnosed with Dissociative Identity Disorder as the result of long-term trauma. It was her way of coping with her father's physical and emotional abuse. From a young age, she made up alters to let them experience the pain instead of her. She says at first the alters were three of her Catholic ancestors: a cavalier killed in the battle at Hawksmoor, a persecuted monk who'd died in a priest hole, and a Victorian child, the victim of diphtheria. But after her twin, Alice, died at the age of fifteen, she became the main alter.

It seems that the patient's symptoms worsened after she discovered that her abusive father had an undisclosed first marriage and committed his first wife to a mental asylum. The patient has admitted to feeling extreme homicidal feelings towards her father after this revelation. However, the patient convinced herself that if she murdered him, her father would 'win' because she would be unredeemable. She says she needed Alice, 'to keep us safe. If I could get her to take control of our identity, I'd disappear.' When I asked her what she meant by disappearing, she replied, 'locked away in the darkness of my mind.'

During my initial conversations with 'Alice,' she appeared to be completely unaware of her host, maintaining her twin existed in the world as a separate entity. But I am not convinced – I think she is more aware than she would like me to believe. Certainly, 'Alice' is the personality and voice that's presenting more in the patient/host than the patient herself, which is unusual. The patient's schisms of understanding seem to allow some command over swapping identity, but never enough to fully control it. There are, as with most DID patients, hallucinations and memory blanks that further confuse the patient's understanding of reality.

I have explained to the patient and her husband that she will have to co-exist with her alter. There is no cure for DID. No drug to make it go away. Talking is the recommended therapy. She has been encouraged to keep a diary as part of her therapy. Both the patient and her alter are continuing to write each other letters.

ACKNOWLEDGEMENTS

Thank you to the Boldwood team. And a huge thank you to my editor, Isobel Akenhead, for your passion and commitment to this novel, not to mention all your astute editing.

Thank you to Eve White, my wonderful agent. I am so lucky to have you.

Thank you to those who played a crucial part in the shaping of this book, from my scruffy first draft to the finished manuscript: Sara Sarre, who read several drafts with her usual heart and intelligence, and gave me brilliant editing ideas; my husband, Alex Marengo, who listens to my plot conundrums in the middle of the night and on dog walks and never fails to come up with excellent advice; fellow writers, Mary Chamberlain and Viv Graveson, for generously reading the whole novel and their thoughtful editing suggestions; Sam Hayward, Hannah Hayward and Ana Sarginson for reading drafts and providing encouraging feedback.

Mary Chamberlain for being my in-house expert on the Catholic faith. Any mistakes are my own.

Love and thanks to my family and friends who put up with me being in a different world at times.

ABOUT THE AUTHOR

Saskia Sarginson is a bestselling author whose debut novel, *The Twins*, was a Richard and Judy Book Club pick. Saskia started her career as a Health and Beauty editor on women's magazines, and then became a freelance journalist. Saskia grew up in a Suffolk pine forest but now lives in London with her husband.

Sign up to Saskia Sarginson's mailing list here for news, competitions and updates on future books.

Visit Saskia's Website: www.saskiasarginson.co.uk

Follow Saskia on social media:

instagram.com/saskiasarginson
x.com/SaskiaSarginson
facebook.com/SaskiaSarginsonBooks

THE SECRET OF WINNING

Learn how to use your setbacks to Design a life you always wanted

Learn how to use your setbacks to Design a life you always wanted

AMANDEEP THIND

Published Internationally by

PENDOWN PRESS

***Powered by* Gullybaba Publishing House Pvt. Ltd.,**
An ISO 9001 & ISO 14001 certified Co.,
Regd. Office: 2525/193, 1st Floor, Onkar Nagar-A, Tri Nagar, Delhi-110035, (From Kanhaiya Nagar Metro Station Towards Old Bus Stand)
Branch Office: 1A/2A, 20, Hari Sadan, Ansari Road, Daryaganj, New Delhi-110002
Ph.: 09350849407, 011-27387998
E-mail: info@pendownpress.com
Website: PendownPress.com

First Edition: 2020

Price: ₹499/

ISBN: 978-93-89601-32-9

Layout Design: Pendown Press Publishing

CONTENTS

DEDICATION

I would like to dedicate this book to my parents, my sister, my lovely wife and my daughter Muskaan, and all my teachers and students who have given me immense support and helped me become the version of the man I am today.

"A lot can be achieved by being a Progressivist rather than a Perfectionist"

–Amandeep Thind

"If there is a book that you really want to read but it hasn't been written yet, then you must write it"

–Toni Morrison

PREFACE

Being overweight or the word will be fat, I found myself discriminated and alone. It made me feel like a loser in my life until I realized that the true winning happens when you stay persistent on your journey of facing the odds and overcoming them. Once you overcome them, you become a winner.

I did my research and couldn't find a book that gave a message of " How you can win in life against all the odds you face in life" in a very clear way. That's why I decided to write this book. The only way you can win in life is to remain persistent. The only time we lose is when we give up!

The purpose of writing this book is to make readers understand that they never really fail until they give up and label themselves as a loser. There is always a way to fight back, no matter how many times you failed, there's always an opportunity to win it back.

Understand this: the only way we can win a game is by playing it. The winner is inside you!

This book shows you the path especially if you've or you're giving up on your dreams and aspirations.

Writing this book has been a challenge and there were days when I wanted to give up this idea of not writing this book, only to realize that the essence of this book itself is to persist and that is what I continued to nurture. This journey of writing a book has helped me discover the deeper layers within me and made me grow as a person.

I invite you to share these tools & techniques with me through this book and nurture the skills to become a winner.

This is not just a book. This is your practical guide to set you on the path of becoming a winner through practical exercises and inspirational quotes which lay down a roadmap to where you can only win, win and win.

I eagerly look forward to hearing all your feedbacks and success.

FOREWORD

There are many teachers, masters, guides and healers. I truly believe that the best ones are those who have experienced it all, who went through the ups and downs of life and turned it into a formula that you will find in Amandeep's book.

This book will guide you how to create win-win situations through learning from your own experiences in life, whether in business or relationships. Through this book, you will find your own winning code. You will expand your communication skills and improve your confidence in dealing with your challenges.

When I work with people, I usually find that they find it difficult to deal with past experiences especially. These memories give them a sense of loss, a sense of failure.

Amandeep is a fresh voice that helps you to access your own brilliance. As a speaker, he passionately speaks from the heart.

May his book touch your heart as well.

Sidra Jafri,

Author of "The Awakening - 9 Principles for Finding the Courage to Change Your Life"

ACKNOWLEDGEMENTS

This book is a product of my 42 years of experience. This book is a way for those people who want to overcome all the odds in their life and become True Winners.

I would like to acknowledge Sidra Jafri, Santosh Sagoo and Lucy Spencer who supported in getting the book out of me. To encourage me; to go deeper into my thoughts to bring those pearls out, that can serve millions.

To all the individuals I have had the opportunity to teach, I want to say thank you for being the inspiration and insight for me to get better with my techniques.

A special mention of gratitude to my Parents, my wife Jagpreet Thind, my sister Ranjit Kaur, my niece Amarjot, my nephew Harmandeep Singh and my daughter Muskaan. I am able to lead this life because of their incredible love and support.

A big thanks to my ex-boss and my current business partner, Veronica Tan & Richard Tan (owner of Success Resources) who have always pushed me to Dream Big in life.

In my life, I always chose to remain a student. A special thanks to all my mentors and teachers Tony Robbins, Dr John Demartini, Les Brown, T. Harv Eker, Blair Singer, Clinton Swaine, Dan Lok, Joel Bauer and many more who have changed my life through their coaching, teaching, training, seminars, and mentoring programs.

I also want to give a huge shout-out to the entire team of GullyBaba and Dinesh who contributed their effort and expertise to this book.

Special thanks to Supreet and my team (Heena, Gaurav, Abhyant, Shiva, Akanksha) for supporting me immensely and putting in so much more than time.

Finally, I am deeply grateful to Rohit Bose (our book cover designer), Gagan Arora (who took the pic for the book cover) and all my students who attended my live workshops. Without them, this book won't have been possible.

INTRODUCTION

> ***Winning is being open to new learnings, finding the growth in our experiences and following our passion to create more.***
>
> ***–Amandeep Thind***

What is Winning?

The word winning can be defined as the correct or desired result of an attempt. In fact, almost every action that we perform right from waking up to going to sleep is an attempt. In an attempt to get out of the bed, I asked my wife to prepare coffee. In an attempt to fetch a glass of water, I moved my hand to pick the bottle. In an attempt to sleep, I tried to tune my mind off. In an attempt to secure good Return on Investment (ROI), the company started to outsource some services. In an attempt to curb corruption, the government is encouraging online payments. In an attempt to check pollution, the government has put a ban on crackers. There is an inherent motive with every effort that we make, and when that motive is met, we call it **winning.**

It is not only apparent in the external world, winning is in fact in our DNA. That's how we came into being at the first place when running a race with millions of sperms to be the one who made it, makes us a winner by birth. This basic instinct of winning is what creates the winning attitude that can be cultivated through daily habits and simple practices.

By taking time out to read this book, you have already started the journey of winning.

Before I tell you how you can cultivate the winning attitude, let's explore what exactly is "winning."

A quick search on the Internet and in the dictionary reveals numerous ways to describe "winning".

Some of which are as follows:

- To finish first in a race
- To succeed by striving or making an effort
- To gain victory
- To overcome adversary
- To achieve any goal
- To be successful in something

Deep down in every human soul is a hidden longing, impulse, and ambition to do something fine and enduring. If you are willing, great things are possible to you.

–Grenville Kleiser

Since the word **Winning** is one of the keywords in my training programs, I often call my participants to the stage and ask, "What is winning?" Having asked more than 1,000 participants, I have developed one clear notion about the word. Its meaning varies from person to person. Moreover, it is based on the **Winning attitudes** of our parents, teachers, family, culture, religion and most importantly, our own environment.

After listening to my participants' interaction with the word **Winning** with rapt attention, I start saying something like this:

Use this book as a tool to unlock the true winner in you by defining your own meaning of winning and describing how **Winning** would feel to you. Life doesn't end when you lose a game or fail in business or an examination. It presents you with an opportunity to own the true winner in you. You can use your winning attitudes to become resilient enough to not get carried away with the past failures and instead bring your business back on track in a surprisingly short amount of time. For that you will have to change what is called the "Belief System." You will have to learn by heart this statement: Winning or losing a business deal or an exam doesn't define you as a "winner" or a "loser." It's rather your attitude towards that occurrence that makes you a "winner" or "loser".

> ***It is your effort that defines you - not the outcome.***
>
> ***–Amandeep Thind***

Everytime, you have a 100% 'winning attitude', you are bound to win.

There are 3 key attitudes of a human body that enable him to emerge as a true winner.

1. Explore: Attitude of learning from mistakes
2. Expand: Attitude of growing from every event
3. Evolve: Attitude of creating from passion

If you observe this diagram, you will see that all the three circles intermingle, clearly suggesting that a winning attitude requires all three elements.

By embodying these three attitudes, you will master ***the secret of winning*** which will allow you to win in any area of your life.

When will you know that you have mastered the secret of winning?

Take some time to ponder this question.

Now, grab a blank piece of paper and write,

I will feel like a winner when I am......................................

Or,

I will feel like a winner when I have...................................

Or,

I will feel like a winner when I achieve................................

Is Struggle Optional?

I hear some senior citizens glorifying their life as "a life full of struggle." They even tend to mock those younger than them who they think are not struggling the way they did. With just this parameter, they prophesy the life of people today. I want to tell you unequivocally that there is nothing noble about working hard. It either shows your alignment to an old school of thought or old technology. If you are able to shun both of these, struggling will be optional for you. All that you need to do is to place yourself in that success set and you will emerge as successful.

There is science behind everything that happens, this is why if you take action in line with what you want to manifest, you will get your results. If not, then your actions were not those you could take. To prepare tea is a set of steps; if taken at the right time, in the right order, and at the right intensity, the result is always as desired. You may use it as a template, a blueprint, or a pre-defined format.

Struggle will become alien to you if you just fit yourself in the pre-defined format.

I am toying with the idea of making a video on **How to achieve success in life with the right tools and techniques** and give exclusively to all my readers (you will not find it on YouTube, or any online platform).

-1-

MY JOURNEY OF WINNING

> ***When you overcome your fears and get out of your own way, you become a Winner.***
>
> ***–Amandeep Thind***

The most important thing that you need to know about winning is that it's personal to you.

It is about:

- overcoming your inner demons and,
- addressing your deepest fears and challenging them.

> ***The greatest pleasure in life is doing what people say you cannot do.***
>
> ***–Walter Bagehot***

My deepest fears were:

- Not being able to become somebody.
- Making my parents fail who did their best to educate me.
- Confirming that my critics were right about me.
- Being publicly humiliated and embarrassed because I didn't know how to behave in public.

Story of Overcoming Fear of Public Speaking

My fear of public speaking first became apparent when at nine years old, my parents decided to move me to an English medium school where all the other children were fluent in English. My English was limited to few basic words like yes, no, please and thank you, as my earlier schooling took place at a local community school where most teachings were delivered in the local language. Having no exposure to English until that age, I hardly understood the language.

I remember being very nervous, in my school dress (uniform), as it felt very rich on my poor body. Even my brown pants with a white shirt and stylish tie failed to make me feel confident about myself.

Just looking at the tall school building, I felt even smaller. My heartbeat was running fast and my mind was becoming heavy with thoughts like:

My Inner Voice

"I better live up to the expectations of my parents. They have sacrificed everything to get me here."

The school day started with assembly which was very foreign to me at that time, since both the prayer and the speech given by the school principal were in English and my language of praying was limited to Bengali, Hindi and Punjabi.

After assembly, my English teacher, 'Sir Simon', made me stand up, as it was the first day of my new class and asked me a question. Since it was being asked in English, it was beyond my understanding.

I was already very afraid, and because of my lack of understanding, I came up with a one-word answer that was totally the opposite to the correct answer. The whole class laughed and, one of the pupils sitting three rows ahead of me nudged the pupil sitting next to him and said: "Ish motte ko kuch nahi aata." (*This fat guy knows nothing.*)

Unbeknown to me, I was tasting the bitterness of defeat and was starting to think that it was painful to speak in public. The change of school had brought more challenges than my young mind could cope with.

In this new school, I was labelled as fat, dark-skinned and dumb. My existence was ridiculed every day and I was making decisions in my subconscious mind about myself and the people around me.

Each day my self-esteem was shattered and as life moved on, I continued to be lonely, defeated and low on self-image.

It was this experience on the first day at the school that destroyed my confidence in public speaking, as a part of me felt embarrassed. The embarrassment conditioned my mind not to speak in public ever again. I shut down my inner voice so I was not heard amongst groups and at gatherings. I stopped expressing the opinions I had inside me.

From that time, I lived with the FEAR of public speaking for many years. Even the idea of facing an audience would give me tremors inside my heart. I would sweat and get shaky with the slightest thought of facing people to speak.

Since this traumatic incident at school, I had created a shield around me to keep myself safe and away from every opportunity that necessitated any kind of public appearance or presentation. I was comfortable being not seen, but very miserable inside as my inner voice was dying. I was losing my voice without physically losing it, but silencing myself seemed to be the only plausible solution at that time.

Story of overcoming the fear of being a "loser"

Alongside my fear of public speaking, the other major challenge that I faced on my journey was 'the fear of becoming a loser.' This fear psychosis pulled me out of activities where there was even the slightest possibility of losing. I had probably picked it up from my parents, which formed the conditioning of always 'playing it safe'. They lived a life with many financial difficulties, so they would avoid risk and anything which could bring a challenge or opportunity. Having modelled my parents subconsciously, I had taken on their way of thinking.

Time glided by. I somehow graduated with a Bachelor's degree in Computer Application (BCA) in IT through distance education. Now getting a job became my first priority. I started going from pillar to post to find something suitable, eventually having almost 100+ interviews. I vividly remember how I would dream of having a great interview but would come home crestfallen, dejected and rejected. One question that the interviewer would invariably put was "What's your experience?" The answer already in my mind was, "How can I get any experience unless I get a job?" but I didn't ever say that in the fear of creating a wrong impression. My failure in passing an interview started making my mind heavy. I slipped into the state of a complete failure.

In order to save myself from further rejection, I started looking for other options as well. That was the time when call centres were booming in India. After few rejections, I got selected in an outbound call centre as a tele-caller.

The job, for me, was like a long-cherished wish being granted. Graduating through distance education mode allowed me to enjoy my job which required daily attendance, a considerable amount of time in the office and incentives galore. As my interest picked up, so my knowledge about the workings of my company and my KRAs (Key Responsibility Areas) grew up. I focused on my job and that translated into better performance.

I was thoroughly enjoying my role and was gaining high sale figures. I was surpassing most of my colleagues in energy and sales performances.

This was soon noticed by the management team and led to the CEO of our company, Pujan Dargan informing the top managers that he would fire everyone but retain Arthur Ashford—it was an alias name which was given to me during my International call-centre days.

This news was conveyed to me by some well-wishers who valued me and appreciated my energy in achieving high performance and gaining positive results. It was due to this massive energy drive that I was later headhunted to work for another company through a member of my team (who later became my good friend).

My friend's Jiju (brother-in-law) named Mr Bajpai had returned to India from Ireland and was highly motivated to join this amazing boom of call centres which were opening up all across India. He found an investor and started a Call Centre called Aarohi. I left my comfortable Team Leader position at a well-established call centre and joined this start-up company. We operated from a lease centre where we were given a few seats to telecommunicate from. I believed that I was a Business Partner at this new centre, but later I realised it was just a cooked up story to make me join the company.

When I first joined, I had a fear within me that I must make this venture successful at any cost. This must be a success story irrespective of the lead (client database) quality, the voice quality of the lease line and, the product we were selling. So, I started showing up not to lose, which led to me becoming bitter and stressed out. The energy which I had at my previous call centre role started to fade and I reached a low point.

I saw one of the junior colleagues from my previous role got promoted as a trainer for external clients, which I had always wanted to be as I love training others.

When this colleague would make surprise visits to check the quality of our work, it would give me shivers of jealousy. I would hate welcoming him in a hospitable manner while thinking evil thoughts about him. I started pushing my team too far and crossed the line to become that bad manager who would just want results at any cost. The people who had left their high-paying jobs and followed me because they believed in me, they loved me for my leadership skills, trusted that my energy could drive a team forward, started losing their hope and trust in me. Slowly, they started leaving the call centre.

Even the friend who had brought me into the role left the company, despite the fact it was his brother-in-law's venture. He wanted to help me, but he couldn't take any more of the environment where everyone was playing not to lose at any cost.

Eventually, I lost! I was fired from that position.

The news was like a bolt from the blue. I had never imagined even in my wildest dreams that I would have to see this day. I had joined the company with the belief that I was going to be the system in that company, not part of the system. The word "fired" started echoing in my mind. I was told by my managers (there were two, I remember vividly) that they no longer needed me. My services were over. They were now looking at me, rather gazing at me anticipating that I would leave the office within no time.

I did what I was told. I took the little kit that I used to carry during office hours and left the company with a very heavy heart. I had tears in my eyes as I walked down the stairs. I felt like I had lost everything in this world as if my whole world had collapsed.

I vividly remember the place where this took place; there was a village nearby, in South Extension, Delhi. Travelling from my office to the bus stop was like a long arduous journey.

Ohhhhhhhh.... the mere thought of that incidence still gives me goose bumps.

I felt like such a big failure and was mad at myself for trusting people blindly and for not reading the contract clearly. I left with a lot of bitterness in my heart and lost some valuable relationships (friends, colleagues well-wishers and admirers) in the process.

Eventually, a few months after I was fired, the call centre was shut down.

When this news came to me, I felt very bad for all my friends who were still there. I then sat down in silence, gave myself a pep-talk and soon realized that probably God had to save me from seeing this day, that's why he conspired to get me out of that job. The bad memory of being left out had gone. I had come a long way in a more secure and enriching path. I thanked the universe and God with folded hands.

A few days later, the thought of that call centre again crossed my mind. I realised everyone in that call centre was showing up not to lose and yet we all lost. Had we shown up just planning to win no matter what, the outcome could have been different. If we had been able to connect with the people behind those voices, we could have got more sales. If we had dug deeper on the lead qualities, if we could have shown faith in other products/ processes we could have narrow marginal difference (0.000001%) but this is what makes the difference between losing and winning in life.

Though some may think that both these things are different, but it means the same thing...

I was born and brought up in the outskirts of Kolkata, not very far from the international airport of the city called Dum Dum Airport. When I was growing up, I lived with my parents and one room house.

This single one room, we called our home, had a shed outside to use as a kitchen where my mother cooked. During the heavy rains, cooking would become difficult for my mother. I still remember we did not have my furniture as such. We had a rolling mattress which my mom would roll out in the night and roll back in the morning.

As I grew up, we continued to face many financial difficulties. I used to wear old clothes borrowed from my neighbours as those were free. The only day in the year when I would wear new clothes was at the festival of Durga Puja, so, Durga Puja has a very special place in my heart. My parents were and still are illiterate. My father was used to drive a taxi for a living. If you are illiterate in a country like India and especially during the 70s and 80s, all you could get is a job of a labourer or a driver.

My parents always believed that their children must have an education so they could have the best possible future and not just a basic education, rather an education in a private English medium school so that the best was available to us. (In the Indian or Asian Education System, it is very important to having English Education to get a better job or a better life).

They wanted to send me and my sister but when they looked at their earnings and savings, they realised that they didn't have enough funds. Somehow, they gained the courage to take some loans from neighbours so they could send one child to a private

English medium school. I was chosen over my sister because I was 3 years younger than her and could better adapt to the change from a local government medium school, where the lessons were in Hindi, to a private English medium school.

Yet, the biggest reason why I was chosen was because in the Indian culture, a male child gets priority over a female child. I'm not proud of what happened but I'm grateful that it did happen. Otherwise, I wouldn't be writing this and communicating to you in English.

And that's how my journey of learning English started. All my school life, I got second-hand books from my seniors as it used to be very cheap to buy them, or they were free. Throughout my school life, I was conditioned to write with pencil on my books.

All the challenges that I have shared with you so far were not my personal challenges though. They were part of the difficulties; my parents were going through while I was a kid. My personal challenges were different. As I mentioned earlier, I was overweight as a kid which made my life difficult. I easily became a target for my peer group so I was often laughed at and teased. My biggest challenge also caused the most pain, but that has made me what I am today.

India is a diverse country. You can see diversity all around, be it language, skin colour, culture or its topography, and that is why we call it Incredible India.

India has 29 different states (counties) with 22 different languages spread over 4,000 km from north to south and 3,000 km from east to west. There are different shades of India within

India. I state this with a great sense of pride because I am a part of Incredible India.

As a child, I was the only mixed child around. My dad is Punjabi, fair in complexion and my mother is Bengali, dark in complexion. This combination of cultures and colours made people treat me differently as they decided that there was something wrong with me. I was made to feel that I wasn't pure enough as a human being from the perspective of the people around me. I had questions for God/Universe; "Why had you made me like this? Why am I not normal for the other kids?"

When I was sixteen years old, my father had a major accident with his taxi (cab). After the accident, my father had no choice but to move to a remote district Sangrur (Punjab, India) which is 50 kilometres from Ludhiana (Punjab, India). This proved to be a big change to my life. In 1994, there was a big contrast between city life and village life. There were many challenges in the city, but in the village I experienced a whole new kind of challenge and life became horrible. The guys in my peer group were little stronger and bit taller than me, because, they'd grown up farming and milking buffaloes. Most of them had beards and they wore Patka (a small piece of cloth which is tied around the head) or turbans. They made me feel like a complete stranger. I was getting mocked, teased, bullied and abused by these macho boys. As I was new to the village, I had no friends, so I had no one to turn to, for support. I was all alone.

I knew I had to find a way to make things better. At the tender age of 16, I developed a strategy that would help me fit in and to combat that, I started growing beard, and wearing a turban. I wanted to show my peers that I was one of them.

> ***No one can make you feel inferior without your consent.***
>
> ***–Eleanor Roosevelt***

Six months later, I gave up on life. This became a deep and dark secret which I didn't share with anyone until I started training. I started looking at myself in the way others saw me. Their voices became my voice. All the voices started echoing in my head, "You are dumb, you are stupid, you are dull, good for nothing. You cannot make a difference to your life, to your parent's life. Nobody wants you, bloody soul. You are an impure version of human being". Let's face it, no matter how positive your attitude is, if the colleague next to you is criticising or blaming, that is bound to impact your life.

I thought there was no point in living because I couldn't make a difference. As I grew up watching Bollywood movies at a neighbour's house, I figured out that the easiest method to commit suicide was to cut my nerve in the middle of the night when everyone was sleeping; when they'd wake up in the morning, I'd be gone forever. I'd be a history.

When everybody was sleeping, I found the blade and held it on my wrist. My hands were shaking and there was an inner voice which was saying, "Just Go for It." Press it once, and all your miseries, sorrows and, questions to God will vanish. But at the same time there was another voice talking to me. We all have that voice, "The voice of fear". It said, "It will pain a lot. A lot of blood will spill out. Maybe, you can do this tomorrow night."

When I woke up in the morning, I was the most miserable

person in my world. Few days passed, and I was still contemplating. I kept on looking for enough strength to take action. And then something magical happened. I received a letter. Until this day, I have no clue how they got my name and address, but that letter saved my life. The letter came from a company named Amway. That time, I thought the letter was very personally written for me. Now, I realise that the letter contained alluring marketing lines. The letter read- "You are special; the chosen one for great International Business opportunities. Come, attend the meeting and you'll be rich and successful........."

I couldn't ignore the letter. It fulfilled a desire for the first time in my life to feel significant. All of us like to feel significant. We human beings have 6 human needs. And, one of these needs is to feel significant. It is true for all of us.

So I travelled 160 kilometre from Sangrur (Punjab) to Jalandhar (Punjab, India) and attended a seminar by Amway. Dr. Braich, the guy who presented the workshop, became India's first Amway Crown. He came all the way from Canada for this seminar business and at the end he said, "It's up to you whether you join the business or not, but I will recommend you to pick at least one book before you leave." I was going through their collection and I picked two books—one was "Think and Grow Rich" by Napoleon Hill and the other book which I picked up (since its title resonated with my life) was "How to Stop Worrying and Start Living" by Dale Carnegie. When I read these books, I realised that the power to change my life was within me. It didn't matter which religion I followed, how I looked, what my height was, what my complexion was or where I came from. Everything was inside me to change in my life. And my journey of change never stopped. Since that day, I have been reading books and I continue to learn in a training room. I haven't stopped reading or learning because I want to remain a student.

Story of Finding My Win

The attitude that allowed me to keep going despite the challenges is my ability to smile in the face of adversity. The smile I am talking about is not as a result of the 17 muscles that move your lips. It's the smile of passion that comes from the heart. When you know deep inside of yourself that it's all going to be OK in the end, you shun the habit of living in the shadow of fear. My biggest win in life was to be ok with being who I was. My winning attitude was deep in my heart. My quest for winning made me accept myself as I was. My life started to turn around the day I started practicing self-love.

> ***Difficulties come. But they do not last forever. You will see that they pass away like water under a bridge.***
>
> ***–Sri Saradamani Devi***

In my heart, I knew that things would get better eventually, even when I faced major adversity.

I came from a part of India (on my father's side) where going abroad was considered as a big prestigious achievement. Most Punjabis from Punjab (Northern India) are known for settling abroad. So, with that vision and mission, I too ventured abroad and came to the UK for a better life. Settling in a foreign land became easier for Indians after the boom in IT. This was one of the reasons why I did Bachelors in IT but I knew I was never made for IT. I didn't understand coding and, a part of me would die whenever I was sitting at the computer to design a program. Without having the backing of higher education, settling in a foreign land was an uphill struggle. Therefore, I had no choice but to come as a student to the UK. I had no money; and neither did my parents.

For Punjabi families, the trend at that time was to sell their farming land in order to send their children abroad, but my family owned no farming land.

My cousin Gurminder Singh Thind, who was then an Aeronautical Engineer employed with the British Airways (Now retired) gave me a whooping £5,000. I am using the word whooping here deliberately, because at that time it was an astronomical amount to me. He has not yet asked for the return.

My financial situation forced me to book my journey on 25th December (2006), as it was available at a discounted price. Had I dared to take a ticket for a normal working day, the ticket would have been prohibitively expensive. When I landed at Heathrow Airport, the airport was deserted; only Sardars were seen there. (The people of Sikh religion wearing a turban are commonly known as Sardars in India.) My friend, Ankit Mishra from my call centre days was with me. So he cracked a joke by asking, "Yaar... Amritsar mein hi utar diya kya?" (*Have they landed us in Amritsar?*) Amritsar is a big city of Punjab, India where most Sikh people reside and they have Golden Temple (holy temple). We both burst into laughter.

Soon after, Bhabhi (*my cousin's wife*) arrived to pick me up in her Mercedes. And that is how my journey to the UK started.

Once I arrived in UK, I went to a town, New Castle, in the north east of England for further studies. I was determined to find a way to take care of myself without relying on my cousin (as he had already done so much for me). This led me to gain my first job in New Castle. Though it was very good news for me, it also had its difficulties; the accent of people there was very different from those in London. At times, it was easier to put the phone down as I could not make out what the Recruiting Officer was saying. I somehow landed a labourer job which was a very bad choice since working as a labourer in the UK in the cold is a very tough task. Your hands freeze and your body gives up after a few hours of working. Wearing thick long boots was not the fashion but a necessity, as a part of health and safety.

Time passed by and I started getting some grounding in this foreign land. After a year or so, my Visa was about to run out and I needed to renew it in order to legally stay in the UK. I gained some bad expert advice, which recommended that I stay illegally, living in the UK without any confirmed timeframe as to when I will return to my homeland. I met people from Punjab, who had not gone back home for 10, 15 or even 20 years. It must have been a very painful experience. The mere thought of it made me feel sick. However, I wanted to follow the process legally. So, almost every year I had to renew my Visa under the pretext of further studies. In 2010, due to lack of funds in my bank account, an attempt to renew my visa was rejected and my whole world turned upside down. It felt as if someone took away the earth underneath my feet. I was miserable and stressed. I did not know what to do, whom to ask for help, where to go.

But, deep down, I knew that one day I would be a trainer and will end up teaching; this is what made me feel alive. So, after those initial moments of panic, I smiled; that smile of Brilliance within my heart told me that it's going to be all OK. It shifted my belief from helplessness to being empowered. That smile made me pursue my journey to the UK and remain there legally. After 4.5 long years, my legal Visa was reinstated. My smile made me a winner and my passion for the bigger picture kept me going. I could survive the toughest onslaughts in my life. I invite you to join me in this practice to smile at your challenges because when you can truly smile you will find the path of perseverance; it will enable you to stick to your dreams.

Many told me that I could go back to India or remain as an illegal immigrant in the UK because it was easy to do so. Had I done what was easy, then you would not be holding this book right now reading my journey of how I created my masterpiece. I had to keep my SMILE alive even in the face of adversity so that one day I could live my passion. Most of successful people have the ability to face adversity and still find a way to come out of it. They are the people who kept on wearing a smile on their face when most of the things were hard on them. I recommend you to keep this skill of smiling even when you're facing adversity in your life.

This is such a deeply profound understanding of my life that I wanted to give myself a constant reminder. With the intention to take this learning deeper into our life, we named our daughter, 'Muskaan'. Muskaan means smiling. And that's what our daughter is for us. Every single day when we wake up, looking at Muskaan reminds us to smile, irrespective of what the situation is. It is the most universal language, a human being can speak.

So, I invite you to put a strong reminder either in your calendar, or in a diary, or on the laptop screen or in a wallet about the power of smile. Smiling doesn't mean adversity will become weaker or smaller. It's just that smiling gives you the strength to face adversity and overcome it. And your win lies ahead of the adversity.

I'm very grateful to my daughter for she gives me a very strong reminder of this principle of smiling every single day irrespective of what the outcome they could bring. She reinforces the feeling of winner in me. So, the choice lies within us as to how we show up every single day of our life.

I believe it doesn't matter how many times you fail at anything. As long as you are putting in your best efforts every time and learning from the event, you are a true winner in every sense.

Notes:

Notes:

-2-

WINNING AND LOSING

Losing is not too far from winning. It's just a difference of one goal or one run or one mark. It's a difference of one nano second between a gold winner and a silver winner in an Olympic.

> ***Take what you get till you get what you want.***
>
> ***–Jamaican Saying***

So, losing is not losing unless you accept it. Till the time, you feel you have the winning ability, no one can take you out of the game or no one can take your winning spirit. It can never be NO. It turns into the Next Opportunity. It gets you closer to your Win. There's a very small distinction but that makes all the difference. The day we stop working on overcoming our limitations or fears, we start losing. When we stop adding new elements to our craft, we start our journey of losing. In the words of Napoleon Hill, "Whatever the mind of a man can conceive and believe, the mind can achieve". It works both ways. If you think you are a loser, or you think you are an achiever, you are right in both the cases. Our journey of failure starts with our acceptance. And the same is true for winning.

It's not what happens to you; it's your attitude towards that loss which will make you a 'true winner.'

Dr. Wayne Dyer, who is known as the godfather of self-development talked about how our reaction can turn every loss into an opportunity of growth in our attitude and by evaluating the loss and learning from it, we still win.

The most difficult part of winning and losing is finding the right balance between the two.

If you keep on losing then you need to learn more about the reason why that is happening.

For example, failing a driving test for the first few times, is part of the learning experience but if this happens too often, it clearly suggests that there is a flaw in your learning system and a better attitude to learning is needed.

However, the contrary is also correct.

If you are winning and achieving all your targets all the time, this indicates a lack of relevant growth in the winning attitude. Your job is too easy for you and there is untapped potential for the attitude of growth.

This brings me to the most important point in the book; as a human being, we are bound to experience both winning and losing. It is our reaction to the events which defines our true character.

The good news is that our mind has Free Will. It can choose Winning as a response to all good and bad, right and wrong, ugly and beautiful, all following the same law of opposites. By training our mind through effective tools and techniques consistently, we can create processes that would increase the chances of Winning.

I remember lying awake in my one-room house, a small space that I shared with three other family members.

Each day was bringing more and more disappointment over the deteriorating living conditions of my family.

Every night, I would look up, staring at a lifeless fan in the hot summer as I felt the heat of the ground through the back of my hands, which I was using as a pillow.

I would say to myself: "I have had enough of losing!"

I could see the days turning into weeks, the weeks turning into months... and nothing was changing.

> ***Nothing changes if nothing changes.***
>
> ***–Courtney C. Stevens***

That was the birth of the true winner within me, regardless of what was happening around me, every night I would stare at the empty ceiling and say to myself, "I have to make a difference." "I have to change this."

If you are familiar with the laws of the universe, you may know the law of intention, which states that everything starts with an intention. As soon as I set the intention to make a difference within me, I found a new sense of desire to explore by learning, to expand by growing from my learnings and to evolve by creating my life exactly the way I want it.

This desire led me to attend countless workshops and seminars in the areas of training and business. After going through this rigorous training in my field, I have found a motto for the game of winning and losing.

> ***Make it personal, Don't take it personally.***
>
> ***–Amandeep Thind***

Here, I want you to understand this: Make it your business to give your best shot in everything with the remembrance that winning and losing is not personal. It is a result of your daily winning habit. You should be indifferent towards winning or losing.

Notes:

Notes:

-3-

LEARNING THE LESSONS

As Vincent Lombardi said: "It's not whether you get knocked down; it's whether you get up". It is safe to say that all of us have faced difficult situations in our life, but we don't take on the situation head-on every time and emerge as a winner.

We face losses in different shapes and forms until we learn our lessons, just like successful people do. The same has been true for me. I wasn't saved from the adversities of life. I kept losing in life until I learnt the lesson of building 'Context over Content' in Life.

> ***Seek first to understand,***
> ***then to be understood.***
>
> ***–Stephen R. Covey***

My entrepreneurial career started very early in life. When I was 10 years old, I used to sell He-man and Spiderman cartoon stickers to my classmates in my 5th standard. I would buy a whole sheet for Rs. 4-5 and sell the individual stickers for a 10-20% margin. Soon the other children found my source and started buying directly from the shop. So, the business died in the first few months. I didn't know how to package it and market it, therefore I lost that business.

So, I opened up a tuition centre in my village when I was 17 to raise the funds for my education. I did very well in that and enjoyed the whole process as I love teaching. However, after 2 years, I had to relocate due to my further education and I didn't know how to delegate or scale the business by adding employees or building a team. I lacked the thought of creating a vision for the business, therefore I lost the business.

Then at the age of 20, I opened up a Computer Centre in my nearby town. That too failed after 12 months. I was in major debt and in immense pain.

> ***There is no education like adversity.***
>
> ***–Benjamin Disraeli***

Although I knew the art of raising funds, I kept failing in my business ventures for a period of 20 years from my school days, until I learnt from the right mentors and created an exit strategy.

It still took me 5 years to implement an exit strategy. With this learning (explore), growth (expand) and progression (evolve) within me, I was able to give up my normal 9-5 job in 2016 to live my passion for training people and delivering workshops across the globe.

> ***With ordinary talent and extraordinary perseverance, all things are attainable.***
>
> ***–Thomas Fowell Buxton***

Every lost point is helping us to get closer to our next win in life provided we are willing to accept it. Our losses teach us powerful lessons about Winning. Our duty is to open up to those learnings and embrace them as priceless gifts that the universe has provided to us. Most people love to stay in denial or in victim mode as they pass the blame to their father, mother, business partner, life partner, their kids, their friends, their teachers and the list goes on. If we blame the people who we believe have treated us badly, then we must also appreciate them for making us tougher and stronger in the process. If it was not for them, we would not be who we are today. They facilitated the growth in our strength to face life's adversities.

Real lessons of life are the ones we act upon and not just those we are pondering or forever analysing. Just knowing doesn't give us the lessons, it only gives us information. Most people believe that knowledge is power. But in today's age, there is no lack of information due to easy access to the Internet. The biggest scarcity in this information age is to experience the knowledge at an experiential level, as it is only at the experiential knowledge, where the real power is gained.

So, this book would only provide you the knowledge, but it will be your responsibility to experience it. I recommend you to come to my Live Workshops to take these learnings deeper and make them experiential.

Despite having all these challenges in my life, with poverty being the main one, I refused to give up as I knew I could change my future.

> ***We always attract into our lives whatever we think about most, believe in most strongly, expect on the deepest level, and imagine most vividly!***
>
> ***–Shakti Gawain***

It took me 25 years to see the lesson in every event of my life and today with full authenticity, I can thank all those people who bullied me, ridiculed me and caused me pain because they were the real teachers who taught me the lesson of self-acceptance and self-love.

It's only when we learn the lesson from the existing challenges, that our life changes. Otherwise, we keep on attracting the same problem with different people and different situations.

For example, at work your boss is bullying you and instead of learning the lessons of empowerment and balance in the relationship, you change jobs. Chances are that even in the new job, you will find yourself in a situation that will ask you to stand in your power.

This concept comes from the idea that every situation in life is there to teach us a lesson about our self, which means that the journey of winning is the journey of learning. If you are currently going through challenges or things are not going as per your plan, then sit down and reflect on what the situation is telling you?

I recommend this exercise.

Find a nice and quiet place; somewhere where you can relax. Take a pen and paper and write down the three biggest challenges you had in your life.

1. ....

2. ....

3. ....

Now, look at these challenges which were gifted to you and reflect...

- What was the biggest learning which came out of these challenges?
- What were the lessons you learnt from these challenges?
- What changed in you as a person?
- What did you do differently after you faced these challenges?

Take a closer look at these challenges now. Draw out the learnings which can help you to become a better version of you because that's what winners do in their life. They learn from their setbacks and make it better. So you're never failing; you're either learning or winning.

Notes:

-4-

THE 'BIG DREAM'

I'm sharing one of my favorite poems which always inspired me to live my dreams, 'I have a dream today' written by Dr. Martin Luther King, a world-renowned freedom fighter who stood for the equality of the people instead of the skin color.

I have a dream that one day this nation will rise and live out the true meaning of its creed: "We hold these truths to be self- evident; that all men are created equal."

I have a dream that one day even the state of Mississippi, a state sweltering with the heat of injustice, scorching with the heat of oppression, will be transformed into an oasis of freedom and justice.

I have a dream that my four little children will one day live in a nation where they will not be judged by the color of their skin, but by the content of their character.

I have a dream today. I have a dream that one day down in Alabama, with its vicious racists, with its governor having his lips dripping with the words of interposition and nullification, that one day right down in Alabama little black boys and black girls will be able to join hands with little white boys and white girls as sisters and brothers.

–Dr. Martin Luther King

It all starts with a Dream. Just like Martin Luther King, I had a dream; mine was not to be discriminated against for my darker skin or bullied for being overweight. Dreams can be as powerful as Dr. King's and, they can be as simple as letting the life flow naturally, which is being in the moment, for the moment.

Dreams are free, so why not Dream big? It's only when you have the audacity to Dream big, you get the courage to make them real. It's like you have to put every scene of that movie in sequence so that you can make it happen in the real world. It's something you see and feel day in and day out until the rest of the world starts seeing that movie with you. Winners are the big dreamers. The former President of India Mr A.P.J. Abdul Kalam, rightly put it, "Small aim is a crime." When we are born to do great things in life, then why would we want to settle for less.

I come from a land where we believe in karma; all our achievements are linked to it. It's also said that we always have Free Will, and so, the desire to dream abundantly. If we dream with our purest energy, the universe will conspire to make it a reality. Dreaming is our ability to channel the Free Will which God has gifted to every human being. Yet, every dream has a price tag. The question is: Will you pay with your determination, sweat, commitment, courage, and faith?

We often use the phrase "like a dream" to refer to something exceptional and out of this world. This is because our dreams are, in fact, beautiful, exceptional and out of this world. Dreaming doesn't cost us anything financially, yet our dreams are priceless.

Not only are they our door to the world of wonder, they, at times, are also our aspirations, hopes and desires. Dreams inspire us. Dreams motivate us. Dreams drive us. In the words of Anatole, French poet and author,

"To accomplish great things, we must not only act, but also dream; not only plan, but also believe."

When Walter Elias 'Walt' Disney started out on his professional journey, working with a newspaper as a cartoonist, he was fired by the newspaper editor for his lack of imagination and good ideas. He always dreamt of having a successful career with his cartoons. He learnt animation, struggled to keep a job, and went bankrupt a number of times, but he eventually achieved his dream. "All our dreams can come true," he said, "If we have the courage to pursue them". It was his courage and his ability to dream big that the world got 'Disney Land'.

My dreams were an outcome of my circumstances as a child. Being poor was difficult, being treated like an outsider was challenging, being fat was unwanted and, having dark skin was difficult to accept. But I dealt with all these obstacles and emerged triumph against all odds. What I couldn't deal with was the helplessness; there was the helplessness I felt as a child to change the attitude of people towards me, the helplessness of my parents in not being able to provide the basic requirements for their children, the helplessness that drives the poor to emulate the rich, just to fit in. So my dreams went far beyond my reality.

> ***Each day silently affirm that you are the type of person with whom you would like to spend the rest of your life.***
>
> ***–Bob Moawad***

I remember sleeping on the floor of our tiny little room and looking through the window at the stars and dreaming of making it big one day. I did not know exactly how would I do it, but I knew in my heart that I would make it one day, rubbing shoulders with the educated, civilised, rich people of society.

> ***The troubles that chase you away also show the road.***
>
> ***–Kigezi***

I knew that I would take charge of my life and not let circumstances dictate my life. Like I said before, I've always believed that Karma plays a role in our life; however, we can't use that as a pretext to not go after those big dreams. Let Karma play its role and let us play our role in achieving our big dreams. What frustrates me is people not executing the Free Will which God has given us to change the path of karma. The pettiness and excuses of putting things on karma and sitting back and not taking action towards your dreams is something I feel strongly against. My attitude of not giving up on the name of circumstances but to go out of the way has helped me carve out and design my life to a place where I am financially free and able to live my passion every single day of my life. I no longer need an alarm clock to wake me up in the morning. Things are naturally and organically flowing into life rather than me running after them. This is what can happen for your life once you Dream Big and show perseverance, courage and faith to make your dreams a reality.

> ***Do little things in an extraordinary way; be the best one in your line. You must not let your life run in the ordinary way; do something that will dazzle the world.***
>
> ***–Paramahansa Yogananda***

The reason I resonate so much with Martin Luther King's speech is that my dreams are not too different from his. I also dream of a world of equality and fair treatment for all regardless of their skin colour, religion or origin. I know the pain of being told off for not reflecting a certain stereotypical look that people dictate for your community or religion. If you are a mixed culture child, people make you doubt your identity. I grew up believing that there was something really wrong with me, that I was not pure enough as a human being. These were some learnings I picked up from the people around me. They were not my learnings, but I started believing in those voices and eventually, they became my voice.

The day the Amway letter stopped my suicidal thoughts, I felt as if the universe was guiding me.

It was the catalyst to create a big, audacious Dream. That's when I started believing in dreams, that dreams do come true. I didn't receive any money directly as a result of working with Amway, but it set me on a path of self-discovery, the path of learning and growing.

Here, I am, almost 2 decades later, writing my own book. It would not have been possible if I had not started with a big dream in my mind. You have to see first and feel it, before the world sees and feels it.

I urge you to sit down and write your big, audacious Dreams. For now, you don't have to know "How" but go deep and ask yourself "Why." My Why was that I didn't want anybody feeling helpless in their life, no matter what their circumstances are or where they were born. I have good reason to believe that in life there is no poverty except for disempowerment. You can't Dream big in your life if you're disempowered. You must empower yourself to dream big as that's where a Winner starts his journey. So, Come! Join me on this journey and write your big Dreams.

I recommend you to take advice from the people who have travelled a similar journey to the one you plan to travel.

Notice how people have pursued their dreams against the odds faced. As they have the experience and learning, they would be the best people to teach you from their real experiences. A person who has achieved, something similar to what you want to achieve has earned the right to share their learnings with you.

Most people end up taking advice from the people who have never achieved their dreams. And that is why their dream dies. The best guidance or mentoring you can receive is from someone who has earned the right to be a Role Model by their actions. People tell you what you can't do for what they couldn't accomplish themselves, so don't pay attention to what they say. If you want to become a Winner then start Dreaming Your Dreams. Never let anyone tell you that you can't make your dreams come true.

When I was a child, I often looked out from the wooden window of my house, up at the stars in the sky above and wondered if there was a world beyond the big blue canvas. I used to dream of being in a position in my life where I wouldn't have to worry financially. I used to dream of a world where I wasn't helpless, a world where I had the power to change things for myself and my parents. My dreams were born out of my pain and poverty; I dreamt of being successful, rich enough to afford good meals, good clothes and a nice house. I didn't know anything else; I just didn't want to grow up continuing to be the same helpless and poor person looking out of that tiny window.

From that tiny room in Calcutta, I went on to magnificent stage shows in London. I have come a long way. If it wasn't for my dream of leaving my old world behind, I wouldn't have travelled beyond the sky to find this new world, where I am not helpless (I am capable), I am not powerless (I am empowered), I am not poor (I am financially stable) and I am not insecure (I am confident). I still look out of the window but now from my own home in my room in London, I look at the sky and dream of bigger and better things. Now, I know that the stars are just an arm's length away. What I am today is what I dreamed about yesterday; what I will dream tonight, I will be tomorrow.

> ***Genius is the ability to put into effect what is in your mind.***
>
> ***–F. Scott Fitzgerald***

I have to warn you that it isn't easy. When you go out fighting for your big dreams, there will be challenges. Things will come up which makes you feel frustrated, angry, depressed, and helpless at times but that's all part of the journey.

The question is: Are you willing to pay the price? It's natural for any human being to feel fear whenever you aspire to do something big. Remember, courage is defined by a determination to keep marching forward despite the presence of fear.

Most people who you admire for their achievements or who you consider to be winners, went through immense fear but they kept marching forward. That's how big things are achieved in life. That's what Mahatma Gandhi, Martin Luther King, Abraham Lincoln, Nelson Mandela did, and that's what you've got to do. Feel the fear and do it anyway. On the journey of achieving big dreams, it's natural to face fear. As the famous saying goes "Dar Ke Aage Jeet Hai". It means your Win is beyond your Fear. And for every individual to win, it's alright to face your fear. You have to be in it to win it.

In my early years, I was surrounded by people who would run from fear, especially coming from an Indian culture where survival is so tough, you're ingrained to stay from anything risky or anything which might destabilize your security. So, I was conditioned that way myself but staying there was no fun. Living in fear and giving up on your Dreams are the worst gifts you can give to yourself. It can cost you your life. I made a conscious choice to move away from safe learnings and from those people who played it safe and were miserable inside. I went on the journey of learning every single day and becoming a better version of myself. I felt that it's better to be dead rather than living a Dreamless Life. I advise you to become friends with fear. Be aware that if you are feeling scared, you are making progress, you are showing courage and growing closer to your Dreams.

Perseverance, Courage & Faith

When you show courage, the universe will send its angel to support your journey. That is where faith kicks in. When something really matters, then you can't help but keep going for it, even when you get failures or rejections or are beaten down.

There are no coincidences in life. Everything happens for a reason. You attract everything you are truly looking for. On my journey, I fell many times and made many mistakes. I wish that I had someone present like me, guiding me along the path.

That's what I am doing for you here. When I realised that there are people who could benefit from my learnings and experiences, I decided to reach out through this book. I know if I had the right guidance during my early days, I could have avoided those losses and mistakes. I am happy to be your guide, your mentor, if you choose me to be one. If you want to learn these strategies experientially, then I encourage you to join me at my next events. Find out where I am in the world, and I would love to work with you in person sharing my teachings and lessons in an experiential way. So come and join to share your big Dream with me, and let's make it happen.

In the meantime, sit down with a pen and paper and let that dream come out on the piece of a paper. When you write things with your own hands on a piece of paper, magic unfolds in my experience. It's like asking the universe for exactly what you want. As in the movie, 'Aashiqui 2' (a famous Bollywood movie), there is a song "Sun raha hai na tu ....." which means the universe is listening and when you write a big dream on a paper, you're giving a crystal clear command to the universe for it to become a reality.

> ***There is nothing like a dream to create the future.***
>
> ***–Victor Hugo***

The main reason a person may not achieve their big dream is that they are distracted; they've taken their eyes off the target. This happens as human beings, especially the modern educated beings go through immense 'Browsing Blackout'. Browsing blackout is when you enter your Facebook or Instagram space with a promise of being there for 15-20 minutes but end up being there for longer hours that impact your results in life. This way, you end up having a mediocre life because dreams would take your efforts and your time.

When people meet me in the live events, they say, "You are a charismatic personality and you have got great energy." So, I wanted to understand how it happened. One day, I sat down and started decoding my life to see how from a big, dull, dumb boy, I became a charismatic person.

I discovered five steps, which I applied to become laserfocussed. These five steps helped me to change my reality and the way people perceived me. This can help any human being to build a laser focus and be perceived in a more effective and influential way. I'll be sharing these five steps later in the book.

> ***If you are born poor, it is not your fault. But, if you die poor, then it is your fault.***
>
> ***–Bill Gates***

Notes:

-5-

TENACITY—THE UNBREAKABLE SPIRIT

Movies based on the real-life stories of ordinary people who became extra-ordinary and winners despite all the odds, have always been inspiring for me. Then it didn't matter to me whether it is a Hollywood movie or a Bollywood movie as the inspiration is universal, just like the secret ingredients in this book. Movies entertain us and take us to an imaginary land, but at the same time, they teach us lessons. Some of these lessons are so profound that they stick with us and become a part of us.

It was never a walk-in-the-park for me, and I'm sure it isn't for most people. The challenges were endless: from miserable poverty to finding a progressive company. One of the painful things about being poor is that you land up being a part of the system that is not in your favor. Also, it limits you to who you can become and who you are as a person. Your ability to do something gets judged by the amount of money you have in your bank account, which is sad, but we live in a world like that.

Breaking away from the confines of these set parameters has been the most difficult thing in my life because it felt like I was fighting everything and everyone to break out of this box that restrained me while everyone kept trying to push me back.

If it wasn't for my undying ambition to achieve what I have achieved today, I would have given up a long time ago as it had been the easy thing to do. However, I transformed into an unstoppable force and went through all the obstacles head-on without paying much attention to what people thought about me. To be able to live the life that I wanted, I lived a life that nobody would want to live and I did that for years and years. I still fight to be the best that I can be because I'm not done yet. I keep improving, one day at a time; breaking barriers and moving ahead in life. I have been tenacious and that is one trait that you will find in every successful person in the world. Successful people don't know how to give up or stop achieving. They will keep pushing through until they are out of the box and then, they will push a little more.

> ***We are what we think. All that we are arises with our thoughts. With our thoughts, we make the world.***
>
> ***–Buddha***

I managed to stay on my path to success because I made a promise as a child that I would never let money define my worth.

I didn't want to be judged based on the bank balance that I had. So, I had to break my financial barriers. I wanted my parents to never worry about money when it came to buying food or buying clothes. I wanted to have holidays and travel freely. Bringing my parents to London was one of the best experiences in my life. Taking them to Kolkata by flight was priceless. My parents, my sister, my wife, my daughter, my niece, my nephew, my village, my city, my country, they all became the reason why I would perform outside my normal office hours. They gave me the energy to push harder even when it got tough. They kept me marching forward when I got hit by challenges on my path. They made me move despite the resistance that I faced in my life.

All our life, we get conditioned with how things will work out based on what our parents were taught, so it's what they in turn teach us. But how will this ever serve us? If Wright Brothers had not only focused on how they fly a piece of metal, they would never have achieved what they did. Edison would never have discovered the light bulb if he had not kept his mind focused on the why.

HOW is important but it only comes after we've established our WHY. Why we want to achieve what we want to achieve? For me, it was a promise for my daughter who was born after years after I had originally made that promise. I wanted my kids and my niece and nephew, to never go through what I had gone through. My WHY was, and still is to help those people who are deprived due to their financial or social circumstances and think that they will never make it. I want to reach out to all those, who contemplate committing suicide every day, just because someone has told them that they are not perfect.

What's your Why? The bigger the Why, the better. So, take a pause here, open up your diary and write down your WHY. If you're not clear on it for now, then that's OK, at least now you know that you have to figure out first before you work on your HOW. Your HOW will only be effective when your Why is clear.

Notes:

Notes:

-6-

LEARNING—THE STAIRCASE OF WINNING

> ***Learning is a treasure that will follow its owner everywhere.***
>
> ***–Chinese Proverb***

True learning is the path to a fulfilled life. As per NLP, (Neuro Linguistic Programming), there are four stages of learning that one has to follow in order to learn properly. These stages must be approached and conquered one by one in order. One cannot skip any of the steps if one has to learn comprehensively.

The four stages are:

1. Unconscious Incompetence - you don't know what you don't know

2. Conscious Incompetence - you know what you don't know

3. Conscious Competence - you know what you know

4. Unconscious Competence - you don't know what you know

Unconscious Incompetence is the stage where you are not aware that you lack certain knowledge. Let's take the example of science: A scientist, who hasn't heard of a certain new scientific method, doesn't know of his lack of competence in that method as he does not know the method even exists.

If he knew about this new method and understood that he lacked knowledge of this method, he would be at the second stage of learning - Conscious Incompetence.

Conscious Competence is the stage where you have fresh knowledge and have to actively apply that knowledge to get something done. At this stage, as the knowledge is fresh, you are not very sure of yourself and are very self-conscious and nervous while applying that knowledge. This is what happens when you have learnt how to drive but feel nervous while driving in traffic during the first few days. You have to be fully attentive to process all the acquired knowledge and apply it. Eventually, with practice, you become comfortable with driving and find yourself at ease behind the wheel. This stage is called Unconscious Competence.

Unconscious Competence is the final stage of learning, where the knowledge has been embedded into your subconscious. Once this happens, you do not actively need to recall what you have learnt. Instead, the knowledge in your subconscious mind allows you to automatically take action. This means that even if you were to take a year's break from driving, you would still be able to drive comfortably once you resume, provided the knowledge of how to drive was embedded in your subconscious mind. This is when you are at your best state; even the most novel of processes and actions become a routine.

These stages of learning are clearly apparent in your childhood. Remember being introduced to the world of education, learning your ABCs and numbers, knowing how to spell and form sentences; being taught table manners and how to greet your elders and the other people you connect with respect. What was such a chore at first now, comes naturally to us with enough time and practice.

As children, our subconscious mind is programmed with information by our teachers, parents, books, environments, etc. and that is who we go on to become; it is such an important part of us that it becomes us.

Most of the decisions that we take and our mannerisms today are all a result of our childhood programming. Most of this programming takes place during the first 7 to 10 years of our life. I call this "The Box Theory", which I cover in my Live workshops and will cover comprehensively in my next book, "Screw the Positive Attitude". If at any given point within this book, you feel like you can't agree with or accept something, it is because your unconscious programming (I call it subconscious programming) prohibits you from doing so.

> ***Your world is as big as you make it.***
>
> ***–Georgia Douglas Johnson***

It is believed that the subconscious mind can be deprogrammed. However, I personally feel that it is better to reprogram it. To erase something from the subconscious is almost impossible or at least extremely difficult; however, it is easier to reprogram it. For instance, if you switch from a manual car to an automatic, you may find it difficult to make the transition at first, always looking for the clutch and the gear. It is only after repeatedly reminding yourself of the transition that you get used to it. Now, this is what I would call reprogramming; modifying the information without trying to erase it. It is obvious that it would be extremely difficult for you to unlearn driving a car with a manual transmission to adapt to an automatic, but it is relatively easier to just reprogram yourself for the new vehicle.

This doesn't only apply to driving cars; every bit of information and each belief in your subconscious mind can be reprogrammed by putting in adequate time and effort. So, to make it easier on yourself, it might be good to deal with the changes in your life, like you would deal with a change of car: Persistent Reprogramming.

It's the principle of Persistent Reprogramming that helped me to venture out onto the path of training and teaching as an International Trainer. It's the same principle which helped me to become rich, famous and successful. It helped me live my life on my terms. Most days when I wake up, I am not rushing to work; I am busy playing with my 23-month-old daughter, at the time of writing this book.

During my education days, I didn't know something called, Effective Communication Skills. Within the few years of starting my professional career, I knew that I would have to become a better teacher than others in the same arena. So, I went on a journey to learn from the masters, those who are world renowned trainers. I learnt the skills of great Speakers to bring my message in such an impactful way, that it would not just make the participant think; it would move them to action. Now, after speaking and training for 10+ years in 500+ workshops, in 20+ different countries, three continents and directly speaking in front of nearly 1 million people, it has also almost become my second nature. I am so engaged in the process of training that I no longer think about it. Sometimes, my students ask me this question: "You have been with us for 12 hours, standing throughout the day delivering the content and you don't seem to be tired. How come? You look at no notes and manage to train for 12-14 hours." Even I didn't realise this until my students brought into my notice. My love for teaching just takes over all my timely distractions.

You can model this to master any skill. Think about a skill you want to master. This is one thing you must know that will become the foundation of your path. Without this component, your rational mind will give up. It is the only way to master you. Read on to find out how to achieve this!

Notes:

-7-

PASSION—THE KEY INGREDIENT OF WINNING

Have you ever had moments where you lost the track of time? Something that you did or created where you were so comfortable and you felt one with the process?

Something which felt like perfect to your heart?

Yes, my friend! I am talking about Passion, finding something which you were born to do.

Passion is the energy that keeps us going, helps us feel filled with meaning, and gives us a sense of purpose, happiness, excitement and anticipation. Passion is a powerful force in helping us accomplish anything we set our mind to, experiencing work and life to the fullest extent possible.

If life was a car, then passion would be the steering wheel, the driving force behind success and happiness that allows us to live better and more fulfilled lives.

> ***I have no special talents. I am just passionately curious.***
>
> ***–Albert Einstein***

Again I am talking in the context of creating or doing something productive. Many people like to doing nothing, by which I mean they don't want to do anything physically or mentally, which they don't enjoy. We are all born with a purpose. Those who keep that question alive in their consciousness and thrive for it, eventually find themselves in the Passion land. Having a passion helps you find yourself. It is about finding something important to you with no obvious value other than the mere fact that it gives you joy. Passion is something you care about, it's something you are dedicated to, and it is something you become a part of who you are.

Once you fall in the alignment with your life's purpose, then things don't feel like an effort anymore. You feel a higher energy which drives you to accomplish your goals. If you are playing the wrong game, it's almost impossible to win, so you've got to play the game of life which is meant for you and not just something you were told to play.

Although it is natural to have a desire to win, succeed and be on the top, this single-minded, resolute, unwavering desire to be triumphant all the time also takes us away from reality. It distances us from the knowledge of losing and failing. In reality, where there is a rose, a thorn will always be nearby. Similarly, where there is a desire and an effort to win and succeed, there is also a chance to lose and fail. The more you want to succeed and make an effort, the more are the chances to lose and fail.

> ***As a man acts, so does he become.***
> ***As a man's desire is, so is his destiny.***
> ***–Brihadaranyaka Upanishad***

The secret is to avoid being attached to negative facets of achieving a goal, while chasing the positives. It is important to stay detached from the process of achieving the goal. This doesn't mean to work half-heartedly towards its achievement. It means giving it your hundred percent without making the outcome of the process. It is the sole factor by which you can measure the success of your effort, and it is the only process that should count.

There are two ways of getting involved in any process: the first is with your head and the second is with your heart.

Our head is responsible for assimilating and processing information that eventually forms our preferences, our likes and dislikes. Most of the time, the negative or an unexpected outcome of any process (say, a game) is assessed by the head and registers it as a failure, which brings us pain that is hard to handle.

The heart, on the other hand, is like a child; it's carefree, curious, enthusiastic and loving. The lack of care makes it possible to play the game without thinking about the outcome; the curiosity makes us venture into places we thought we would dare not to go and try things we are uncertain of; the enthusiasm makes us work hard and gives our best till the very end; and the love takes us back to the playfield, irrespective of the challenges that we have to face.

> ***You must begin to think of yourself as becoming the person you want to be.***
>
> ***–David Viscott***

In order to be winners, we must work hard, play smart, have fun and do it all together. I found this to be as good advice as one can come across. It dawned on me that before anyone would ever want to commit to all the hard work required to win, something else would need to be present. The reason we become real winners and champions in sports and life comes down to this: apart from committing to hard work, playing smart, having fun and, all the rest, we truly have to love what we are doing.

When you love what you are doing, you become one with it. You are so engaged in the process that it is the only thing that matters and you will lose track of time while doing it. When you are truly passionate about it, it becomes easier to put in the hard work, rebound from failures and return to the playing field, time and again.

Have you ever heard great athletes or film actors say that they do not love what they do? Probably not! People who excel in any field usually love it and are enthusiastic about being a part of it. Champions do not become champions just by doing what they are required to do. They become champions by loving what they do and doing it over and over again without quitting or slowing down.

Almost all great people have been down the road of struggle. They have faced obstacles, challenges and failures. However, they had discovered the art of playing the game with their hearts and not with their heads. They would use their hearts, as compasses or tools to navigate their way to success. This also happens to be one of the most valuable lessons I've learned from life; I've followed my passion despite all the odds. So, I would urge you to reflect on your life and find something that you are truly passionate about.

Take a moment now and look back upon your life and write down 3 things you are most passionate about.

1. ....

2. ....

3. ....

Now, look at your job or any area of activity and see if your passion is being reflected in your chosen career. In other words, answer this question, "Are you living your passion while on the journey of winning?"

Take the thing you love and make it your life. Once you start following your passion and devote your time and energy to it, your mind will expand, allowing you to reach the heights, you could only dream of. It is this passion that brings joy to your work and leads you to glory. Winning is only possible when you follow your passion. Even if you are in the process of training, passion leaves you feeling as if you are fulfilling the purpose of your life. It brings a level of fulfilment that no amount of money can buy and nobody working outside their passion can match.

> ***It is never too late to be what you might have been.***
>
> ***–George Eliot***

The Power of the Mind

> ***Once the mind expands, it can never return to its original state.***
>
> ***–Oliver Wendell Holmes***

Plutarch, a Greek essayist and historian, once said "The mind is not a vessel to be filled but a fire to be kindled."

I truly believe that the human mind is an absolute genius; all we need is to nurture our thoughts. It's all about our own mindset. Once we make our brain believe that we can do it, your journey of change starts.

It's about breaking your limitations.

When you're able to break your own limitations, you tap into the higher power of the mind. Until you face a tough situation in your life, you don't know how tough you are. To prove how capable the human mind is, we bring 'Firewalk Experience' for our attendees. So, during our training programs, our attendees walk on the hot burning coals as a metaphor to break their limits.

For most human beings, it is like we're afraid of fire and we are conditioned to stay away from it. So, we create a situation for a human mind to face that fear of fire and walk across hot burning coals. So when they walk on burning coals, they feel that their bigger self has come out. And they feel as if they've conquered their fear. Most people, after Firewalk look back and think, 'If they can walk on the burning coals, what else they can achieve in their lives?'

Some people also share Firewalk as a spiritual experience of letting go of the energies which were not serving them and tap into the higher power of the mind. Doing such an experience 12+ years back, I was able to break my limitations and tap into the higher power of my mind. Now, I bring the same experience to my students. At times, depending on the context of the training, attendees go through board-breaking, brick-breaking, arrow-breaking, or glass-walk, rod-bending and many other such physical activities that support participants to break their limitations.

As I previously mentioned, the mind is a powerful tool, which is why Napolean Hill said, 'Whatever the mind can conceive, and believe, it can achieve'. The mind will perceive something as true or false, good or bad, whatever you tell it to. This means that if your mind 'thinks' there is a threat to you, your body will react in fear. For example, if you are in a room and someone says to you that there is a man with a gun waiting outside for you, whether this statement is true or not, your mind will start producing 'threat sweat' in response. Therefore, a mind, on its own, cannot tell the difference between reality and what you imagine the reality to be. Depending on what thoughts we think, what things we imagine, and what perspectives we feed, our mind can be forced to accept whatever reality, we establish.

It is like training a specific muscle, say the winning muscle, of your body. The more you train it, the bigger, and the stronger it gets. It is the most essential component in your journey to winning as it is the mind that helps you make those important decisions. Thankfully, one of the best things about our minds is that while it guides our actions, we, in turn, can also direct them.

Thoughts become your feelings, feelings become your actions and actions become your results.

This statement can be deconstructed into three different parts,

1. Thoughts; what you think about all the time.
2. Feelings; how you feel about those thoughts.
3. Action; how you act upon what you feel gives you the ultimate result.

This has also been reiterated by Richard Bandler, a world-renowned author and trainer in the field of self-help, who emphasised that your thoughts create your feelings and those feelings create your reality. It is important to think the right thoughts to have the right feelings and so to act rightly. That's the kind of attitude you need to carry with you on the path to winning. The next section covers the importance of attitude in the journey leading to winning and reveals how to develop the ultimate, unshakeable attitude.

Notes:

-8-

FOCUS—THE HIDDEN WEAPON

The successful warrior is the average man, with laser-like focus.

–Bruce Lee

The Oxford dictionary defines focus as "an act of concentrating interest or activity on something". As per this definition, how many things do we focus on every single day? In an ordinary household, the average human being focuses each day on what to eat, what entertainment to consume, what to wear to the office, the work in the office and socializing. While you are focusing on all these monotonous routines and activities, you often stop focusing on your life goals.

Whatever you focus on becomes your reality. If you focus on the pressure of work, you are inviting in more pressure. Similarly, if you are focusing on your lack of wealth, you are inviting more misfortune and tough financial times. For me, my parents always used to focus on the lack of financial resources available to us, and it became our reality. Similarly, there are hundreds of thousands of people around the world who believe their circumstances are bigger than they are, and hence they keep focusing on this, and guess what, these people end up becoming slaves to their circumstances.

So, do we just stop focusing on things that are not productive or good for us? It is not that simple, because whatever we choose to not focus on ends up as our primary focus. It is just natural that we cannot think about something without thinking about it first. Let's use an example to understand this better: Clear your mind and take a deep breath in. Let it out. Now, do not think about a red pen. You will think about something else in a moment and for that, you need to refrain from thinking about a red pen.

What happens here? In order to avoid thinking about the red pen, you cannot help but to think about it. Those who think visually can even visualise a red pen right now. This is our subconscious mind at work. As soon as we say 'red pen', the subconscious immediately brings up information related to the word in the form of words or pictures similar to how the RAM (Random Access Memory) works in a computer. This ends up becoming our reality because we cannot think beyond it. As soon as we say it, the subconscious perceives it as reality even if it isn't so. Similarly, when we keep thinking that we cannot do it, or our circumstances are bigger than us, it becomes our reality.

A little story is in order here. One of my friends took her son to learn to climb on a climbing wall. He was doing really well and making his way up with confidence, with the trainer encouraging him to go further. As the boy got closer to the top, his mother shouted, "don't be afraid son, don't be afraid." That very moment, the boy stopped climbing and started trembling because the only thing he could think about was being afraid. He realised he was doing something he'd never done before and he couldn't help but be afraid.

What we learn from this story is that focus is a very powerful thing. We need to change our focus if we want to move forward. So, if we want to be financially successful, keep telling yourself "Money is coming in" or "I am doing things that are going to bring money into my life." It's important, however, to be modest and realistic. You cannot keep telling yourself that you've become a millionaire. That would be lying to yourself or a sign of delusion.

Focus on whatever good is happening and build on it. These little things will accumulate over time and the smaller dollar bills will become stacks of larger dollar bills. The things that make it almost impossible for us to focus, is distractions. Nowadays, with the Internet and the various Apps being downloaded on mobile devices, it has become easy to be engaged in avoidable and mostly useless activities throughout the day and often late in the night. Whether it's engaging games on our mobile phones or the networking Apps (if it's available for download), it is on the device and, we are using it. The distractions are endless, from television soaps to sitcoms on Netflix, from newly-released movies to sports, from blog posts to online discussions, from social networking to picture sharing, from YouTube to live streaming. The possibilities are endless.It is estimated that an average person spends around four hours watching television each day, which amounts to nearly 13 years of a human life (should a person live beyond 70). By adding to it the time spent on the various Apps on your phone and the Internet, you get to know yourself that a staggering amount of time you could have utilized in a more productive manner. While entertainment is good for your mental health, excessive amounts of idle consumption of entertainment can be counterproductive as well, if not harmful.

As already mentioned earlier, this is known as Browsing Blackout whereby every day we spend hours of our time, on our mobile devices, or computers, accessing blogs, pictures and videos, with no clear recollection of what we saw or learnt by the end of the day. This means a lot of intelligent and capable people lose years of their lives that could have been spent earning thousands of dollars in wages, making new friends, travelling, learning new languages and art, being more productive and enjoying life. In today's age, where there is so much distraction due to technology, it becomes very difficult to stay on the path of success.

Browsing blackout is a household issue, given the distractions that it brings, creating and maintaining focus is both hard and important. If focus is necessary for success, laser-like focus is necessary for an exceptional success story. All that you need to do is to follow the five simple steps (listed below) to achieve laser-focus in life.

I. Set a specific goal in your life

Most people wish for great things in their life, but very few create specific goals in their life. Harvard University researched that people do better who write their goals than those who don't write it. Creating a specific goal is the first step to create a laser-focus in life. If you are not aiming at a specific goal, that means you're very scattered and distracted in your life.

When you want to reach somewhere in your life, you got to follow a path. If you want to become a winner, there is a certain path you need to follow. One of the most important steps for the winner is to set a specific goal in their life. Have you taken a bus, train or a flight you don't know where it is going? I'm sure the answer is no. The same is for life. If the word goal has some negative connotations for you, then you can replace it with words like target, map or design.

You need to know exactly, what it is that you want to achieve and accordingly take actions to achieve that goal. When you direct your energy for a specific goal, you become laser-focused. If becoming rich is one of your goals, you must specify how much money you want to earn. Some people have this belief that if they make more money, others will lose out.

For your information, 14+ trillion dollars exchange hands every single day in trading. There is enough abundance for 7+ billion to become millionaires.

> ***If you are born poor, it is not your fault. But, if you die poor, then it is your fault.***
>
> ***–Bill Gates***

So you have to be very specific, exactly how much money you want, how much weight you want to lose, which places you want to visit, and which targets you want to achieve within a specified period. Set a specific goal and believe in that goal, so that the universe conspires to get you there. There are a few precautions that I would recommend you to keep in mind while setting a specific goal:

- **Set a realistic goal**

  When I am asking you to set a realistic specific goal; it doesn't mean that you need to play a smaller game of life. Create a specific goal that will stretch you, but at the same time, it has to be realistic. A goal that will up your game; and it must be achievable. Because if your mind knows that you're aiming for something which is not possible at all, it will not make enough efforts to achieve it. For example, if you've made, £50,000 last year, you can aim to increase it by 30-50% or even double it for next year. Even if you want to triple your income, it is possible depending upon who you are, how you show up, the actions you take and how much pressure you can sustain. Keeping it realistic helps the mind to keep you in the game. It draws evidence that it is possible and it will make its best efforts to achieve that goal.

- **Know your starting point**

To know your starting point, you must know who you are as a person. And that's where most of the people are going wrong. So, understand your starting point right now at this moment. If you set on this path of creating realistic and stretchable goals, you would have to define your journey from this moment onwards. As a human being, you don't have any power to go back in the past and fix it but you surely will have the power to change your future. So, set your goals based on the point where you start and what you start with.

If you've ever run a race (sprint or marathon) or even witnessed one, you probably know that the starting point of that race is as important as the finish line. Without the starting point, the race cannot begin and, you'd never know how long the race is going to be. To measure that distance between point A and point B, point A is as important as point B. Without either, the progress or distance to the goal cannot be measured. Being a human being, you've got a unique journey. So, be aware of your point A. When you know your point A, you can define point B.

Success is important, specifically, in terms of how much you have improved yourself and, not by how much better you can do in comparison to others. Your success is never ever in comparison to the person sitting next to you or your cousins, or brothers or sisters or your colleagues. Success is always from where you start and what you start with. Others are insignificant to your success curve; the only person who matters is you. Even for twin brothers or sisters their journey is not the same.

- **Find out your Bigger WHY**

This is the most essential part in your goal setting. We have been conditioned from school & college to get stuck up on the how. But you have to work on your WHY first for the HOW to show up. When I figured out my WHY; the How didn't matter anymore. The how came; I'm not saying how is not important; it's just not 'the most important thing'. You need to work on your Why and it has to be bigger. And why isn't about you or your immediate family. It's about you, your relatives, your cousins, your friends, your neighbours, your community, your city, your country and above all, the universe. The bigger the Why, the easier the How would be. That's how the most successful people are successful because they've figured their bigger WHY. And that's how things will show up.

This is where the "why" comes in. Why have you set the goal and why do you want to achieve it? Let's say you want to make a certain amount of money in the next two years; why do you want to make that money? Is it for your first car, a new house for your parents or maybe a much-needed vacation with your partner? When you have an emotional connection with your goal, you are motivated to go a long distance to reach that goal; letting go or giving up isn't an option. For me, I wanted to be successful in general, but had two specific goals I dedicated my life to. I wanted to become an internationally-recognized speaker and come out of poverty. I had a deep emotional connection with both of these goals. The first goal of becoming an internationally recognized speaker was close to my heart as I was either bullied and ridiculed or just excluded from everything, throughout my childhood. I did not exist for others. It was important for me to be recognised and affect the lives of others in a positive way. The second goal was crucial for me because of my parents. The effort and resources that they put into me despite financial hardships deserved positive returns. I remember my parents going out of their way to place me in a private school so that I could get a quality education. It was important for me to respect that effort and make something of myself so that I could come out of that world of poverty and bring my parents out with me. And since then I am so emotionally attached to my goals that not a single day passes by when I don't do something to get closer to the goal, meet it and exceed it.

II. Write your Goal

Once you have set a specific goal, you need to write it down. As I already mentioned in one of the previous exercises, when you write things with pure intention, something magical happens in your life. So, I highly recommend you to write your goals with your own hands. As when you write it down, you are letting know the universe what exactly you want from it. Once you have decided on your goal and are absolutely sure about it, write it down. Consider this a finalizing ritual, indicating that once you write down the goal, you cannot change it. Writing has more impact than reading and speaking; as written information stays with you longer, which is why this exercise is important. Remember writing down important points from your lessons back in your school days? That was you, trying to get more involved with your lessons by taking the initiative and creating your content. It gave you a better understanding of the same information provided in your book; allowed you to remember it better, for a longer time.

Once you've written your goal down, make it a habit to spend some time with it every day. Write it on a big piece of paper and frame it. Put it up on the wall of your room where you will see it at least once a day. Better still, make multiple copies and place them around the house so that you will often see it. The more you see your goal on a daily basis, the more you'll know what you need to do to achieve it. You can also use pictures and objects that remind you of the goal. These reminders will keep you focused and reduce the likelihood of you being distracted. If you reach a milestone, where you realise that you could aim higher, or need to tweak the goal, go for it. While you have written and finalized your goal, it isn't written in stone that you cannot change it if the need arises.

III. Declare your goals

The third step is a very powerful mechanism. It can put anybody into action. It's very important to declare your goals aloud to the people who truly matter to you the most. Remember, I don't recommend you to set up an unrealistic goal. If you set realistic and stretchable goals and you let your near and dear ones know about it, they will hold you to higher standards. Most will hold you with the wrong kind of support. Very few would understand you; and they will hold you accountable in a nice way and encourage you. Most of them are fearful; they will project their own fears on you and will overprotect you. Now that you have decided your goal and have made sure that you are focused on achieving it, share it with your friends and family. If you have a social networking profile, raise the ante by putting it up there and letting everyone know about it. At first, it may seem odd and could even lead to a few raised eyebrows, doubts or ridicule.

However, this is just going to keep you on your toes and make you accountable to everyone who knows about your goals. They will question you every chance they get and, you will need to strive for answers and answers that lead towards the fulfillment of your public proclamation. When I publicly declared my goals, it was my close friends and colleagues, out of all the people, who made fun of me. When they came to know that I aspired to become a renowned international speaker, they would taunt me by calling me "Speaker Sahib"; this was meant to mock me and question my ability to become a speaker. Their laughter motivated me to work harder as I had a point to prove. Even now, whenever I announce my goals to people around me, there are some who doubt my abilities and question me. I am grateful to such people because if there were no questions, there would be no answers to seek. If your goal is bigger than you, people will laugh at you. If they don't laugh at your goal then maybe your goal is not big enough and if it is not big enough, there is no point striving to achieve it. So, make a goal that is bigger than you, write it down, declare it and believe in it. Others will follow.

IV. Measure your progress

The fourth step towards creating a laser-like focus is to measure or track your progress. The point of measuring goals is to understand your progress i.e. how you are doing and how far you need to go to reach the destination. Consider a plane ride to a distant location. It takes a certain amount of time to get to that destination. However, we should always be aware of how much distance we have covered and how much is still left to go. Some people prefer to notice the time taken instead of distance travelled, "three hours gone, three more to go before I reach the destination". What really helps to keep track of the distance on a journey, are the milestones and major stops on the way.

Understand this, it's just not the progress; it's also regress which is the opposite of progress. It could be more losses in the journey than wins. The best part is you need to focus on the bigger win. You need to be okay with the pain in the path. However, as long as you are moving towards your goal, it's alright. When you get on a bus to travel to a particular place, an hour's delay in departure or a brief traffic jam on the way shouldn't matter as long as you reach your destination safely.

Remember that the only person who you are in competition with is you. Keep measuring it on a regular basis. When you measure and improve it; you'd achieve more in your life. You also need to measure your goals via the milestones that are required to set along the way. For example, to become a billionaire, you need to become a millionaire first, and to become a millionaire, you need to bank your first 10,000 pounds or dollars first. So, you tick off the milestones after achieving them and keep moving ahead, with the knowledge of how much distance is left to cover and how much has already been covered. Some of the milestones will be harder to achieve than others and some will take more than one attempt, but you keep going and moving towards the final goal, one milestone at a time.

V. Celebrate all successes

And the final step of creating laser focus is that you should celebrate all your successes. It doesn't matter how big or small it is. Every time you reach a milestone or achieve something along the way to your eventual goal, you should take the time to celebrate with your colleagues, friends or family. Success is great, but celebrating makes it even better as you feel good about yourself and the festivity of celebrating can go a long way to keeping you motivated and focused. The happier you feel about moving closer to your goal, the more distance you will be willing to cover in the near future. However, if you keep focusing on 'what you have not achieved', you will get stuck. So shift your focus to 'what you've achieved'. And don't just celebrate your own successes; celebrate everyone's success around yourself. If we can get a habit of celebrating each and every success happening around us; we can't help but get charged up in our life that we can achieve whatever we want to achieve in our life.

> ***The key is to keep company only with people who uplift you, whose presence calls forth your best.***
>
> ***–Epictetus***

Notes:

-9-

CONNECTIONS—THE FLUID OF ALL WINNING JOURNEY

Alfred Lord Tennyson famously wrote, "I am a part of all that I have met." This simple phrase from his widely loved poem Ulysses, zeros in on one of the most empowering truths of life.

The people we meet and surround ourselves with play a huge role in: what we do with our life, who we become and, how we shape our dreams. Research studies show that we become like the people we surround ourselves with. It also suggests that if we take the income of the 5 people we spend the most time with, add them all up, and then divide it by 5 to find the average, it will more or less equate to our income. The truth of life is that if we hang out with quitters, we will soon become one. The same is true when we hang out with winners who are not ready to give up on their dreams; we become like them. So, in this chapter, whenever I mention people; I'm talking about the people with progressive mindset. They're the people who are open to learning, growing and, always willing to become their better version in life.

While it's true that nothing and nobody in life can keep you away from your dreams, it's also true that the quality of people you know can really help you move closer to your dream. Remember, a champion is remembered for his individual glory, but most champions have a team of great people around them. If there's one thing you must start building today, it is your very own 'Championship Team'.

Life has taught me that no matter what path you set foot on, people are your most valuable currency, capital and source of strength. I love meeting and interacting with people from all walks of life. Once you start opening yourself up to the idea, you will see that everyone you meet has the potential to teach you something wonderful and useful.

People will help you find solutions to the problems you face on the way to your dream. They'll give you practical and moral support. They'll give you great ideas or help you hone in on your own. And never forget, people will help you make connections and contacts that you can transform into more successes. I know from first-hand experience that meeting people can change your life forever.

I must share that it's people who will support you to grow. People who hold themselves to higher standards will lift you to higher standards. People who play a bigger game in life may also make you feel uncomfortable, but it's required as when you challenge your comfort zone you'll be directed towards your highest potential.

Think of meeting people as a life source for the energy that you need to fuel your Winning Journey. Connecting with the right people will transform you as a person and expose you to so many great new ideas and possibilities.

I strongly recommend that you use every opportunity you get, to step out and meet with people.

During my journey of self-discovery, I was attending many training programs and courses. While attending a business seminar on strategy in London, I learnt one very important life lesson, which really stood out for me: 'Stage time being Wealth Time'. I thought further about this principle realising that it's not just applicable to money, but it can also be applied to all types of wealth in life from health to well-being to Winning in Life.

This mantra reminds me that if you want to Win in your life, you must make sure that you've to turn up everywhere else first. From one-to-one interactions to meetings and workshops, you must look at every interaction as an opportunity to learn and grow.

As Tony Robbins says, "Proximity is Power". Communication is more than mere words. It includes body language, facial expressions and voice modulation, amongst other things, which can help the communicators to understand each other better and leaving little scope for misunderstanding and misinterpretation.

The concept of verbal versus non-verbal communication was researched and studied by Prof. Albert Mehrabian of the University of California. In the 1970s, he suggested that we tend to deduce our feelings, attitudes, and beliefs about what someone says not by the actual words spoken, but by the speaker's body language and tone of voice.

As I stayed open to learning on my journey and always looked to connect with the big winners of life, I happened to come in to close proximity with Veronica Tan & Richard Tan of Success Resources which opened up the doors of being one of the trainers for Tony Robbins. While working with Success Resources, I met Michael Burnett, which opened the doors for me to work in Australia. It also led me to meet some great Winners in my industry like Tony Robbins, Joel Bauer, Les Brown, T. Harv Eker, Jordan Belfort (The Wolf of Wall Street), Richard Branson, Donald Trump, Alan Sugar and Sebastian Coe (London Olympic Organiser). It crafted a path for me to become friends with some wonderful people like Sidra Jafri. I also met Surendran Jayasekhar of Success Gyan leading me to share the stage with Dr. John Demartini and Ashish Vidyarthi (Bollywood Actor).

This one little principle has created so many wins in my life that I now train people on the 'Power of Connections' during experiential workshops and help people realise that Connections are a Catalyst to winning. I train attendees to learn the art of connecting with people who will support them on their journey of winning.

I also use my experience from such meetings to teach others the value and power of connections through interactive sessions such as 'Treasure Hunt'. My aim is to share everything that I've learned and to make it experiential, as I believe that experiential knowledge increases the chances of Winning.

Winners are known to seize every opportunity by the horns, and believe me, in just a few short weeks of imbibing this, you'll notice how far you've progressed. While human interaction is of the essence here, it isn't always possible to meet people in person. That is where technology and a great personality come into play. With the right amount of coordination and charisma, the Zoom and Skype meeting can be very fruitful. I often connect online with my 1-1 clients and conduct online seminars too. I even connect to my mentors online when I look for answers to win further in my life.

Once you start implementing this principle, you will make huge progress in moving closer to your goal in a very short span of time.

When it comes to building connections, we don't ignore the power of learning from those who have made it big themselves. Some of the biggest ideas and sparks of inspiration in my life have been a result of learning from people who are successful in their chosen fields. In this day and age, when you have the opportunity to attend seminars and hear successful people share their stories and strategies, it's almost criminal to pass up on the chance. Half of the road to success is paved by just showing up, and I have used this principle to guide my life.

During my early days in London, when I was newly immigrated to UK, I made it a mission to attend every training, seminar, workshop, course which I thought could help me to become a speaker. I have participated in many workshops and seminars, met many trainers and thought leaders across a range of industries to find an answer to what makes a person Winner. Following each event, I would go back to my little room to research further into the priceless insights I'd gained. I delved into books that spoke about Winning and watched videos that could give insights on winning. I reached the following conclusion, 'It's your Powerful Connections with people, which will raise your Game of Winning.' I wish I had a resource on becoming a Winner in Life.

In 2003, I attended one of the events in Delhi where I discovered Tony Robbins' book and then later I attended his event in 2007.

I've had different results from the meetings that I've had with these great speakers. Some meetings I attended translated into direct opportunities, while others laid the foundation for great things to come. Whenever I think of the days when I was reluctant to go out, it scares me because, now it's so clear that if I hadn't shown up, my life could have been completely different. That realisation paints a dismal picture: I would have been working at a call-centre answering calls all day and feeling miserable about missing out on the life I could have had.

Now, you might ask why I chose to share this with you? It isn't only because I want you to use every chance you get to learn from other people. It's also because I know how safe you can feel staying within your comfort zone and turning your back on meetings and events. However, if you take away anything from this section it should be this: every time you have the opportunity to attend an event or meet a person, make a pact with yourself to go, even if you don't want to. Look at it as a personal commitment to yourself. You owe it to yourself to follow up on all avenues that lead to your dream, (the dream of Winning) and just as you would honour a commitment with someone else, you must do so with yourself. Once you know your dream, you'll find opportunities hard to resist. Indeed, it is staying away that will be harder because once you're passionate about something, every fibre in your body will urge you to move in its direction. I want you to listen to your inner voice and never stop moving towards your dream.

Earlier I shared that I believe in Experiential Knowledge; so now it's time to bring that into action. You may pause at this point and go to Google and search for events, trainings or meet- ups in your field of interest that are happening in your area this week or this month, or this quarter, which you can attend. And if you live in a small village (like I used to) then what's the nearest city you can travel to. Perhaps, you can jump on a Webinar. You may have a local club or a meeting place frequented by influential people. Find something which you can belong to.

I also want to caution you here against attending seminar after seminar with no actions. When you attend your next seminar, then note your key learnings and start applying at least 50% of them in your life. Grow through events; not grow into event. Remember, Winning occurs through our actions. Connecting with people enables you to travel on your journey smoothly. It makes an effort, much more effective and focused.

New places, events and people can be scary at first, but you must constantly remind yourself that only by moving forward, you can reach somewhere. Whether you don't like where your life is right now and you want to move away from, or you're happy with all that you have achieved, but you want to take your dreams further, the first step is to take action, greet every opportunity with open arms.

I'm sharing my personal experiences with you because I've experienced the wonders that can happen by opening oneself up to the world.

Experience is more useful than knowledge since the real world often behaves differently than the textbook, online or offline information.

You need to consider who you need to connect with and where you need to go for your dreams to come true, and once you've figured that out, let nothing stand in your way. This book will help you on your journey but know this: only you can reach your destination and for that, you need to get moving and meeting people today!

> ***Faith is the bird that sings***
> ***when the dawn is still dark.***
>
> ***–Rabindranath Tagore***

Notes:

Notes:

-10-

UNIVERSAL POWER— THE DIVINE DOORWAY

> ***Once you make a decision, the universe conspires to make it happen.***
>
> ***–Ralph Waldo Emerson***

A varied version of this quote is found in a famous movie. 'Om Shanti Om' which talks about how *when you desire something intensely, every part of the universe works to make you one with this desire.* Here's the original quote for those who would appreciate the language.

> ***Itni Shiddat Se Maine Tumhe Paane Ki Koshish Ki Hai... Ki Har Zarre Ne Mujhe Tumse Milane Ki Saazish Ki Hai.***
>
> ***–Shahrukh Khan's Voice***

Once you set out for a destination, the universe lays down several paths for you to reach there. But what does 'universe' mean here? Does it mean the flora and fauna around us, the mountains and the rivers or the earth and the stars? It can mean different things to different people.

Universe, here, refers to the higher power, the power that is bigger than all of us, and the power that governs this world– The Universal Power. One important aspect of winning is tuning in to this universal power and becoming one with it. You may know and recognize this power by many different names, such as, God, Jesus, Allah, Angels, The Field, Source, Buddha and—in my native Punjabi language—Waheguru.

All these names, although different, refer to a common power that governs this universe. Kenneth Clark "Kenny" Loggins, a famous American singer, songwriter and guitarist, once remarked, "There is trust in there being a Spirit who loves me and wants me to have love in my life. I trust in this higher power, it is what keeps me moving forward, no matter what happens."

Once your mind connects with a higher consciousness, you become aligned with a deeper understanding of the nature of reality, the self and various spiritual aspects of life. As a result, you come closer to self-realization. This creates a strong grounding to boost your career or profession. It doesn't matter what name we call our universal power, as long as we accept that there is something bigger than us that can support us provided we keep our faith alive.

This universal power can be a strong guiding force that can keep us moving forward. All that we need to do is to have belief. You cannot reap the benefits of this power unless you put your faith in it, and so become one with it. However, it's not a switch that you can turn off and on. It's a process—a gradual and fulfilling process. Through the insights of some of my teachers, I was able to tap into this Universal Power. All I needed to do was to channelize that higher energy to support me on my way to Winning.

Just as my teachers and research opened me up to this Power, I want you to tap into this Power too. This is what lets you breathe, lets you see things, and lets a seed turn into a tree. It's the same power which lets the stars shine, holds the gravity together, keeps the moon going, and holds the galaxies and solar systems together. I believe it's the same Power which is speaking to you through this book and has asked me to build your Faith in it. I want you to enjoy the same uplifting Life force particles that I'm able to enjoy. I had to start somewhere and for me, it was my friend and mentor Sidra Jafri, who ushered me into this beautiful world of belief and trust. When I was first introduced to this concept of Universal Power, I was taken aback and immediately wanted to change the way I looked at things, and what I believed in.

However, at first, it was confusing and not everything was falling into place. I was eager to see results but impatient to put in the effort and wait. It was only when I fully started trusting this process that my world changed. Everything started making sense and people started popping into my life out of nowhere to help me succeed and win. I believe it's only when you start trusting the universe, it's willing to help you. If you want to win and succeed in life, you should also tap into this Universal Power by becoming one with it, by trusting it and believing in it. Just as the universe conveyed this message to me through its different sources, I feel that by writing this book, the universe is conveying it to you through me. I am nothing but grateful for having been chosen to deliver this message.

Now, I understand that my journey to this point has been meaningful. All my sorrows, grief and suffering were for a reason to make me appreciate the joy and happiness I find in simple things. I can enjoy my success, but only because I have known failure. For if I hadn't burst the blisters on my hand while tilling my land, how would I have reaped gold from my harvest? For if I had not fallen on gravel and hurt my knees, how would I have learned to get up and walk in pain?

It was 2009 when I took an admission to a new college after struggling to find the one, offering a course that I could finish in 6 months. UK Home Office Visa regulations were about to change in April, 2010. So, I didn't have long time to complete my studies. The UK Home Office had decided to stop PSW (Post Study Work Permit) for the students who were graduating from their Colleges/Universities. Coming to London had been a big dream for me since childhood. I had seen my cousins do so well whenever I saw them during their stay in India. I was fascinated with their clothing, perfumes, and even the razor my cousins would use!

I naively thought that coming to London would solve all my challenges and I'd become rich overnight, but, I learnt the reality of London within a few months of landing there. From being in the wrong course as the college misrepresented the value of the course to get another college was just another scam, to eventually getting into a college which was duly affiliated to a proper university. Going down the college route was my only option for higher education. I couldn't get admission to a UK university as the fees were too high, so my best hope was getting into a college that was affiliated with a university. I also had to be near London so that I could continue my part-time job which would pay for my living expenses and also an installment for a £30,000 'world-class speaker' program which I'd signed up for.

Just imagine, how far my part-time salary had to go! It had to cover my college fees, my rent, and food and also to pay for the public speaking program. For almost 2 and half years, I ate in the Gurdwara (Sikh temple) most days as the food was free there. In return, I would do some voluntary work. I couldn't ask my parents for any funds as they had none. Also, I didn't ask my cousin who sponsored when I came to London. He had already paid £5,000 for me, which I think had been a huge help.

With so much going on in my life, I still had to meet a deadline to complete my Masters before April, 2010 so that I could qualify for my Post Study Work Permit. Things didn't go smoothly! I had a visa rejection letter posted to my house. At first, the Home Office couldn't charge the visa fee from my account and then my bank balance dipped below the amount I was supposed to maintain during the visa process. But, despite all these challenges, I kept my dream alive. I believed that I would be successful in London. Some people showed up as guardian angels, supporting me when I needed some relief, something which I have covered in the chapter about Connections.

I persevered and kept my faith alive; as it was going to be alright. I fought back against the visa rejections and got my visa reinstated after five years of fight. I lost at the lower tribunal and then finally won at the upper tribunal. Imagine being in a foreign country without a job for five years with no one as such to help me with money. Faith got me through it. I was aware as a result of what I'd learnt and my growing attitude that there's a lesson in everything. I had to overcome my own battles so that I could go out and teach the world.

My challenges gave me answers of Faith when everything was falling apart. There were many nights in the dark, small, lonely room in London when I would cry my heart out. I feared being deported back to India where I would again be laughed at and made fun of. Traveling to a foreign land is a huge achievement for the place I come from (Punjab), so the thought of going back to these people and sharing that I had been deported filled me with fear. I didn't even share my situation with my parents as it could have caused them stress and grief.

I am grateful for my insight of faith as that kept me going. Each morning, I would wipe off my tears and get out of bed and back to fighting. Being able to afford the high lawyer's fees was very painful but I badly wanted to stay in the UK, so I stuck with it. I knew from Tony Robbins that people who had achieved this before were nothing special, yet they persevered with courage and kept their faith alive.

So, that's what I did! I modelled the people who had been on the same journey before me. I had heard many stories that I could learn from regarding immigrants coming to the UK and making it big using their courage and faith to help them persevere. Just have faith that even if things go wrong, it will eventually all be OK. You have played small for too long. It's time to raise your game. So, commit to that big Dream. Open up the Divine Door which is for the souls who have Faith. With ordinary talent and extraordinary perseverance, anything is attainable!

> ***...to learn and not to do is really not to learn. To know and not to do is really not to know.***
>
> ***–Stephen R. Covey***

By now, and in many instances, while reading this book, you may have started feeling as if you already have the information and knowledge you need; you just need to find a way to reinforce it so it gets embedded in your system. This is where experiential learning comes into play; what you can learn by doing, you cannot learn by reading alone. Reading can help you gain information but unless you implement this information, you won't completely understand it and over time the information will fade away and maybe forgotten.

This is the information age. Through information from all over the world, the internet has brought the planet closer, only a few clicks away. However, not many of us attempt to gather and connect with this knowledge. Of the ones who do, only a few choose to put the knowledge into practice. This results in superficial knowledge, which eventually, will fade away. The information age has also somehow become an age of overwhelming information. So much information is available that it becomes difficult to choose, filter and retain the information that's truly valuable. I'd like to share a short story to explain this better.

Once there was a young boy who liked to read all kinds of books. While reading the story of an avid traveller, he became fascinated with the concept of traveling to unique and less-travelled places. He wanted to uncover all the hidden secrets of nature. He was a curious little boy. So, he started reading about all the exotic places he could visit. Once he had shortlisted a few places, he got his brother to join in on the plan. His brother was not like him. In fact, he was quite the opposite; enjoying spending most of his time outside the house, experiencing things first hand. He wasn't interested in learning from books; he liked to learn things by doing them. As the summer vacation approached, the brothers started pestering their parents about letting them travel alone for the first time in their lives. They wanted to spend a week in the wilderness close to where their house was located. The parents were sceptical, yet, gave in to the persistence of the boys. The boy who liked to read, started to read everything he could about surviving in the wilderness and started putting things together.

By the time summer vacation was around, he was brimming with knowledge. There was no more information he could take into his mind regarding the topic. They left on their first adventure, saying goodbye to their worried parents, promising to take care of themselves and stand by each other. After a good day of walking in the woods, the boys got ready to sleep. As they were almost done pitching their tent, which took an awfully long time, as it was the first time they'd done it, a wolf came out of the woods and started growling at them.

The boy had read a lot about how to deal with wild animals. However, the fear got to him and he froze, unable to think. His brother quickly picked up a few stones and started pelting them at the wolf. The wolf, after being hit a few times, turned away and left. The boy was shocked. Despite all his knowledge and information, he'd been unable to think, let alone do anything to thwart this situation. His brother was brimming with pride, knowing that he was the hero of the day. As soon as his brother was about to enter the tent to sleep, the boy stopped him and told him that they had to leave immediately. He had read that wolves almost always hunt in packs.

Now that he was calm, he could think and knew that the wolf would come back, but, this time, there would be more. They couldn't run either, as the wolves would follow their scent, and catch up with them. He discussed the best options with his brother and they both decided to climb a tree and stay there for the night. The wolf did return and with four other wolves. The boy and his brother were terrified; however, the brother seemed to be relatively calmer as he had been in similar situations with dogs in the neighbourhood. He said that if they stayed still on the tree long enough, the wolves would get bored and eventually leave.

It took them almost 16 hours for the wolves to become bored and leave. The boys waited another hour after the wolves had left and quickly climbed down, picked up their bags, leaving their pitched tent behind and ran home. Only when he got home did the boy remember the pepper spray and cymbals he had packed to dissuade any attacks in the wild. This is when he realized that just reading could not prepare him for the practical challenges and examinations of life. If he wanted to be truly knowledgeable, he needed to put the information he gathered into practice. If it hadn't been for the quick thinking of his brother who had been in similar situations before, they could have been badly hurt. This reminded me of something he had read in a book titled 'The 7 Habits of Highly Effective People: Powerful Lessons in Personal Change' by Stephen R. Covey.

At the same time, his brother realized that if it wasn't for the young boy's thirst for knowledge, they would have either been set upon in their sleep or caught on the run. It reminded him of the inscription on the library wall at his school by the famous artist Leonardo da Vinci, which read: "He who loves practice without theory is like the sailor who boards ship without a rudder and compass and never knows where he may cast."Together, the boys combined knowledge with experience and learning with practice to face a challenge and emerge as winners. This holds true in our world as well. It's as important to put your knowledge into practice, as it is to gain that knowledge in the first place. My workshops are designed to give participants this experience of 'learning by doing' which proves to be highly beneficial for them.

Without knowledge action is useless and knowledge without action is futile.

–Abu Bakr,
famous Muslim Caliph during 632 AD.

If you think you can do a thing, or think you can't do a thing, you are right.

–Henry Ford

Let's look further into the mind. Buddha once said, "The mind is everything. What you think, you became." So, what exactly is the mind and how does it work? Our minds are divided into two distinct parts: the conscious and the subconscious (also known as the unconscious). Commonly, only 10% of your mind is conscious while performing any activity, such as, reading this book. 90% of the mind is subconscious. To understand how this works, let's consider the example of driving. Driving, at first, is a challenge. When you are learning how to drive, you are introduced to the ABCs (accelerator, brake and clutch) and then you learn to shift the gears, reverse and parallel part. Initially, it is such a strenuous task concentrating on all these things individually: press the clutch, change the gear, press the accelerator while letting go of the clutch and so on. However, as you practice and become comfortable with your driving, you can easily deal with all these aspects of driving and can even change a music station on the radio while on the road. In terms of conscious versus subconscious, when you were introduced to the basic aspect of driving, you used your conscious mind to absorb information and implement them. With time, you became more comfortable with these aspects, as they were fed into your subconscious mind. Once thoroughly embedded in your subconscious, driving seemed to come naturally to you and your conscious mind could focus on doing other things such as changing the radio station or talking to the fellow passengers.

It doesn't only work with driving, but almost every other aspect of your life, such as, tying your laces, swimming, cycling, knitting, and typing. If you learn the difference between conscious and the subconscious, and learn how to control them or, in other words, learn how to use them in tandem, you will come to know about the limitless power of your mind. You'll be able to do and achieve things you couldn't even imagine. Remember, on a day-to-day basis, the conscious mind does not have any control over the subconscious which allows your past experiences to dictate your present and your future. However, with this knowledge (the difference between the conscious and the subconscious), you can channelize your thoughts, i.e. use your conscious mind to process thoughts over and over again until they are embedded in your subconscious and become your reality. This cannot be done over a day or even a week. It's a continuous process that will work only if made into a recurring habit, a way of life to speak. So, be patient and be aware.

A man is but the product of his thoughts.
What he thinks, he becomes.

–Mahatma Gandhi

> ***When the student is ready, the master appears.***
>
> ***–Buddhist Proverb***

> ***Once you make a decision, the universe conspires to make it happen.***
>
> ***–Ralph Waldo Emerson***

Hopelessness is a terrible affliction, a black hole that continuously sucks us inwards until it completely devours us. Hopelessness breeds more hopelessness and it is the loss of hope, not the loss of lives that determines the outcome of a war. Many of us have faced hopelessness at certain moments in our lives. However, we have behaved differently in such situations and so seen a different outcome. Some of us were dipped into the abyss and became morose, feeling defeated, while others battled their way out and came out stronger on the other side. Either way, anyone who has ever entered this void of hopelessness in their lives, has come out as a changed person.

My tryst with hopelessness took place when I was just over 16 years old. I remember having to remove my glasses every time I entered the village just to avoid looking bookish or weak and to escape being further preyed upon. I was called "Chashmish", which is a derogatory slang used to identify someone who wears eyeglasses. The connotation is that you are weak and deformed and do not deserve the same respect as everybody else; you should be treated differently. As I have already shared, my way out was to take my own life, by putting an end to the misery.

Fortunately, I didn't go through with it and had a life-altering letter arrived just the next day. The possibilities for my future completely changed. The letter for some reason made me feel significant; the Universe hadn't forgotten me. Now looking back at that incident, I realise how important it is for human beings to feel significant. After reading the Dale Carnegie and Napoleon Hill's books, which I felt resonated so much with my own story, I started taking responsibility for my actions, and my own life. I became proactive and started striving to improve my life.

In London, I got an opportunity to attend a workshop by Tony Robbins. It was a four-day program called "Unleash the Power Within"; I even did a firewalk, a part of the program where the participants breakthrough anything which were keeping them stuck by walking on the burning coals. The moment I completed the firewalk, I made a decision, "It doesn't matter if I don't have the necessary background, extraordinary linguistic skills or an affluent family to support me, I will be a world-class speaker and I will travel around the world inspiring people".

> ***Destiny is as destiny does. If you believe you have no control, then you have no control.***
>
> ***–Wess Roberts***

That one decision changed my life. I heard Tony Robbins say in the workshop, "It is in one moment of decision-making that your destiny is shaped." Now that I do preview workshops for Tony in London, I'm a living embodiment of this statement. And I would like to thank you and congratulate you for making the decision to pick up this book and gear up for an adventurous journey leading to success, wealth and prosperity.

Notes:

HOW YOU CAN USE THIS BOOK AS SUCCESS LADDER?

At this age, I believe that I've gained some maturity, thanks to the various challenges in life that I've had to face. I'm no longer sensitive to what's said about me as long as I'm happy with each day in my life. The purpose of writing this book is not to glorify my life to boost my image in your eyes, nor is to capitalise on my adversity. To trigger emotions in someone is easy. You tell someone about how you or your family have faced pain, and suffering in a certain period of your life, and you will see so many misty eyes around you. In fact, what has driven me to write this book is the unquenchable desire to change the life of those who read this book. By frankly telling you my story, I want to assure you that what seems impossible today will certainly be possible for you, provided you create the right conditions for it.

Just read the tips provided below as if you're reading the holiest books and follow what's said in these tips religiously.

Your life will then touch a new high every quarter.

- **Create a Clear Picture of Your Present Situation**

  What's your current situation? You can look at your economic situation, your preparation level for an ensuing examination, or imminent problem, challenge, anything you fear, anything you think needs caution. Write it down in your diary so that you're 100% clear about your starting point. Remember, a fault recognised is half corrected, fault ignored is twice corrected.

- **Nothing Changes if Nothing Changes**

  As mentioned in Chapter 2, Winning and Losing, nothing changes if nothing changes. If you sit back once you've achieved something, you'll end up like a one-hit wonder. You'll emerge as a star, but your charisma will blow out like a candle. Likewise, if you're not resolute enough to take your challenges head-on, you'll not be perceived as a person with winning ability. Here, the word winning should not be limited in definition. It could relate to something as small as being able to fetch something in a crowded shop to being number one at a global sporting event. So, after analyzing your situation, the next thing is to develop a winning attitude.

- **Your Future Account is Empty**

  Lots of people have said to me, "I am doing my best Amandeep, but I don't know what the future has in store for me." I'm telling you, the future is empty for those who think it's already filled with a fated destiny. You're never destined. If you pull your socks up and prepare today, you're the winner tomorrow. Your insurance for tomorrow is what you do today.

The future is destined.

Then strike it through.

Now, write

The future is the sum total of your present. There is no such thing like "already decided."

- **Chalk out a Sure-fire Strategy**

Create an air-tight strategy to meet your goal, or achieve what you dream for. Your style of functioning, your way of thinking and each next step, should be in alignment with the desired outcome. If these three are in harmony, you'll be able to achieve whatever you set your mind at.

- **Know the Power of your Mind**

As I've already discussed, your mind is powerful. It's just your ability or inability to acknowledge the true potential of your mind that makes or breaks you. If you accept and believe that you are capable enough to perform a particular task diligently and, possess a positive outlook, no circumstance will be able to divert you from your commitment to achieving something "extraordinary."All that I have written is an honest effort to help you meet A Man DEEP inside you.

If Amandeep can do, so can you.

CALL OF THE FUTURE!

Stay in touch with Amandeep

Email: info@emergingbrilliance.in

Phone nos.: +91 8585993007

+44 7550 671695

Website: https://successmastery.in/

Social media platform

Instagram : @amandeep_live

Facebook : www.facebook.com/AmandeepLive/

LinkedIn : http://linkedin.com/in/attitudeguru

If you are reading this book, take a picture and share it with us. We'll publish it on our social media channels.

To attend Amandeep's Live workshops, visit https://amandeepthind.in/

See what our students have to say!

Amandeep is a man one should look for a mentor. He over-delivers what he commits. He is superb.

–Asootosh Kkant,

An Entrepreneur, Author, and Influencer

Amandeep is a true giver. He not only teaches you how to be a trainer but also teaches you 'How to be a World-Class Trainer'. He comes from the space of complete authenticity where he is totally and fully available for all his students. As a trainer, as a guru, as a teacher, he will be by your side. Not only that, he will show you the path and equip you with so many skills that you will be confident enough to walk.

–Gayatrri Vaidhya,

A Trainer, Hypnotherapist and Life coach

Once you are in his shadow, you will actually get those positive vibes very strongly. He will be there to guide not to spoon-feed you but then to push you, that kick is really necessary for you to perform sometimes.

–Sanchita Chakraborty,

Project Manager

In each of the stages, Amandeep helps us to understand what has to be done, when it has to be done, how it has to be done. So, hats off to him and his team for great work. He has been with Tony Robbins and he is training worldwide. So that is the cream he brings in helping the Indian trainers to get this learning and become a world-class trainer.

–Sachin Gurav,

Investor and Financial Coach

When I started reading the book, I was trying to focus more on the external sources of inspiration to help me achieve my goals and uncover the secret of winning. While reading the book, I realised that it's extremely important to focus on what's within you, the strengths and goodness which we often tend to overlook. As I have attended Success Mastery Workshop conducted by Amandeep Sir, I can very well connect the topic of the "Invisible Prison" to every aspect of the book. It's been a great read. Thank you for publishing such an amazing book. Amandeep Sir is truly an epitome of inspiration.

–Neha,

Digital Creator

See what thought leaders say about Amandeep Thind

Amandeep is very hard-working. When he speaks, he speaks from the heart. He really has very powerful message to share and he has earned the right to share it with you and teach you what to do. I want to congratulate Amandeep for his success. He learned and got better and better. Today, he is travelling all over the world sharing the same mission and changing lives.

–Veronica Tan

Co-founder of Success Resources

Amandeep has a special gift and an amazing ability to empower and inspire people to live more fulfilling and joyful lives. Listen to him, he knows what he's talking about.

–Mac Attram

Business Coach & Millionaire Entrepreneur

Where you can meet me?

↓

Do you want to discover the path to your success?

↓

Do you want to get rid of procrastination?

This Success Mastery Workshop is about discovering the blocks that have been stopping you from creating the quality of life that you desire and deserve.

This one day workshop will take you on a journey to uncover a new way of thinking. It will give you the tools and techniques that will allow you to easily create a progressive mind-set and succeed in every area of your life.

We all have fears, but what you do with those fears will make the difference. If we focus on our fears, we will get nowhere; however, if we focus on what we want, we can get anywhere!

With that in mind, build enough courage to walk barefoot over the bed of hot coals, and discover the unlimited power that lies within every one of us.

Be a FIRE WALKER and turn the impossible into possible.

Once you start doing the impossible (what you thought was impossible), you can conquer the other fears of life with ease!

I'm truly excited and privileged to have this opportunity to share with you the best of what I have learned about personal growth and improvement.

Let's make a commitment today to participate together with a progressive mindset and new levels of energy. Through our outrageous and passionate levels of energy, we can make this workshop a life-transforming event you will never forget!

Event Link:

https://successmastery.in/

Art of Becoming Million Dollar Speaker

Do you want to share your powerful message with the world but aren't sure where to start?

I believe that each one of us has some message to share with the world and inspire people. If you succeed in doing so, you can help others and in the process, your life becomes magical & phenomenal.

In this workshop, I will teach you 'how-to' deliver compelling messages with real-world strategies, that will captivate and mesmerize your audience. It will teach you by getting you to do the material, making learning fun and engaging completely in the process.

Through Accelerated Training Methods and interactive knowledge, you will be able to clearly communicate valuable content, hold people's attention and easily implement these tools and techniques once you return to your business.

By the end of this workshop, you'll increase your value as a professional by brilliantly presenting your own powerful programs that will leave your audiences wowed. You will receive a fail-proof template that you can use to create any presentation for any industry and leave your audience asking for more.

Highlights of the Event

- Dissolve all the fear & design an invincible presentation from start to finish
- Earn up to Rs. 9 Lakhs within a weekend
- Master your body language and exhibit power and confidence
- Unlock your true communication ability & present yourself with more clarity
- Make your presentation more effective and memorable
- Learn state management for your audience and channelize the energy in the room!

Event Link:

https://amandeepthind.in/art-of-becoming-million-dollar-speaker/

Milton Keynes UK
Ingram Content Group UK Ltd.
UKHW020700231023
431165UK00015B/570